WHEN THE WIND

WIND

BLOWS

WHEN THE WIND BLOWS

ZACHARY ALAN FOX

Kensington Books
http://www.kensingtonbooks.com

Grateful acknowledgment is made for permission to excerpt *Death in Venice* by Thomas Mann, a revised edition of the authorized translation by Kenneth Burke. Reprinted by permission of Random House, Inc. © 1970 by Random House, Inc. © 1970 by Alfred A. Knopf, Inc. © 1924 by the Dial Publishing Co., Inc. © 1925 by Alfred A. Knopf, Inc.

KENSINGTON BOOKS are published by

Kensington Publishing Corp.
850 Third Avenue
New York, NY 10022

Kensington and the K logo Reg. U.S. Pat. & TM Off.

Library of Congress Catalog Number: 98-065257
ISBN 1-57566-335-X

First Printing: October, 1998
10 9 8 7 6 5 4 3 2

Printed in the United States of America

For Dan and Kristina,
friends forever

Prologue

—Now he watches: *feels*—

An almost paternal affection for the girl.

—That was it, was it not? Paternal?—

There was a stirring in the secret reaches of his soul, a pleasurable hardening of desire. But something in his consciousness suddenly began shattering, violently breaking apart, like a plate thrown against the wall.

Feel it?

Feel it?

Shattering.

He began to shake, and the skin all over his body tingled as though a thousand spiders danced on naked flesh . . . lightheadedness . . . a terribly heightened sexuality— (Out of control, though, hard throbbing, feels it, an embarrassment. Would the nurse notice, tell the doctor?)

—He hates it, this loss of control. But prays for it. Maximum pleasure. Designed for few—

(The elite.)

Damn medicine makes him forget. *Where's the nurse?*

He stares at the child with mounting excitement; she came back! I knew she would. Couldn't stand to be away. *The way you fought, and cried, and tried to hurt. It was all an act, wasn't it? You need me.*

(Sounds of love. Moaning.)

Her mother pretending not to hear.

(Throbbing.)

This time I won't lose you. You're mine. Forever. *Don't struggle, damn it.*

Forever.

(Dreams.)

I

1

Only seven years old and already arguing about mortgages and money, Mark thought as his daughter gave him a satisfied look, and tapped the card on the table. "You're going to have to pay, Dad. You still owe me for Ventnor Avenue."

Mark sighed and looked at his meager cache of folding money. "How much is it?

Lisa consulted the card. "Tennessee Avenue with three houses . . . Nine hundred and fifty."

"I don't think I have it. I guess I could—" But Lisa had already begun to shake her head when real life intruded in the form of a ringing telephone. "If my banker will excuse me . . ."

Going into the kitchen, he picked up the receiver, said, "Mark Ritter," then felt a chill, like ice scraped along his spine, as he heard the words he had been dreading for years. His eyes squeezed closed and his head fell back as he listened, said, "Yes . . . Thank you. . . . Of course, Eleanor," then put the phone down, but didn't move from where he was standing.

A moment later the swinging door opened and Lisa said, "I have six thousand, three hundred dollars . . . " She stopped as she saw her father's face. "What's wrong?"

How do you explain death to a seven-year-old? Mark felt his insides tighten. The finality of it—of someone suddenly no longer *being*—had to be incomprehensible to a child, even a child like Lisa whose mother had died when she was only one, and who existed only as an abstraction and in pictures in the bedroom and living room. But what alternative was there?

"That was a lady in South Dakota who knew your grandma."

Lisa at once picked up on the past tense. Her brow furrowed and eyebrows moved together in a way Mark usually thought so comical, so grown-up and full of worldly-wise knowledge.

"Grandma died, hon."

The girl looked at him with half-comprehending eyes that began to water. Grandma Ritter was the only relative other than her father she had ever known. For a long time she said nothing, processing the information, trying to salvage some meaning from the unfamiliar words. Then she started to sniffle but fought against crying.

Mark put his arm around his daughter, felt the terrible racing of the girl's heart and the confusion in her face. He lowered himself to his knees and hugged her close. "Let's go in the living room and talk."

That night, lying in bed, staring at the darkness of the room, he thought, *Only sixty-three. . . . Too young. Too damn young!* What was the cliché people usually trotted out at times like this? *It was really a release. She had been in such pain since the last stroke.* Maybe so. But she was a woman who loved life and who had the energy and determination to run their farm by herself since Mark's dad had died more than ten years ago.

But he had seen it coming. Last summer when he and Lisa went back to Dexter to visit, his mother could hardly get from one room to another. A home-care nurse came by weekly to check on her but his mom wouldn't hear of having a housecleaner, or someone in to cook. Somehow, though, the house, the house where he had spent almost every night of the first eighteen years of his life, and which he was destined now to see one last time, was always spotless, and his mother, despite her obvious pain, as cheerful and optimistic as she had always been.

Suddenly his mind filled with the thought that he had been trying to keep away: the single constant in his life, the *only* tie to the past, to a childhood that had been happy to a point almost impossible to believe, was now abruptly and irretrievably gone. And his life—his and Lisa's—was about to change in ways he couldn't foresee but unexpectedly began to fear.

2

"Amber waves of grain, hon," Mark said, gesturing grandly with his arm as they shot past the seemingly endless stream of South Dakota farms in the silver BMW Z3 convertible that still made him feel embarrassed. The car was a bit showy for Mark, who tended to see autos primarily as a way to get from point A to point B. But he had won it in a sales contest from the Seattle office of Merrill Lynch where he was employed as a stockbroker, and Lisa had fallen in love with it at once. "It's James Bond's car!" she squealed the first time she saw it. "Put the top down and let's go for a ride."

"How do you know about James Bond?" he had asked, and she said, "I saw the video at Ashley's."

Great, he'd thought. *It's tough enough monitoring a child's movie-viewing at home; you have to worry about her friends, too.*

He turned now to Lisa in the passenger seat. "Do you remember being here from last year?"

"Sure," the girl said, but without conviction, "last year" being an eon ago to a seven-year-old. Mark, first with Beth, then with Lisa, had made this trip every summer since getting out of the Air Force five years ago to visit his mother and help with chores that had piled up from the previous year.

"Will Monster be there?" Lisa asked, turning suddenly from the sea of wheat and soybeans to look at her dad.

Well, at least she remembers that, Mark thought with pleasure. Monster was an aging golden retriever who had been on the farm for at least a dozen years. "I don't know. Maybe. But someone probably took him in. There wouldn't be anyone to feed him now."

"I like him," Lisa said cheerily. "He was fun."

"Yeah, I like him, too," Mark said, and again it hit him that an entire portion of his life was forever lost. It wouldn't have been so bad if there were other relatives to provide some tie to the past—aunts, cousins, grandparents—but there was nothing, and never had been. A family alone, and seemingly reveling in its isolation in the bleak Dakota prairie, where even TV-sitcom families could seem closer than the nearest neighbors. Staring out at the checkerboard fields and farms with their silos looking like upended caskets flying by in the morning air, he wondered if he'd ever return once the funeral was over. Probably not; his life now was Lisa, and the arcane world of stock options and short sales and junk-bond financing.

An hour later he swung off the highway onto the familiar gravel drive and eased to a stop as the house where he grew up rose suddenly in front of him. For a long moment he sat staring, the engine humming in neutral as a hot dry wind blew down from the north and tousled his and Lisa's hair. The only sound they could hear was the car's engine, and a flock of ravens circling the fields like buzzards over carrion. The house was like thousands of others in rural America—white clapboard weathered to a dull gray, two stories high, with three small bedrooms, and a basement used for storage. It hadn't been painted for years and looked as if the next big storm would blow it into Nebraska. The barn in the rear was in even worse shape, sagging badly, half its roof and both main doors long gone. Some farm equipment and a forty-year-old Ford without an engine rotted in knee-deep weeds off to the side. Only the towering elms next to the house, elegiac and funereal in their timeless majesty, offered a hint of the care and concern and sweat several generations of owners had given to the property.

The surrounding hundred and fifty acres that his mom had worked with a succession of hired hands was planted in corn and looked as it had always looked, though for the last three years it had been leased to the farmer next door. Mark supposed it now belonged to him, and wondered briefly how he'd go about selling it and what it'd bring. Maybe one of the neighbors would be interested, though every year there seemed to be fewer and fewer family farmers.

"Eighteen years," Mark said without thinking.

"Huh?"

"That's how long I lived here. Until I went to the Air Force Academy." Most of that time, certainly when he was Lisa's age, it would never have occurred to him that he wouldn't be living here the rest of his life. One more night and he'd never see it again. And life goes on. Or does it? *Jesus, where did that come from? You're getting morbid.* Maybe a parent's death does that to you. Especially if it's your last blood relative other than a child. Makes you walk up to your empty coffin and stare death in the face, whether you want to or not.

"Where's Monster?" Lisa asked.

"If he was here he'd be slobbering all over us by now." Mark tapped the gas and rolled up behind his mom's old Chevy, and killed the engine. Lisa was out of the car and trying the front door by the time he reached the raised front porch.

" 'Door's locked," he said, and retrieved the spare key from under a flowerpot where it had always been kept. The familiar scents of childhood assailed him the moment they stepped into the darkened living room, the "front room" his mother always called it: red wood polish and musty carpets, thirty-year-old upholstered furniture that seemed to be rotting from the inside out, and the warm fruity scent of decades of home canning. But also this time the foul stench of death lay everywhere; it had been three days before a neighbor had found his mother crumpled on the kitchen floor, the victim of a massive stroke. The woman had called the police and an ambulance, and later Eleanor Dahlquist, the family attorney, had come out to lock up the house to keep any valuables from disappearing. *At the same time trapping a century's worth of ghosts inside,* Mark thought ruefully as he walked around, throwing open windows while Lisa ran through the house yelling for Monster.

"He's not here," the girl said unhappily as Mark came back to the living room.

"I'm sure one of the other farmers took him in. Let's see if there's anything in the fridge for lunch."

Mark made sandwiches from cold cuts and they took them on the porch and ate in the pale afternoon sunshine. Afterward, Lisa went exploring out by the barn while Mark tried to mentally arrange what he had to accomplish before going back to Seattle. Since the funeral was tomorrow it didn't give him much time. Eleanor Dahlquist could take care of putting the farm up for sale. She could also sell the car and farm equipment. That meant today and tonight to go through the house and see if there was anything he wanted to ship home. How much crap can two people accumulate over a lifetime, especially after living in the same place for thirty years? A lot, if he knew his parents. But other than a few pictures and mementos he couldn't think of anything he'd want to keep. Might as well get to it.

Is anything more depressing than going through a dead parent's possessions, especially personal things put away over the decades because they once had some significant, if private meaning? While Lisa explored the deserted barn Mark walked through the house and did a quick mental inventory. The furniture was nice, sturdily built, mostly of oak: big oversized beds, a farm-style dining table where he vaguely remembered a dozen people sitting at Thanksgiving or one of their rare dinner parties, a huge desk that looked as though it had come from a bank. Some of the pieces must have been a hundred years old, but he didn't want any of it. *Let it go with the house.* Same with the few pictures on the walls, and the kitchen appliances, and all the little knickknacks his mother had collected over the years; she must have been on every mail-order "collectibles" list in America, and he remembered as a child his dad having a fit whenever he found one more plaster angel or baby raccoon on an end table. Finally he'd had to buy a wood-and-glass curio cabinet to collect all the clutter in one place. Hell, the next family can decide what to do with it. But he'd have to do a room by room check of the more personal items. *Hurry it up, though,* he told himself; *get it over with and get out of the death house.* It was giving him the creeps.

He started with his old bedroom. The aged pine dresser had been cleaned out long ago and there was nothing in it but an old album of photographs he'd taken when he was thirteen or fourteen: friends of his, camping trips, the high school. God, he hadn't seen those pictures in years! He smiled—what had happened to all these people?—and put the album aside; maybe Lisa would be interested in it someday. No clothes in the closet, but it was crammed with camping equipment—tents, backpacks, cooking gear—all too old and decrepit to be of any use now. And that was it for the entire room. A photo album. It seemed a letdown somehow, but he supposed he'd taken everything worth saving when he graduated from the Academy.

The second bedroom had been used as an office by his dad and held two dusty file cabinets and a desk with twenty years' worth of paperwork and canceled checks and receipts, and God knew what else. This room had been off-limits to him as a child, and always held an air of mystery as he peeked in from time to time. It looked like his mom hadn't been inside in years so the task of cleaning up and throwing away had fallen to Mark. But he wasn't ready to tackle it yet, so he went instead to his parents' bedroom.

The double bed that had been there since his childhood had been moved from the center of the room to the far corner, and a metal rail attached to the open side to keep his mother from falling out. He hadn't seen the bedspread before, a bright-yellow–and–brown sunflower design that didn't look like something she would have chosen; probably a gift. A maple double-dresser bought the year he left home stood against one wall, the straight-backed wooden chair she needed to get in and out of her clothes in front of it. An easy chair, too soft for her to use, sat empty in a corner along with her aluminum walker.

This was going to take awhile. He went to the kitchen and found some plastic trash bags and came back, filling one with clothes from the dresser. He could drop them off at Goodwill in town tomorrow. Some of the stuff was pretty good, expensive even, underwear from a mail-order store in Chicago, and three or four silk blouses. At the bottom of one drawer he found some loose pictures of himself as a child, and quickly flipped through them, keeping only one that showed him in his high-school football uniform; that would give Lisa a kick: macho papa.

The closet was packed with more clothes, most of which she hadn't worn in years. The good stuff he shoved in trash bags but the rest he left hanging. The new owners could take care of it, make it into rags if they wanted. There were two jackets and an overcoat, both of which he saved, draping them over the wooden chair. A dozen pairs of boots and shoes went into a bag, along with three purses which he first looked into to ensure that they were empty. He wondered where his mother's current purse was. Perhaps Eleanor Dahlquist had retrieved it when she came out to close up the house.

As he ran his hand over the closet shelf his fingers touched a cardboard shoebox in the rear and he took it down. Dust covered the top. Had Mom been hiding it up there? He opened it. More old photographs. His mother and dad, back in the sixties from the looks of it, his dad with those bushy sideburns he wore to the bottom of his ears until the day he died. Mom and Dad holding Mark as a baby. Another half dozen pictures of Mark as a child in his mom's arms. Why was she hiding these? Maybe Eleanor Dahlquist could shed some light on it; she'd known his parents for years. He found a rubber band and snapped it around the pictures.

His mother's jewelry case was also on the shelf. He took it down and rummaged through it. There were some inexpensive earrings, some pins and brooches, and three gemstone rings. He put the rings in his pocket; maybe he'd keep them for their sentimental value if nothing else.

A chill suddenly ran along his spine and made him shiver. *Something's wrong,* he thought at once, and his heart began to race. *Something's not right around here.* His eyes darted from the closet to the bed to the door as a feeling like dread grew in him, and he shivered again as though a chill wind had blown in from a window. *It's the house,* he decided: *it's not mine anymore, not the place where I grew up. It's a crypt, where Mom and Dad and God knows how many more before them died, and where no one lives now. More tomb than home.*

And something else, something else was wrong. A feeling. But what?

Don't get morbid, he warned himself. This had been a wonderful place for his family, and probably for the families before, and would be again for whoever bought it next. *You can't allow your mom's death to make you look at everything through a cloud.*

An hour later he had put aside all the clothes worth saving. Might as well check out the bathrooms and living room before tackling the den. The small bathroom in the rear that he had used as a child was completely empty, not even toilet paper on the roll. The larger main bathroom had been altered recently, a chrome support bar anchored on the wall next to the toilet and another on the rim of the tub to provide a handhold. The medicine chest was full of pills of various types, all of which he flushed down the toilet before dropping the bottles in the metal trash can. The hair dryer and portable radio he briefly considered saving, then decided against it; it seemed ghoulish to be salvaging items of day-to-day use from a deceased parent.

He looked at his watch. Almost four o'clock. Where had Lisa gotten off to? Grabbing the bags of clothes he trudged out to the car. "Lisa! . . . *Lisa!*"

No answer. He popped the trunk and put the clothes inside. Turning toward the barn he yelled, *"Lisa—"* just as a clod of rich South Dakota soil splattered against the BMW's polished silver hood. He turned to see the top of a small head behind the rusted out Ford.

"Watch it, kiddo," Mark said. "I don't even have two thousand miles on this. I don't want to have to pay for body damage already."

"Do I have to come in?" the girl asked from her hiding place.

"No, but don't do anything stupid out here. The nearest hospital's forty miles away."

"I'm going to look for Monster again."

"Okay, but stay out of the fields. You smash any cornstalks and old Mr. Jorgensen will come after you with a shotgun."

Lisa promised she wouldn't, and Mark went back inside, stopping in the living room and looking around. There were some knickknacks on the mantel that he'd skipped over earlier—a carved wooden eagle that had been in the exact same spot as long as he could remember, a black-and-white picture of his dad in his Army uniform, and a formal photograph of Dad and Mom at their wedding. He wanted both pictures and set them aside. There was nothing else in the room of interest so he decided to take a look in the basement.

As soon as he opened the door Mark remembered why he had always hated to go down there. The smell that greeted him was like a mixture of wet soil, rotted fruit, and bat guano. He flipped the light switch and wasn't surprised when nothing happened. In the kitchen he found a flashlight and a spare hundred-watt bulb, and began to slowly descend the darkened stairs. How long since he'd been down here? Fifteen years? As a child he'd had nightmares about the place—monsters called Gikes lived under the floor and would slip up at night to look for little boys to steal and take back to their hiding places. He let the beam of the flashlight play quickly around the room. No madmen or monsters. Not even the stray serial killer. Still, he shivered. *You watch too many horror films,* he told himself as he went to work unscrewing the burned-out bulb and inserting the new one. *Or you haven't grown up yet. Take your pick.*

The light came on abruptly and he started as memories returned in a flood. The basement had never been used as a living space because it was so poorly constructed. Moisture bled from the cement walls, and the ceiling beams were rotting away like a diseased body. *Another expense for the new owners,* he thought. There was a wooden table where his mother stored preserves, a banged-up chest-type freezer, some ancient fan-backed metal lawn chairs, and a black-and-white television with a thirteen-inch screen that probably hadn't worked since the days of Ed Sullivan. And that was it. A faint noise from somewhere startled him and he spun around, his heart racing, and saw two field mice scurry across the floor. *Basements,* he thought. He took one final look to ensure that he had missed nothing, and hurried up the stairs in time to see Lisa tracking mud through the living room. "Hey, where have you been?" Mark asked.

Lisa turned around and Mark could see that her T-shirt and shorts were also caked with mud. "I fell down."

"Yeah, I guess you did."

"Should I take a bath?" she asked plaintively.

"You know the drill," Mark said, and led her into the main bathroom with its old-fashioned claw-foot tub and shiny new hand-holds.

Lisa waited while Mark drew the water. "Can we have dinner when I get out? I'm hungry."

"I still have one room to go through," Mark said, thinking of the den. "You clean up and I'll take a look at how big a job it's going to be. Maybe I can be done in half an hour."

But only if I set fire to the place, Mark decided as he stared around the previously inviolable room. Where to start? He threw open a window that hadn't been touched in years, then sat at the desk, feeling an odd, almost fugitive pleasure as he did so—the always out-of-bounds desk in the off-limits den—and stared at the broad walnut top. There was enough dust to write his name. How often did Mom clean up in here? Probably never. When his dad had been alive she was as afraid to enter as Mark was. He pushed the chair back and pulled open the center drawer. So what was Dad's big secret? *Were you a Soviet spy, Pop? A money launderer for the mob? A big-time dealer in dope for South Dakota?* He rummaged inside the overfull drawer. Pens, pencils, a few old coins, and an uneasy clutter of miscellaneous junk: paper clips, rubber bands, old keys, wooden rulers, crumpled-up receipts and bills and scraps of paper. Feeling something of a letdown, he reached for the top left-hand drawer. A spiraling of dust fluttered up as he opened it. Typing paper, curled and brittle with age. Next drawer, ancient magazines; third drawer . . .

Only in the bottom right-hand drawer did he discover anything of interest. Mixed in with files detailing crop yields and prices was a folder marked PAYMENTS RECEIVED. Odd. It looked like his mother's handwriting, not his dad's. He pulled it out. Empty.

Payments received from whom? And for what? He stared at it a moment, then shoved it back in the drawer. There was no time to worry about it now. He still had the two file cabinets to look at.

"You okay, Lisa?"

"Yeah."

"Well, splash once in a while so I know you didn't drown."

The girl hit the water with her hands and laughed.

"You got it, kiddo. Maybe you could sing, too."

As Lisa began singing the theme from *Sesame Street* Mark tackled the first of the file cabinets. Farm reports, contracts, product guarantees—year after year after year. . . . He sneezed twice from the dust he was kicking up, and continued rifling through the drawers. Canceled checks for three decades, records of small investments in mutual funds, newspaper and magazine articles on farming and gardening and home repair.

In the second file cabinet there were copies of letters to local newspapers, all on Dad's favorite topic: government interference in farmers' lives. Well, hell, it was every farmer's favorite topic; even when cashing government support checks. Also a drawerful of travel brochures—England, the Caribbean, Australia. All his life Dad talked of traveling the world when he finally gave up farming but it never happened. Farmers don't live long enough to even *have* a retirement.

Lisa was singing "Blue Tail Fly" as Mark opened the closet door and sighed aloud: thirty years' worth of Dad's hunting and farming clothes. Let someone else sort it out.

"Okay, honey, time to get out. There's some clean clothes for you in Grandma's room. After you get dressed we'll eat."

Lisa pulled the plug and scurried out of the bathroom while Mark finished up in the den. When he walked into the bedroom the girl was wearing shorts and a T-shirt and jumping on the bed. Mark picked up one of her shoes and tossed it in a lazy arc in her direction. *"It's a long pass to the famous Seahawk wide-receiver Lisa Ritt-errrrr—"* The girl squealed and snagged it with one hand, leaping off the bed and upsetting the old-fashioned black telephone on the nightstand. She halted at once and looked at her father, chagrined.

"It's okay, hon. Pop's fault for playing football inside. Time for Dad to grow up." Maybe. Then again, maybe not.

While Lisa hurriedly pulled on a shoe, Mark walked over and picked up the phone. As he started to put it back on the nightstand he froze. A key was taped to the underside of the base. A strange feeling moving within him, Mark pulled it free.

"What's that?" Lisa asked as she put on her other shoe.

"A key. Go ahead and finish dressing."

It was flat, made of stamped metal, and had "183" impressed into its head. A safe-deposit box? A mailbox? Obviously something valuable or why would his mother hide it? And why hadn't she mentioned it to him, especially in later years when she knew she could go at any minute? What was she hiding?

"Are we going out to dinner?" Lisa asked, pulling Mark out of his reverie.

"Huh? Yeah. We'll go into town. Let me call someone first. Maybe we'll have dinner with her."

Eleanor Dahlquist picked up the phone on the first ring; small-town attorneys seldom have secretaries, Mark supposed, or any other kind of help. Yes, she said, she'd be happy to have dinner with them if they didn't mind the Red and White downtown. It was the only restaurant open for dinner now. Could he be in town at six o'clock? He said he could, if they left right away. After hanging up Mark stared at the key again, turning it over and over in his hand. Why the hell was his mother hiding something from her only child?

3

The Red and White was on Main, one of the few businesses not boarded-up in what used to be Dexter's three-block shopping

district. It looked exactly as Mark remembered, a white stucco building with a large red-rimmed picture window in front allowing pedes-
trians, if there were any, to peer through at the diners inside. But
now the stucco was falling off in chunks and the red paint was faded
to a bloodless dull pink. A bell over the glass door jangled when
opened, causing the dozen or so customers to glance up in curiosity
as he and Lisa entered. Eleanor Dahlquist, heavyset and probably in
her mid-sixties, was at a booth in the corner, and she smiled at once
and waved them over.

"I remember when Lisa was born," she said in a husky voice after
they sat down. "I sent her a crib blanket with little bunnies on it, I
think. Or was it clowns? Crib blankets all look alike, don't they?"
Eleanor was one of Mark's mother's oldest friends and one of those
people he still couldn't help thinking of as an "adult" while he,
presumably, was something lesser.

"Bunnies," Mark told her. "She still has it. It's one of those things
you never throw away."

"Do you know where Monster is?" Lisa asked abruptly. "I can't
find him."

"No, I'm sorry, honey, I don't. Mrs. Dyer—you remember her,
Mark; she has a farm about ten miles from your mom's—volunteered
to take Monster in but couldn't find him when she went out there.
But dogs can be funny when their master dies. Oh, hi, Ruth. You
recollect Mark Ritter, don't you?"

The waitress who had approached looked at him with surprise
and said, "Land sakes, Mark Ritter," and they went through the
same sort of mini-reunion that happened at least twenty times every
year when he came back to Dexter. Yes, yes, he was doing fine, considering. Yes, this was Lisa. And how was Ruth getting along . . . ?
After about five minutes Ruth remembered that she was here to take
their order. Eleanor and Mark ordered pot roast while Lisa, as usual,
wanted fried chicken and french fries.

When the waitress left Eleanor said, "You sounded a little strange
on the phone. If the funeral's worrying you, forget it. I've got everything taken care of."

"It's not that," he said, and took the key out of his pocket, laying
it on the red-checked oilcloth in front of her. "I found this taped to
the underside of her phone, as if she was trying to hide it."

Eleanor picked up the key, turned it over a couple of times, and
looked over her glasses at him with a shrug.

"It goes to something," he said, and began to feel a little foolish though he didn't know why.

"Well, of course it goes to something!"

"It was *hidden,* Eleanor."

She put it on the table in front of her as though uninterested. "Safe-deposit box? That's what it looks like. Kind of old-fashioned, though."

"I thought you might know where she had an account. A bank here in town, I suppose, or—"

"There's only one bank left in Dexter and that's Farmer's, down a block, in the same building it's always been in. She had a checking and savings account there. The final balance together only came to about five hundred dollars, but you'll see it all spelled out when I get done handling the estate. I'm the executor, you know. I don't know why she didn't appoint you. It would have been easier all around but she wanted me to handle things, maybe because you live so far away. This isn't a Farmer's key, though. Theirs are about half this size."

"Could she have had an account you didn't know about?"

"Look, Mark, I've handled your mother's business matters since your dad died. All of them, such as they were. There's *nothing* about her life I didn't know about."

"So what's it to?"

"How old was the phone it was taped to?"

"Oh, I don't know. It was a rotary type. Could be twenty years, maybe older."

Eleanor said, "Then the key's been there for decades. She probably completely forgot about it. You know how people are when they get old."

"It still opens something, Eleanor." Lisa had begun to look bored. Mark pulled her close and gave her a hug. "Hang on. Food's always been a little slow coming here in Dexter."

"Well, it's not *fast food,* if that's what you mean," Eleanor said with some asperity. "People here still like to taste what they're eating. Anyway, the burger and pizza joints don't think we're important enough for them. Thank God—"

As though on cue Ruth appeared with the food. Lisa's fried chicken was brown and sizzling and had actually been pan-fried, unlike the franchise places. The pot roast came with gravy and mashed potatoes and mixed vegetables, and suddenly Mark was five years old sitting on an *Encyclopedia Americana (A to Ava)* at the dining-room table and enjoying Sunday dinner with his family. *Paradise lost,* he thought with a sigh.

"Let me know if you need anything," Ruth said, and disappeared after giving Lisa a pat on the head that made the girl wince. Eleanor picked up the key and started to drop it in her purse but Mark put his hand out. She looked at him questioningly. "My mother thought it important enough to hide so I guess it's important enough for me to look into."

Eleanor started to say something then changed her mind and said instead, "I'm her attorney."

"I'm her son."

She turned the key around until she was holding it by the tip as though studying it, then reluctantly let it drop into his hand. Mark could sense everyone else in the restaurant watching them. The mood at the table seemed at once to sour. The conversation stopped and the three of them made a show of eating; even Lisa managed to finish her chicken though she made little attempt to diminish the mass of peas and corn on her plate. After a few moments of desultory conversation Ruth strode up. "Apple pie for everyone?" She gazed expectantly around the table.

Lisa gave her a devastating smile. "Yes, please."

Mark glanced at the girl's plate and shook his head. "Eat some vegetables first."

"Oh, come on, Pop!" the waitress said. "She can eat veggies the rest of her life. Helen's apple pie can only be had at the Red and White."

His temper already on edge, Mark felt like throttling the waitress; having strangers contradict his instructions in front of his daughter was about as welcome as Eleanor lecturing him on life in South Dakota. "Eat half the vegetables," he said, looking at the adult-sized portion and compromising. Lisa grinned, certain that she had won, and began to attack the peas and corn.

After Ruth left, Eleanor sank back against her seat and frowned. "I assume you want me to put the farm up for sale. I don't know what you can expect in this market, though. Times are tough out here."

Mark told her he didn't want to hold out for a high price. "Make sure one of the agents who specializes in farm properties handles it, and not a residential agent. I know there's five or six specialists—"

"There's exactly two left," Eleanor snapped. "Old Tom Dunphy, who's got one palsied foot in the grave, and Ed Whitson. I'll let Ed take care of it. Not many farmers left, either. Most folks work in town and lease out their land. At least you know you won't go belly-up that way. Won't get rich either, of course."

Ruth returned with three pieces of pie, deftly removing Lisa's plate before Mark could pass judgment on her vegetables. The apples were a luminescent amber, soft and steaming, and the dough flaky and warm, and after one bite all seemed well with the world again.

Ten minutes later when they made ready to leave, Eleanor said, "You sure you don't want me to check on that key? Could be you're the one she was hiding it from, you know. Might be something best left undone."

"I'm sure. What time did you say the funeral was?"

She spoke coldly. "Ten o'clock at Hansen's Funeral Home. No graveside service. Your mom didn't believe in that. Said it was barbaric. I completely agree."

Back at the farm Lisa watched TV while Mark went on his daily three-mile run, though he had to estimate the distance by checking the time, twelve minutes out and twelve back, all along the shoulder of the highway. It was just after nine when he returned. When he emerged from the shower Lisa was asleep on the couch. Mark gently carried the girl into his mother's room, laying her in the middle of the double bed. "Monster . . ." Lisa said, her eyes still closed, and rolled onto her stomach. *Sorry, hon,* Mark said to himself. *Monster's gone, gone, gone. . . . Along with the rest of our life in Dexter.*

In the living room Mark stayed up until eleven, finishing packing the few things he wanted to take home. Finally getting under the covers in his old twin bed he fell asleep at once, thinking, *Sorry, hon, Monster's gone, gone gone. Just like the Gikes.* Almost instantly he came awake. *No, it couldn't be, could it?* Turning on the light he hurried into his pants and walked barefoot to the cellar door. *It's my imagination,* he told himself. *Too much brooding on death and family and endings.* Opening the door, he flicked on the light and walked quickly down the stairs, his head swimming from the nauseous smell. *My imagination, wild flights of fantasy . . .*

Where?

The freezer was against the wall. He pulled up the door. Packages of wrapped meat neatly labeled VENISON, ELK, HAMBURGER. He let the top drop and looked hurriedly around the damp room. The smell was far worse than this morning. Or was that his imagination, too? His gaze settled on the cabinet under the table where his mother stored canning supplies. He yanked the door open and instantly felt sick. Monster. A single bullet hole in his head. *My God . . .*

The body was stiff.

He shut the door at once.

It must have happened yesterday.

But who would kill a harmless dog? And why?

4

There were only about thirty people at the funeral the next morning, one for every year his mother had lived in Dexter, Mark thought darkly. Not a very profound send-off after sixty-three often-difficult years on this earth. Besides Lisa and himself there were no relatives, of course, adding another somber note to the occasion. The pastor from Grace Methodist didn't look older than twenty-five, and couldn't have known her long. Most of what he had to say sounded as though it came from the book of boilerplate funeral clichés. It all seemed very sad; a life whimpering away in the northern prairie winds.

Afterward Mark stood on the sidewalk and shook hands with everyone, renewing a few acquaintances and taking the opportunity to do what he enjoyed most: show off his daughter. But there seemed to be a reticence in the people he talked to, men and women he'd known most of his life, almost as though they were going through a social convention by being here, and wanted to maintain their distance from him. Curious about the lack of evidence of any life prior to Dexter at his folks' house, he asked a few of the older people if they knew anything of the Ritters before moving here. The answer was always the same: They had been dairy farmers, hadn't they? Over in Wisconsin?

Why was he asking? an older man wanted to know. Didn't his mom and dad ever talk to him about the old days? Well, no, not really. He knew about the dairy farm, of course. They'd evidently sold it for a lot of money and moved here because Dad was tired of dealing with livestock. "Corn and wheat don't run away or poop on your shoes," he liked to say, though he'd insist that if you stood in the middle of a field in summer you could hear cornstalks growing.

Eleanor Dahlquist waited until everyone was gone, then wandered over, a grim look on her face. "Ed Whitson's going to stop by the farm tomorrow and tell me what he thinks it's worth. What have you been bugging people about your parents for?"

"I wasn't bugging anyone, Eleanor. I'm just curious. My folks didn't talk much about the old days. I don't even know where they were married, except that it was someplace in Wisconsin."

The lawyer's eyes darkened in anger. "Sometimes I just don't understand people. Always butting their way into others' lives. Your parents were just plain old farmers, Mark. There's no secrets, nothing hidden away. They're dead. Let them lie in peace. Christ sakes!"

Mark shoved his hands in his pockets and stared at her without expression. "I found Monster last night."

"Monster? Came home at last, did he? Well, I figured he would. Probably just got spooked when your mother collapsed on the floor and wouldn't get up. Dogs are funny like that."

"He's dead. Someone shot him and hid his body in the basement."

She looked at him as though he were hallucinating. "*Shot him?* Monster? Who would . . . ? That means someone got inside the house after I locked it up. Unless your mom did it. Maybe she felt herself going and didn't want to leave Monster alone. Old folks think like that sometimes."

"He'd only been dead a day or two. Anyway, my mom wouldn't have touched him. You know that. And getting inside wouldn't be a problem to anyone who knew her. She kept a key out front. Probably half of Dexter knew where it was."

"But no one here would shoot her dog! And the only burglaries we ever have are teenagers looking for booze. They sure wouldn't kill a harmless old mutt." Suddenly she screwed up her face and looked as though she wanted to hit him. "It's that damn key, isn't it? It's making you look for *mysteries* where there aren't any. My God, how I wish you'd never found it! You think this is some kind of *plot*, that that dog's death has something to do with your mom or that goddamn key! Mark, your folks weren't hiding anything from you! Forget it. Act like an adult for once. Go home!"

Mark's anger instantly flared. Maybe it was Eleanor's out-of-place hostility, or finding Monster, or the final impact of facing his mother's death. But he was definitely upset. "You take care of the will, Eleanor.

That's where your duty begins and ends. And tell Ed Whitson to call me in Seattle before he puts the farm up for sale. Maybe I'll hang on to it after all." He seized Lisa's hand and began to walk toward his car. Suddenly he turned back. "Someone was in that house when the dog surprised him, Eleanor. Kind of looks like he—or she—was looking for something, doesn't it?" He started walking to the car again, jabbing his other hand in his pocket and turning the key over in his fingers. *If there aren't any secrets,* he thought, *what the hell were they looking for?*

Back in his mother's house, staring at the boxes of papers and documents he'd removed from the den, Mark felt a growing fury at the attorney. Ever since he'd arrived in Dexter she had acted as if he were an intruder whose only obligation was to put the farm up for sale and get out of town.

Screw it, Eleanor. I don't need you making my decisions for me.

His gaze fell again on the crates he was going to take to the dump. Maybe . . .

He dropped to his knees and began going through the boxes of canceled checks. It wasn't hard because his mother had saved them according to date, a different year in each box. He started with the oldest checks—1967—and glanced at each one. It was almost as good as a diary, and certainly more honest, since checks don't lie. Each year was laid out in black-and-white as if he were there. Grocery bills, utilities, insurance, car payments ($137 a month for their new Ford Fairlane), supplies, seed, fertilizer—there was an eerie fascination to it all, watching his folks' lives progress, if that was the word, month by month: refrigerators, TVs, cars, down payment on a tractor. Deposits in savings accounts as crops were sold, payments to the bank when storms wiped everything out.

But was it really progress? Did things get better, had their lives improved over their four-plus decades farming? Or had it all been a holding action, a frantic attempt to keep their heads above water as they fought the soil and the weather? Finally, shortly after six P.M. he found what he had been looking for in a series of checks to the Rapid City Merchants and Farmers Bank.

Moving quickly to the door he yelled at Lisa who was playing in the barn. "Hurry up, hon, get your clothes. We're leaving."

5

The voice on the phone said, "Now just calm down," but Eleanor Dahlquist was incapable of calming down.

"Look, I'm telling you he knows something's wrong."

The voice remained unaffected. "That's not the same as knowing *what*, is it? Let him muck around. Everyone covered themselves thirty years ago. You know that as well as anyone. He's not going to find anything."

"But the key—"

"That may be a problem," the other conceded with reluctance. "But only if he finds the bank where the box is. It might not even be around anymore. You say she never mentioned anything about it to you?"

"Never! That proves she was hiding something!"

"But in a safe-deposit box! What could it be?"

"It's something from the past." She began pacing in front of her desk, gripping the portable phone tightly, as if to cut off its life as her eyes lost their focus. "It has to be. That key had to be twenty or thirty years old!"

"Even if it were, Eleanor—"

"Damn it, don't you see what it means? What if he somehow discovers what happened? You know the law as well as I do. I can't take any chances. You have to *do* something."

The line went silent for a moment, then she heard a sigh. "I was up there a couple of days ago."

"In Dexter? Why?"

"I thought I better have a look at the old lady's house, make sure there weren't any loose ends hanging around."

"The house! Then you killed Monster."

"That ugly dog? He got in my way. I wasn't about to wrestle him."

"Did you find anything?"

"Anything? Indeed, indeed . . ." Pleasure and fear animated the voice. But he didn't want to tell her too much. "Nothing incriminating, though. Forget about the safe-deposit box. It's probably nothing more than baby pictures."

That's what I'm worried about, Eleanor thought after she hung up. Her heart began to race with fear and she was suddenly warm. *That idiot doesn't understand how this could screw up everything.* She needed help, but who could she turn to?

6

For the second time in three days Mark found himself and Lisa hurtling through midwestern farm country, this time heading toward Rapid City. It wasn't until he was on the road that he realized the bank might not be open tomorrow, this being Friday. No matter. He had to get on with it. If the bank was closed they'd stay over until Monday.

It was after midnight when they pulled into town. Mark checked into a Best Western, looked in the phone book for the number of the Merchants and Farmers Bank and immediately dialed it. A recorded voice said it was open Saturdays from nine A.M. to noon. Relieved and tense at the same time, he lay on his back and stared into the darkness. *What were you hiding there, Mom? What didn't you want your only child to find?*

At five minutes to nine the next morning Mark and Lisa were parked on the street a half block down from the bank with a bag of donuts and two Cokes. Mark was anxious to get inside but wanted the bank to be busy enough that they'd give him little attention when he asked for a box registered in a name different from his. At nine the blinds snapped open, lights flicked on, and the door jiggled as it was unlocked. Two minutes later a middle-aged woman entered. Shortly after a couple with a child went inside and the woman left.

He waited, drumming his fingers on the steering wheel while Lisa finished her Coke. Two men in overalls parked in front and hurried inside, talking volubly and gesturing to each other. The couple with the child came out, laughed at something, walked down the street. Nine-fifteen. Goddamn it, didn't people in Rapid City need to use a bank?

"I have to go to the bathroom," Lisa said.

"Hang on awhile," Mark told her and flicked the car radio on. A classic-rock station: REO. Elton John. Stones. Janis Joplin. Nine-thirty; no customers. Beatles. Bad Company. Cream. A teenager went inside, followed by a man wearing a suit and carrying a briefcase. Two women with a baby carriage . . . Still not enough. He felt warm and put the window down.

At five after ten there were nine customers inside. *Now!* "Come on, hon." They walked quickly down the street, following a young couple through the door. *Safe-deposit boxes.* There was no sign. Mark glanced surreptitiously for the vault—*Act like you've been here before*—and found it at once, next to the tellers' windows, the shiny stainless-steel door ostentatiously open. He walked over to the counter and after a moment a girl of about seventeen came up to him and smiled. "Can I help you?"

He smiled back and showed her the key. "I have to get some papers from my box."

"Sure. I need to see some identification."

Trying to mask his nervousness Mark fished out his driver's license while the clerk tore a form off a tablet and said, "You'll have to sign."

Praying his father had been a cosigner, Mark quickly scratched out his dad's name while the girl smiled and said hi to Lisa. He handed the slip across the counter. She glanced at it and then at his license, evidently not seeing any difference between Mark's and Matthew Ritter's signatures. "Hang on," she said, and stepped over to a file cabinet where she bent to check the signature against the card inside. A moment later she straightened and gave the cabinet a puzzled look. Kneeling down she started going through the files again. After two minutes she eased to her feet and turned to him with a frown. "Can't find your card."

Mark could feel his anxiety ratchet up a notch. "Maybe it's misfiled. It was here when I was in a year ago."

The girl shrugged apologetically. "I'm going to have to ask the manager."

Mark watched, his heart pumping and hands sweating, as she disappeared across the marble lobby to the other side of the bank. Lisa pulled sharply on his shirt. "I have to go to the bathroom." There were only two customers now and Mark began to feel as though everyone was watching him. "Just wait," he snapped. A moment later the clerk returned with a balding and unsmiling middle-aged man. He was holding the signature slip Mark had signed. "Mr. . . . Ritter?"

"Yes." Mark wiped his hand against his slacks, held it out, and the man reluctantly shook it.

"We seem not to be able to find your card. Very strange. *Very.* . . . We don't lose things. This is an extremely efficient bank."

"Well, it happens, I guess." Mark didn't know what to say; he couldn't tell what the man was thinking.

"Yes—" The bank manager looked around in mild agitation as though he didn't want other customers to hear. He turned at last to the clerk, his tone clearly annoyed. "You checked his identification, didn't you?"

"Uh-huh." She sounded defensive, as though used to being blamed for any problems that sprang up in her workday.

"Well, have him fill out a new card. And make *sure* you file it in the correct place this time." He shoved the signature card at her, nodded abruptly, and walked away.

"An unpleasant man," Mark said, hoping to get on her side.

The clerk handed him a blank signature card and pursed her lips. "My father."

"Sorry." He signed the card and she buzzed Mark and Lisa through to the back.

"It doesn't matter. I get blamed for everything at home, too." She led them into the vault and scanned the box numbers. "One-eight-three, one-eight-three . . . There it is." While Lisa stared around the odd-looking area the girl went up on her toes and inserted a key. Mark put his key in, turned it, and pulled out the eighteen-inch box.

"You can go in there," the clerk said and pointed toward a small room with four tiny booths like library study carrels.

Feeling warm, Mark directed Lisa to one of the chairs, then sat next to her and didn't move until he heard the door shut. For a long moment he remained frozen, his eyes fixed on the gray metal box. What had his parents been hiding these last thirty years? And why in Rapid City, rather than Dexter?

7

——Walking—*striding*—eight steps up, fourteen back— hurry, hurry—felt it coming on this time, felt the *swoosh* of convoluted thoughts rushing toward him since returning from Dexter: *Tried to keep it from me, keep* her, *didn't they, didn't they?*

(Looks at the picture.)

Eight up. Fourteen back. *Stride, stride, stride.*

But they always tried to keep her from me. Couldn't. I had her. God, it's hot!

Fourteen back.

Had *her!*

—He saw the photo—like a lightning bolt to the head— (Hear it crack? Smell the sizzle. Brain cells snap.) . . . electricity flowing to nerve endings, toes and fingers, all body parts tingling, alive, like power lines snapping in a storm. *But it's getting away from me, can't concentrate—*

(Venice, the humid, putrid, Mediterranean beach. . . . The face— Tadzio's—"pale and reserved," smiling at him, beckoning. . . .)

So hot. So hot.

My gifts? Prophecy. I see ahead.

To pleasure in all its forms.

Eight up.

—Stops suddenly, jerks his head back, eyes to the blazing Venetian sun, but closed, infinite, the sky of limitless beauty, blue in thirty-two shades across the years, and pallet—

Such soft skin.

My craft? Love. . . . Oh Lord, oh Lord.

(Leaves his body now. . . . Dreams . . . soft skin, touching, tracing his fingers across lines; ins and outs. Tactile. Lives!)

Fourteen small. *Stride.* Eight.

Madness is relative, its meaning defined by the times, and the times-tellers in the Ministry of (This) Truth. (This) Time.

Should take my damn pills. Forgot. Difficult thinking if I don't, connections fade.

—The picture, three-by-five, printed at Kmart, sits, at rest, in his trousers pocket now, against his thigh. Hard. Feels it through the fabric of his pants, feels himself, fools himself, feels foolish himself—

Our experiences, like a thousand random pieces of sky falling to the earth around us, arrange themselves not in the seamless fabric of life, but end in no-bliss ignorance unless organized, ordered—*life* must be ordered—the past and the present, this chunk, that, or else it is meaningless.

Eight big up. Sees her nude, his mind saying, *Yes, yes. You must!* Touching.

Out of breath. *Try. To. Relax.*

8

Mark could feel sweat collect on his ribs as he drew the metal safe-deposit box near him and slowly lifted the lid.

A legal-sized white envelope on top—or rather it had been white years ago. It was now dull with age. He lifted it out. Another envelope below, smaller, brown, fragile, as though it had been opened and closed many times.

And that was it.

His stomach clenched and he felt a spasm of disappointment. What had he expected? Deeds? Gold coins? A map to a buried treasure?

The larger envelope was unsealed. He picked it up and removed four old photographs. More baby pictures: Mark as a newborn, stretched out in a bassinet in a hospital. A blue blanket indicating a boy. A hand-lettered name tag on the bassinet: RITTER, MARK. He looked at the pictures closely and for a reason he couldn't fathom began to feel a chill trace its way along his spine. They were like a hundred other photographs of him as a baby. But somehow they weren't! They were different . . . wrong, as though taken by someone unfamiliar with photography. His heart began to speed and his torso was swimming with perspiration now. Hurriedly, as though not wanting to look at them again, he shoved the photos back and grabbed the other envelope. It was sealed but so brittle around the edges that it practically fell apart in his hands as he picked it up. Ignoring Lisa who began to wander around the small room, he carefully pulled up the flap. There was an official-looking document inside, folded, and then folded again and again to fit the envelope.

His head suddenly light and hands trembling, Mark gingerly opened it. STATE OF IDAHO, it said in fancy letters at the top, and below it, CERTIFICATE OF DEATH. It had been issued thirty years ago in the name of a child who had died at the age of seven months: Mark Alan Ritter.

He could hear his own sudden intake of breath.

Mark Alan Ritter.

He was dead.

* * *

How long did he stare at it? Two minutes? Five? His eyes closed involuntarily and he felt his body rock back and forth in the chair, felt his pulse beating through his fingertips, blood roaring so loudly in his ears he couldn't think.

Slowly his senses began to return to normal and he opened his eyes, breathed deeply, and stared at it again as Lisa mumbled something and tried to hug him around the waist. "Mark Alan Ritter. Age: seven months. Cause of Death: congenital heart failure. State of Idaho." . . . But his parents had never lived in Idaho. They'd lived in Wisconsin and South Dakota. Or *were* they his parents? Suddenly he didn't know. He didn't even know who he was.

Mark Alan Ritter. Age, seven months.

His shock was turning to anger. Fingers trembling, he stuffed the death certificate back in the envelope, shoved it and the other envelope in his pocket, grabbed the safe-deposit box and slammed the top down. "Come on, Lisa."

The clerk saw him come out of the room and hurried over to help lock the box in the vault. When she saw his face she looked concerned. "Are you feeling okay? You're a little pale."

"Fine," he told her and turned the key on the box. "Fine! Great!"

She smiled reassuringly. "Guess what? I found your old card. Someone put it in the Deceased file. Isn't that wild? Who'd think you're dead?"

Two minutes later in the car, his heart thudding against his chest, Mark pulled the brown envelope from his pocket and stared again at the death certificate. "Mark Alan Ritter. Age seven months. State of Idaho." Goddamn it, what could it mean? *Mark Alan Ritter.* The name he'd lived with all his life. Had there been another child with that name? Did he have an older brother who had been given the same name? Or had that Mark Ritter been born into a different family? "Name of Parents of Minor Child: Ritter, Matthew M. and Helen L." His parents. His!

Now what? His fingers tightened painfully on the steering wheel. He needed to *do* something, to talk to someone, but who? He was lost. *State of Idaho.* Maybe that was the key. But why Idaho? He shoved the death certificate back in the envelope and noticed a penciled phone number faintly scribbled on the flap: (970) 555-7126. The area code meant nothing to him. He reached under the seat for his cell phone and dialed the number. It was answered on the first ring, a woman's voice. "Law Offices of Mason Hightower. Can I help you?" Without thinking, he hung up.

A lawyer! Now what? Area code 970! Grabbing the phone, he punched out the number again. "Law Offices of Mason Hightower. Can I help you?"

"You certainly can," Mark said, attempting to sound far more cheery than he felt. "This is Tom O'Neil at Haskins, Dorset, and Fell and I need to send some papers to your office and I just can't find the mailing address anywhere. Can you—"

"Of course. It's 100 Adams Street, Harmony, Colorado, 82706. Is this something that—"

He hung up.

Colorado?

Goddamn it, what *was* this?

He'd never even heard of Harmony. He pulled a road map out of the glove compartment. The town was in the mountains, maybe seventy miles west of Denver.

Harmony!

What the hell is going on?

He turned the key and started for the motel. Thirty minutes later they had checked out. By noon they were heading toward Colorado.

9

Mark and Lisa reached Harmony shortly after six o'clock, at the same time a mountain rainstorm kicked up and almost at once turned to hail that rattled like millions of BBs against the surface of the BMW. Trying to peer through the hail and semidarkness at the town he felt a strange feeling move through him, almost like a virus, prickling the surface of his skin and making the fine hairs along his spine erect and icy with anticipation. *Something's waiting for me here, waiting* . . . Something he would be better off not discovering. But it was too late to back away now. He was trapped in its web.

He passed a sign: HARMONY, A GREAT PLACE TO LIVE . . . A GREAT PLACE TO PLAY. Attached to it were plaques from service organizations: Lions, Rotary, Elks.

The storm had lessened by the time he found the center of the obviously schizophrenic town. The west side was made up of three or four blocks of century-old wooden buildings with false fronts and wooden sidewalks, and looked as if it had been lifted in toto from a failed Hollywood movie lot. The eastern part of town was an Aspen or Vail clone: a score of German-Swiss–inspired condo developments, probably in the $400,000 to $600,000 range, mostly grouped near the massive Eagle Point ski resort, now oddly barren and deserted in midsummer, its numerous runs like treeless swaths of earth scratched out of the greenish blue blanket of pines and spruce by an angry giant hand.

Stretched along both sides of the highway there was a mile-long procession of upscale motels and restaurants, probably also mostly barren and deserted this time of year.

Mark pulled into a three-story ersatz Swiss chalet called The Mountain View and took a room for two nights. The coffee shop was closed so they drove to Denny's in the old part of town, and had dinner, then came back and watched TV until ten when he turned off the light. Lying on his back in the darkness, he tried to sleep but couldn't, couldn't calm the cauldron of emotions his mind had become. Rolling over, he faced the window where a splash of red, the *L* from the motel sign, bled through the blinds and made a stain on the bed.

As a kid in Dexter the only thing he could see from his bedroom window had been stars. If he went outside he could find the Milky Way, something impossible in Seattle or any other big city. When he was small, Lisa's age, his mother would come in each night and sit on the edge of the bed and read to him. Even after he could read for himself she'd spend twenty or thirty minutes reading aloud from one of her own childhood books, and spending time, just being together, the way Mark did now with his own child.

What had his mother been thinking, sitting there staring at him, looking so small in the large bed and ignorant of the lie he was a part of? Was she thinking, *You're not mine but I love you?* Or had she been fabricating stories of his birth—*"Seven hours I was in labor!"*—in case the question ever came up?

But why would it come up? Mark would never have had reason to question his parentage if he hadn't found the key. He was certain his mother had never intended him to find it. It was her private link to a past she needed to keep alive. Then why hadn't she thrown it out before she died? Maybe she was waiting for someone to drive her to Rapid City. She couldn't drive on the highways anymore. Perhaps she was hoping one of her friends would take her so she could close out the safe-deposit box and destroy the death certificate she had held on to all these years.

He angrily rolled onto his other side, facing Lisa, and almost at once a calm began to come over him. Fatherhood had been the one great revelation of life. Marriage he had been ready for, preparing for, in a way, for years. But a child, a part of you, someone who depends on you and loves you without condition . . . Sometimes he felt he loved his daughter too much, that she would be spoiled for marriage because no one could give her this much devotion again. Perhaps it was a poor inheritance to have, and unfair to a future husband.

He felt a recurrence of his earlier fears. *What else have I left you, Lisa? What genes lurk in our shared backgrounds, perhaps forever hidden from us because my mother wasn't honest with me?*

Why the secrets, Mom? What was so important you couldn't tell me?

He twisted onto his back again, feeling warm, and kicked off the sheet. A new anger began to grow in the darkness. His life was being stolen from him bit by bit—his past, his parents, his *being*—all those things that make up who we've been and who we're becoming. It was all slowly disappearing, a little more snatched away each day, as though someone had turned the clock back and was now erasing entire blocks of memory, obliterating his history.

And for what?

Why had Eleanor Dahlquist been so antagonistic when he'd told her he was going to try to find the safe-deposit box? Did she know something about the death certificate? His heart began to race. Of course she knew! It was the only explanation for her hostility. Damn her! Turning on the light between the beds, he grabbed his wallet and rummaged for Eleanor's number, then snatched the phone and dialed while Lisa slept. No answer—and he didn't know her home number.

Goddamn it, she's keeping something from me. She knows! And doesn't want me to find out. But find out what?

Mason Hightower.

It was only seven-thirty A.M. but Mark sat on the edge of the bed and rifled through the white pages until he found the name and address, then turned at once to the yellow pages where Mason Hightower, Attorney-at-Law, had a half-page ad. *Lifelong Harmony native,* it said. *Criminal and civil law. Divorce. Bankruptcy. Foreclosure. Free half-hour consultation. Office open nine to five weekdays.*

Today was Sunday. More than twenty-four hours to kill. Christ! His frustration and anger were mounting again, his body temperature rising with them. He flipped back to the white pages to see if Hightower's home phone was listed but it wasn't. Now what? He came to his feet and began to pace the small room while Lisa said something in her sleep and rolled over in the other bed. They couldn't stay cooped up in here all day; both of them would go nuts. Might as well play tourist and take a look at Harmony.

But already he knew he wasn't going to like it.

Lisa finally woke at eight. *My God,* he thought, it coming as a new revelation each morning, *how sweet she looks when she awakes, just as her mother did.* She rubbed sleep from her eyes and smiled in a way that was going to break a thousand hearts someday.

"Hi Daddy."

Mark sat on her bed. "Did you have a nice sleep?"

"Uh-huh. What are we going to do today?"

"Walk around town. See the sights. Whatever sights there are."

"Can I have an omelette?"

"You can have whatever you want. All you have to do is say 'please.' "

After breakfast at the motel coffee shop Mark drove toward the small downtown, jammed between the older and newer sections of the city, then through the upscale condo developments on the south side of the highway. His initial impression had been correct—almost everything was closed down for the summer, though he saw half a dozen cars at the ski resort; maintenance workers, probably. The newer residential neighborhoods were clean and perfectly maintained, obviously the consequence of substantial association fees. Cobblestone walkways snaked between two- and three-story buildings with balconies and small walled yards. Huge masses of red and yellow summer flowers blazed from perfectly-tended beds or dangled from a thousand hanging pots, and pine and aspen and fir trees were shaped and fussed-over as though nothing could be left to chance or nature.

He stopped the car, put down the top, and let the sun warm them. "Beautiful, isn't it?"

"I like to look at the mountains," Lisa said, and indeed there was much about them to appreciate. Harmony sat in an east-west rift between two ranges that towered two or three thousand feet over the city, giving it the feel of a remote and isolated Swiss village, cut off from both time and tourists.

"I like to look at them too, hon. It's quite a view." Though it was not why they were there, and he fought off thoughts of Mason Hightower and the death certificate, determined to have a good time for Lisa's sake.

Back in the center of the business district he found the older four-story redbrick structure where the attorney had his office. Mark parked in front—when was the last time he'd done *that* in Seattle?—and he and Lisa walked up to the double glass-door entrance with gold lettering that spelled out HARMONY PROFESSIONAL BUILDING. He shook the handle. Locked. A directory on the wall to the right listed a dozen doctors, a dentist, a large Farmers' insurance agency, and Mason Hightower.

As they walked back to the BMW Mark noticed a police car parked up the block. A uniformed officer was inside, smoking a cigarette and evidently wanting to know why anyone would be rattling the door of the Harmony Professional Building on a sleepy Sunday morning. *Good question,* Mark thought. *I don't know why I'm doing it, either. But I do know there's something or someone inside I need to see.*

He started the engine. A whole day to kill. Might as well drive around. West of town he found a new shopping area with an upscale supermarket at one end, a small department store at the other, and a dozen smaller shops catering to skiers and other overly-affluent yuppies sandwiched between. None were open this early. Everyone was at church or asleep. *Or counting his money,* he thought.

Two or three times as he drove around he noticed the police cruiser some distance behind. At first it was amusing ("What are you doing in Tombstone, stranger?"), then it began to grate. What the hell did he think Mark was going to do? Stick up a frozen yogurt store?

To hell with him. It was only ten o'clock and they had nothing to do until tomorrow. Can't sit in the motel all day. Going back through town, he found the highway and headed west. Might as well see the sights.

Lisa loved it, they both did—the top down, sun on their heads, mountains thrust up majestically on all sides. He could spend his life in a place like this, he thought, except that there probably weren't enough full-time residents to support a stockbroker. Still, he could dream.

It was after six when they got back to Harmony. He felt a sudden plunge of emotion as they crossed into the town. Lisa was chattering about something but he didn't hear her. *Tomorrow morning . . .* he was thinking, and felt his heart speed up.

Tomorrow morning I'll find out who I am.

10

——Sitting in his car he tries to slow his racing heart. It can't be. Can it? He blinks, blinks again. Then his fingers close on the steering wheel, gripping it so tightly he can feel the pain shooting up his arms to the back of his head, feel the pulse throbbing in his neck. He switches off the engine and tries to catch his breath—

My God, he thinks: *It has to be!* Has to be!

He should have known, been ready.

Grabbing the door handle he starts to get out, wants to *run* to her, then checks himself. Wait! Who's that man she's with?

He watches as they rattle the handle of the Harmony Professional Building. What could they be doing here? Seeing a doctor? Or Hightower? Was that it? But it was Sunday. Didn't they know that?

They turn and begin to walk back to their car, the man holding her hand, and again his heart begins to beat out of control.

It *is* her!

—Suddenly he's suffused with a joy such as he has never felt before, his body so light he could float—

She *has* come back. He knew she would, he had always known it. Cheryl's returned because she loves him.

So pretty she is in her white shorts, and T-shirt, and white sneakers. So pretty. Just as she's always been.

—Then a piercing of pain, like a needle suddenly plunged deep into his heart, makes him moan aloud, the sound at once filling the car. Who can that man be? What is he doing to her—?

It can't be her father. He's long gone, dead certainly.

Wait . . . And watch. Like you used to do. Remember? Remember?

—He sits frozen now on the seat as the girl and the man climb into a fancy-looking silver sports car. It draws out into the street and comes slowly in his direction. He starts the engine, is about to follow when a police car also pulls out and begins drifting in the same direction—

Wait. And watch.

The small car turns south, the police cruiser following.

Harmony's best, he thinks with a lump of contempt, demonstrating their innate distrust of all outsiders.

He swings his own car around and heads in the same direction. Hang back until the policeman loses interest, which shouldn't be long. And then see where she's going. Sweat begins to swim along his cheeks and his ribs; even his fingers are wet as he turns the steering wheel.

The sports car drives slowly through town, then out to the shopping mall, and finally back to the highway, by which time the police car has disappeared.

Now where?

The car turns west, its top down, the backs of the man's and the girl's heads visible, hair askew.

He can't stand it any longer, puts his foot down on the accelerator, pulls up next to the car, and looks at the little girl. *Looks* at her!

(Heart racing madly.)

She's smiling and talking and pointing excitedly, and then she makes eye contact with him, and smiles again, and he has to let his car drift back, he's shaking so badly.

—*My God,* he thinks—

11

Sometime after three A.M. Mark woke to the sound of his daughter screaming. Leaping out of bed, he flipped on the bedside light. Lisa was shrieking and flailing out with her hands, and saying, "No, no, no."

Sitting on the edge of her bed, he shook her gently by the shoulder. "Wake up, honey, you're having a nightmare. Wake up."

The girl's whole body shuddered violently, her eyes squeezing tightly shut and mouth grimacing. Then suddenly she was awake. Stiffling a sob, she bolted forward, grabbing her father tightly.

"It was a dream, hon. That's all. A bad dream. We all have them sometimes. Even I do." Though hers seemed more frequent, as well as more frightening lately.

Her grip eased but she held on to her father as though to let go was to lose him forever, and he could feel the sweat from her forehead on his chest. After a moment her breathing began to slow. Mark did not want to disengage from her, letting Lisa decide when she felt comfortable enough to break their bond. Finally her fingers loosened and she sank onto the bed. Her voice was so strained and tiny that it made his heart ache. "I was scared."

Mark smiled and tried to put her at ease. "What were you dreaming about?"

"Running. Someone was chasing me."

"Who?"

She looked at him a moment without expression, then gave a small smile. "I don't know. I forgot. A monster, I think."

"Monsters are only in stories, hon. There aren't any in real life. And if there were, I'd smack 'em dead if they even looked at you."

She smiled thankfully at him, and Mark marveled, as he had so many times before, at the enormous trust children feel for their parents, those "big people" who can do no wrong. Or so they think.

He touched her on the tip of the nose. "Go back to sleep, dollface. No more monsters. Dream of . . . chocolate cake, or Barbie Dolls, or . . ." He made a face and began to sing. " 'George, George, George of the Jungle.' "

Lisa laughed, closed her eyes, and was asleep within seconds.

Mark turned off the light and fell back on his bed, listening to his daughter breathe. He'd been unable to tell her: when she woke him up he was having a nightmare. People were standing in a heavy gray fog, looking at him, talking angrily among themselves. When he approached they quickly concealed something, turned away, and suddenly were gone.

II

12

Something's out there, Mark thought the instant he came awake the next morning. *Waiting. . . .*

Hiding. . . .

Expecting me.

He must have been dreaming again, he realized, drifting in and out of that languorous zone between sleep and wakefulness, because the same images he had awoken to earlier were still alive in his mind: people moving about in the fog and darkness, anxiously concealing something as they whispered his name and glanced over their shoulders to ensure they weren't overheard. *Hurry,* they seemed to be saying. *Hurry, before he awakes.*

Dreams as metaphors, he thought: explaining and obscuring at the same time, drawing open the curtain just a little to give a quick glimpse of the truth, then snapping it shut.

But the curtain had parted enough to reveal the obvious: *Something happened here thirty years ago. Something my parents were part of.*

Something involving a baby.

Me.

Stop it, he chided himself. *Your nerves are already on edge; you'll end up talking yourself into a frenzy.*

And the best antidote to that was running: *Wear yourself out.* Since he had been an underclassman at the Academy he had exercised strenuously at least five days a week. Yearly survival training in Guatemala (which he had to volunteer for specifically) further fixed him in the habit. Now, two or three days without pushing his body and he began to feel uncomfortable. After a week his muscles ached and his mind became jumpy and clouded, like someone trying to withdraw from a heavy caffeine addiction.

He dropped to his knees next to Lisa's bed, and gently rubbed her shoulder.

"Ummm?"

"I'm going running, honey. I'll be back in a bit. Don't open the door for anyone. Okay? Not anyone."

Her eyes struggled to open, but she had heard the same words a thousand times. "Okay," she murmured, and immediately fell back to sleep.

Mark put the door key in a holder around his ankle, and quietly let himself out. Four miles out and four back today. He stretched for five minutes even though his running partner at home, an M.D., told him the notion that stretching prevented injuries was a myth that had long ago been exploded by the "experts." Then he took off slowly, letting his muscles ease into it; after a quarter mile he picked up speed. The sun wasn't visible yet but it was becoming light toward the east, the firs and pines a soft matte-black against a sky just now becoming striated with thin lines of white. *The most beautiful time of day,* he thought, as he always did, and took in his surroundings as he ran up and down the unfamiliar hills that made up the land south of the highway: the edge of a park, a gas station that tried to look like something else, boxy faux-European condominium buildings. Again he noticed that flowers were everywhere—in garden beds, window boxes, ceramic pots, hanging baskets. But there were few businesses in this part of town, and no one outside. He had Harmony to himself.

It was twenty minutes after six when he let himself back in the room. Lisa had not awoken yet, probably wouldn't until seven. Time for a shower. He was just coming out of the bathroom ten minutes later when the phone between the beds jangled. Lisa moaned in her sleep and rolled over. Mark grabbed it before it could ring again. "Hello?"

"Mark Ritter?" A man's voice. With an odd, compelling urgency that demanded attention, and breathing so deeply and rapidly Mark could almost see his lungs rise and fall. He had a quick flash of a face—middle-aged and covered with sweat as it bent close to the phone, not wanting to be overheard. Why? Where was he calling from?

"Yes."

Whispering now. "Such lovely skin your daughter has. How fun it's been to feel, my flesh against hers, hard against soft."

Mark's body grew cold. He couldn't reply.

The man's words rushed out. "Her thighs so white and warm, a small imperfection only, a freckle—"

"Is this some kind of joke?" Mark didn't know how to react. He felt as though he was in the midst of a particularly stupid dream. This was ludicrous.

The voice hurried as if he had just seconds left. "She has to die, of course, like the others, like your wife and mother. But I'll make her last day enjoyable. More fun than a picnic at the zoo."

"*What—?*" Mark's voice wavered and died in his throat. Finally he said, "This is absurd. Who the hell are you?"

"Just like your wife and mother had to die."

The dial tone hummed in his ear.

Mark was stunned. His heart was racing, more with anger than fear. This is idiotic, he thought. Why would someone . . .

A man's voice. . . . Distorted, anxious, intent. Or not a man, a young person, a kid, pretending.

"*Such lovely skin your daughter has.*" Jesus, was he supposed to believe the man had actually . . . Actually what? He couldn't bring himself to even think the words. It was sick beyond comprehension, and almost childlike in its attempt to frighten him.

A soft, well articulated pronunciation. Overarticulated. Not like normal conversation. Almost as if it had been recorded and played back. Maybe it had. The voice had not responded to anything Mark said.

"*Just like your wife and mother had to die.*"

He began to pace around the small room. Why the hell would anyone do something like this? Who even knew about his wife and mother—and Lisa? Except someone from Dexter—one of those dour "friends" of his mother's who treated him so distantly at the funeral. Or Eleanor Dahlquist.

"*Just like your wife and mother.*"

But he hadn't told anyone he was coming to Harmony. He hadn't known himself.

Goddamn it! If this was meant to scare him for some reason it was pathetic. No one had done anything to Lisa. He was her father, he'd know if someone had tried to . . .

"Ummm." Lisa rolled onto her back, rubbed her eyes with tiny knuckles, and smiled spontaneously when she saw her father. "I'm hungry."

"You're always hungry." Mark forced himself to sound natural as he sat on the girl's bed. "But you're also a beauty and a joy to behold. Did you know that?" He bent down and kissed her forehead.

"Can I watch cartoons?"

"Never again as long as you live."

Lisa looked at him in alarm.

"Hey, just kidding. Go to the bathroom and get dressed. Then we'll rustle up some grub."

"Huh?"

"That's how people in Colorado talk. Get used to it."

Only an attempt to scare me, Mark told himself again as Lisa disappeared into the bathroom. *But scare me from what? I don't know anybody in Harmony and no one knows me.* What the man said—it was idiotic; he'd probably never even seen Lisa. *"A small imperfection."* Christ! *Couldn't you come up with anything better than that?*

When his daughter came out of the bathroom Mark relaxed back against the headboard. "Hey, hon, do you remember much about day care?" Two years previous, Mark had worked out a deal with Merrill Lynch: as a single dad responsible for a five-year-old he wanted to spend more time at home. With computers and modems there was no reason for someone with his customer base to come into the office anyway. So Mark worked out of his den now, beginning at six A.M., an hour before the market opened back east, and was home after school so Lisa no longer had to go to day care, which she had always hated, and which he had never felt good about anyway.

She gave him a look and glanced around for her shorts. "It was stupid. I told you."

"I know, but what was it like there? Did you mostly play with other kids, or watch TV or play with adults?"

"I played with Mendy and Kristina. Sometimes Kenny." She found her shorts and pulled them on.

He didn't want to go on—this was ridiculous—but couldn't help himself. "Did you ever play with big people? . . . I'm sorry—adults!"

"You asked that. Where's my shoes?"

"Under the bed, I think. Were there games with adults?"

"Mrs. Williams played jump rope sometimes."

"Was Mr. Williams there much? Or any other men?"

"I don't know."

He forced a smile. "There weren't any games where you had to take off your clothes, were there?"

This time her look was almost disbelief. "They tell us about that in school, Dad."

"Good. So that never happened. . . . Did it?"

Making a face, she pulled on her shoes. "I want an omelette, with chili and cheese. Or crepes with strawberries and whipped cream."

"So that never happened? No undressing games?"

"Nope. When are we going to eat?"

Mark stood too quickly, and felt suddenly dizzy. "Now."

They went to a place called Aspens just north of the highway, and ordered breakfast crepes and orange juice. Mark tried to concentrate on reading the *Denver Post*. But after a minute he tossed the newspaper on the adjacent chair; he couldn't keep from fixating on the phone call. Why in God's name would someone do something like that? Damn it, no one even knew he was here.

"Why haven't you eaten anything?" Lisa asked.

"Not hungry, I guess."

"What are we going to do today?"

He tried a smile. "Solve a mystery. Sound okay to you?" He patted her hand.

"I'd rather go swimming."

"We'll see. Maybe we can find a swimming pool later." He glanced at his watch.

She gave him a pouting look.

"What's wrong, hon?"

"When you say, 'We'll see,' it means no."

He laughed and stood up. "Come on, kiddo. This time 'We'll see' means 'Absolutely, positively, yes.' But first we have to see the man." *And,* he thought, *find out why I've suddenly become a danger to someone; and why he would try to get at me by threatening my child.*

13

Impatient, anxious, Lisa in tow, Mark was at the Harmony Professional Building at nine, riding the elevator to the fourth floor where Mason Hightower's office took up the entire northwest corner. He half expected to find the door locked but it swung open into a large and very neat outer office. Stepping in, he let it bang loudly enough to announce his presence.

"Sally?" a voice from beyond asked, and when Mark said, "Nope," a surprised head popped through a half-opened doorway behind the desk.

"Oh, sorry," a middle-aged man said, and came out with his hand extended. He was tall and thickly built, dressed in gray slacks and a white shirt with no tie. "Figured it must be my secretary but she normally doesn't come in till noon on Mondays. Thought for a minute last night's Jack Daniel's was still eating away at brain cells and I'd forgot what time it was." He chuckled happily and stared from Mark to Lisa and back to Mark. "Mason Hightower. Do I know you? Don't think so, though you do seem sorta familiar."

Mark introduced Lisa and himself, and Hightower considered a moment, then shook his head. "Ritter, Ritter, Ritter . . . Nope. Here for business? Might as well come on back and sit a spell."

He led them into his private office, a cheerful area of wood and leather and light pine paneling. The wall of glass behind the desk overlooked the older part of town and the sudden dramatic rise of trees climbing the undisturbed mountains to the north. The two interior walls were decorated with lawyer-trash: diplomas, certificates, awards—*look at me, look at me, look at me*—and a few color photographs signed *M.H.*, showing the surrounding countryside—ranches, ski slopes, the Rockies in winter. It was all very comfortable and affluent.

There was something comfortable and affluent about Hightower, too. Fifty-five or so, with an easy smile and crow's-feet fanning out from his eyes onto puffy pink cheeks. He settled himself behind his granite-topped desk and rested his feet on a pulled-out drawer as though about to take a nap. "So what can I do for you, Mr. Ritter? You're not a Harmony resident, I take it."

"I live in Seattle. I'm hoping you can help me. Are you sure the name Ritter doesn't mean anything to you?"

Hightower squinted, pursed his lips, and tilted his head toward the ceiling as he thought about it. "Nope. Was a TV actor named that, but he doesn't look like you. John Ritter, I think. Wimpy guy, always whinin' about something. What was the name of that show? *Three's Company.* That was it! Remember?"

"How about Dexter, South Dakota? That mean anything?"

Hightower's gaze slid down from the ceiling as he refocused on Mark. "Dexter, Dexter . . . Don't think so. Should it?"

Mark took the envelope of baby photographs out of his sport-coat pocket and put it on the desk. "Would you mind looking at these and telling me if they ring a bell?"

Hightower stared at the envelope as though it were a subpoena and stiffened in his chair, placing his hands deliberately in his lap. "Maybe you better tell me what this is all about before we go any further. You an attorney?"

"No—"

"Cop?"

"I'm a stockbroker. This has to do with my family." As Lisa pushed from her chair and began to wander around, Mark explained about finding the pictures among his mother's possessions. Then he mentioned the death certificate and Hightower dropped his feet to the floor and came forward in his chair. "Jesus," he said softly. "You do have a problem, don't you? Got a birth certificate?"

"Back in Seattle. I haven't looked at it since I got my marriage license."

"Man!" Hightower stood up unexpectedly, rumpled and worried-looking, and shook his head. "I can see where you've got some worries. It's like you don't know who you are. Gotta be one weird feeling." He started to step away, then shot Mark a look. "Why are you coming to me with this? Seems like if you wanted a lawyer you coulda got one in Seattle or Dexter." He smiled. "Not as good as me, of course. But *something* brought you here."

Mark took the other envelope out of his pocket and laid it on the desk directly in front of the man. Hightower sat down and looked at it. "That the death certificate?"

Mark nodded. "Look at the envelope."

Hightower stared at it without picking it up. "Kinda looks like my phone number on there, doesn't it?"

Mark didn't say anything. Hightower finally picked it up and extracted the death certificate, carefully unfolding and flattening it on the desk. " 'Mark Alan Ritter'. That you?" Almost against his will, it seemed, the lawyer's eyes went to Lisa standing by the book-case, then swung quickly back to Mark.

"Yes."

"Must be really something—seeing your own proof-of-death like this." He leaned across the desk with sudden enthusiasm. "Tell me: What's it like on the 'other side' of life? Big flash of white light, sense of well-being and calmness folks talk about? Hell, never mind, I'm just being rude. I really do feel for you, though. Gotta be one hell of a shock. You have to wonder what in the sam hill your parents were up to. If they *were* your parents. You look like 'em?"

Mark waved an arm toward Lisa who had pulled a magazine off an end table and pretended to look at it. "Like most kids, I guess— a little bit. Nothing distinguishing like red hair or big ears or freckles. They both were middle-sized, dark hair and dark eyes, like me. Just sort of typical midwestern farmers."

"Grandparents?"

"Both my parents were orphans. Or so they said." A feeling almost like shame came over him as he spoke to a stranger about his mother and father as though he couldn't trust anything they had told him. Picking up the envelope, he dumped the photos onto the desk, and Hightower slowly flipped through them.

"You think this is you?"

"Hard to say. If they are, why'd my mother hide them?"

Hightower moved them around on his desk. "Got us a real mystery, don't we? Not a who-done-it but a who-am-I?"

"That's why I'm here."

"Well, I can clear up the phone number, I reckon. Had to be my dad, Julian Hightower. I took over his practice twelve years back when he retired. I'd been down in Colorado Springs, in the Public Defender's Office. Daddy wanted to take off and spend the rest of his life trout-fishing so I came up here and took over. Isn't a hell of a lot to do, as you can see, except wills and real-estate law. But the building's mine free and clear, and the docs downstairs keep me in lunch money with their rent. This here law practice is all gravy and there's no heavy lifting so life's good."

"Could your dad shed some light on this?"

"Could if he was alive, but he had a heart attack three months after retiring. Isn't that the way it always is? No, Daddy can't help but Daddy's files sure as hell can. Let me rummage around and see what I can come up with. Ain't nothing else to do this morning. Might be fun and maybe we can clear up your little problem. Come on back about three. Ought to be done by then. On the other hand, there's no telling what shape those files are in. Didn't have computers back when Daddy was here. Good thing, too; if they'd had, he woulda put a .thirty-eight slug in every one he saw. Kind of an old-fashioned cuss, if you get my meaning."

Mark did, he told him. His father had been the same way. If Matthew Ritter *was* his father.

Hightower started to rise but Mark said, "One more thing."

The attorney settled back in his chair. "Shoot."

"Someone called me at the motel this morning." He slid a quick glance at Lisa playing with her magazine and dropped his voice. "He said my daughter was going to die."

"What?" The word came out as a low-pitched wheeze.

"Just like my wife and mother."

"Those were his words?"

Mark nodded. "It got cruder than that. A suggestion of molesting. But there was something almost ridiculous about it. Like he was playing at being a pervert but wasn't quite sure how to do it."

"But why do it at all? Your wife died—"

"In an auto accident."

"There was no doubt it was an accident?"

"None. And my mother died of a stroke." He paused, flipped his hand over. "If she was my mother."

Hightower was clearly confused. "So maybe he does mean someone else. Or maybe he's just trying to frighten you. I guess the question is why? You don't have any idea?"

"Not at all."

Hightower looked as if he didn't believe him. People whose lives are threatened normally know why. "And you don't know anybody from Harmony?"

"Not as far as I can tell."

The large man settled back in his chair. "A kook? Someone taking a shot in the dark?"

"I would have thought so, but he knew my name. And that my wife and mother are dead."

"You've got to have some idea." He fixed Mark with a look that said, *Stop screwing with me.*

"None whatsoever. No one even knew I was coming here. I didn't know until I found your phone number."

"Doesn't really seem to be a threat against the girl, though, does it? More like a threat against you. The girl's too young to upset anybody."

"That's what I figured. So I guess we wait and see. Curious, though, isn't it? In a town where no one knows me, or knew I was arriving, someone is aware of both." He rose to his feet, feeling no better than when he had come in. "So now what?" he asked the attorney. He had six hours to kill. "How do people spend a day off in Harmony?"

Hightower's chair rocked forward and his face lit up. "Well now, myself, I like to drive east about thirty miles where there's this right nice cattle ranch—Herefords, mostly, though there's a few real handsome Black Angus, too. I just pull off the road and go up to the fence and let the cattle stare at me for two or three hours while I chew tobacco. They just love watching my jaws work. Sometimes I spit for them but—" Suddenly he started laughing. "Hell, I'm just kidding you. Don't look at me like that. What do you think tourists do? In the winter they drink and ski. Rest of the year they drink and say, 'Ain't nothin to do here.' You get bored, drive over to Denver and watch our elected representatives misrule us. Or I can point you to a real sweet house of what some bad-tempered folks call 'ill repute' in Georgetown. Otherwise there ain't much but watching *The Price is Right* at the Mountain View."

14

Mark felt a sudden plunge of emotion as he walked out of the Harmony Professional Building. Taking Lisa s hand he started walking toward the car, torn between disappointment and anger, feeling as though he would like to throw his head back and scream at the top of his voice. But what had he expected from Hightower—a sudden revelation, something life-changing? *Yes, I remember. Your real parents are descendants of the Emperor Franz Joseph who were just passing through town and decided to put you up for adoption. . . .*

Hightower had probably been in his early twenties thirty years ago. Was he living here then, or away at college? And what was he likely to find in his father's files from the sixties? Who even *has* files from thirty years ago?

"Come on, Lisa." They crossed the street and were almost to the car when he saw a sales rack for the *Harmony Courier,* and stopped abruptly. Of course—a local newspaper! They'd have back issues. If something happened here in 1968 that had caused a parent to give up a child . . . or resulted in the death of the parents, leaving the child an orphan, it almost certainly would have made a small-town paper.

He shoved two quarters in the rack, pulled out a copy, and hurriedly looked for an address. It was on page 6 of the eight-page first section: 360 Adams Street. Less than three blocks from here.

"We're going to visit someone," he told Lisa as he began to walk quickly. "Hurry up."

He could see the building from a block away, a single-story adobe structure on the other side of the road. Grabbing Lisa's hand he crossed in the middle of the block, just as an elderly man dressed in buckskins, boots, and a floppy leather hat appeared from a side street. Mark felt his daughter's hand tighten in his as the girl noticed him. "Just some local color, kiddo. Don't be alarmed."

The old man halted in front of the *Courier* building as Mark and Lisa approached. He had to be in his seventies, Mark thought, tall and thin, with skimpy, shoulder-length gray hair that hadn't been washed in years, a long, limp mustache and wispy goatee. His buckskin clothing seemed almost as old and brittle as he was, and the stench of tobacco was evident from a dozen feet away. He swept off his aged hat and bowed grandly from the waist. "Welcome to Harmony, folks. Name's Bill." He straightened and beamed at them from a face weathered with a million wrinkles.

"Wild Bill?" Mark hazarded warily.

He winked at them. "Well, it's what folks call me. That was really my grandpa, though, the *first* Wild Bill. Died up Dakota way, holding aces and eights."

"Dead man's hand," Mark said.

Bill grinned with the several teeth he had remaining. "You know your history. A rare thing today."

"Every poker player knows Aces and Eights." He stuck out a hand. "Mark Ritter. And Lisa." They shook hands, then the old man bent down. "Lisa, you say. . . ." He stared at the girl with an intensity that disturbed Mark as he remembered, *"Such lovely skin your daughter has"*.

"Lee-saaah . . ." the man repeated softly. A thin, dirty hand reached out and the girl shook it reluctantly. "Lisa! Yes, indeed. You're a real looker. Freckles too. But you must not have washed today. Look what's in your hair." His fingers brushed the top of her head, hesitated, then produced a quarter. He held it in front of Lisa's face. "Go on, take it, it's yours."

The girl's eyes went uneasily to her father, who nodded. As Lisa pocketed the money Bill said, "Let's see if there's anything else," and pulled a ten-inch black-and-gray feather from behind her head. "Now, how do you reckon that got there?"

Lisa looked at the feather in wonder while Bill fluttered it across her nose, making her giggle. Then he stuck it in Lisa's T-shirt pocket. For a long moment the old man seemed frozen as he stared into the girl's eyes, then he pushed to his feet and stared over at Mark. "Your people from around here?"

"I'm not sure."

"She don't much look like you. Blue eyes and fair. You're a little dark. Must favor her momma." He took an old Polaroid camera from a leather pouch around his waist. "Why don't you two stand in front of the building here and I'll take your picture. No charge. It's courtesy of our friendly Harmony Chamber of Commerce."

But Mark wasn't paying attention. His eyes were riveted on a green Land Rover turning off Main a block away. It couldn't be, could it? Probably just someone who looked like her.

"Something wrong?" Bill asked, looking in the same direction.

Mark turned back to him. "Just thought I saw someone I know."

"What? That lawyer lady in the four-by?"

"You know her?" Mark was surprised.

"Know *of* her. 'Dollkiss' or something like that. Lived here years ago, I think. Someone told me she has a time share over at the resort— a week in winter and a week in summer, August, I think. Don't know why she'd be here now."

"Interesting." Mark turned back but the car had disappeared down a side street. "Funny, she never mentioned Harmony to me." But his musings were interrupted by an angry voice from behind. "Damn it, Bill, how many times have I told you to stop bothering kids?"

Mark turned to see a policeman standing with his hands on his hips, glaring at the old man. He was about thirty, tall, Greek-looking, with black curly hair, and a tightly muscled body.

Bill put his finger to his lips as he pretended to ponder. "Well, now, I think it's eighty-five. . . . No, no, wait, I forgot about last Tuesday. . . . Eighty-six times! That right, Officer?"

The cop rested his right hand on his baton. "Want me to run you in again?"

The old man took off his hat and crushed it against his chest. "Oh, please, sir, don't do that. This noble old heart couldn't stand such a shock. My untimely death would be on your hands. And conscience, if you had one."

The cop turned to Mark. "Chamber of Commerce pays this old fart to walk around and play-act at being Wild Bill Hickock, and take pictures of people. They don't pay him to annoy kids." He turned back to the man. "Go on, get the hell out of here. I mean it. Tired of seeing your ugly face. And don't let me catch you putting your hands all over kids again. I saw what you were doing."

Bill put his hat back on, bowed with an infinite grace, and smiled at the cop. "I believe I will exercise my constitutional right to stand awhile on a public walkway."

The cop's baton was suddenly in his hand. "Goddamn it, I'm not kidding. Get your smelly ass out of here. Now!" He prodded the old man in the chest with the end of his stick.

Mark was annoyed with the cop's *"I'm the law"* attitude. He said, "Leave him alone. He was just talking to us."

The man's pale face flared as he spun around. "Keep the fuck out of this." There was a blue-and-white name tag on his uniform pocket: SAMPLE.

"A lovely day the Lord's given us," Bill said, glancing happily at the perfect blue of the sky. "I could stand here for hours and stare at it. Fact is, I think I will."

The cop pushed again with his baton. "Out of here, you goddamn bum. Get moving!"

"Wait a minute," Mark said, his anger mounting. "Is there a law against talking in Harmony?"

"And who the fuck are you?" Sample demanded, turning his full attention on Mark now. Lisa, suddenly frightened, put her arm around her dad's waist.

Mark smiled. "I'm the president of the American Civil Liberties Union. And you're out of line."

"All right, smart-ass, let me see some identification." The cop had lost all interest in Bill.

"Let me see some probable cause."

Sample raised his baton, Lisa shrieked loudly, and the door of the *Courier* suddenly opened. "What's going on out here?" A young woman in her mid-twenties, thin and willowy, wearing slacks and a blouse, looked from Bill to Sample to Mark.

Bill removed his ancient hat, bowed smartly, and smiled through yellow teeth. "Our uniformed thug here is fixin' to arrest us for talking to each other on this fine Colorado morning."

She stared without surprise at the cop. "Oh God, Bobby. Now what?"

He flushed a sudden red. "I don't hafta explain nothin' to you, Karen. It ain't none of your damn business."

"Bobby—"

"Don't give me that, Karen!"

"What did they do?"

" 'Interfering with police work.' "

"Bobby—"

"This asshole," he angrily pointed his baton in Mark's face, "is impersonating an attorney."

Her face clouded over. "Well, why didn't you say so? That's serious stuff. Put him in jail for bad taste if nothing else. I get to keep the cute one, though." She bent down and tried to look at Lisa but the girl retreated behind her father's leg.

"Don't joke, Karen. Both these guys is giving me trouble."

She walked up and stared in his face. "Bobby! Hello! Is anyone home in there? Are you listening? Go . . . Away . . . Now."

"Damn it, Karen." His thick fingers tightened around the baton.

Karen nodded at his hand. "Very Freudian, Bobby. Cops like to play with their rod in public, don't they? Makes them such a manly man."

"Shoulda fuckin' expected this from you, Karen."

"I know what," she said brightly. "Let's put your picture in the next issue of the *Courier*. How about 'Local Officer Sued for False Arrest'? Don't like that? How about 'Bobby Sample Fired for Gross Stupidity'?"

The policeman stared hatefully at her a moment, then spun around and stomped across the street where his car was waiting. The woman smiled at Bill. "Better disappear for a while. He's going to be in a bad mood. Not that his good mood's much better."

The old man said, "I'm already gone," and hurried down the street, singing to himself.

She shook her head as she watched him disappear. "I don't know about Bill sometimes. He's fun but just a little too off-center." Suddenly she remembered herself and turned to Mark, sticking out a hand and smiling beautifully. "Karen Paige. A reporter on the *Courier*. *The* reporter, actually. Don't worry about Bobby. He's just trying to play grown-up and finding it difficult." Her eyes locked on his.

"Mark Ritter. This is Lisa."

She shook hands with both, giving special attention to Lisa again, but the girl was still unresponsive, holding on to her dad with her left hand.

"Actually, this is where I was headed," Mark said. "I need to see back issues of your paper."

"That's a new request. For me, at least. Well, come on in and we'll see what we can do." She grabbed the door and held it as they went inside to a reception area with a counter but no place to sit. She retreated behind the counter and said, "You're not from around here, are you?"

"I don't think so," Mark said, surprising himself. Think so! Why did he say that? "I'm from Seattle. South Dakota before that. Actually that's why I'm here. I'm not sure where I was born. Or who I am." Hurriedly he told her about finding the death certificate and his feeling that his parents might have spent some time in Harmony. Maybe he could find something in the paper about them.

Karen shook her head. "Sounds weird. Coming across your own death certificate, I mean. But it'll make a great story for me, won't it? If you find something, that is. Let me ask Noel Atchison. He's out back. He's the *Courier*'s editor. And publisher. And owner. He'll know how far-back we keep things."

She disappeared through a rear door, returning a moment later with a red-faced blimpish man in his late sixties wearing twill pants and a sweat-stained sport shirt. He squinted at Mark and Lisa through his bifocals but didn't offer to shake hands. "What'd you say your name was?"

"Mark Ritter. I think my parents might have lived here thirty—"

"Yeah, yeah, Karen told me. Weren't any Ritters I remember and I've lived here since 'fifty-nine."

Mark could feel himself becoming agitated. He put his hands on the counter and tried to keep his voice steady. "Look, I know this sounds strange to other people but it's important to me. I have to know where that death certificate came from. What were my parents keeping from me? If I'm not who I thought I was, who am I?"

The publisher frowned, clearly unimpressed. "Seems pretty obvious: you were adopted."

"But I don't *know* that! Can't you understand? If the people who raised me weren't my parents, who were? Who died at seven months? And why didn't they tell me? Why all the subterfuge?" *And*, he didn't add, *why did somebody try to frighten me this morning?*

The older man shook his jowly head and shoved his hands in his back pockets. "Hell, makes sense, I guess. If it was me I reckon I'd be doing the same thing you are. If you're really serious, though, you might want to get an attorney to dig into the legal stuff. You're not likely to find what you want in a newspaper."

"I know that. I've already talked to Mason Hightower."

The man gave him an agitated look. "Hightower! He send you over here?"

"No. He doesn't know. I didn't even think of it until a few minutes ago."

The man's face eased and he stuck his hand across the counter. "Name's Noel Atchison. Come on back and I'll show you what we got." He lifted a board in the counter, allowing Mark and Lisa through.

"I've only owned the *Courier* for twelve years. Had a hardware store before that but sold out when I saw Wal-Mart rolling west like a herd of crazed buffalo. Pretty obvious that small retailers were going to get trampled like grasshoppers on the prairie. Ed Rausch who owned the paper died about then so I bought it from his widow. Been learning ever since how to run it."

He pushed open the door to the back and smiled at the two Ritters. "Come on, young lady. And you might as well see too, Karen." The four of them moved down a bare hallway past a single large office. Atchison waved a proprietary hand. "The city room. Where the ink-stained wretches—meaning me and Karen—toil. She writes and I correct. Ain't that right, Karen?"

The young woman laughed. "Noel never says 'ain't' unless there's visitors around. I think he committed Fowler's *Modern English Usage* to memory. He just likes to play the hayseed to outsiders."

Atchison shook his head sadly. "Being accused of histrionics by this neophyte."

They had stopped in front of a closed door. "Come on, Karen. Let's see what secrets we've got hidden back here."

15

Karen Paige stepped forward and opened the storage-room door. Atchison reached a hand in and flipped on a light. "This is it, the sanctum sanctorum of the *Harmony Courier*. Storage, files, and assorted detritus from the soon-to-be-vanished Age of Print. I haven't been inside for five years. What do you think, Lisa?"

The girl looked around and frowned. "I don't like it. It's spooky."

Atchison laughed. "I don't much like it either. It's an unholy mess. Well, let's see what's here."

The room was so crammed with boxes they could barely fit in; most were marked on the outside with a black felt tip pen: 1979, 1980 . . . "Receipts, office crap, payroll records. Suppose I can get rid of most of it. Just never had the energy to go through it all. Let's see: back issues, back issues . . ."

Metal shelves sagged with dusty keyboards, typewriters, telephones, and other random leavings of office life from the sixties and seventies. Stacks of old-fashioned green-and-white computer paper overflowed from another bookcase.

"Ah-ha!" Atchison said abruptly and pointed to a shelf of stacked canvas bindings. "These are the volumes for—let's see . . . goes back to 1976. You want the sixties, though. It was a weekly back then, just eight pages. I went to twice weekly in 'eighty-nine. Actually made money out of Wal-Mart and the new supermarkets, with all the advertising they do. The little guys never wanted to spend the money. Let's see . . . pre-1976 is over on this other shelf, I think."

He bent and pushed some heavy boxes away from the shelves. "Here we are. Let's see what we got: 1975, 'seventy-four, 'seventy-three— looks like it goes back to 1960. I guess anything earlier must've gotten thrown out. Doesn't matter to you, though, does it? Reckon this'll do?"

"Yes," Mark said at once. "Great. Mid- to late sixties."

Atchison came laboriously to a standing position, and looked around with a sigh. "Suppose you can take this stuff to the city room if you want, but Karen and I got work to do."

"No, no, this'll be fine," Mark assured him. "I can sit on the floor."

The publisher glanced dubiously at the clutter. "That would be best. If you can *find* the floor. Guess we ought to get back to work, huh, Karen? Happy hunting."

Karen smiled at him. "Let us know what you discover. I'll want to do a story on it."

"Sure," Mark said, but he was only half paying attention as he pulled a dusty keyboard from a shelf and handed it to Lisa. "Write a letter, kiddo. I have things to do." He bent and pulled out three bound volumes at once: 1967, 1968, 1969. Moving aside some boxes, he settled on the floor, his back against the wall, and laid the middle volume on his lap. His stomach tightened and his mouth went dry as his hands held it. *The year I was born . . . something happened, something my parents didn't want me to know—or, the people who* said *they were my parents.*

The Harmony Courier, 1968. Price ten cents.

He flipped the cover back and began to quickly scan the headlines. Snow storm . . . high-school basketball . . . crop news . . . taxes. A whole page of letters to the editor—mainly diatribes against politicians in Washington. His interest quickened as he saw a weekly "Police Log" that listed every call the department responded to. Reading carefully, he scrutinized each entry but most were uneventful—burglar alarms, drunk driving, husband-wife disputes, cars stuck in the snow.

There was little national news even though the country had been in the throes of a popular upheaval not seen since the Civil War— a disliked president and a detested war, drugs, civil-rights demonstrations, a recent assassination, the sexual revolution. Little evidence of any of it appeared in the *Harmony Courier,* though. People probably bought the *Denver Post* for that.

The final three pages were given over to classified advertisements and closely-printed legal notices—loans in default and applications for business licenses, mostly. Quickly scanning them, Mark's heart skipped a beat as he saw a two-inch column headed "Vital Statistics." Maybe that was what he was looking for: births and deaths. Just one child born that week, a girl named Kimberly Ann Dunnett. Two deaths, both in their seventies. And that was it. But this was what he needed! An official record of births! If whatever he was looking for was not in a news story, maybe it would be here. The seven-month-old child—Mark Alan Ritter—who died in Idaho might have been *born* in Harmony.

He moved to the next issue and quickly scanned the headlines and police log: a schoolbus accident, no one hurt. A citizens' meeting about taxes. The "Police Log." Impatient, anxious, he flipped to "Vital Statistics." No births. A thirty-seven-year-old woman died at Memorial Hospital. No cause listed.

Feeling a knot growing in his stomach he hurried through issue after issue, quickly glancing at headlines before turning to "Vital Statistics." Only the weather—always on page one—seemed to change as the year progressed. Most of the paper was given over to blatant promotion of local businesses—a new restaurant, a new retail outlet, beauty shop. Every real-estate agent in town seemed to appear at one time or another holding an award they'd won, and every local youngster who finished military basic training was pictured, steely-eyed and unsmiling in an official photograph, standing in front of an American flag. Even the ads varied little from week to week.

Occasionally there was something of local interest—a miner claiming to find silver down by Beaver Creek, the owner of the ski resort thinking about expanding, the town's only bank being robbed by two men who were later tracked down by dogs. But clearly there was little real news in the little town.

He finished the volume. Seventeen boys had been born during the year. Mark jotted down the name of each along with the parents' names. But there was nothing out of the ordinary, nothing relating to anyone named Ritter, nothing about a child born under unusual circumstances, or a child dying at seven months. No crimes or disasters or accidents or . . . Or *what?* Damn it, what was he looking for? He had no idea. But whatever it was, he felt certain, it was *here,* in this room, in this volume or one like it. He *knew* it.

He put the book down and grabbed 1967. January 5. "Mid-Winter Blizzard Buries Harmony" . . . "Area Scholar at State Spelling Bee" . . . "Real Estate to Recover, Expert Vows" . . . Issue after issue after issue. A pattern soon became apparent in the "Police Log," though: Home burglaries and "shots fired" in the summer turned to spousal abuse and an occasional suicide as the dour winter months proceeded. But again there was nothing even remotely concerning an orphaned or abandoned baby, or a couple losing a child. Fourteen boys born; again he noted their names.

He began to feel panicky. He should have found something by now.

"You okay, hon?"

"Can I have a telephone?"

He got up, grabbed two old phones off the shelf and handed them to his daughter. "Call Mrs. Campbell, tell her where you are." Mrs. Campbell was a next-door neighbor who frequently watched Lisa.

"Where am I?"

"Harmony, Colorado. Thirty years ago." While Lisa played with the phones Mark grabbed 1969 and sat down again. January 2. "State Suffers Under Severe Storm" . . . "No New Taxes, Vows County Leader" . . . "Harmony Resident Accepted at West Point." More national news now. Nixon taking over from Johnson, farmers and ranchers complaining about Washington. "Seniors May Not Graduate": a dozen kids at the high school who walked out to protest the Vietnam war; the school board, stunned at such impertinence, immediately suspended them. "Vital Statistics." Twenty-three boys born—many nine months after the "Severe Storm," a local official, who refused to be identified, noted.

Something was desperately wrong. Mark came to his feet, went back to the shelves, grabbed 1965.

"Can we go?" Lisa asked.

"Surprising Mild Weather" . . . "Need for New School Questioned" . . . "Fire Guts Gas Station." No serious crimes. No Ritters. Fifteen baby boys.

Goddamn it, it's here, I know it! His eyes swept around the cluttered room. *It's here! Somewhere. . . .* His gaze settled on the discarded volumes. Maybe! Snatching up 1968 again he began to flip through it: January 4 . . . January 11 . . . *Maybe!* . . . January 18 . . . January 25 . . . In another minute he found it. June 20. Next issue July 11. He hadn't noticed before because it hadn't occurred to him to check the dates. He slammed the cover shut. Two issues missing. *Goddamn it!*

His heart was heaving as he gathered up the book and hurried down the hall, Lisa trailing silently behind him. Noel Atchison and Karen Paige looked up suddenly from their desks as he stood red-faced in the doorway. "Where the hell is it?"

Karen turned a surprised expression on her boss, who looked both confused and annoyed. "I suppose you figure we know what in blazes you're talking about."

Mark came up to Atchison's desk and dropped the bound volume with a thud. "Two issues are missing. June 27 and July 4. Where the hell are they?"

The publisher adjusted his glasses and moved the book around to look at the date. "Nineteen sixty-eight. Interesting. But how should I know where they are? I didn't even own the *Courier* then."

Mark felt like grabbing the older man by the shirt but managed to dampen down his anger. "But you own it *now!* Goddamn it, it's your paper! What the hell happened to them?"

Karen came over and began to flip through the pages, looking for the dates in question. "Maybe they're just bound incorrectly."

Atchison said, "What I bought is in that room back there. I've never even *looked* at those back issues. Got no reason to. If there's something missing it was missing when I took over. Might be, they aren't missing at all. Paper could've missed publishing a couple issues—it happened sometimes. It's always been a shoestring operation."

Karen Paige had spread out the book on an empty desk and was staring closely at the binding where two issues met. "I don't think so, Noel. They've been cut out, all right. Look—"

Both Noel Atchison and Mark bent over the volume as Karen pushed the two sides flat against the desk. Atchison squinted and ran his finger along the crease. "Yeah, there was something there, for sure." He brushed tiny fragments of paper onto the desk. "Cut with a razor blade, most probably. Years ago, from the looks of it."

"Who else would have back issues?" Mark asked at once.

Atchison straightened and shrugged his shoulders as Lisa began to spin herself around in a swivel chair. "I've never heard of anyone. Like I said, it was an eight-page weekly—that's pretty much the definition of 'ephemeral' you know."

"Is there a library here?"

Atchison shook his head. "No money for it in Harmony. No call, either. Folks ain't much for reading."

"Goddamn it!" Mark's fists clenched at his sides. He felt like hitting something.

Karen said, "You know the time period you're interested in now. You don't need a newspaper. Ask some people who lived here then what they remember about late June or early July 1968."

"Good idea," the publisher said. "There's still a fair number of folks from the old days. Me included."

Mark jumped on the idea. "Do you recall anything? Something unusual—maybe something about a boy being born or . . . I don't know—*anything!* Nineteen sixty-eight—the summer! Think!"

" 'Sixty-eight . . . Vietnam . . . God, wasn't that the Summer of Love and all that: San Francisco and a flower in your hair?"

Karen looked at Mark and smiled. "Our hippie publisher."

"Oh, not me," he said at once. "Christ, I was trying to keep alive selling tools and feed over on Main and Third. Wouldn't have gone to San Francisco on a bet. Still wouldn't. L.A., either."

"But do you *remember* anything?" Mark pressed.

Atchison shook his round head and frowned, clearly annoyed. "Nope. Of course, you yelling at me isn't bound to refresh my memory. Let me think on it a bit. Maybe something will pop up."

"Who, then? Who around here can help me? There must be someone!"

"Well, your attorney pal, for one. Hightower spent his early years here before going over to Colorado Springs for a bit. He wasn't practicing law back then, but he might have heard his dad talking about anything unusual. Old Julian knew everything that happened in town, including things that never made the newspaper."

"I've already done that. There must be someone else."

"Well, of course, there's still a few old-timers. Doesn't mean they'd remember anything. It's been a long time."

"What about B.J.?" Karen asked Noel.

"Yeah . . . maybe. He was only a kid back then. But his parents lived here, and he knows most everyone from the pre-resort days."

"B.J. Blake," Karen said to Mark. "A real-estate broker. We usually have lunch with him. Come over to the Rocky Mountain Cafe at one. We'll hold him down while you grill him."

"The Rocky Mountain. Where is it?"

"Second and Main. And don't forget I've got a story riding on this. Maybe I'll be able to parlay it into a job on a real newspaper." She smiled at Atchison who said, "Yeah, sure, Karen. A year at the *Denver Post* and you'd be beggin' me to take you back. But, hell, I want to hear what B.J. has to say, too. Those two issues were cut out for a reason. Like to know what the hell it is."

Mark took Lisa's hand. "One o'clock. We'll be there."

When the door shut behind their two visitors, Atchison put his feet up on his desk and shook his head. "I hope I didn't just see what I think I saw."

Karen turned to him. "What's that, Noel?"

"The little light of love—or was it lust?—gleaming in your baby-blues. Even the hair on the back of your neck vibrated."

Karen batted her eyes at him and smiled beautifully. "Don't be foolish. I'm just trying to help."

" 'Foolish' is exactly the right word. You've got enough troubles without adding Ritter to them. As you damn well know." *And,* he thought but didn't add, *Ritter doesn't need your kind of trouble, either. He's gonna have enough as it is.*

16

"Dang fools," Wild Bill muttered to himself as he hobbled along the rural road to his cabin a mile west of town. "I *knew* it'd come to this. Had to. *Had* to! 'Goes around comes around,' is what they say. 'Goes around comes around.' " And this had definitely come around. " 'Bout knocked me on my ass," he said aloud, and grinned as he imagined others' reactions. *They're going to be scared shitless and witless.* "Like to see the looks on their faces. Be better than a picture show."

He turned off the road and followed a dirt path down a gully overgrown with waist-high weeds and occasional aspens that fluttered in the slight breeze. "Ritter, Ritter, Ritter . . . Never would have given him a thought. Just another fool outsider coming to waste his money. But the *girl*—yes, sir! That's a beauty—a real beauty. Skin like a princess. And great big eyes the color of a Colorado sky." He began suddenly to whistle and a dog barked a greeting and exploded out of the underbrush. "Howdy, Deadwood. Papa's home early. Got us a thing or two to do."

Rounding a bend he came upon his cabin. Just one room, it had been built from logs in the 1890s. Somewhere along the line electricity had been added but not plumbing. Surrounding the house on all sides was a lifetime's collection of junk—wheels, bicycle parts, pipes, a washing machine, two couches, stray pieces of wood and metal.

Bill limped up on the porch and pushed on the door where he'd nailed two aces and two eights. "Come on, dog, we got something to do."

Inside, things were, if anything, messier. Trails had been cleared between boxes of clothes and old books and kitchen utensils so he and Deadwood could maneuver from one end of the cabin to the other. A television sat on a wooden crate, with an antenna wire running out a window, a ripped green leather chair in front of it. A card table stood off to the side, along with two mismatched kitchen chairs.

Deadwood barked, wanting to be fed, something Bill had forgotten to do for two days. He had also forgotten to take his medication for two days, he realized. He'd have to get to that. But first—

He sat down at the table, moving aside rubble and grabbing the phone. He remembered the old phone number—ought to, he'd called it enough, almost daily for a year—but it would have changed since the last time he made this call, twenty-nine years ago. He rose and rummaged around until he found a two-year-old phone book under some ancient *Life* magazines and hurriedly flipped through it, looking up the number.

Then he sat at the table again, whistling as he dialed, and waited until it was finally answered. "Well, hi there! Remember me? Sure you do. I'm the one that saw you kill Carl Stark thirty years ago. I'm *ba-aaack!*" He couldn't help but chuckle with pleasure, then added sweetly, "Did you miss me?"

17

Only ten forty-five. More than two hours to kill until Mark met Karen and Noel Atchison at lunch. So now what? He didn't want to go back to the motel. Waiting in that small room with nothing to do would drive him nuts. "How about a drive?"

"Can we put the top down?" An excited if predictable reaction.

"Sure." They headed west, higher into the Rockies. Between Copper Mountain and Vail, Mark turned north, found a single-lane Forestry road, and followed it past a metal No Trespassing sign. It was a beautiful midsummer day in the high seventies, with a clear blue sky and gentle breeze. Lisa, still unused to the convertible, was more entranced with the car than the scenery. "How fast can you make it go?"

Mark started to answer flippantly before being halted by the weight of responsible parenthood. "As fast as the speed limit."

She rolled her eyes and brushed the hair back from her face. "Daaaad."

"Life has limits, hon. Ours is about forty-five on this road." But even that was a bit much as the single lane twisted and turned through a series of switchbacks. After three miles the pavement ended and the road became rutted dirt with a layer of dust that swirled up and landed on the car and its occupants. "Far enough," Mark said, and pulled to the side next to a meadow of wildflowers surrounded by blue spruce and pines, and a huge stand of aspens that twitched nervously in the breeze.

"Look at that bird!" Lisa burst out of the car, and raced into the meadow, hoping to catch it. Mark got out and rested against the front fender as his daughter laughed while black-and-white magpies landed around her and pecked at the soil, ignoring the girl until she got too close, then leaping more than flying to a nearby spot. Finally, exhausted from running, Lisa plopped down on the ground, surrounded by blue columbine, goldenrod, and purple larkspur that rose to her shoulders and brushed against her bare arms.

It looked like a picture on a calendar, and Mark's heart went out to his daughter. Then she shrieked as a huge gold-and-black butterfly landed on her bare knee, another on her head, and after a moment, a third on her upturned shoe. Within seconds another dozen or so had landed on the flowers next to her, their wings pulsating in the clear, morning sunlight. It was as perfect as life could get, Mark thought, watching as Lisa grinned and desperately tried to hold her body absolutely still, but couldn't. The butterflies hesitated, moving their wings as though communicating to one another, then took off together. Lisa leaped up, her joy at its limits, and raced to Mark, hugging him around the waist, as though he had arranged this display of nature's delights especially for her.

Mark found the Rocky Mountain Cafe without trouble, parked on the street, and was inside by five after one. Karen Paige waved from a table where she was seated with Noel Atchison and a heavyset man in a cowboy hat.

"B.J. Blake," Karen said, introducing the stranger as Mark pulled out two chairs next to her. "We just ordered. I'll get the waitress."

"So you're the one Noel's been telling me about," Blake said as they shook hands. "Sorry I can't help you none. Sounds like you got one hell of a problem. But I was crawling around in Pampers in 'sixty-eight." He offered a huge hand to Lisa. "Boy, you're a cutie, aren't you? Bet you're breaking hearts in the first grade."

"Second grade," Lisa said with hurt feelings. "And I don't."

"Don't what?"

"Break hearts."

"Yes you do," Blake laughed. "You just don't know it."

The waitress came over with a menu but Noel Atchison said, "Unless you want breakfast, get the steak sandwich and cottage fries. Can't be beat."

"Too heavy for me right now," Mark said. "I'll just have coffee and a salad. You want a hamburger and Coke, Lisa?"

She did.

"Eats like a city fella," Atchison said, and winked at Blake.

The other man agreed. "Damn cities will put anyone off their feed. If you ever decide to turn to small-town life, you come and see me at the Century 21 down the road. I'm the top real-estate agent in the area. 'The Land King of Central Colorado.' Get you a real nice 'gentleman's ranch' where you can relax and raise a kid without big-city crime. Friendly Harmony, the sign at the city line says. No drive-by shootings, or gangs, or welfare leeches living off your taxes. Well, hardly none."

Mark shook his head. "I lived in a small town for eighteen years. I'm a city boy now."

"That's an Air Force Academy ring, ain't it?" Blake nodded at Mark's hand.

Mark said it was.

"Why'd you get out? It's a good life. Up, up, and away, people snapping to attention when you walk into a room, good benefits."

Mark glanced at Lisa who was squirming in her chair and not paying any attention to the adults. "My wife passed away. I needed something more steady than flying F-16s. Also something that would let me be home more often than the Air Force did."

"You still fly any?"

"I own ten percent of a Bonanza. Haven't got much time to take it up, though."

Blake smiled. "Well, you'll be wanting to get out of Seattle some-day, even if it's just a vacation home. I could put you into a real nice place around here with a landing strip for a small plane. Or build your own house. Get outta town and there aren't any building codes to speak of. Pretty much do what you want." He began to laugh. "Come on out with me this afternoon. We can go up in my Cessna and I'll show you what we got for sale."

"Come on, B.J.," Karen said with impatience. "Back off. The poor guy's looking for his parents, not a home." Mark felt a foot nudge his under the table, then move away.

"Hell, I'm sorry," Blake laughed. "That sales stuff just kinda comes out natural, like sap from a maple."

"Or piss from a horse," Atchison said softly, and waved for more coffee as Karen excused herself to go to the restroom.

Mark asked Blake, "Did your parents live here in the sixties?"

"Oh, hell yeah. There's been three generations of Blakes in Har-mony. Came over from Nebraska in the last century, Kentucky before that. Had relatives on both sides in the Civil War. What'd your people do in the Civil War, Noel? Sell maggoty meat to the troops?"

"Do you think your parents could help me? I'm looking for—"

Blake nodded, his head bobbing up and down. "I know, I know. Missing newspapers and mysterious parents. I'll ask 'em. But if Noel doesn't remember, I don't know why my folks would. It was a long time ago."

"Couldn't have been too many people living here then," Mark said. He could feel himself becoming annoyed at everyone's lack of interest in his problem. "People should remember anything unusual."

"Back in the sixties? Not much here but hippies and cowboys. That was a weird combination, I bet. Head shops and feed stores. Incense and horse poo. Hippies probably destroyed their memories with LSD, and the cowboys were riding herd, or whatever cowboys do. 'Course, all that changed in the seventies when Walter Lowndes bought the old ski resort. He's the guy you ought to talk to. Wasn't no *resort* here back then, just a tow rope and a couple of wimpy runs. But ol' Rottweiler—Lowndes, sorry—put in a bunch of high-speed lifts and built the lodge, and the town took off like a rocket. Guy's a marketing genius. You've got to give him that. He flew in a bunch of millionaires from the coasts every year—writers and movie stars and TV people and such—and the resort started getting mentioned in the gossip columns, and the town just exploded, especially in the eighties. Wish I'd bought some property back then but I wasn't interested in nothin' but women and beer."

"Some things never change," Karen said, pulling out a chair and sitting down. "Are you giving Mark your local history tour?"

"Just telling him about Rottweiler and his big bucks. Didn't say anything *nasty*."

The food arrived with a clatter of dishes and Karen hummed some spooky music and said, "Tune in next week for . . . *The Nasties*."

"You wanna bring me another beer, Mary?" Blake said over his shoulder as the waitress started to leave.

"Look," Lisa said, joining the conversation for the first time and wriggling a front tooth at Mark.

Karen stared gravely into the girl's face. "Oh my, you're going to lose that pretty soon. Does the tooth fairy come to your house?"

The girl gave her a look with a forbearance that she thought was very grown-up. "Dad's the tooth fairy. But I get a dollar. Then I buy candy."

"Makes some sort of sense, I guess."

"Symmetry," Mark told her.

As Lisa made a production of taking the pickles off her hamburger

Blake went on with his story. "The man—Lowndes—is tenacious as hell. That's why I call him Rottweiler. He gets his teeth in something and won't let go. But, heck, most entrepreneurs are like that. You think Trump or Steinbrenner back away from trouble? Most new millionaires in this country have made it because of real estate, you know. They buy, they develop, and watch the value shoot up, then they sell and do it all over again. Except ol' Rottweiler hasn't sold. He hangs on—"

"And squeezes every damn penny he can get out of his investments," Atchison said. "As well as being a blight on the landscape. Look at that damn Ice Castle restaurant he's building on top of the slopes. How many trees died so his friends can gargle with twenty-year-old brandy while watching folks ski?"

"Lighten up, Noel. The man's a genius. Not just a businessman but an artist. That's what they say in New York."

"New York!" Atchison said the two words like a doctor might say "bubonic plague."

Lisa said suddenly, "I'm not hungry," heaved back in her chair as though pushed, and let her arms dangle loosely at her sides.

"Man's an obnoxious thug, B.J.," Atchison went on. "You wouldn't give him the time of day if he didn't have forty million dollars."

"Hell," Blake snapped with surprising emotion, "wasn't a damn town worth talking about until he came back. You were here then. Land wasn't worth a hundred dollars an acre in the sixties. Lowndes has made a lot of folks rich, Noel. Done okay by your paper, too, so don't go knocking him."

"Harmony in microcosm," Karen said brightly. "The Lowndes-haters and Lowndes-lovers. Most of the old-timers—except hot-shot real-estate salesmen—think he's some sort of ogre who's bulled his way into an earthly paradise, knocking down trees and destroying a way of life."

"On the other hand," Noel Atchison said, "are the condo-yuppies, the bottled-water-and-Volvo crowd who come in to ski and then forget about us the rest of the year."

"We do keep the Swedish auto industry alive," Blake laughed, relaxed again. "Volvos and Saabs. Every once in a while you see a troublemaker in an Audi. The old-timers are driving ten-year-old Ford F-100 pickups with a rifle rack and bale of hay in the back."

"A town divided," Karen said in a singsong voice, and put her hand briefly on Mark's, a movement only Atchison seemed to notice. "Sounds like a movie of the week, doesn't it?"

"Don't let Noel fool you," Blake said to Mark. "Old Lowndes has made a lot of folks rich. Even some that hate him."

"I want to go outside," Lisa announced, tired of being ignored.

Karen said to Mark, "Why don't I give you a short tour of the town? I think Lisa would like that."

Atchison threw a glance at B.J., then shook his head. Mark, looking the other direction toward his daughter, said, "We better go to the restroom first but I think we might be able to fit a tour into our busy schedule. What do you think, hon? Want to see where the Old West meets the New West?"

Lisa smiled with enthusiasm and jumped off her chair. "I'm hungry. Can I get an ice-cream cone?"

18

Caroline Bellamy's hand shook as she squeezed the cordless telephone. "Jesus Christ, Micah, I couldn't believe it—even the hair is the same. And her dad—I guess it's her dad—is with her."

"Caroline, I know, I know. Relax! I saw them yesterday and talked to Eleanor Dahlquist."

"Dahlquist? Oh lord! What'd she say?"

"What do you think? He's on a quest, he's looking for his folks. Always figured something like this might happen."

Caroline was verging on hysteria. "His folks! What are we going to do?"

"We are not going to panic, that's what. We'll take everything easy and rational and make calm decisions. Where were they when you saw them?"

"At the cafe having lunch with Karen and Noel. B.J. was there, too."

"You talk to them?"

"Hell no, I didn't talk to them. I came back here as soon as I could and called you."

Micah Rollins leaned back and put his feet up on the desk. "You and Karen are close, aren't you? Give her a ring, see what the hell he's planning to do."

"Of course I will. That's not why I called you. It's the little girl."

"Yeah, I see that." Resignation in his voice now. And maybe sadness.

"You're going to have to do something. You know how he is."

Rollins sighed. "I don't think he does that anymore, Caroline. You're talking about the old days. That's all water under the bridge."

"Damn it, listen to me! He's getting more bizarre all the time. He has got to be watched. And you're going to do it."

There was a pause, then the man said, "All right, I'll see what I can do. There'd be hell to pay if he *does* go off the deep end."

"More than that, Micah. It's our *lives* I'm talking about now— all of us. I'm not going to risk my life because that slimy son of a bitch can't keep his hands off little girls. We should have done something years ago."

"I truly don't think it's any little girl that's the problem, Caroline. Never has been far as I can tell. It's *this* little girl."

"I know that!" He acted as if she were an idiot. "Then you'll do something? You're not just playing along to calm a hysterical female?"

"Leave it to me, hon. I'll take care of it."

Micah Rollins put the phone down and began to pace around his office. No sense getting Caroline all upset but he damn well wanted to know what was going on around here, too. It'd been thirty years— he figured they were out of the woods by now. Was he going to have to start worrying all over again? Goddamn it, it just wasn't right! He deserved better out of life at his age.

He halted, closed his eyes, and tilted his head toward the ceiling. Lisa Ritter! *Think!* he told himself.

Don't jump into anything. And don't panic. You'll come up with something. Always have.

19

"'A tale of two cities,'" Karen Paige said as they stood on the sidewalk and looked east. "Behind us is Old Town, mostly dilapidated brick buildings about a hundred years old. And in front, what the old-timers call Yuppieville, mostly put up since the mid-eighties. With Pioneer Park in between like a demilitarized zone. Which way do you want to head?"

"I want an ice cream," Lisa repeated.

"Sounds like a wise choice. There's a Häagen-Dazs a couple of blocks up. Okay with you, Dad?"

"Sure," Mark said. If Lisa wouldn't eat lunch maybe milk products would substitute. Wasn't ice cream one of the five basic food groups? Just then a boom resonated overhead and Mark looked up to see a cloud of dust rise from the mountaintop.

"The restaurant Noel was talking about. Walter Lowndes is having it put at the highest point on the mountain, about a half mile from the Express lift. You'll be able to see it from anywhere in the valley. As you can imagine, not everyone is pleased."

"Developers versus environmentalists?'

"More or less. Or Lowndes-haters versus Lowndes—I guess '-lovers' is too strong a term. . . . '-tolerators.' "

They started walking east. Almost immediately a black-and-white police car eased away from the curb and began to follow them, rolling slowly along the street.

Mark halted, feeling a mix of irritation and curiosity. "What's with the cops around here? Someone followed me around when I got to town yesterday, and Sample started hassling us this morning. Don't they believe in tourists?"

Karen glanced at the car and her face flushed with anger. "That's not Sample. It's worse. His name is Todd Kachen and he's an asshole. Sorry—" She glanced apologetically at Lisa. "But he is."

The car rolled up next to them, shifted into neutral, and the engine roared like a teenager's hot rod.

"Ignore him," Karen said, and stared straight ahead as she began walking again.

"What's his problem?" Mark asked.

"His *problem?*" She was almost shrill and her arms began to flail. "Stupidity. Testosterone imbalance. Distrust of outsiders."

The black-and-white was drifting along, even with them, its side window up and blurring the view of the driver. As they stopped at the intersection Lisa sensed that something was wrong and began looking at the car with alarm. Karen took the girl's hand, put her arm aggressively through Mark's, and stepped off the curb. "Come on. Pretend he's not there. It's what most of us do."

When they reached the far sidewalk Karen dropped Lisa's hand but kept her arm in Mark's. "The biggest disadvantage of small towns is the police. Every damn one of them is convinced he's Clint Eastwood or Steven Seagal."

Mark turned his head. The car had slipped slightly to the rear. He could vaguely make out the driver's wraparound dark glasses, blocklike head, and thick shoulders.

"And Les Cady is up ahead," Karen muttered uneasily as a dumpy, middle-aged man came loping toward them on the sidewalk. "Jesus! That's who the cops should be watching."

"Who is he?"

"I'll tell you later." She had dropped her voice as the man approached and gave her a fierce look. Karen pretended not to notice him, and said, "There's the Häagen-Dazs." Lisa whooped loudly and began to run ahead of them toward the small shop.

"We can eat in the park," Karen added. "It's too nice to stay inside."

"Hey, slow down," Mark shouted to Lisa, but she had already disappeared inside the store.

"Ah, to be seven," Karen said with a tight-lipped smile, "where life's biggest problem is choosing what flavor of ice cream you want. It's all downhill after that. Physically, anyway. You've stayed in good shape, though. You're a runner, aren't you?"

He glanced at her in surprise. "You saw me this morning."

"No, you have the taut, masochistic look of the fanatically fit. I used to see it at the university all the time. The early-morning Gatorade-and-pain crowd. Lean muscles and no body fat. Most of the guys I know around here are bodybuilders. They go over to this co-ed gym on Main and grunt and lift weights in front of the women riding their exercise bikes. They all end up with thick upper bodies, and arms bulging like zucchini through their T-shirts. Deltoids on parade. But if they have to walk up two flights of stairs they're huffing and puffing. And they hate mountain-biking. It's a hobby of mine. It helps work off the calories from a serious ice-cream addiction."

They took their selections—gooey chocolate concoctions in a cup for the adults, a cone of mint chocolate-chip for Lisa—across to the park. The police car was nowhere to be seen. Mark and Karen sat on a green bench but Lisa wanted to sit in the sand beneath the playground equipment thirty yards away. "Okay, but stay where I can see you," Mark said. "Don't go in the bushes or wander away."

"I won't."

Karen said, "You keep a close eye on her. It's nice to see. So many parents today see kids as an obstacle they'd rather be without."

Mark watched as the girl ran toward the play area while trying to balance the double-dip ice-cream cone. "Is it too melodramatic to say she's the only reason for living?" He turned to look at Karen, his jaw tightening and his tone going flat. "Someone called the motel this morning and threatened her life."

"You're kidding!" But she could see he wasn't, and her voice rose with concern. "Why would anybody do that?"

"He made some vague sexual references but they were so general he was probably just taking a shot in the dark—as far as Lisa, anyway." Mark told her what the man said.

"Les Cady." She shuddered. "The man we saw by the ice-cream shop. God, I hate him. He knows exactly how much he can get away with and not get caught."

"What do you mean? Why would Cady call me?"

"He's a child molester, a pedophile. He chases after little girls. I guess Lisa caught his fancy. A new kid in town, someone who hasn't been warned about him—"

Mark looked over at his daughter as he thought about it a moment. "Or someone trying to sound like a pedophile. There was something distinctly unreal about it. It would have been comical if it wasn't so pathetic."

She looked at him questioningly.

"Maybe whoever did it thought threatening my daughter was the best way to intimidate me. If so, he's right. *If* I believed the threat. But I don't for a minute think the day after I wander into town Lisa has suddenly become the target of a child molester, Les Cady or anyone else. It's *me* that concerns someone—the fact that I showed up in Harmony and started looking into my background."

"But you hadn't started looking. Had you even talked to anyone?"

"Not a soul."

She shook her head. "Have you told the police?"

"I'll get to it this afternoon. But what can they do, other than take a report?"

Karen ran her hand through her hair. "God, what an introduction to Harmony."

Mark twisted his spoon through his ice cream and realized he was losing his taste for milk products. A sign of age? Or a sour stomach developed since finding the death certificate? He put the cup down on the bench with revulsion. "Have you lived in Harmony all your life?"

She smiled beautifully. "You're questioning me? It's supposed to be the other way around. I'm the reporter."

"I guess we're both looking for something."

She paused a moment as she thought about it. "I guess we are. All right, I'll show you mine if you show me yours. Sound okay?"

Mark looked at her as if for the first time, taking in the flawless skin, deep-blue eyes, and full lips. She was wearing her shoulder-length hair back, held by a blue elastic band, and he had a sudden fantasy of it coming loose and swinging forward over her face as he lay on his back and she lowered her lips from above to meet his. Immediately he felt angry and embarrassed at himself. "Okay," he said stonily. "You've lived her since when?"

"Just ten years. Lawrence, Kansas, before that. A farm in Oklahoma until I was eight."

"Then your parents couldn't help me?"

"I'm afraid not. There actually aren't that many people left from the sixties. It was just a wide spot on the road then, you know. Caroline Bellamy, I suppose. She's a good friend of mine. She owns a restaurant called Trees over by the slopes. Walter Lowndes, of course, if he's in town. Les Cady. I don't think you want to talk to him."

"How do you know he is a pedophile? Has he ever been institutionalized?"

She waved a hand. "Everybody knows. He's been arrested quite a few times, once a few years ago when a little girl was molested and killed. He's been hospitalized but I don't think he's ever been actually convicted. It's tough, especially in a rural area like this. People don't want their kids exposed to publicity or a trial. I can't blame them. But you saw what he looks like—that bear-cub face and baby fat, and the weird mustache you can hardly see. He's just creepy. He works at the resort as some sort of maintenance person—dealing with machinery and not people. It's Walter Lowndes's one attempt at charity, I guess. He's showing us how open-minded he is, not listening to scurrilous rumors, and daring to hire someone no one else would take a chance on."

"You don't like Lowndes." It was a statement, not a question.

Karen seemed surprised. "I don't know. I guess he's got good and bad points. Like most people."

"Tell me a good point."

"He's rich."

Lisa hurriedly licked ice cream that was dripping from the cone onto her hand, and frowned because it never tasted good that way, with sweat mixed in with it, but it was hot here in the sand and there wasn't going to be any ice cream in a minute if she didn't hurry and eat it.

She glanced back over her shoulder. Her dad was still talking to Karen. She wasn't sure if she liked that. It probably meant that Karen wanted to be his girlfriend. Women were always doing that. It was dumb because Daddy didn't need a girlfriend. At least he never said he did.

Ice cream again dribbled on her fingers and she bent her head all the way around the other side of her cone and tried to lick the mess off. Too yucky. She wiped her hand on her shorts. Now she was going to get in trouble for messing up her clothes. Where was the paper napkin Karen gave her?

Maybe she'd go on the slide when she finished the cone. Usually she didn't like slides when it was hot because it made her legs burn. On the other side of the park she could see a mom pushing a stroller with a baby in her direction. Behind her a little boy about five, probably still in kindergarten, was trying to keep up. Maybe there'd be someone to play with. Even if it was a boy. It was boring just having adults around. They never wanted to do fun things.

"Good afternoon, Lisa."

Who said that? She looked around but saw nobody.

"Over here." The voice was low, almost like a loud whisper—or the way Miss Carnover read *Goosebumps* books in class. It made Lisa shiver.

"Here," the voice persisted. "In the bushes."

Lisa stared toward the trees and bushes bordering the sand pit. A man was sitting there like she was, legs crossed, looking at her. What a funny place to sit. It was hard to see his face because of all the shadows, but she was sure it was a man. It sounded like a man, anyway.

"Did you like your ice cream?"

Yuck! It was getting on her hand again. She shoved the cone in her mouth and began to chew with a vigorous up-and-down motion that made her want to laugh at herself. Then she tried to shake the melted ice cream off her skin.

The man said at once, "Let me lick it off," sounding almost panicky; then he angrily chided himself for his eagerness. *Don't be a fool! Slow down. Remember where her father is.* Trying to sound jovial, he said, "That was good ice cream, wasn't it? Very cold. I have lots of ice cream at home. Every flavor."

"No one has every flavor."

"I do. Promise."

"Do you have licorice and pumpkin and blueberry?"

"Yes. All of them."

"And baseball?"

"Yes."

"Liar! There is no baseball flavor."

"I have a hundred and one different flavors of chocolate. Would you like one?"

She swallowed the last of her cone, and fixed the man with a determined look. "I'm not supposed to talk to strangers."

"I know that, Lisa. I'm not supposed to, either. But I'm not a stranger. I even know your name."

She bent forward, challenging him. "But I don't know *your* name."

"What would you like my name to be?"

"Yucky. Because you're funny-looking." In truth she wasn't sure what he looked like because of the shadows. But he *sounded* funny-looking.

He drew back, hurt; Lisa seemed to sense it but didn't care. Or wasn't sure if she cared. It was just too bad if he was hurt. She didn't know him, whatever his name was. And he probably *was* funny-looking. A lot of big people are, with hair on their face and big stomachs and fat legs. She looked over to where the mother and her baby were sitting down on the grass. The woman's son was wandering around, looking bored. He'd come over here pretty soon and she'd finally have someone to play with. She glanced back at her dad. Karen was laughing at something. Maybe it wouldn't be bad if Daddy had a girlfriend. They could go places Daddy didn't want to go. Like to a mall. But when *she* grew up she didn't want a boyfriend. She just wanted children, maybe twenty of them. Or forty-five.

The man was whispering at her again. "You can trust me, Lisa.

I'm a policeman. Policemen are good people. Didn't your daddy tell you that?"

"If you're a policeman where's your uniform?"

"It's at home. Maybe I'll show you someday. Would you like to see it? It has shiny belts and a holster and a gun. I'd let you hold it if you want." His breathing increased to where she could hear it.

"I don't like guns."

"I don't like them either. Guns are bad."

He shifted position and she said, "What are you doing?"

"Touching myself. Do you ever touch yourself?"

Lisa wasn't sure what he meant but she decided to get up. She didn't like this man. Maybe she'd go back to her dad.

Just then the little boy came over. "Hi. Want to play?"

Lisa frowned. "I'm going back to my daddy."

"Don't go, Cheryl," the man muttered, alarm growing, and he started to rise. "Please—" But she turned and walked away. Watching her, he had an experience that made him shiver—his whole body trembling—and he turned at once from the ugliness of the boy heading across the sand toward the swing set to the retreating form of the girl. He rose, and trembled again, with ecstasy—

"I think he was stupid and funny-looking," Lisa said as she rejoined her father.

Thinking she was referring to the little boy, he said, "You shouldn't talk like that. We don't want to hurt anyone's feelings." Which in fact, Mark believed, was one of the great moral lessons parents had an obligation to teach their children. Lisa's comments had surprised him greatly.

Karen said, "Look at you. Your hands are covered with ice cream." She reached for one of the napkins she'd grabbed from the store.

"He wanted to lick it off."

Mark's eyebrows lifted but Karen laughed. "His mother can buy him his own ice cream. Let's get you cleaned up."

She had to wet some of the napkins with water from a drinking fountain but working with Mark they managed to get her clean.

Karen said, "You didn't lose your tooth in the ice cream, did you?"

The girl stretched open her mouth and moved the tooth around with her tongue. "Still there. I hate it. I look like a baby."

Mark's mind had reverted again to the problem of his identity. "There must be someone around here I can talk to. What about Walter Lowndes?"

"Not a chance. He hardly talks to anyone anymore. I'm not sure he's even in town."

"Then how about that 'Wild Bill' character?"

Karen smiled. "Bill's a lovely old man but he's spent half his life in and out of mental hospitals. It's hard to tell where reality ends and fiction begins with him. Like with that story about the real Wild Bill being his grandfather."

"It's not true?"

"Who knows? I doubt it. Bill inhabits his own, very alternate, very weird, universe. The Chamber of Commerce likes him because the kids like him. But a lot of parents in town *don't* like him for the same reason."

"You don't think he could help me, then?"

"I don't know if you can believe whatever he says." She took three steps to a trash can and deposited the napkins.

Mark felt his frustration rising. Why did everyone treat this search of his with so cavalier an attitude, a minor whim of no real importance? "You must know someone. Come on, this is important. I'm trying to find my parents, Lisa's grandparents!"

They began to walk out of the park. "Yeah . . . well . . . Caroline Bellamy, like I said. B.J., you've already talked to. . . . I know! Janis Lowndes. No one should visit Harmony without meeting Janis. It would be like going to London and not seeing the changing of the guard."

"Walter Lowndes's wife?"

"Daughter. She's only twenty-seven or twenty-eight but she's lived here most of her life. And of course she would have heard her father talking. We can try it, anyway. She has a bookstore—books and art. She'll like you. You're a man."

Mark's eyebrows went up and Karen put her arm through his. "Don't worry, I'll protect you if she gets too aggressive. And don't forget your part in our bargain."

"My part?"

"You've been questioning me. Remember our agreement? Now you have to show me yours. We'll set up a time."

When they reached the sidewalk, Mark looked around. "My pal in the black-and-white is gone."

"Don't kid yourself," Karen told him. "Todd Kachen is no one's pal. Neither is Bobby Sample. They're thugs, the triumph of steroids over brain cells. Most of the department's like that. Come on, we can walk to Janis's from here."

On the sidewalk Mark glanced around at the smart-looking shops in the new part of town: Prada, Cartier, Coach, Armani. There was a certain look to them, a just-scrubbed, faux German/Swiss sameness that couldn't have been accidental, and which he also found mildly annoying. "Who designed this place?" he finally asked. "Martha Stewart or Laura Ashley?"

Karen jerked playfully at his arm. "Don't be silly. They only did the stores and restaurants. Calvin Klein and Ralph Lauren were given control over what people wear—east of Fourth Street, anyway. In Old Town, of course, it's Levi's and T-shirts with pictures of motorcycles or dead animals. But over here, for the men, it's slacks, boat shoes, and knit shirts with the appropriate logos on the left breast. If you're incorrectly attired—as you are now—you go straight to jail."

Lisa said happily, " 'Do not pass Go'; 'Do not collect two hundred dollars' . . ." She screeched suddenly and pointed across the street. "Is that Tom Cruise?"

"Close. It's Zeke Daniels. He owns a liquor store."

Lisa frowned, and her voice became whiny. "Well, he looks like Tom Cruise."

Karen said, "Actually quite a few movie stars do own places here, but you never see them in the summer. People say Barbra Streisand owns a condo but I don't believe it. I think Walter Lowndes started the rumor to build up interest in the resort back in the early eighties. He's always doing things like that. He's quite a showman."

As Lisa began to skip ahead of them Karen said, "I should prepare you for Janis, I guess. She's a sort of nineties version of a hippie. Harmony used to be a hangout for the tie-dye–and–handicraft set. There's still a few of them living up in the hills, throwing pots and wondering what the Beatles' *White Album* really means. Janis isn't dumb but her mind doesn't progress in a linear fashion. She thinks . . . creatively. She's also been keeping company with Bobby Sample. If you know what I mean."

"Doesn't sound promising for my problem."

"No, but you'll like her. She's an artist. She don't look back."

"What?"

"She paints. And sings old Bob Dylan songs. And sells books, and her dad's supposedly famous photos. But she's an *artist* of sex. Or so I am reliably informed."

"By whom?"

"The owner of the Rocky Mountain Cafe let me go into the men's restroom once—for research! The toilet stalls extol her skills highly. I'm sure she'd accommodate you if you care to test their veracity."

Mark felt a prickling of unease but tried to play along with what he assumed was a joke. "Well, I'm free tomorrow from two to two-thirty."

"Not nearly long enough. She'll demand a whole evening. Multiple orgasms are her right. After all, she is a Lowndes."

20

The Songs of Innocence Book and Art Store was in a newer building on Main. The front was blue-tinted glass with several posters of paintings by artists Mark had never heard of. One showed a red background with a small white ball in the bottom right corner; another was white behind old-fashioned rabbit-ears television antennae. Mark shrugged. Some things aren't worth pondering over.

A bell over the glass door tinkled gently when they entered. The store smelled of incense, marijuana, and a not-too-distant cigar. Books were displayed on shelves around the periphery of the square room, and in revolving racks in the center. More than a hundred oil paintings, framed and unframed, leaned against bookcases, counters, and chairs. One entire wall held framed photographs under the legend WALTER LOWNDES ORIGINALS—all black-and-white, all very stark—people, vaguely familiar, sitting in completely empty rooms; what looked like electrical generating plants in some sort of montage; flies nibbling on dead fruit.

Karen followed his gaze. "He's supposed to be one of the world's top photographers. So much for the state of the art world, huh?" Hidden speakers were softly dispensing Big Brother and the Holding Company. Something moved at the edge of Mark's vision, and a man—bearish, vague-looking, untidy—emerged from behind a rack near the front door, and disappeared.

"God," Karen whispered, and shook her head. "Les Cady again.

I don't know why he hangs around Janis. Just being in the same room with him makes me feel like spiders are crawling all over my spine."

Beads covering a rear doorway suddenly parted and a woman from a pre-Raphaelite painting materialized in front of them. Red wavy hair almost to her waist, mid-twenties, barefoot, pale, pale skin that screamed out to be touched, held, experienced. "Karen—" She smiled at her guests as she floated in their direction.

"Janis," Karen said, and introduced Mark and Lisa. The young woman leaned slightly forward to shake hands, the movement strangely like a curtsy. She was stunning, Mark thought, but in an emaciated, magical way: thin and ethereal, almost fragile in her movements, though with a supple figure that she showed off under a tight blouse and peasant skirt. After greeting Mark she seemed to melt in layers toward the floor where she put pale, red-tipped fingers on Lisa's tiny shoulders. "Oh, you're so pretty."

"Thank you," Lisa whispered, obviously not sure what to make of this apparition.

Janis Lowndes smiled, rose, and turned again to Mark. "What brings you to Harmony? We don't see many tourists this time of year." The softness of her voice gave her an air of vulnerability Mark had not expected after Karen's preparatory comments. Not wanting to go through it again, he glanced at Karen, and she briefly explained, ending by saying, "We were wondering if you remembered hearing anything unusual about the late sixties, something that could help Mark."

"I wasn't born then."

"Yes, Janis, but you could have heard something from your father. It would have been the summer of 1968."

The young woman's face seemed to go trancelike. "No, nothing, I'm sorry. He never talks about the old days."

Karen said, "Could any of your customers help? Do you see many of the old-timers in here?"

The young woman's eyes widened, and her still-soft voice became almost wondering. "Does your boss count? He's been in every day for two months. But I think he wants something a little more primal than books on art."

Karen's jaw dropped. "You're kidding. Noel?"

"You needn't worry, Karen. I won't seduce him behind the Erotica section. But if you know any sexy widows—"

"What's 'seduce'?" Lisa asked in a way that sounded as if the word were not unfamiliar to her.

Janis added, "On the whole, though, I don't see many people from my parents' days. A few of the old artisans come by from time to time, however. I'll ask them. Summer of 'sixty-eight, you say?"

Mark said that was correct, then asked, "Can you ask your father for me? It could be that he'd remember something. Or maybe I could talk to him."

Her expression briefly tightened, but she said, "I'll see what he says. I doubt if he'll see you. He's very busy. And somewhat reclusive. But come by tomorrow. Are you going to be in town long?" Her green eyes looked straight into his, as though reading his thoughts.

"I don't know. A few days."

"And your wife?"

Karen suppressed a smile, stuck her hands in her jeans pockets, and stared at her feet as the music changed to the Doors' "L.A. Woman."

"I'm a widower," Mark said as Lisa began to wander around the store, touching things.

Janis considered a moment. "Maybe I could take you around to some of the artists who live in the hills outside of town. There's still a few counterculture types from the sixties out there who wouldn't talk to anyone who just walked in, especially someone who looks like you. They'd think you're FBI or DEA. Maybe one of them would remember—or has heard talk of something. Tonight maybe—"

"And I could watch Lisa!" Karen said brightly.

"Oh, that would be—" Janis stopped suddenly and gave her a pitying look. "We're having our little joke, aren't we? Anyway, Mark, do think about it. There are people out there in the hills who wouldn't talk to you—people who knew my folks when this was just a village. They'd talk to me."

Karen touched Mark on the arm. "I'm going to have to get back to work. Noel's going to be in a mood."

"Tell him you were talking to me," Janis suggested. "Then give him a wink." She turned to Mark. "And if you ever do need anyone to watch Lisa while you're in town just bring her by here. I'm here until five or six most nights. It won't be any trouble."

"Thanks," Mark said. "Maybe I will." He raised his voice to the girl who had disappeared into the back room. "Come on, honey. Time to go."

Lisa pushed her way through the curtain of beads to the front of the store. She had been wondering about that man in the bushes at the park. Why had he called her a funny name when she started to walk away? He knew her name was Lisa. She tried to remember the funny name but couldn't.

Mark was standing at the door. "This is getting old," he said to Karen as he saw the police car sitting across the street.

Janis Lowndes came over and shrugged. "He's not looking for you, is he?"

"I don't know what he's looking for. He and his buddies have been on my tail since I got to town. I guess they don't have anything else to do."

"Why don't you see Eldon Stallworth? He's the chief. There must be some reason they're following you. If there isn't, he'll get them off your back. He doesn't put up with any nonsense from his people."

Mark took Lisa's hand and stepped outside. "Come on. We've got to get to Hightower's."

Janis squinted in the direction of the police car. "Isn't that Todd?"

Karen threw her a look.

"Well, that's—"

"It's harassment, Janis! It's as simple as that." She turned quickly in Mark's direction, her voice rising with emotion. "Janis is right. Talk to the chief. Tell him he's got a bunch of thugs working for him and the *Courier*'s going to do a story on police misconduct if they don't knock it off."

Mark looked at her, surprised at the sudden vehemence in her voice.

"I've got to get to work," she snapped. "But I'm serious about this. This crap's got to stop. If you don't tell Stallworth, I will."

21

"Screwed up again, didn't you, Bill? You crazy old fart! Just can't leave well enough alone."

Moving his hands furiously, he shoved aside trash and clothing and old magazines and boxes full of junk as he looked for his ancient .45. Deadwood barked at the excitement as though this were a game rather than an old man's sudden recognition that he had done something irrevocably stupid with that phone call. Even so, it'd taken an hour before the realization hit him.

"Stupid old goof," he said aloud as he pushed away boxes of books and travel folders he'd found in a downtown alley. "You shoulda known better! Just couldn't keep your mouth shut. Yakety-yak. That's old Bill." Of course, it was seeing the little girl that made him do it. "Dang fool! No wonder folks think you're crazy."

Nothing good was going to come of it, that was for sure. "Shoulda disguised your voice like you did in the old days. Do that real low whisper. That always brought a shudder from the other end of the line, didn't it? Almost made the phone shake." He giggled to himself momentarily, then started searching again. *Too late to worry about it now, of course. The creepy bastard knew who it was soon as I started talking. Where the hell's that gun?*

"Deadwood! Where'd I put that old forty-five?" *Dang thing ain't been fired in twenty years. Too bad the Chamber of Commerce didn't let me wear guns out on the street. Bunch of pussyfootin' sissies thought I couldn't be trusted and would start to shoot up the city."*

Maybe I ought to call that girl's dad first. His heart started racing. *Shoulda told him this morning, of course. Thought I'd have a little fun first. Stupid old fart! Had the sense to warn him, though.* That was when Bill realized what a fool he'd been. Shoulda said it right out when he was talking to the man earlier in the day but Sample showed up, then Karen Paige. Wasn't about to do it then.

The more he thought about it, the better contacting Ritter sounded. Stopping his search, he grabbed the phone book off the table. "Staying at the Mountain View, someone said." He found the number and dialed. When he was connected to the room the phone rang and rang. *Damn it, damn it, damn it! The man's gotta know about the trouble that gal's going to cause.* And the *subtle* approach had been just plain dumb. *Gotta come out and tell him. Even if it does get me in trouble.* "No, damn it, no message." *Not this message, lady.* "I'll call later." *Or go over there. That'd be better. Ain't going naked, though.*

He started throwing things aside as he looked again for his old revolver. "Damn it, dog, where the devil is it? It's got to be here somewhere."

Then he heard a sound from behind and realized it didn't matter anymore.

22

This time Hightower's secretary, a middle-aged woman with a cheery smile, was in the outer office. "Mason said you'd probably be back before three. Have a seat while I ring him. My, you're a lovely one, aren't you? Betcha look like your mother." She bent and shook hands with Lisa who moved behind her dad's leg.

"Shy," Mark explained.

"Nothing wrong with that," she said as she picked up the phone. A minute later the attorney came out to greet them. "Come on back. Hope you had a nice day seeing the sights. Such as they are." They retreated to the cozy, wood-paneled office with its photos and diplomas. Hightower closed the door and waved Mark and Lisa to leather chairs. "You should have taken me up on that little house on the prairie, though," he said with a wink. "Sure beats the Mountain View for putting the rosy glow of satisfaction on a man's cheeks."

Mark wasn't in the mood. "Look, Mr. Hightower—"

"Mason," the older man said and smiled as he lowered his bulk behind the desk. "Just like the jar."

Mark leaned forward. "Did you find anything?"

Hightower's smile faded with reluctance. "Well, I'll tell you: This here was no small job. I started with 1965 and went all the way through 1970. Six years. My father was a very meticulous man. Saved every piece of paper that might ever have any significance at all. And I *looked* at each one. Took me most of four hours to do it. Big-city law firm would've charged you three or four hundred dollars an hour, so I figure I just saved you about fifteen hundred dollars. Good thing, too, because I turned up squat."

"Damn it!" Mark pounded his fist on the arm of the chair and felt like screaming. Lisa, looking tiny in the chair next to him, began to squirm.

"Well now, don't go getting all agitated. Just because Daddy didn't have anything to do with your problem doesn't mean you can't find someone else around here who'll be able to help."

"But your *phone number* is on the envelope."

"Well, there is that. Doesn't necessarily mean anything, of course.

Could be someone told your mother about a good lawyer in case she ever needed one, and she jotted down the number."

"Five hundred miles from where she lived?"

"Well . . ." Hightower sank back in his chair and waved an arm weakly. "Doesn't sound too likely, does it?"

"It didn't have to be an adoption. Your father could have handled something else for my folks. Was there anything at all relating to a Ritter?"

"Nope. Not a thing."

"Anything dealing with Idaho? Or South Dakota?"

"Again—" He waved an arm.

"What about 1968?" Mark came to his feet and began to pace. "Was there something unusual about that year? Especially the summer?"

Hightower stirred. "What's so special about 'sixty-eight?"

Mark sat at once and quickly told the attorney what he'd discovered at the newspaper. Hightower's face clouded over. "Well now. . . . That is a mystery, isn't it? Missing newspapers. Kinda makes a body wonder."

Unable to stay in one place, Mark got to his feet again. "They were definitely cut out. Someone was trying to hide something." He started pacing once more, crossing and recrossing the area in front of the bookshelves. "Atchison says the bound volumes must have been that way for years. Maybe so. Or maybe *he* cut them out—"

"Whoa," Hightower said, and came forward in his seat. "The worst thing you can do right now is start accusing people of something you got no proof of. Especially in a small town like this. You do, and you aren't going to get anyone to help you."

"I know, I know," Mark said, still pacing. "It was a stupid thing to say. But I'm running out of options. The key is in those two newspapers, but Atchison says no one else would have a copy. He told me there's no library here. Is that true?"

Hightower nodded. "Never has been. But I bet the library at Colorado State or the University of Colorado has a copy—on microfilm, if nothing else."

Mark came to a stop. "Of course! A university. . . ."

"Give 'em a call. One's up in Boulder, the other in Fort Collins. They'll be able to tell you. Old Atchison wasn't any help, huh? Doesn't surprise me. Of course, him and me hasn't gotten along since high school so I'm not exactly impartial here."

"He said he couldn't remember anything about the summer of 'sixty-eight. He thought I should ask people who lived in Harmony then."

"Yeah, right. Like folks can remember something that happened more than thirty years ago. Hell, most people can't remember what they saw on TV last night." He picked up the phone and hit a button. "Could we see you a minute, Sally?"

The secretary came through the door a moment later and Hightower said, "Nineteen sixty-eight, Sal. What were you up to? And keep it clean."

The woman laughed. "Well, I was married in 'sixty-six so I don't suppose I was doing anything very exciting. Fact is, I was pregnant. Cassie was born in February of 'sixty-eight."

"Remember anything unusual about the summer—June and July in particular? Mr. Ritter is pretty sure something important happened in town about then. Guess I agree with him. Something important enough to make the newspaper."

"Summertime. . . ." She moved her gaze toward the window and the mountains beyond as she pondered. "No . . . nothing comes back."

"Births, maybe," Hightower prompted. "Mark thinks he may be adopted."

She looked back at them and shook her head. "Can't think of anything."

"How about a child dying?" Mark asked.

"Sorry—"

"Okay," Hightower said with some exasperation, then added, "What'd you watch on TV last night?"

The secretary smiled. *"The Magnificent Ambersons* with Orson Welles. It's a wonderful movie. A love story."

Hightower waved a hand and smiled at Mark. "Okay, so I was wrong about that part." He turned his attention to the secretary again. "Why don't you kinda call around to some of the more *mature* folks here in town, Sal—people who were here in 'sixty-eight. Ask them if they remember anything in particular about that summer— especially a child being born, or a child dying. This is mighty important to Mark here and maybe we can help him."

"Sure," she said and turned to Mark. "What a job! I can gossip on the phone all day and still get paid."

After she left, Hightower said, "This is getting sorta interesting, isn't it? Too bad my dad's files didn't help. He was the only lawyer in town back then, too. Got about six now. Even got some crime, not that I care. I don't handle criminal cases anymore. Got tired of playing cops-and-robbers at my age."

Which reminded Mark: "What's going on with the police around here?" He sat down heavily. "I can't take a step without a black-and-white trailing along behind me." Briefly, he told the attorney about Sample and Kachen harassing him since yesterday.

Hightower shook his head dismissively. "Hell, ol' Bobby Sample isn't exactly the smartest guy in town. Folks used to call him Bobby Simple. The police force here doesn't pay much better than driving a snowplow so it's hard to get good people. They all pretty much follow Chief Stallworth's orders to be visible. 'Cops should be on the street so folks can see they're being taken care of,' the chief keeps saying." Hightower laughed. "You'll notice there's none of that 'To Protect and Serve' nonsense on the squad cars here. It says 'Enforcing the Law.' Stallworth says if you want to be 'served,' go on down to the Rocky Mountain Cafe; his job is to keep the city as free of crime as possible. Doing a pretty good job of it, too."

Mark came to his feet, and stalked over to the window, Lisa quickly getting up and following. "They couldn't get away with that crap in most of America."

"Well now," Hightower said, not smiling, "this here ain't 'most of America.' It's Harmony. Colorado. Folks do things different here from New York or Cleveland or L.A. You should try to remember that."

"Yeah, yeah, sure." Mark turned around and rubbed the back of his neck.

"Headache?"

"It's what you get when you bang your head against a wall. Which is what I've been doing since finding that death certificate last week."

"Seems to me it's early days yet. No need to get all worked up."

Mark walked quickly back to his chair, lowering his voice so Lisa, still at the window, wouldn't hear. "I'm thirty years old and I suddenly find out I'm not who I thought I was, my parents were not the loving loyal people I thought they were, my daughter's been threatened, and someone went to the trouble to cut up old newspapers to keep me from finding something. I've got a right to be worked up, angry, pissed off."

"Seen the cops about the threat yet?"

"Not yet." He rubbed the back of his neck again, and winced. "Who exactly is this Walter Lowndes everyone talks about? Besides being the resort owner and Janis's father."

Hightower's eyebrows went up. "Whatever made you ask that?"

"He seems to be a *presence* in town." He said the word with sarcasm. "An omniscient aura that hangs like a radioactive cloud over the whole place."

"He is that."

"He lived here thirty years ago?"

"Well, let me think. 'Sixty-eight. Yes, I reckon he did. Started moving away after that. Not all at once but it seemed he kept getting more distant."

"What do you mean?"

"Walter was always sort of different—more cosmopolitan, I guess you'd call it, than most folks around here. He's the only person I knew in those days to go to college out of state. And not just out of state, but to the Ivy League. Dartmouth, I think. He was definitely the local artsy intellectual. It didn't keep him from raising hell and drinking with his buddies, and fighting rodeo cowboys on Saturday night, though."

"But he left town?"

"Not exactly. He was developing the resort in the seventies, of course. But he also got into some sort of publishing business in New York. I think some of his rich college friends helped him raise money to start a small firm that puts out poetry and art books. I don't know much about it but you can get their stuff at his daughter's store on Main. It's probably the only place in Colorado outside a university that would carry it. He's also a photographer of some note. I saw a story in the Denver papers years ago, on a show he had in New York, museums and others snapping up his pictures.

"That part of his life would have begun in the early seventies, I think. He started spending some time here and some in New York every year. As he became more well-known it got to be less time here and more there. I guess he liked hobnobbing with the literary set more than with folks with brambles in their socks or hayseeds poking out of their hair.

"He still comes out here for a month or so in the summer and two months during the ski season but folks hardly see him anymore. Stays holed up in that lodge of his, doing whatever local royalty does.

How's that nursery rhyme go? *'The king is in his counting house counting all his money'* . . ."

"And the queen?"

"Oh, died years ago. Mid-seventies, probably. Beautiful woman. My gosh, you wouldn't believe it. You've seen Janis? Well then, you know what I'm talking about. Ariel would've knocked your socks off. That's where that red hair and body-to-die-for comes from. Society gal from Denver. Oil money. Thought Walter was some sort of romantic character, I guess, with his wavy hair, and poetry and art, and dreams of Eagle Point."

"She must have been right."

Hightower smiled. "Put it that way, I guess so. Successful at just about everything but his kid. He can't be too happy with her lifestyle. On the other hand, he helps support her, I hear. That bookstore can't be doing all that well. This is not exactly a town of readers or art buyers. And she's been helping run the resort when he's not here. Anyway, I reckon her reputation's a mite exaggerated."

"Is Lowndes a friend of yours?"

"Shoot, I haven't talked to Walter in—I don't know—six or eight years, maybe."

"You don't do his legal work?"

"Nope. I think he and my daddy had a skirmish about something years ago. The sins of the father are the sins of the son, you know. No, Artie Thirsten, who's got an office over next to Trees restaurant, does his local stuff. Some New York firm with fifty names handles his big-time work. Can't understand those New York lawyers. Probably never get a chance to go fishing or see bears chase their cubs up a tree. What's the point of all that money if you can't watch the sun come up and smell the piney air?"

"Did you go to school with Lowndes?"

"No one went to school with him. He was home-schooled until college. It's why he was so damn smart—sat home reading books and doing math problems while the rest of us were learning 'social skills' or making little clay dinosaurs and papier-mâché volcanoes for Science Day. No, his momma had a list of books long as a flagpole he had to read and understand. And he did. I heard somewhere when he got to college he'd already read everything assigned in his English and History courses. Knew more than some of the professors.

"Anyway, he was older than me by a few years. I knew about him, though. Every kid in town did, because as long as he read his books his momma let him do what he wanted all day. So we'd see him go fishing or hunting while we were sitting in school watching a film strip on personal hygiene or the Great Barrier Reef."

Lisa, still standing at the window and tired of being ignored, had a pout on her face. "I want to go. There's nothing to do here."

Hightower laughed. "Nothing more honest than a child, is there? Maybe that's why I never had one. All that truthfulness goes against the principles of my profession."

Mark stopped by the police station, a one-story adobe building off Main. The patrolman on duty behind the counter had a baby face and looked as if he hadn't started shaving yet. Mark said, "I want to report a threatening phone call."

The cop looked at Mark as though he had never taken such a report before. "Someone threatened to kill you? That's assault."

Mark looked at Lisa who had wandered over to a model-police-car display. "My daughter."

The policeman's eyebrows went up, and he reached under the counter for a report. "Fill out the top three lines." A pen was attached to the counter by a chain.

When Mark finished the cop picked it up. "Ritter?" His eyes narrowed as he studied Mark for a moment. "What'd this caller say?"

"That my daughter was going to die. Just like my wife and mother."

"That's it?" He put the report down.

Mark felt himself getting warm. "It's a threat."

"Yeah, I suppose it is. Your wife and mother dead?"

"Yes."

"Murdered?"

"No."

"Kinda takes the sting out of the threat, doesn't it?" He looked at Mark as if he was being kept from more vital work.

"They're dead!"

"Okay, okay. Tell me the exact words."

As Mark did the cop wrote them down. Then he straightened and put his pen down. "I'll give it to the assistant chief when he gets back. He can decide what to do with it. Probably nothing since this sounds like a prank. Where are you staying?"

"The Mountain View."

"We'll call you. Or not. Depends what the chief says."

He walked back to his desk.

"Friendly Harmony."

"What's that?"

"The sign outside of town. It says, 'Welcome to Friendly Harmony.' "

"Does it? I've never seen it. But I wouldn't believe everything I read."

23

—Pain in the right eye. Hand trembling, won't stop. Anticipating, waiting—

—A new lock put in yesterday (rush job). Ten push buttons arranged in a circle, that had to be punched in correct order for the door to open. One-nine-seven-one (important date)—

—Lets the door slam behind him. Stands and admires. Feels pride. At feeling pride—

Look: Black drapes, a couch. *Her* room!

Suddenly dizzy, sits on the couch.

—*Can't take that medicine anymore. Confuses me. Relaxes, but makes it hard to remember*—

Closes his eyes now to the light (has learned how to do this), squeezes darkness into his mind like paint from a tube, squeezes it all the way back until it hurts. Then flashes his eyes suddenly open into the girl's magical face. A picture. More than life-size. Staring, wide-eyed. At him! Holding a rose. A smile.

Force the memory to return. Force it—

The ideal, perfect beauty.

And he does remember now. Does: How the mother said it was okay as long as she wasn't there with them. *Close the door* (doesn't want to hear). *The two of us.*

the sounds

(of love)

enjoying

. . .

—Dizziness once more. Pain. The darkness bulls its way through, angrily extinguishing the light—

(Sighs softly.) *"Rockabye baby, on the treetop, when the wind blows—"*

"When the wind blows—"

He was like her daddy, wasn't he? Almost. . . . Which made it all right to possess, *own* her.

Separate the child from Ritter. This room is hers. Keep her. Forever.

Lisa, he thought.

Lisa

. . .

Cheryl

Mine

24

Mark put the key in the motel door, let it swing open, and said sharply, "No, Lisa! Wait!"

Something's wrong. He could feel it on his skin, like a shock from a live wire.

"Stay here."

Keeping the door open behind him, he took a step inside and stared around. Everything was exactly as he had left it this morning. Except . . .

Except what?

The room hadn't been made up yet, both beds in disarray, his shirt from yesterday still draped over the chair.

He felt the hairs on the back of his neck stiffen.

The TV remote control was on the night table where he'd left it. A couple of dollars of change on the dresser, air conditioner rattling in the window. . . .

Someone's been here.

Trying not to show his concern, he said, "Hang on a minute, hon." He tried the bathroom. Electric razor where he put it this morning. Toothbrush. Water glass. Washcloth hanging on a chrome rack.

Everything unmoved.

Still, someone had been here. He began to feel warm with rage. *Friendly Harmony!* They probably came in while he was at the restaurant, or walking around town with Karen Paige. How did they know he'd be gone long enough to search the room? And what the hell did they expect to find?

His fury mounting, he stormed outside, leaving the door open and Lisa waiting on the landing. The maid was two rooms down, bringing out an armload of sheets. He caught up with her as she was about to go back in. "Did you see anyone go into my room?" He gestured toward his open door. "Number 206."

The woman smiled without comprehension and shrugged her shoulders.

"My room," he repeated. "Did anyone go in this morning?"

"Your room? *Si. Triente minutos.* Thirty minutes."

"No, no," Mark said. He could feel himself losing control but didn't care. "Did anyone go *inside*? . . . In my room? . . . Did someone go *into* my room?"

The maid frowned with annoyance. "Finish here. Then go."

Mark tried to recall his high-school Spanish, but was too upset to think clearly. "Man," he tried again. *"Hombre!* Go into . . ." Goddamn verbs! He mimicked walking through the door, then pointed to himself.

The phone in his room rang. Mark gave up, shook his head. *"Gracias, señora, gracias—"* and hurried back. "Come on, Lisa." He slammed the door behind her and grabbed the receiver as it rang for the fourth time.

"Mr. Ritter," a man's cheery voice said. "I'm Micah Rollins. I understand from Noel Atchison that you're looking into something concerning a death certificate and events here in Harmony back in the late sixties."

An iciness seemed to surround Mark. His fingers tightened on the receiver; he couldn't speak for a moment, then said, "That's right."

"Well, I might be able to help. I've lived in Harmony most of my life. I reckon I know what you're after. It has to do with your parents, doesn't it? Matthew and Helen Ritter. Those are your folks, right?"

"Yes!" His heart was beating wildly now.

"Well, I knew them, knew them real well. Knew you, too, when you were a baby. Noel tells me you're anxious to find out about them."

"Of course. Do you mean Atchison knew them too?" Mark felt a wave of anger for the publisher: He had known all along. . . .

"Well, Noel was living here back then but he said he doesn't recollect anything. Of course, I was more involved in it than he was. You sure you really want to follow up on this? It's kinda complicated, more than complicated, to tell the truth."

"Of course I do," Mark said at once.

"Don't be so sure, now. I've seen people start to poke around in their family's history before, and wish to heaven they hadn't. Sometimes it's a sinkhole and not a treasure chest at the end of the rainbow, you know. I suppose most of us would find more embarrassments than anything else. But if you really want to—"

"I *do,*" Mark said.

"All right, then. Tomorrow, let's say. How does nine o'clock sound?"

"Tomorrow? Why not right now? I don't want to wait until tomorrow." He knew he was whining like a four-year-old, but didn't care. Sweat, warm and tingling against icy flesh, rolled toward his waist, making him shiver. "I've been trying to dig into this for a week! You're the first real lead I've had."

"Well, then, another day won't hurt, will it? Noel tells me you used to be in the Air Force so I reckon you're used to waiting. Anyway, I want you to sleep on it. Maybe you'll decide this is not something you want to do. On principle I'm against adopted children seeking out their 'real' parents, so called. Sister of mine had a son out of wedlock twenty-some-odd years ago and last summer he managed to find her. It's caused nothing but trouble since. The poor gal didn't *want* to be found."

"Then I *was* adopted? And my parents are still alive?"

"Oh, Lord no. Been dead for years. But I want you to *think* about this, what it might mean to you. These sorts of things don't end with the child finding out who his folks are. It affects your family, too."

Mark wasn't listening. "Where at nine o'clock?"

"Come on out to my place. Might as well do it here."

"Tell me how to get there."

The man chuckled. "Forgot to explain myself, didn't I? Rollins Construction. Gray, two-story glass building just off the highway west of town. You can't miss it. We're the biggest construction company in this part of the state. Just ask to see the president."

When Mark hung up his heart was racing as though he had just finished running up hill. *So I was adopted!* As Lisa flipped on the TV he began to pace the small room, his feet pounding angrily on the thin carpet and his fists opening and closing at his sides. *Adopted! Why didn't my dad and mom—damn it, they're not my dad and mom—why didn't the Ritters tell me? Why the big secret? They should have let me know. I had a right to know! What if my real parents had some sort of genetic disease, or a history of cancer or mental illness? Shouldn't I know that? Doesn't my child have the right to know?*

But that wasn't the real cause of his agitation, he knew. What bothered him most was not knowing why his birth mother and father had given him up. Why didn't they want him? And why South Dakota? Wasn't there anybody in Colorado who'd take their child? Didn't his parents have any friends?

He tried to force his mind back to childhood—eighteen years living with "Mom and Dad" and not a hint, not even a *hint*, that he wasn't their natural child. And there were never any other relatives to let something slip. His parents, *adopted parents*, had been orphans, both of them. Or so they had told him. Suddenly he didn't believe anything they said. They had lied about the most important thing in his life, they might lie about anything.

But maybe that's why they didn't tell me. They were orphans, they knew how tough it was to grow up without parents and didn't want me to feel the same pain.

Then what am I feeling now?

How did you expect to keep it a secret? And why hang on to that death certificate all these years? You must have known I'd find it! Did you want me to? Was that it? —But why?

Tomorrow at nine o'clock. Goddamn it, why not today, right now? Suddenly he remembered: I *have* a birth certificate. From South Dakota. With my parents listed as Matthew and Helen Ritter. *Birth* parents! Where the hell did that come from if I'm adopted?

He snatched the phone off the nightstand, punched out the number for Mrs. Cameron, the woman who lived next door at home. "Bessie, I have a favor to ask of you." He explained about needing a copy of his birth certificate and how he kept it in a fireproof box under his bed.

"Fax it to—" He tried to think but only came up with one place. "Fax it to the Harmony police station. I don't know the number. Call information, get the fax number, and send it in care of me."

While Lisa sat at the end of the bed watching TV he began to pace once again. Kicking at a towel on the floor, he suddenly froze, the Cartoon Network blasting kaleidoscopic fragments of manic sound and color all around him. Bending down as though in a haze, he picked up a photograph that had been underneath the towel. His knees went suddenly weak and he thought he was going to be sick. It was a Polaroid photograph of Lisa in front of the ice-cream parlor this afternoon. There was a hole (a bullet hole?) all the way through the picture where her head was, as if half her face had been blown away.

His hand shook and he felt dizzy.

Is this supposed to be a threat? Like that idiotic phone call?

Suddenly anger roared toward him in a single huge wave. What else could it be? Someone had come in this room and left it for him.

But why threaten a seven-year-old child that no one here even knew? It had to be the same person who called this morning. But who . . . ?

Wild Bill had a Polaroid camera but Mark couldn't picture him doing this. Bill had never even seen the two of them until yesterday. Though he did seem fascinated by Lisa. Even that cop noticed how he had reached out and touched her.

Mark went to the window, looked out, and shivered. The Flintstones were yelling at each other. Lisa laughed, and bounced on the end of the bed. Think back: Who was around the ice cream shop this afternoon? Karen. But she was with me. . . . The policeman who had been following them, Kachen. Some hostility there between him and Karen. . . . The dumpy middle-aged guy Karen said was a pedophile. He didn't have a camera with him, did he? Mark couldn't remember. But they saw him again at Janis Lowndes's bookstore. Hadn't he been carrying a bag then? Still, this photograph wasn't the work of a child molester; it wasn't the sort of thing they'd be interested in. It wasn't sexual. . . .

He suddenly straightened as he remembered someone else he'd seen today: Eleanor Dahlquist. He felt warm at the recollection. He hadn't any idea what the hell was going on around here but was confident Eleanor did. His longtime family friend!

He blew out his breath, closed his eyes, and let another thought bubble up from where it had been kept down since this afternoon. Karen's crack about Janis and the graffiti in the men's restroom at the cafe. Mark had been in there and seen no graffiti. It was as clean as his bathroom at home.

So, okay, maybe it had been painted over, though the white enamel looked at least twenty years old. Or it was never there in the first place. He tried to remember if there was any point this afternoon when Karen had been away from him long enough to take the picture. Probably not. But she had excused herself at lunch to go to the bathroom as soon as Mark had arrived, and could have phoned someone to search his room. And she had suggested showing them around town afterward, making sure they found the Häagen-Dazs and stayed away from the motel.

Forget it. You're becoming paranoid.

If someone was trying to keep him from finding out about his parents, they'd failed because tomorrow he would see Micah Rollins.

One week after finding that key in Dexter.

Whatever his mother had been hiding, whatever she had been keeping from him, he was about to discover it. The threats had been for nothing.

At nine P.M., after warning Lisa again not to open the door, Mark went into the bathroom and took a shower, letting the hot water drill into his neck and back while he tried to relax. But it did no good. When he came out ten minutes later he sat at the end of the bed next to Lisa, and pretended to watch television. But the mutilated photograph was like a huge stone pressing down on his chest, slowly taking his breath away. Someone was threatening him, and using his daughter as the target.

He closed his eyes: *All I'm doing is looking for my parents.* Why would this upset someone enough to threaten a seven-year-old?

Or is there some other reason I'm being threatened?

Maybe it's not *me. Maybe the threat really is aimed at Lisa.*

He felt sick, and put his arm around his daughter's waist, pulling her toward him. It can't be her—

"Is there something wrong?" Lisa asked, suddenly looking at him.

"No, no, hon. Nothing." He squeezed again; then, to change the subject, said brightly, "I think we need room service. What do you say?"

Lisa's eyes widened and she clapped her hands. "What can we get?"

Mark could never understand this mania for room service, but was more than happy to give in to it. He grinned at her. "What are you in the mood for?"

"Ice cream!"

"That's all?"

"And pizza!"

"I don't know. Sounds pretty yucky together."

She bounced on the bed. "Pleeeeeze—"

"No. I changed my mind. Let's go to sleep instead."

She attacked him with her small hands, pulling at his arm and shirt. "Daddy!"

"Okay, okay, I give up. Let me see what they have."

He went over to the phone, punched a number, and smiled at his daughter. "Yes, room service. We'd like two Brussels sprouts sandwiches, and warm tomato juice, and some raw carrots—"

"Daaaad!"

"All right, forget all that. How about two small pizzas with everything, two hot-fudge sundaes made with French vanilla and chocolate–chocolate chip ice cream—it has to be Häagen-Dazs. . . . Well, go down and get some, it's not that far away. And make sure the fudge is really hot, and *real* whipped cream on top, not that stuff out of a can—"

"And a cherry!"

"And three cherries on top of each. And some coconut sprinkles."

While they were waiting for the food, the phone rang. When he heard Karen Paige's voice Mark felt a spark of pleasure that startled him with its intensity. But when she said, "I've been thinking about that story I might do—" his spirits plunged.

"Forget it. I don't want a story." After finding the picture of Lisa he wasn't sure he wanted to do anything to bring himself, and especially his daughter, to public attention.

"But maybe someone can help you."

"No! I mean it. I—" He hesitated in mid-thought. Maybe she was right. He might still need help, depending on what he learned in the morning. His tone softening, he told her about the call from Micah Rollins. "Call me again tomorrow. After I find out what he has to say."

"That'll be fine," she said at once. "You and Lisa can come to my house for dinner. We'll eat in the backyard and I'll ask you all the girl-reporter questions from high school: your favorite color; what music you listen to; if you could be a tree which kind would you choose?"

"Deep stuff."

"Well, I can get personal if you want: Why you never remarried? What you find sexy in women, besides long red hair and a perfect body? What you think of assertive but sensitive female reporters?"

"We'll stick to the simple questions. Check with me tomorrow. I'll decide then." He hung up.

Why hadn't he told her about the photo he found? Why was he wary of Karen Paige? He was, though, and it bothered him, because along with the wariness was an unexpected and surprising attraction.

When the food arrived forty-five minutes later Lisa was so excited Mark thought she wouldn't be able to eat it. But she did. All of it, laughing almost the whole time.

And, because it would make her happy, Mark forced himself to eat, and tried to pretend that someone had not twice threatened to take away the one person in life he loved.

Deep into the morning hours the same dream as before revisited his sleep: A dozen people standing about in the fog and darkness, but this time he could see they were in front of the Eagle Point Resort. They turned away when he saw them, and whispered his name, and Lisa's this time, and dissolved into the mist as he came forward to ask what they were doing.

But also tonight another dream: Karen Paige holding his hand, leading him down a long corridor to a room. As soon as they stepped inside she was kissing him and he responded eagerly, for once feeling no shame or guilt over betraying Beth. And then, in the disjointed fashion of dreams, Karen was nude, in a huge bed; he went to her, and woke up, and at once felt his embarrassment. How many years since *that* has happened?

He rolled over, angry; he hadn't come to Harmony for romance, and damn well wasn't in the mood for it. He had more important things to accomplish. Clearing his mind, he made everything go blank, and while sinking once more into sleep saw Karen Paige, nude, in a huge bed, and he went to her.

III

25

Don't get upset about things you can't change, Mark's mother used to tell him. It was a tiny nugget of advice that had served him well over the years, especially in the Academy where hazing and mindless harassment were a long-established part of the curriculum and lifestyle.

But he couldn't help being angry as he stared at the two-month-old Z3 with four slashed tires and a windshield with a spidery web of cracks on the passenger side. Staring down at the car from his room when he opened the venetian blinds at seven A.M, he had thought it didn't look quite right, but he wasn't ready for this. A voice behind him said, "Haw! Knew I heard something out here."

Mark turned to see the motel desk clerk, a man about seventy, propped on a three-legged cane. He was looking at the car and shaking his head.

"Last night?"

"Couple of hours ago. Just before it got light. Opened the office door and came out but didn't see anything. Good thing for you I did, though. Must've scared him away. Another minute and you wouldn't have a windshield. Hard suckers to break, aren't they? Got that lamination to hold them together."

"I've got a meeting in less than two hours. Do you know where I can get four new tires by then?"

"Sure. My son-in-law's got the Conoco station out east of town. He won't be in yet but his boy opens up at six for the truckers, and two more guys come in at seven. Let me get the size here and I'll call him. Fast service, reasonable prices." He bent down and read the numbers off the sidewall. "Small tires, aren't they? But he'll have them in stock. He's gotta keep odd sizes for the winter crowd. They've all got weird foreign cars. Ain't worth a bucket of piss in the snow but they like the way they look."

The tires were replaced by eight forty-five. Mark handed the young man his Visa card and waited while he made an impression of it with the back of a pencil.

"Nine hundred and forty-six dollars," Mark said. "Not exactly what I'd call reasonable prices."

"Don't know about that," the young man replied as he handed the card back. "Seems like you got off easy. Someone don't like you. Coulda been a lot worse than just tires and a window. I was you, I'd lock the car up at night. Probably carry a twelve-gauge, too."

"Well, I'll try," Micah Rollins's secretary said, but already there was the tinny ring of apology in her voice. "He's on the phone to Houston, though. And there's these gentlemen ahead of you." She pointed to three middle-aged Japanese men in identical black suits sitting on a brown leather couch, staring straight ahead without emotion.

"Look, he's expecting me," Mark told her, already feeling annoyed. He'd had only three hours' sleep and, after a week of frustration, threats, and slashed tires, was in no mood to be put off for even a few minutes. He added, "Rollins set the time. There's no one ahead of me." *And goddamn it, he knows who my parents are.*

The woman wearily ran inch-long nails through her stylishly short hair. "Have a seat. I'll check."

Mark and Lisa sat in matching leather chairs next to the suspicious but stoic Japanese, and waited while the secretary picked up her phone just as another line began ringing. They had already made their way past a half dozen offices where men and women hunched over drafting tables or sat at desks, talking on phones or staring into computer monitors. All this activity, this hubbub of people in motion, had surprised him. He wondered what he had expected from a construction firm. Two guys in hard hats smoking cigars and scratching themselves?

The secretary put the phone down. "It'll be okay but he'd like the little girl to wait out here."

For Christ's sake! "She's not 'the little girl.' She's my daughter. And why should she wait out here?"

The woman's face became vaguely alarmed as if she feared he was going to get violent. "Mr. Rollins just thought it best. Maybe I can find a magazine for her to look at."

Mark sighed. "All right. Stay here, hon. It won't be long."

The secretary looked relieved. "The door's unlocked. Go on back."

Micah Rollins was sitting behind his desk with his feet on a pile of blueprints stacked on the desktop, talking on the phone. He smiled, rolling his eyes theatrically and waving Mark to a chair, then said into the receiver, "Yeah, yeah, sure, Phil. Look, I gotta go. The governor's here and . . . What do you mean, 'What governor?' The governor of Colorado, for Christ's sake. What do you think—the fucking Federal Reserve. . . . Yeah, of course. I'll call. But first I'll call your bank. You get me?" He slammed the phone down and almost bounded over the desk to greet his visitor. "Micah Rollins. Happy to meet you."

He was a huge man, maybe six-four, two hundred fifty pounds, in his mid-fifties, wearing a western-cut embroidered sport shirt, casual slacks, and no tie. Mark shook hands and Rollins waved toward the chair again, then took the one across from him. Between them sat a coffee table that had been made by resting a glass top on a pine frame containing an ornate silver-studded saddle. "Used to belong to Gene Autry," Rollins laughed as he saw Mark staring at the saddle. "Bought it at a charity auction over in Denver and had this table constructed to show it off. Got all kinds of cowboy stuff from the forties and fifties around here. Let me show you." He jumped up, full of a contagious enthusiasm, and went to the far wall. "Just look at this. Framed original lobby poster for *Springtime in the Rockies*—1937. This one's from *The Fargo Kid*, Tim Holt, 1941. These here guns"—he took a badly weathered leather gun belt with two holstered revolvers off a shelf—"came from *The Squaw Man*—one of the first full-length movies ever made. God, I love this stuff. Got a lot more at home." He led the way back to their chairs.

"Used to just *love* going to the movies when I was a boy. Folks your age can't understand how important movies were to children in those days. No TV, of course. A kid could go to a matinee for a quarter and lose himself in someone else's more exciting life." He waved a possessive hand at the side wall. "Autographed pictures of Roy and Dale, Lash LaRue, Tom Mix. Real movie six-shooters, lassos, spurs, saddles, hats. Hate to tell you what this stuff costs nowadays. The wife says I'm nuts but I figure it's my money and my office and

I can do what I damn well please." He relaxed back, his booted feet stretched out in front of him. *Younger than my parents,* Mark thought. Soft and paunchy despite his size, but with keen dark eyes that were watching him closely though pretending not to.

"Damn, you do look like him," Rollins said, hunching forward and rubbing his long hands together. "I'll say that. You got some ID, I suppose. Don't mean to get ticky-tack with you but I don't want to go spillin' family secrets to the wrong people. How about a driver's license?"

Mark took out his license and, as Rollins examined it, stared at the pictures on the walls. The only non-western article in the room was a photo of an attractive young woman with shoulder-length brown hair. Daughter or trophy wife?

Rollins handed back the license and smiled broadly, pink cheeks rising toward his eyes. He seemed thrilled with his guest. "Noel said you went to the Academy downstate. Your dad woulda liked that. Yes sir. Woulda been proud. A pilot! Damn! This is pretty exciting for me. Never had anyone else from Harmony make it to the Academy. Hell, tough enough to get Harmony kids to finish high school. Everyone wants to go out and make money, even if it's five bucks an hour at Burger Crap. That's why we got a city full of Beavis and Butt-head look-alikes. I guess I shouldn't complain, though. I quit school at fifteen."

Mark tried not to show his anxiety. "You knew my dad and mom?"

Rollins wiggled back in his chair and his face turned serious with obvious reluctance. "You sure you want to go through with this?"

"Dead sure."

The man nodded and frowned. "Hell, reckon I would if I was you, too. It ain't pretty, though." He looked at Mark.

"Please."

"All right, all right." The large man slowly lumbered to his feet, looking lumpy and beer-bellied, his hair somewhat askew. "You want a drink? Just past breakfast but—"

"No!" Mark's fingers tightened on the arm of the chair. The offer seemed more like an attempt at putting off the inevitable than a desire to be hospitable. He felt like screaming but clamped his teeth together and stared at the big man.

"Yeah. Okay." Rollins began to walk, taking half a dozen steps away from his chair, coming back, then repeating the trek, his eyes fixed on the floor as he spoke. "It goes back to 1968. I was working on my own as a carpenter." He shook his head, staring back at the memories. "Man, that was a long time ago! Not much work, of course. That was before Walter Lowndes took over the resort." He looked over at Mark with pride. "Walter Lowndes is the reason I'm where I am today. The only reason. Soon as the resort got under way I started my own construction company. Three years later I put up the first condos in Harmony and things just sorta took off. Those explosions you hear from time to time come from the restaurant we're building for Lowndes on top of the mountain. The Ice Castle. Rollins Construction was the only firm willing to do all the excavation necessary to anchor it into the mountain like the damn state insists on.

"Anyway, we, me and the wife—first wife—lived out on Archibald then, just east of town. Little bitty two-bedroom place, all we could afford. One night in the summer, must've been late June or thereabouts, when I was mowing the back lawn I saw smoke coming from about five miles east of town. So I figured, shoot, I'd pop over and see what it was. Just being nosy, I guess, like folks are when there's a disaster. Turned out to be an old cabin, probably eighty years old. It was burning like nothin' I'd ever seen. Hell, you could see the smoke from anywhere in town by then. I remember standing out on the road with about thirty other folks watching the fire department trying to get it under control. But it was hopeless. Only time I've seen a fire act like that. The whole house was burning and *whoosh*ing and tumbling down. It was noisy as all get-out and hotter than the dickens even where we were out on the road. It was clear there weren't going to be any survivors." He glanced quickly at Mark, still pacing. "That was your folks' place.

"Wasn't much of a house, more like a cabin, and forty acres of scrubland. Wasn't worth all that much, still ain't 'cause the town grew in the other direction. But your dad was up-to-date on the payments, I guess. It wasn't an easy life but they were making a go of it. Of course it helped that your mom had a job. She worked at Donner's department store. I recollect when you were born. She only took a week or so off, then was back to work because they needed the money. Your dad tried to watch you during the day and also do something with the land. Had a few head of cattle, some alfalfa if I remember correctly, but this really isn't ranch or farm country around here."

He stopped pacing and put his hands on the back of a leather chair as he stared at Mark. "The next day, after it cooled down enough to get inside and poke around, the firemen found your folks' bodies. Burned real bad but they were identifiable. Also found a baby. Still alive, believe it or not. A big metal utility cabinet had fallen over the kid and evidently it provided enough protection so the flames couldn't reach it. The doors had come open when it fell and it kinda cocooned the baby on three sides. Must've been hotter than hell, of course. The kid was burned on the feet and hands but not too seriously. Had to be hospitalized for a while, though. But no one could believe it: a miracle baby, everyone said. Anyway, that was you." He looked at Mark, the surprise still evident on his face. "The miracle baby."

Mark sank back in his chair; he was flushed and lightheaded. *Miracle baby.* A fire, both parents dead. He felt his body stiffen with emotion. A goddamn *fire!* Why had this been such a secret for thirty years? What had people been hiding from him? He began to feel racked by a storm of emotion—anger, confusion, fear—and glared up at Micah Rollins, his voice cracking. "There's more. Something else. Has to be!"

Rollins nodded reluctantly. "Once we start, we gotta follow it all the way to the end. Hell, yes, there's more." The phone rang, suddenly shattering the mood. Rollins stalked over to the desk, reached across and grabbed the receiver. "Jesus Christ, Gloria, what'd I tell you? . . . I don't give a damn! I'll call her back." He rammed the phone down, and resumed stalking around the room, the fingers of his right hand unconsciously striking his leg.

"Well, while everyone was oohing and ahhing over you and making plans to take care of you in the hospital our local police were poking around in the ashes. Took your folks' bodies to Haskins's funeral home, of course—you've seen it over on Main—but the chief at the time was curious because they were both in the bedroom, fully clothed, your mom sprawled across the bed, or what was left of it, your dad on the floor. Didn't seem right. If they weren't asleep why didn't they get out?"

Rollins's eyes were fixed with an odd intensity on the floor. His voice seemed overloud, full of emotion and energy. "It was Deets— that was the Chief back then, old Howie Deets—who found the gun. It had fallen into the crawl space under the floorboards during the fire, then the roof fell on top of that. It was an old thirty-eight revolver with three empty chambers. By the time the chief got back to town Haskins had discovered the same thing. Your mom had been shot twice in the heart, your dad once in the brain, the bullet entering through the mouth."

Mark's eyes closed, then opened onto Rollins's pained face. "He killed her."

"Killed her, then shot himself."

"But *why?*"

Rollins waved an arm. "Who knows? They'd been having some marital problems, according to the pastor at their church. Your mom had been in for counseling but your dad was kinda an ornery cuss and wouldn't go. But he'd never been violent. No one ever expected anything like this, of course. I mean it just floored us all." Rollins came over and flopped down in his chair. "Who can explain these things? They just happen."

Mark sat with his head in his hands, trying to bring some meaning to what he was hearing. But he couldn't, couldn't make sense of any of it. It was just too much to absorb. Finally he asked, "What were they like—my parents?"

Rollins eased back, rubbed his eyes with his knuckles. "Just folks. Name of Contrell. Ed and Ruthann Contrell. Typical small-town people, trying to make a go of it on land too small and too rocky to be much good to anyone. Your dad was never in trouble with the law, if that's what you mean. He wasn't bad—"

"Wasn't *bad?* He killed my mom and he wasn't bad?"

"Now, you know what I mean. He wasn't a bad man. He just flipped out. It happens. It wasn't anyone's fault, it was just"—he waved uneasily—"life. It all just got too heavy, I reckon."

"Christ!" Mark stood up suddenly. *"Goddamn it!"* He felt like striking out, hitting somebody, breaking something. All the time he had spent searching and *this* is what he discovered. And in the back of his mind a glimmer of relief rose that Lisa wasn't here to experience this with him.

Rollins seemed to sense what he was thinking. "I tried to warn you. Some things are better left in the past."

Mark was covered with sweat and his stomach knotted. Rollins was right. It had been a mistake. Better to have never known, to have never discovered the death certificate. Isn't that what everyone had told him? No good could come of it? Then he sank down on the chair as another thought suddenly struck him. "I was supposed to die too, wasn't I? My father wanted me to die in the fire."

Rollins was staring at his feet. He glanced up, catching Mark's eyes. "Looks like."

"God. . . ." His head fell forward. "You're *sure* he started the fire? It couldn't have been an accident?"

"Dumped kerosene in practically every room of the house. That's why the fire department never had a chance."

For a long moment Mark said nothing, eyes closed and breathing heavily, staring at the hands that sat clenched in his lap. Suddenly he looked at Rollins. "So how did I get from the hospital to South Dakota?"

"Well, that was what I gather they call a private placement. Old Julian Hightower—Mason's dad—knew a couple up north somewhere—Idaho, I think—that had just lost their child. It was all kinda done outside of legal channels. Folks here in town had raised some money for your hospital care—held a barbecue and carnival and bake sales, and such. The folks in Idaho were planning on moving away, wanted to start out new, I guess, where they didn't have any memories. They'd already bought a place in South Dakota. I remember when they came down here—real nice folks, the Ritters."

Mark's face flushed. "Real nice folks would have told their son he was adopted."

"Well now, don't go getting like that. You don't know what they were feeling, or what they were thinking. Remember, they'd just lost their own child, and if I remember correctly she couldn't have another; had a hysterectomy after the child was born. This had to be awful tough for them. So you're not the only one who suffered. Fact is, I don't see where you suffered at all. Looks like life's been good to you."

"They *lied* to me, damn it. The most important thing they could have told me—who I am—they deliberately hid."

Rollins shook his head wearily. "I hope you get over this in a few days because if you don't, I'm going to be mighty upset with myself for opening my big mouth in the first place. You sure as hell aren't being fair to those folks."

Mark's anger was mounting. He could feel himself becoming irrational but didn't care. "How do you know I *am* that baby? The Ritters' first child died. Maybe the second one died too. Maybe I'm the third kid they had, or the twenty-third. How do I know the

Contrells *were* my parents? Maybe my father's not a murderer. You're just guessing."

"Easy enough to check. There's a birth record up in Denver. Got your palm or footprint on it."

"But I've *got* a birth certificate with my prints on it. In the name of Mark Alan Ritter, born in South Dakota to Matthew and Helen."

The man was surprised. "You sure?"

"Of course I'm sure."

"And you checked the prints on it against yours?"

"No. Why should I? Have you ever checked the prints on your birth certificate? But I'm sure as hell going to now. I'm having a copy faxed to the police station. They can match it."

"You got a copy of your prints with you?"

"I'll get printed at the station when I get the fax."

"Well, there's only two possible outcomes when you get your birth certificate. Either your prints match, which means it's a phony since it's in the wrong name because you are definitely not a Ritter. Or they don't match. Meaning they'll match the birth certificate in Denver. In which case Mark Ritter—you—is the son of Ed and Ruthann Contrell. Which in fact is the truth."

"Maybe," Mark said. He put his head back, squeezed his eyes shut, and let his breath out in a long sigh. His mind spun and he felt sick. Then his eyes blinked open suddenly. "So why is this important enough for someone to want me not to find it out?"

Rollins's eyebrows drew together. "What do you mean?"

Mark pulled the photo from his pocket and tossed it on the coffee table. Rollins picked it up and squinted. "This your kid?"

"With a bullet hole in her head."

"Maybe not. Could be anything. Where'd you get it?"

Mark told him. "It's probably the same person who slashed my tires, and called yesterday morning with a crude sort of threat. My daughter is going to die. That type of thing."

Rollins shook his head. "Meaning what?"

"How the hell should I know what it means? It was corny enough for one of your old B westerns: 'Get out of town or we'll run you out.' All that so I won't find out my drunken dad shot my mother and tried to kill me? Come on! There's got to be something else."

"Maybe he was trying to protect you."

"Right. Threaten my life to keep me from learning the awful truth. In words of one syllable, bullshit."

"Okay, so there's another reason."

"Bingo. Eureka. You hit the nail on the head. Whoop-de-do. Another reason it is. Shall we try to figure it out or just head on home?" He wasn't sure why he was acting this way. Making an ass of himself was not something he normally enjoyed doing. But he was sure he was doing a pretty good job of it today. Suddenly he wanted nothing more than to get out of Rollins's office. He jerked to his feet. "I'm going to check on my birth certificate. Maybe it's at the police station by now."

"Hope I was some help to you." Rollins rose, sticking his hand out, but Mark had already started for the door.

26

The weight of Micah Rollins's story was like a rock pulling Mark beneath the sea. Numbed into silence, Lisa beside him in the car, he drove a mile to the police station, and asked the uniformed officer at the desk if a fax had arrived for him. The cop gave him a sour look, then went back into the business office, returning a moment later. No fax. And why would he have it sent here anyway? This ain't a secretarial pool.

Harmony, Mark thought out on the sidewalk. A perfect name for a town of such uniquely friendly and helpful people. He felt like going back inside and slamming the cop's head against the desk.

Holding Lisa by the hand, he stood in the morning sun as the dullness grew in his mind; his eyes wondered aimlessly. Now what? He couldn't do anything further until he checked his prints against those on the birth certificate. But why did that even matter now? His folks—Matthew and Helen Ritter—had lied to him. He wasn't who he thought he was. All his life had been a lie. He was Mark Contrell, the son of an alcoholic murderer who had wanted him dead. Or was his name even Mark?

Might as well go back to the room and then decide what to do next. If anything. Stopping at a 7-Eleven, he bought a six-pack of Coors for himself and a Snapple for Lisa. As he was getting back in the car he realized he'd been so angry at the cop about the fax that he'd forgotten to say anything about the photo he'd found, or the slashed tires. Christ, that meant another trip to the police station. But not now. Later, when he was in a better mood.

Back at the motel he flopped down on the bed with a mid-morning beer while Lisa turned on Nickelodeon. His mind seethed. Ed and Ruthann Contrell. The names meant nothing to him. He was sure his parents . . . A sudden surge of emotion overtook him, and the pulse began to throb in his temple. . . . *Parents!* He was sure *the Ritters* had never mentioned them in his presence.

Feeling warm he climbed off the bed, turned the air conditioner to High, then sat down again, propping his back against a pillow. *Contrell!* Did that make him legally Mark Contrell now? Did Lisa suddenly become a Contrell too, grandchild of a murderer?

He finished the beer, opened another, and put the back of his head against the wall. What would drive a man to do what his father had done? What horrors could push someone over the edge like that, where the only way out of his misery is not only his own death but that of others also, including a blameless seven-month-old child?

The miracle baby. Alive only by chance, because a cabinet fell on it. *I was supposed to die too. My own father didn't want me to live.* Almost every room sprinkled with kerosene and torched. . . .

The air conditioner rattled in the window, filling the room with dissonance but unable to cover the shrill sounds blasting from the TV. Still warm, he kicked off his shoes. An anger at Micah Rollins rose but passed over him like a wave. *Can't say he didn't try to warn me. And I would have found out sooner or later anyway.* But the rage for his father, for both fathers, made his heart race.

Someone knocked on the door. Forget it. He wasn't in the mood.

"Dad?" Lisa looked over at him.

He picked up the beer and drank half of it in a single swallow. More knocking. *Go away, damn it, leave me alone.* But the pounding became more insistent. Lisa stood up, looking worried. "Do you want me to open it?"

Furious, he jumped off the bed and yanked on the door. "What the hell—" but stopped when Karen Paige smiled brightly and said, "Hi! Got time to chat?"

Still holding the door, he looked at once back into the unmade-up room, then down at his bare feet, his anger dissipating, but said nothing.

"If you're not up to it—"

"No, hell, come on." He moved aside as she passed in, then shut the door loudly.

"Hi," Lisa said, clearly happy to see Karen.

Karen was clutching her purse in front of her with two hands. "Have you two been exploring Harmony today?"

Lisa scrunched up her nose. "We went to a place with pictures of buildings. It was boring."

Karen looked at Mark who said, "Micah Rollins's."

"Oh," Karen said. "Boy stuff. Tractors and earth movers. Yeah, that would be boring, all right. How would you like to go ice-skating someday? We have an indoor rink."

Lisa spun toward her dad. "Can I? I've never been."

Mark was in no mood for bantering. "If we stay in Harmony. We might be leaving."

Karen smiled at the child. "Let me talk to your dad for a while. I'm sure we can find some time for skating later." Lisa clapped her hands, said, "Yay," and went back to the TV. Karen sat down at the small oak veneer table, looking at Mark with concern. "Noel just told me. I guess Micah talked to him about your folks last night."

He closed his eyes, rocked back on his heels. "Small towns are wonderful, aren't they? Probably everyone in Harmony knows about me now." He yanked out the other chair and sat.

"I don't think it's that bad but the story's getting around. If you don't mind I think we should still do an article on it."

His eyes flashed angrily. "Why?"

She put her hands in her lap. "Human interest. A young man's journey of discovery, or something like that. I haven't worked out the angle yet. I wanted to talk to you first."

"Forget it, there is no angle!" The thought of making his family's history part of Harmony's breakfast-table conversation made him snap at her. "Do runaway-dog stories or pothole stories. Or write about motels with half-assed air-conditioning, or why people in Harmony are so damn unfriendly. But keep me out of it."

Lisa glanced over her shoulder at her father but Karen's expression didn't change. "I'm not trying to exploit you. But I thought if we did an article maybe some people who knew your mom and dad would come forward. Don't you want to know what they were like?"

Putting his back to Lisa, Mark leaned across the table and hissed at her. "My father *killed* my mother! He tried to kill me. I *know* what he was like."

"I think you're being a little too quick to judge, don't you? Whatever happened to your father happened before you were born. You don't know a thing about his life. Do you? Nothing! Do you know the kind of pressures he was under? Or what his childhood was like? Or who *his* parents were? Don't you care?"

"I know more than I want to know. It's enough." He stood up suddenly, tipping the chair back against the bed.

"I'm sorry," she said, looking up at him. "I wish this could have turned out differently for you. Really."

"I never should have come here! That's what everyone told me. They were right, weren't they? It was stupid. What did I expect to find? It was that damn key. It drove me, it *made* me search. I should have thrown it in the trash and gone back to Seattle." He crossed to the window, yanking on the drapes and staring out at the parking lot.

Karen went over to him. "Whatever's happened is not your fault. You did what anyone would have done. It just didn't turn out the way it could have."

He looked at her, then at Lisa staring uncertainly from the end of her bed. Suddenly the fight seemed to rush out of him, like air from a balloon.

Karen smiled, trying to relax him, and he closed his eyes as though to will away the thoughts that had been storming through his mind. "You did what you had to do, what any child would need to do in your situation." But he was only half listening, his palms pressed against his lids. When he dropped his hands and opened his eyes she was standing so close their feet were touching, and he could smell her perfume, hear the soft in and out of her breathing, feel her warmth gather him in. He began to feel dizzy, as he had in Micah Rollins's office, and put a hand on the wall.

They looked at each other a moment, then Mark again closed his eyes as Karen touched his fingers. He couldn't think clearly, felt a shiver as her hand closed on his. His daughter said, "Are you all right, Dad?"

Mark shook his head to clear it, and when his eyes opened Karen was staring into his face. "Yeah, fine, hon." He said to Karen, "Do you know where the Contrells used to live?"

"I can find it. I'll call Noel."

He turned to Lisa. "Do you remember how to put the top down?"

She jumped up. "Sure I do."

He tossed her the car keys. "Do it. We'll be out in a minute. We're going to look at some property."

The girl looked from her dad to Karen. "Neat."

He listened to the door slam, the sound of Lisa's feet pounding on the metal landing, then touched Karen's arm with his fingers. "I guess I'm not much company today. Rollins shook me up. I look like an idiot. I'm sorry."

She moved slightly so their bodies touched, and at once their eyes met. "You look okay to me." And then they were kissing, slowly and gently, their tongues questioning and teasing, softly probing. Her hands were at his back, holding him against her, as if he'd fall to the floor if she didn't.

After a moment, he shook his head. "We've only known each other for two days," and experienced a strange piercing of guilt that made him feel fourteen years old. He wasn't ready for a serious relationship. He hadn't, in his own mind, put away the feelings of betrayal that haunted him every time he showed interest in a woman. It had become easier, he'd learned, not to be interested at all.

Karen smiled. "Even so, you're intrigued by my ready wit, fresh-faced good looks, and scintillating personality. Tell me you aren't!"

"Yes, but—"

"But nothing. You were an Air Force officer. Take charge here." She moved against him, and he did. She held him tighter this time, and felt her passion escalating as his tongue darted a trail of excitement on the inside of her mouth. His gentleness with her was unexpected, and almost excruciating, as her heartbeat rose out of control. Drawing a breath, she smiled, and squeezed his shoulder with her fingers. "I agree with Lisa: Neat. Better than I planned."

"Planned?"

"Shameless hussy that I have become." She laughed, but also seemed uneasy. "I've been thinking about this since yesterday." She smiled again, shrugged, and put her palms on his chest. "Don't look at me like that. Who can explain chemistry, or the mysteries of attraction. I felt . . . I don't know what. Something. The moment I opened the door yesterday and saw you. I figured it had to be you who made my heart go pit-a-pat and not Wild Bill. Though," she added playfully, "I am a sucker for a man in buckskin fringe."

"Which reminds me—" Mark felt a plunge of emotion, and put a hand on his forehead.

"Lisa's waiting. Right? I've got to call Noel first and get the address."

"No," he said. "Wait—" His voice was strained. In the wake of his visit to Rollins this morning he had half forgotten about last night, even now wasn't sure he wanted to confront—why did he use that word?—*show* her. But he had to get it out in the open or continue to wonder about her involvement.

He pulled open the dresser drawer. "Someone was in my room yesterday. It had to have been when we were at lunch or when you were showing us around town." He paused, allowing her to say something but she remained silent.

"Whoever it was left this." His hand shook as he removed the Polaroid picture and gave it to her.

Her eyes went at once to Mark. "In front of the ice-cream shop. This is Lisa, isn't it?"

He nodded, but said nothing. He wanted her reaction, and felt himself growing uneasy waiting for it.

"Is that supposed to be a bullet hole?" She sounded shrill.

"I guess someone tacked it up and took a shot at it."

"But why?"

He took the picture from her. "It has to be the same person who called yesterday and threatened Lisa's life. But like I said, there was something unreal about it, the scratchy voice, the way he implied he'd been molesting her. It's pretty sick."

"Les Cady."

"Whoever. But I talked to her about it again. If she had been molested she'd have told me."

Karen looked at him dubiously.

Mark was annoyed at the implication. "I know my daughter. She's not been molested. Whoever this is, he's trying to scare me. Before I even had a chance to talk to anybody. No one here knew why I was in Harmony. No one should have even known my name. But somehow he did. He said my daughter was going to die. Just like my wife and mother had."

"What does that mean?"

"My wife died in an auto accident. My mother of a stroke. . . . If she was my mother."

Karen sank down on the bed. "But why try to frighten you? What would be the point?"

He put the picture in the drawer and slammed it shut. "I don't know what the point is. But if he thinks he can scare me by threatening my daughter, he's right. If anything happened to Lisa . . ." His jaw clenched and his whole body seemed to stiffen. "My wife, my mother, now Lisa."

"It has to have something to do with your parents, your coming to Harmony."

"That goddamn key."

"Did you talk to the police?"

"I'll go this afternoon. I'm getting to be a regular. Yesterday it was the phone call, this morning a fax, now the photo and my car."

"Your car?"

He told her what happened and she shook her head in dismay. "God, I can't believe this is going on in Harmony." She considered a moment, then added, "The only person I know with a Polaroid is Bill. Do you think he—"

"Lots of people have them. Go ahead and call your boss. I want to see that property."

She dialed the newspaper and made a hurried notation on the cover of Mark's Colorado map. "Got it," she said.

Mark took the phone from her. "I want to try to get hold of Walter Lowndes before we go. Do you know his number?"

"Why do you want to call him?" There was something that sounded like apprehension in her voice.

"Lowndes is the town big shot. Or so everyone says. And he's lived here for years. He can tell me about the Contrells."

"We can try the resort, I guess. He's probably in New York, though. He doesn't spend much time here in the summer."

Karen dialed the number while Mark held the receiver.

"You know it by heart?"

Her mouth tightened into a grim line. "Small town. And I'm a reporter." She turned toward the window, and he couldn't see her expression.

The hotel switchboard transferred him to a secretary. Yes, Mr. Lowndes had recently arrived in town. No, he seldom saw visitors except on resort business. Yes, she would take his name and number and leave a message for him. But her tone indicated a return call was unlikely.

Mark banged the phone down with annoyance. "We better go. Lisa's going to be getting anxious."

Karen turned around. Her voice was suddenly tentative. "Do you know how hard that was for me to do? To force myself on you like that?"

"Very?" he guessed, taking her hand in his.

"My arms are swimming in sweat. I've never even asked a guy to a movie before and here I am practically tearing your clothes off. God, I sound terrible, don't I? I'm babbling! Well, don't mind me. It's how I deal with extreme nervousness. I talk. And talk."

Mark took her in his arms. She smiled, suddenly cheerful again. "Hey! I like the newly pushy me. It gets results." She kissed him slowly and deeply. "Dumb question," she whispered after a moment, "but have you got a girlfriend or . . . whatever? I guess I should have asked before. I don't have much experience as a shameless hussy."

"Beth was the last person I was serious with. After she died . . ." He didn't know how to explain, didn't want to explain, and felt the rising of guilt again. It had just never seemed right, seemed like betrayal to the only person besides his parents and child he ever loved. It still seemed this way; sometimes he wondered if he would ever get over it. And of course he'd worried how Lisa would view a new woman in his life, and Lisa's happiness was the only thing that really mattered. "My daughter . . ." he began awkwardly, and then gave up.

"Your daughter," Karen explained, moving to kiss him again, "has known since I came in the room. That's why she said, 'Neat.' "

27

Karen said nothing as Mark, holding a bottle of Coors by the neck, stood in the field of knee-high weeds and stared around. A hundred yards to the north a barbed-wire fence indicated the boundary line. To the east aspens and pines sprouted in what was once plowed land; to the west as far as he could see there was nothing but mountains. He wiped sweat from his forehead as he walked back and forth, his eyes trained on the ground while Lisa waited impatiently with Karen. "You sure this is the right place?" he finally asked.

Karen shrugged and shoved her hands in the back pockets of her Wranglers. "According to Noel."

Mark kicked at a rock. "There's nothing here. Not a trace."

"It's been thirty years."

He looked over at her. "It would have had a stone foundation. Or cement. A brick fireplace. Something should be left."

"Old bricks disappear into people's backyards—walkways, barbecues, planters. People like the looks of them."

Still staring at the ground, Mark strode toward the fence, then turned across the field and headed in the direction of the pines. Suddenly he stopped. "There's a concrete footing over here." He bent and ran his fingers over it. "Pretty old. I suppose it could be part of the house. The ground's flat enough here." He walked a few steps and kicked at something, then picked it up. "Scissors. Just about rusted through."

Karen came over and looked at them. "Thirty years in the snow and sun."

Mark let them drop to the ground and again wiped sweat from his forehead as Lisa wandered away from them toward the trees. The sun, still not overhead, already beat down intently, and insects swirled around their heads. Mark's eyes slowly traced the outline where the house would have been. His voice dropped, but was without emotion. "Where I was supposed to die. Where my father tried to kill me after shooting my mother."

Karen frowned. "You're obsessing on this. It's not healthy."

"If your father tried to kill you, wouldn't you be curious? Maybe even obsessing?"

He kicked again at the ground with the tip of his shoe. "Not very good farm or ranch land, is it? Rocky, dry, hard to till. I wonder why my folks ended up out here."

"Inexpensive," Karen guessed. "Still is, relatively. Most people who live out here either work in town, or are retired. Land's too hilly for serious farming."

Mark turned toward the road and sighed, but was too numb with the day's events to rouse any anger. "I'm getting real tired of that."

When Karen saw what he was looking at, her anger was enough for both of them. "Goddamn it! I think it's Bobby Sample. Let me talk to him. You stay here."

The black-and-white was parked on the gravel shoulder, engine running so the air conditioner would function. Karen waited for an eighteen-wheeler to rattle by, then crossed over and tapped on the window.

Sample opened the door and grinned. "Whew! Hot out there.

Y'all come around and sit in the front seat if you want to talk to me."

"Bobby! *Don't!*"

But the door clicked shut. Karen stomped around the front of the car and yanked open the passenger door. Sample grinned as she slammed it after her. "You look hot, girl. Why don't you take off your shirt and cool down a bit?"

Karen gave him a withering look. "What the hell are you doing out here, Bobby?"

"Doing? I'm *po*-licing. This here's my beat."

"You part of the state police now, Bobby? Your *beat* ended at the city limits."

"Not if I see a crime being committed. I gotta go where the bad guys go. *Enforcing the law,* you know. It's my sworn duty."

"Bad guys, Bobby? Crime? Are you losing all touch with reality?"

Sample jerked a thumb toward the field. "Well, right now I see a man trespassing. Wondering if I might oughta take him in. You know how it is—a fella starts with trespassing, next thing you know, he's committing serial killings."

Karen slumped back in the seat. "Poor Bobby. Never heard of the U.S. Constitution. Didn't you pay attention in school? Or did you stay home and lift weights that year?"

He ran a hand over his tightly curled black hair. "Then there's the unlawful intercourse."

Her head snapped in his direction. "What? What the hell are you talking about?"

"The Ritter dude. The poor ol' orphan boy with a little girl. You and him, Karen. Seen you come slinkin' out of his room, all smiling like, and smoothing down your clothes. Seems like a real dumb thing to do, you ask me. Things being like they are and all."

"Bobby, I didn't . . . Oh hell, even if I *had,* it's not against the law, for God's sake."

His voice abruptly lost its bantering tone and became aggressive. "Might not be against your law, Karen, but it's sure as hell against mine. Know what I mean?"

Suddenly she was furious. "Bobby, goddamn it, don't give me any trouble. You do and I'll go straight to the chief. I mean it."

He turned his handsome face in her direction, and she could see a tiny scar on his forehead, another on his cheek, and a place where a chunk had been taken out of an ear. He held her eyes with his.

"You think Stallworth's going to be sympathetic to you after what you did? Come on, Karen, you ain't brain-dead. No one in the department's going to give you an inch. And if you keep screwing around with the orphan boy there, he's likely to end up in a ditch with a bunch of broken body parts. Someone already trashed his car, from what I hear. Best thing y'all can do is tell him to take his brat and get his raggedy ass out of town right quick. And I mean like today."

"Bobby, you lay a hand on him and I'll go to the state attorney general's office faster than you can say Rodney King. Remember what happened to the cops who beat *him?* Jail time for the *po*-lice. And you know what happens to cops in the slammer."

Sample's angry voice filled the car. "Tell you what, gal. Since you and me is such good friends, I'll beat in Ritter's pasty face myself. Break a few teeth, bust his nose, bloody up his eyes. Tell him it's a present from Karen. Then let Todd do his arms and legs. This all sound okay to you?"

She pushed on the door handle. "Look for yourself in the paper next week, Bobby. Every word you just said. This all sound okay to you?"

She purposely left the door open and stomped back to where Mark was kicking at weeds. He turned and looked inquiringly as she angrily walked up. "Don't ask," she said. "Bobby Sample's in his own alternate universe."

Mark looked over at the patrol car. "If he doesn't get off my butt his universe is going to come to an early end."

Karen shook her head. "Don't provoke him. Please. He likes to fight. Broke some guy from Boston's jaw last year. Probably because he was *from* Boston. Bobby's specialty is 'resisting arrest.' "

Mark continued to stare in Sample's direction. "Why the hell's he on my tail all the time?"

"Bobby doesn't need a reason."

They both stared at the car but the policeman's face was a blur behind the side window. Karen muttered something that sounded like "Screw it," put her arms around Mark's waist, and kissed him. Lisa came up behind them and said triumphantly, "Caught you! Caught you!"

Mark laughed uneasily and held Karen a moment, then let her go, and tried to change the subject before Lisa became too inquisitive. "Who owns this property now?"

"I can ask Noel. He might know. Why?"

"Because maybe I do."

"Well, it's probably not worth much."

"Maybe not. But I seem to be accumulating real estate. First a farm in South Dakota, now maybe forty acres in Colorado. I might become the next Donald Trump or Walter Lowndes."

"Not a very worthy aspiration. On either side." She looked at her watch. "We're going to have to get going. Noel needs me back at the paper. It's layout time. Want me to drop you at your motel?"

"No, let us off at the police station. Bobby Sample ought to like that. I want to tell them about the Polaroid and slashed tires. And see what they have on my parents' death. There should be a file on it."

He looked again at the field, the weeds and aspens moving gently in the hot breeze. "I don't know what I expected coming out here. Something to show me why my father wanted me to die? A sign? A revelation? Something's here, though. Somewhere in Harmony. I don't know what it is. But I'm going to find it."

28

Taking long rapid strides back and forth in her office at the rear of the vacant restaurant, Caroline Bellamy clutched the phone to her ear as she asked, "Did you talk to him?"

"Hell, yeah," Micah Rollins said from his own office a mile away. "Told him about the little girl and her snoopy dad. But he'd already heard."

"Shit!" Once tall and thin, Caroline had matured into a large woman who affected multicolored tentlike muumuus to disguise her size, and lately had taken to covering her fingers with a gaudy assortment of rings as a mark of some personal eccentricity. *I'm rich and I can do what I damn well want,* they seemed to say. A half dozen rubies and sapphires flashed on and off through the lamplight as she jerked a hand angrily through her hair. "Who the hell told him?"

"Who knows? Maybe nobody. Maybe it's a sensing mechanism he has, like dogs after birds. Ain't his tail that'd be pointing, though." He giggled at his joke. "But, Christ, Caroline, everyone's seen 'em. It's not like a secret, more like the circus come to town, folks going out on the sidewalk to see the parade and scratch their heads at the freaks."

"And what'd he say?" She glared out her office door toward the bar and dining room, where a young man was ineffectively mopping the floor while singing the theme from *Evita*.

"Told me to go fuck myself. Are you surprised?"

"Surprised? Nothing he does surprises me, Micah. I told you, he's losing control, he's living in a crazy-world, a little-girl world. You know that."

"Better than you, my dear. But I still think you're overreacting. Just leave things to me. I'll take care of it all."

"My God, Micah, you are the most optimistic person I ever met. Aren't you ever down?" A long sigh blew through her lips, and she felt like collapsing onto the floor.

"Always up for you, hon. And I'll keep it up anytime you want. You know me. Aim to please and pleased to aim."

Caroline rubbed her forehead, gems and Navajo silver flashing, in no mood for the man's bantering. "Did you talk to the dad?"

Rollins relaxed back, dropping his feet on the top of the coffee table, and admiring the tooling on his $700 cowboy boots. "Yep. Came over this morning. Brought little Miss America, too."

"You think he believed you?"

"Seemed to. Pretty shook-up, in fact. Of course, who wouldn't be, learning old Ed Contrell was his father?" He giggled again and rattled the glacial ice from Norway in his glass of Johnny Walker Blue Label.

Caroline sighed, shut her office door, and came back to the desk. "I hope so, Micah. For our sake. Both of us."

"Coulda told him the truth. That would've been fun to watch, too." Playing with her now, trying to get a rise.

Caroline held her temper in rein. "Sometimes, Micah, you astonish me with the stupid things you say. How did you ever get to be so successful?"

"Same way you did, darlin'. Through hard work, clean living, and acting *real nasty* to my friends."

The dial tone buzzed angrily in his ear. Micah put the phone down with a chuckle, then began to tap a finger on his knee. *You are not thinking very clearly here, Caroline, old gal. The threat's a hell of a lot bigger than you think but it ain't from the kiddy-lover or Ritter— it's coming from a whole new direction, like a snake slithering along behind you and getting ready to crawl up your skirt. Thing is, how am I going to use it to my advantage? I gotta give this some more thought.*

Relaxing back, Micah closed his eyes, and moved it around some.

With careful planning this could turn out okay. Could even be fun.

But he was worried about Caroline. The woman was too damn impulsive. And that was a problem.

29

Karen nodded ahead as she drove Mark and Lisa back to town in her Taurus. "There's an ambulance up there coming from down in the gully. I'd better take a look. Might be a story."

"Are you always on duty?"

"I told you, I'm the only reporter. If I don't do it no one will."

She slowed as the red-and-white vehicle rose onto the highway, crossing abruptly in front of her and turning in the direction of town. "No lights or siren. Not a good sign. It usually means they have a body."

She swung a hard left onto the side road and plunged immediately into a thicket of trees and tall grass that seemed a world away from the neat boxlike condos and restaurants of Harmony. A hundred yards ahead two police cars and a white Jeep Cherokee were jammed into a wide space along the side of the road. "Oh-oh."

"What is it?"

"Bill lives down there. I hope he didn't have a heart attack." As she pulled behind the Cherokee and parked, her demeanor changed in an instant from intimacy to impersonal professionalism. "You two can come if you want. Or wait in the car. I might be awhile."

Just then a black Ford Explorer drew up behind her. As they climbed out of the Taurus, B.J. Blake was getting out of the Explorer. He looked around with concern. "What's going on, Karen? I saw the ambulance—"

"Don't know, B.J. Looks like something happened to Bill."

"God, I hope not," he said. "Can't remember him even being sick. Kind of indestructible, like part of the Harmony landscape." He nodded to Mark and Lisa. "Nice seeing you folks again."

The four of them followed a path that led down through the overgrown hillside to Bill's cabin, where two uniformed policemen were desultorily searching through the mountain of junk outside. Karen was hurrying ahead of the others toward the open front door. Blake glanced at Mark. "Loves her job, doesn't she? Beats the alternative, I guess."

Just then a stocky, hard-looking gray haired man of about fifty walked out. He stepped off the small porch and met them amid the clutter. "Figured you'd show up sooner or later, Karen. What took so long?"

She yanked a notebook and pen from her jeans pocket. "Is Bill all right? Did something happen to him?"

"You don't know? Must've had your scanner off." His eyes flicked past Blake to Lisa and Mark. He hesitated, and his cheeks colored and eyes narrowed.

Karen said hurriedly, "I'm sorry. Hector Chavez, assistant police chief. This is Mark and Lisa Ritter."

As Mark shook hands Karen asked again, "What happened, Hector?"

"Someone killed old Bill. Shot him in the back of the head. Killed his dog, too."

"Killed?" Blake almost shouted. "Like in murder?"

Karen also was disbelieving. "Are you sure? Why would anyone kill an old man like Bill? He was as harmless as could be."

Chavez looked around at the trash surrounding the house. "Believe it or not, we think it was robbery."

"Robbery? Bill?"

"Place is a mess. Someone was looking for something."

"Come on, Hector!" Blake said. "I was in there a couple of times. The place was always a mess."

"I know. I was out here before, too. But this is different, B.J. Someone was definitely looking for something. Don't know if he found it."

"God!" Karen put her hand to her forehead. "Robbery! That harmless old man. The only money he ever had was those coins he'd give away to kids."

"Yeah, well—" Chavez started to say something else, then changed his mind.

Karen said, "Maybe someone thought he was a miser and had a

houseful of cash hidden away. Couldn't be anyone who knew him, though. I don't think he ever had a real job."

"Must have had at one time. We found Social Security check stubs in there. He was only collecting about a hundred fifty dollars a month, though." He turned to Mark. "You're the guy looking for his parents, right?"

"Everyone seems to have heard."

"Small town. People gossip."

"I was talking to Bill yesterday. One of your cops was giving him trouble."

"My cops? Who are you talking about?" His voice became aggressive, and his jaw set in a scowl that had been perfected in three decades of police work.

"Bobby Sample," Karen said with a look that implied he shouldn't be surprised. "Bobby has this weird notion Bill's been annoying children. I've tried to tell him he was *paid* to entertain kids but Bobby's not one to change his mind. Assuming there's one there to change."

"True, Hector," Blake said. "He's had a thing against Bill for a long time. I've seen it, too. I mentioned it to Eldon once but I guess he didn't do anything about it."

Chavez's eyes went briefly to Lisa who had begun to walk around, inspecting the masses of junk surrounding the house. "Maybe Bobby knew something you folks didn't, Karen. Just because he and Todd are friends doesn't mean he's wrong about everything."

"Hector," she said, turning to stare into his eyes, "Bobby is Harmony's answer to the Piltdown Man. He can't even grunt in two syllables."

Chavez considered, then said, "Let's go inside for a minute." He turned to Mark. "You can come if you want but the kid's got to stay out here."

Mark told Lisa to wait, then he and Blake followed Chavez and Karen onto the wooden porch and inside the foul-smelling cabin. "Jesus—" Mark muttered as he looked around. The place looked as if it had been filled with litter, then picked up, shaken, and dropped onto the ground. Bags and boxes had been emptied of whatever they had held, the drawers of the single pine dresser pulled out and thrown onto the floor, dozens of pieces of clothing tossed into a pile. . . .

"Someone was looking for something, all right," Karen said. "And you don't have any idea what?"

Chavez hesitated. "Maybe. Come over here to the kitchen."

They threaded their way around mounds of junk to the tiny kitchen where Bill had installed a hot plate and small refrigerator. Chavez lifted a pile of about a hundred photographs of various sizes from the top of a counter. "We found these hidden in an envelope taped to the back of the refrigerator."

Karen paled as she began to look at them. "Oh, God. I can't—" She dropped them on the counter top. Without picking them up Mark could see what they were: girls from about six to ten, nude, or having sex with men.

"Bobby might've known what he was doing," the policeman said. "Our good friend Bill was one sick puppy."

Mark felt ill remembering the old man with his hand on Lisa's hair, the way it lingered, the way he stared intently into her face for a long moment while he touched her.

Chavez said, "Also makes me feel a little stupid about the way we've been treating poor old Les over the years."

"Les Cady," Karen said to Mark. "The pedophile I was telling you about yesterday." She paused briefly. "Or maybe not. God!"

B.J. Blake had picked up the photographs and was fanning through them. "All the men's faces are blanked out or turned away from the camera."

"Does look like we were wrong about Cady," Chavez said. He glanced at Mark. "We've known there's been a child molester loose around here, or used to be, anyway. People figured it had to be Cady—everyone just kinda *knew* he was weird, you know, even when he was in high school, I guess. He was arrested back in the seventies on the word of a nine-year-old girl whose parents worked in the fields east of town. But they went back to Mexico rather than go through with the disgrace of a trial. Happens all the time in this type of case, unfortunately. A seven-year-old was raped and murdered a few years later but Cady had an alibi. Never had any real proof. But people wouldn't have anything to do with him. If Walter Lowndes hadn't given him a job I don't know what would have happened to him. No one else would hire him. If we *were* wrong I feel real bad about how we treated him all these years. Pretty cruel thing to do to a guy."

Blake shoved his hands in his back pockets. "If it turns out Les was innocent it might be worth doing a story about, Karen. 'Small town crucifies local kid,' and so on. You could interview people, including me, about how they feel about destroying an innocent man's life. Get the right approach and it could be Pulitzer stuff."

"I guess this explains some of Bill's peculiarities, too," she said softly. "But I'm surprised. I never would have guessed it. He always seemed so nice."

"Molesters usually are," Mark said softly. "It's how they get close to kids." He turned to Chavez, wondering how stupid he was about to appear. "My mother died in South Dakota last week."

"I'm sorry to hear that."

"A day or two later someone broke into her house and searched it. And killed her dog."

Chavez looked at him with surprise. "And you think these two events are connected? Because dogs were killed?"

"I don't know. I just thought you should be aware of it."

"Okay." The policeman considered a moment, then added, "Don't get me wrong here but there wouldn't have been any kiddie photos at your mom's house, would there?"

Mark felt warm at the implication. "Of course not."

"No one took pictures of you as a little kid, maybe?"

"Goddamn it!" Mark shook his head. He never should have mentioned the dog.

Blake asked Chavez, "Do you think the killer was looking for these photos?"

"It's possible, of course. But how would he have known they'd be here? And as far as I know no parent's complained about anyone bothering their kid recently. Haven't had a molestation reported in years. I reckon this guy was looking for valuables. Probably some meth freak. Hills are full of them. He sure picked a piss-poor victim."

Mark had picked up the photographs and was quickly flipping through them when his fingers began to tremble. All the pictures but one splashed to the floor as the room spun, and his mind raced through a progression of emotions from denial to rage and finally a limitless black fear.

"What?" asked Karen. She put her hand on his arm.

Blake said, "Are you all right?"

Chavez frowned and bent to pick up the pictures.

Mark handed the single photo to Karen, who gasped. "My God, it's Lisa."

Mark's eyes had locked closed. He rocked back on his heels and felt nauseated as bile rose in his throat, and his stomach cramped.

"In our backyard in Seattle. That's our play equipment. I put it up last year."

Lisa, wearing shorts and a T-shirt, was sitting on the top crossbar of a swing set. Her eyes were turned away from the camera and she had a determined look on her face as though she was trying to decide the best way to get down.

Chavez was confused. "Are you saying this is your daughter, and your backyard?"

Mark nodded, but he was only half paying attention. His mind wouldn't stop spinning questions at him: How . . . Who . . .

The policeman glanced at Karen, then back at Mark. "How could—" He broke off, rephrased what he wanted to ask. "You've never been to Harmony before, right?"

"Just a couple of days ago," Mark said, then steadied himself against the countertop.

"And you didn't know anybody here?"

Mark nodded, thought to himself, *Nobody, we didn't know a single person here. But someone knew us, called me. . . .*

"Never met old Bill?"

"Of course not."

Chavez again looked at Karen. "And you didn't know Ritter?"

"I met him yesterday at the newspaper."

"And you're sure it's his daughter?"

"Jesus Christ!" Mark's voice shot out. "It's Lisa. I know my own daughter."

Chavez glanced down at it again. "It's not like the others. She's clothed. And there's no man in the picture."

Mark just shook his head.

Chavez asked the obvious. "So how do you think this picture ended up in the house of a child molester with a bunch of other photographs? Especially since he lives hundreds of miles from you."

Mark grabbed the photo from Chavez and ran outside where Lisa was looking at an eighty-year-old woodstove. Trying not to give any hint of the fear racking him he knelt down next to her. "Do you know how this stove works?"

"Uh-uh."

"You put wood in it." *Calm down, damn it!* "See—in here." The cast-iron lid felt as if it weighed fifty pounds as he lifted it for her. "You'd put wood down here, light it with a piece of paper, then put the lid back, and wait for it to get hot."

"Neat."

Mark put his arm around her waist, forced it not to tremble as he pulled her against his body. "Hey, hon, look what I found."

She looked at the picture without interest, then opened the oven door and let it slam shut. "Last year. When I was little."

His heart began to pound. "What do you mean?"

"Those red shorts. I can't wear them anymore. They're too small."

Of course, Mark thought. So . . . okay, last year. One day when he had to go into the office, maybe, and Mrs. Cameron was supposed to be watching her. Damn that woman! What was she doing when Lisa was being photographed? He began to feel panicky again. "Did a man ever come to our house and take a picture of you?"

"I dunno." She picked up the stove lid, let it drop loudly. "You took me to Sears for pictures. It was dumb. The lady acted like I was a baby and tried to make me laugh."

"No, no, not that. Did someone . . . Did you ever see Wild Bill before yesterday?"

"Nope. I like him."

"I like him, too. Did he ever come to our house?"

"I don't know."

Oh God, Mark thought. "You don't *know* if he came to our house, or you never saw him at our house?"

"That one."

"You never saw him at our house?"

She nodded, pulled open the oven door, stuck her head in.

"Did you ever see Bill in Seattle?"

"Where do you put the wood here?"

"Lisa, did you *ever* see Bill before yesterday?"

"Nope, nope, nope." Her singsong voice. *Borrrr-ing,* it was saying.

"Then how did he get this picture?" he couldn't help but ask, and his voice betrayed his emotion.

"He likes me!" She smiled. "He took my picture yesterday."

Goddamn it, I know he did. Mark looked at the picture again. It could have been taken from outside the gate if a telephoto lens was used. Whoever took it wouldn't have had to go in the back or even let Lisa know he was there. His body had gone cold. Why would Bill have gone to Seattle? Why would Bill even know him and Lisa? "Lisa, did Bill ever touch you? Did he put his hands on you?"

The girl's face froze up. "Stop asking me that!"

"Did he take off *his* clothes?"

"Don't!" Lisa insisted. "I told you! No, no, no!"

She tried to move away but he gave her a hug. "I'll be back in a minute."

Chavez was waiting for him. "Well?"

"She doesn't know anything about it. *Jesus!*" His hands clenched into sweaty fists and he kicked at a pile of junk on the floor.

Chavez was concerned as well as confused. He held Mark's gaze. "I still don't get it. How could this picture end up here when you don't know anyone from Harmony?"

Mark just shook his head as blood roared in his ears. How was he supposed to answer a question like that? His mind had been bombarding him with questions since arriving in town. Why had his mother hidden the mystery of his birth? Who called, threatening Lisa? Who left him the Polaroid, or ripped out the missing issues of the *Courier*? And all of this to intimidate the son of the town drunk who murdered his wife and committed suicide thirty years ago? It didn't make sense.

He could see Chavez watching him, appraising and rejecting a number of questions as his mind shifted between sympathy and mistrust. Finally the man removed the photograph from Mark's hand. "We better hang on to this for a while. Just in case."

"In case what?" Mark demanded. He felt a sudden and irrational hostility toward the policeman.

"We've got a murder victim here. This might be evidence. Or even help us. You never know."

Mark took a breath, tamped down his emotion, and tried to speak calmly. "That's not the only picture of Lisa." He told the man about the Polaroid with the bullet hole, as well as the threatening phone call and slashed tires.

Chavez looked at Karen, then back at Mark. "In the two days you've been here?"

Mark nodded.

The cop shook his head. "Have you got the other picture?"

"It's in my motel room."

"Did you report any of this?"

"I reported the phone call. I found the picture late yesterday. My car was attacked this morning."

"And you don't know why this is happening?" He looked at Mark dubiously.

"No, damn it. I haven't any idea!"

"And a dead dog," Chavez added, and watched him. But before

Mark could respond, Karen put a hand on his arm. "I'm sorry, I have to go back to the office to get my camera. I can drop you and Lisa at the motel if you want."

B.J. waved an arm. "Don't worry about it, Karen. I'll take them back."

She turned at once to Chavez. "Is the chief coming out?"

"Been here and gone."

"All right. I'll be back in ten minutes or so. I'll want to interview the officers out front, too."

Chavez folded his arms and regarded her stoically. "No need to hurry. I don't know if they'll want to talk to you. You know how they are."

But Karen seemed to be ignoring him. She put a hand on Mark's shoulder, the concern obvious in her voice. "I don't know what to say. I can't imagine what any of this means."

Mark felt a tightening of his intestines. "I *can* imagine. God, I hope Lisa's telling the truth and no one's been bothering her."

"Would she lie about it?"

"Don't child molesters usually tell the victim they'll kill the parents if the child says anything? That's what I've heard."

"But there would be symptoms—odd behaviors, crying fits. Anger. Something!"

Mark tried to think. Were there any signs? Or had he been too tied up with work to notice what was happening to his daughter? There had been the nightmare a couple of nights ago, and some temper tantrums lately. But all kids went through that. And again the thought came: What did any of this have to do with his parents, or Harmony? He didn't know anyone here, had never been here before, had never even heard of the town.

30

Are you taking your medicine?
Yes, nurse, I am (again).

It makes you feel better, doesn't it?

Much. I *think* better. Really. But it makes it hard to remember. And sometimes all I want to do is remember (to live again, experience, feel).

I counted your pills. You missed three days. You can't do that, you know.

I understand. Yes. But I'm better now. Better.

It makes you irritable.

I know that. But I wanted to remember.

I think I should check with your doctor. Maybe he should see you again. It's been awhile.

I'm okay, damn it! Don't do this to me.

We'll see. See how you do.

I'm okay. Please, I only want to remember.

31

The message light was blinking on the telephone as Mark and Lisa entered their motel room. He grabbed the phone off the night table and, still standing, dialed the office.

"A letter arrived for you today. Want me to send it up?"

Mark said he did. A letter? Who would write him here? No one from out of town knew where he was. Not even Eleanor Dahlquist.

Eleanor! he thought, and felt a stab of anger. Somehow the attorney was a thread that connected Dexter and Seattle and Harmony. And she had been here yesterday.

There was a knock at the door a minute later and a Vietnamese clerk handed him an envelope. Postmarked Harmony, yesterday. Still at the door, he ripped it open. There was no letter, only a photocopy of a newspaper article. Dated June 27, 1968. The missing issue. He felt warm as he began reading.

FIRE GUTS MOUNTAIN RESORT

A raging fire early Tuesday morning swept through the local ski resort, destroying the tow-rope and office/home of Carl Stark, owner of the property, and resulting in the death of Mr. Stark.

"We never had a chance," stated Travis Hawk of the volunteer fire department. "By the time we got there the whole place was in flames. We tried to save the house but just couldn't do it."

According to witnesses the entire resort seemed to go up at once, though authorities say there is no indication of arson.

"Just summertime in the mountains," Hawk said, adding, "Folks got to watch out this time of year. Things is pretty dry out there, and there's been a lot of lightning."

It was not until the following day that the badly burned body of Carl Stark was discovered in the rubble of his home.

According to Police Chief Howie Deets, identification of the body was made through dental records.

"It's a sad thing," Chief Deets said. "He was planning on finally doing something with the ski area, maybe put in a chair lift or a restaurant. The town could have used a boost like that. Now it'll probably be years before anyone else is interested."

Mr. Stark had inherited the property from his parents, knowledgeable sources informed the *Courier*. He leaves no family. Services will be Friday at ten A.M at the Haskins Funeral Home.

That was it? That's what someone had been trying to keep him from reading? There had to be something there he wasn't seeing.

His heart pounding he grabbed the phone. Whatever this was, it was one more reason to see the police. This and the photos of Lisa. Suddenly he put the phone down. He needed to talk to the police openly, without upsetting his daughter. Janis Lowndes had volunteered to watch her yesterday. He found the number of her store in the phone book and dialed. Janis answered on the first ring. Would she mind keeping an eye on Lisa while he talked to someone at the police station this afternoon? No, she wouldn't mind at all, would enjoy it, in fact. She seldom had a chance to talk to children. She'd bring Lisa by Mark's motel when she closed up about five, if that was all right. But he should insist on seeing Chief Stallworth so he could tell him about being harassed. The chief needed to rein in his troops before they killed someone.

Mark felt a surge of energy as he hung up. He snatched his keys off the end table. "Come on, honey. I'm in a hurry."

32

Patrolman Rudy Bains, a pleasant-looking young man with blond hair and soft eyes and freckles, had a manner that belied his appearance. He stared dully over the counter at Mark and shook his head. "The chief doesn't see people until they've gone through channels. That means you start with me. What do you need to see him about?"

"A murder-suicide that took place before you were born." Something kept him from mentioning the photographs. The privacy of his family, perhaps. Or the fact that pictures of a fully clothed child, even with a bullet hole through her head, were not illegal, or indicative of anything suspicious. Except to the child's parent.

Bains glared at him, his pale skin turning red.

"You trying to be funny?"

"I'm trying to be accurate."

"What year are you talking about?"

"Nineteen sixty-eight."

"We wouldn't have any records on that. It's too long ago." He turned away.

"Get the chief for me." He was losing his patience—Harmony again—and felt his control slipping away with it.

Bains spread his hands on the countertop and raised his voice. "I told you. There ain't no records."

"Get the chief."

"Listen up, man. This isn't hard to understand. The chief isn't going to see you. Period."

Mark's hand shot out, grabbing the patrolman's thumb, twisting it back against the wrist, then slamming the knuckles onto the counter. The patrolman yelped.

"Call the chief," he said calmly, putting more pressure on the thumb.

The door opened behind Bains, and Hector Chavez said, "What's going on, Rudy?"

Mark released the patrolman, who stepped back quickly.

"Jesus Christ! This asshole broke my thumb." He shook his hand back and forth in the air as if that would relieve the pain.

"What did you say to start it?"

"Start it? Christ, Chavez, this fucking nut case comes in and demands to see the chief about something that happened thirty years ago. And the CIA's transmitting radio signals through your fillings, right Ritter?" He blew on his thumb and continued to shake his hand.

Chavez let the door shut, and came up to Mark. "I already told Stallworth about that photo. We're looking into it."

"I want to talk to him about my parents. My father killed my mother here in Harmony in 1968. Your department investigated. I want to see what's in the file."

"I told him we haven't got anything," Bains snapped, still rubbing his fingers and wrist. "But he just kept pushing and pushing. Thinks we're a bunch of rubes he can order around."

Chavez looked calmly at the young patrolman. "Sometimes we are a bunch of rubes. Go put some ice on that, if you want." His dark eyes came back to Mark and he shook his head. "Thirty years! Chief Stallworth's the only one in the Department who would have been around then. I didn't come over from Colorado Springs until 'eighty-five. I don't know—" He thought a moment. "Let me see what he says. Try to be civil when I'm not here, Rudy."

He disappeared into the back and Bains turned his pleasant, freckled Tom Sawyer face on Mark, while flexing his fingers. "Fucking affirmative-action hire. He likes you, though, doesn't he, Ritter? Maybe he'll invite you over to his *casa* so you can roast a goat and bend a few tacos together."

Mark sat in a ripped leatherette chair, his fingers silently tapping on the arm, until Chavez returned and pushed open a waist-high door. "Come on back. Chief said he'll give you five minutes."

Mark stood up. "There ought to be a fax here for me. A copy of my birth certificate. It was sent from Seattle yesterday. I checked this morning but they said it hadn't arrived."

"Ask Rose in the back. She's keeper of the office machines. The chief won't let us touch any of it. Thinks we're all thumbs."

He followed Chavez into the business office, a large, mostly empty area with half a dozen gray metal desks and a haphazard assortment of filing cabinets, lockers, and office machinery. A harried-looking middle-aged woman in slacks and a Mexican blouse was the only occupant. Mark asked about the fax.

"Don't remember it." She got up from her desk and went to another desk where she began rummaging through a pile of papers. "I'm the only one who files. If it was faxed during business hours I'd recollect it. I'm sure we didn't get a birth certificate. Maybe she got the number wrong."

"It's not likely she would have gotten another fax machine, is it? If it turns up, give me a call at my motel."

"The Mountain View, right?" She smiled over her glasses at him as she continued shuffling through the papers.

Mark shook his head in dismay.

"Well, I heard talk. This is a police station, you know."

Chavez was waiting at an open door in the rear of the room. "That was a neat trick with his thumb. Where'd you learn it?"

"Survival training for F-16 pilots. I went down to Central America and trained with Marines in the jungle. They didn't tell me I'd need it in Colorado."

Chavez said nothing, but waved him inside the office. The man behind the desk—sixtyish, wary-looking, with a ruddy, fleshy face— was coming to his feet as they entered. He jabbed a beefy hand over the tidy desktop as the overhead lights bounced off his bald scalp.

"Eldon Stallworth. Figured you'd show up sooner or later after I heard about your folks from Atchison. Then Hector told me about the picture out at Bill's." He motioned Mark to a seat after they shook hands. Chavez took the only other chair.

"Half of Harmony seems to know who I am," Mark said.

Stallworth dropped into his oversize swivel chair. "If that reporter does a story on you like Atchison says, the other half will know soon enough. You're our summer entertainment, I guess. A man searching for his family—it makes for an interesting story."

"I don't think I want a story. This isn't anyone's business but my own."

"Hell, I'm with you a hundred percent. But I'm afraid we live in an era of terminal snoopiness, don't we? Folks wanting to know what Fergie had for lunch, or what Mel Gibson watches on TV. Or those daytime talk shows: 'Women Whose Husbands Had Sex with the Sewing Machine.' It's a weird, weird world. And full of snoops and busybodies."

"Maybe so. But I want to keep what I'm here for between the three of us."

Stallworth waved a hand in front of his face. "I've got no problem with that. Depending on what it is."

"First, that photo."

Stallworth hunched forward. "Well, the obvious thing is it's no crime to have a picture of a kid in your house. Weird, maybe, but not a crime."

"Depends what kind of picture it is."

"Yeah, those others Bill had definitely are a problem. Would have been better if you'd never touched the one of your kid. But we sent it to Denver for prints anyway. Hector says you don't know how Bill could have gotten it."

"My daughter says she never saw him until yesterday. And I'm sure I've never seen him before. Do you know if he ever went to Seattle?"

"Could've. He'd disappear every once in a while for a couple of weeks. Off on a drunk, I figured. Spent time in a state mental hospital more than once."

"Have you turned up any other pictures?"

"Nope. Be a day or two until we're done out there, though. You saw what it looked like. But if Bill was a molester he could have had designs on your kid and never had the opportunity to do anything about it. Seems like you can breathe a sigh of relief now."

"But how could this man we never saw until yesterday have designs on a child who lived hundreds of miles away?"

Hector Chavez said, "You're going to have to wait until we have a chance to go through his house more thoroughly. There's just no way we can answer that now. Might not ever be able to."

Mark tried not to let his frustration show. "All right. What about my parents, then? I want to see the file on their deaths. And talk to anyone who might have been in the department when it happened."

The chief leaned back and regarded him with curiosity. "And what do you expect to discover from this little archaeological dig?"

"Why my father killed his wife and tried to kill his son." His mouth went dry, the words suddenly hard to form. "And how I ended up living with the Ritters."

"You talked with Micah, I hear."

"He told me what he knows, but it's just an outline. I want the details."

Stallworth rested his elbows on the desk and leaned forward. "Well, I'll be happy to tell you what I know, which isn't much, I'm afraid. I was just a patrolman then, so I didn't get involved in the investigation but I remember it. Not very well, to be honest with you. Hadn't thought of it in years, till Micah mentioned it."

The chief pressed his lips together and his eyes wandered away. "It was just one of those things that happens from time to time, not so much back then but more and more nowadays—guy flips out and starts shooting." He looked back at Mark. " 'Going postal,' they call it in the big city. Too much stress, you know. Everyone figured that's what Ed did. Just flipped. It wasn't a premeditated plan—"

"He poured kerosene in almost every room, and set the house on fire before shooting himself," Mark reminded him.

"Kerosene woulda been there anyway. He didn't go out and buy it. The gun was his, far as I can remember. It was a spur-of-the-moment thing, believe me."

"But *why?* What kind of stress are you talking about?"

Stallworth's chair creaked as he tilted back. "Best I can recollect, we decided it was sort of a male-ego thing. It still happens in rural areas. This was before the ski boom, of course. We were just a dirt-poor mountain village back then. Ed couldn't get any money out of the ground and didn't have a trade to sell in town. He tried to make a few bucks by repairing lawn mowers and gasoline engines and such but didn't have many takers."

"He was from Harmony?"

"Don't remember where he was from. Out of state, I think. Kinda strange the way he just showed up in town one day. Just gotten out of the Army, I think, and was bumming around, riding freights. Hopped off a train here for some reason. Worked for a while over at the feed store on Garfield—can't remember the name of the place, it's long gone."

"Then you don't know anything about him? What his family was like? Anything like that?"

The chief shook his head. "Nothing. Sorry. This was a long time ago, remember."

"When he was here in town, when you knew him, did he seem—strange? Act like the kind of person who might do something like this?"

For a moment Stallworth didn't reply. Then he came forward slowly in his chair, his face troubled. "I guess I see what you're after. You want to know if your biological father had any mental problems that might have been passed on to his son."

The fingers of Mark's right hand closed on the arm of the chair. "And granddaughter."

Stallworth let out a sigh. "Yeah, I guess I'd want to know, too. Kind of a hard thing to face at this point in life, though. Well, I can't help you but there might be something in the file. Everything over twenty years old is in the courthouse basement. I'll go over personally and dig through the boxes till I find it. But, Jesus, man, just because he flipped doesn't mean he was crazy, not in any clinical way."

"He tried to kill his seven-month-old son."

Stallworth shook his head. "Well, let me check into it, see what we got. If I were you I'd check the Army, too. They might have medical records. I'm not sure they'd release them, though. I guess the first thing you gotta do is prove you're Contrell's son. You can get the birth certificate up in Denver."

"I have a birth certificate from the Ritters, too, proving I'm *their* son."

"Yeah, Micah told me about that. Can't be real, though."

"My neighbor faxed it to your office yesterday but it's disappeared."

"You mean we never got it?" He fixed Mark with a look.

"I don't know what I mean. It was sent but no one can find it. I guess I'll have her send a copy by overnight mail."

"Well, I'll dig around the office. Maybe it's out there somewhere. Rose isn't the neatest person in the world." He started to stand but Mark took the photocopied news story out of his pocket and tossed it on the desk. Stallworth picked it up and raised his eyebrows.

"It came in the mail today. Anonymously."

The chief frowned, read the story. "I remember when this happened. About a month before the Contrells' fire, I think. Anonymously, you say?"

Mark nodded.

"Well!" Stallworth picked it up again, thought about it, dropped it on the desktop. "Why do you think someone sent it to you?"

"You tell me."

As Chavez reached over and plucked the story off the desk, Stallworth said, "Folks know you're looking for your dad. You think this has something to do with that? You think Ed Contrell was involved in the resort fire also?"

Mark said, "Two issues of the *Courier* were removed so I wouldn't read about it. Someone else obviously wants me to."

"Noel told me about the missing issues. But it doesn't mean they were taken because of you. Could have been taken anytime. For any reason."

Mark just stared at him.

"Does look odd, though, doesn't it? The resort fire and Contrell's fire. Your dad and Carl Stark."

"Did Stark know the Contrells?"

"Christ, boy, there was only thirty-five-hundred people then. Everyone knew everyone."

"Were they enemies?"

Stallworth shook his head. "You think I'd remember that? Hell, it was thirty years ago!"

"But you remember the resort fire."

"Of course. Biggest thing to happen around here, before or after. Whole ski area burned one night. Lit up the entire town when the mountain went up. Kind of awe-inspiring, in a creepy sort of way. Looked like the end of the world from Main Street. Mostly it was trees and underbrush that burned. Wasn't much in the way of structures or improvements—a tow rope, a little house and office. That's why Stark died. He lived there, was sleeping when the fire started."

"Was Ed Contrell suspected of starting it?"

"Hell, no one was suspected of starting it. Electrical, I think."

"The story said Stark was planning to improve the resort."

"Well . . . maybe. Carl had more ideas than money. Must've been another five years before anything was done to the place."

Mark retrieved the clipping from Chavez. "Why do you think someone sent this to me?"

"Trying to tell you something, I guess. Show it to Atchison, see what he says. It's his paper, he's become our local historian."

"I kind of figured the police department would be the place to start."

Stallworth's face tightened. "I told you I'd look in Contrell's file for you. Don't make me change my mind. By rights I don't have to do a damn thing. This isn't a library."

Mark took the Polaroid picture of Lisa from his pocket and put it on the chief's desk directly in front of him. "Another anonymous message from the good people of Harmony."

Stallworth's face reddened. "You are beginning to be one problem after another, Ritter. This your daughter? Hard to tell."

"Someone searched my room. And left it as a sort of message, I guess. Lisa with a bullet hole through her head."

Stallworth passed the photo to Chavez. "Jesus, Ritter, are you telling me someone sent you an anonymous newspaper story, someone else sent you what appears to be a threatening picture, Hector tells me your tires were slashed, and old Bill has a picture of your kid— all this within, what, two days of arriving in Harmony?"

"And the phone call."

Stallworth sank back. "*What* phone call?"

"I reported it to your department yesterday. Someone threatened my daughter's life."

The chief looked at his assistant who said, "Ritter told me all this out at Bill's, Eldon. I haven't had a chance to check for the report yet."

"So why don't you just tell me?" the chief said to Mark with obvious sarcasm.

When Mark told him what the caller said, Stallworth looked disgusted. "I'm beginning to wish I never saw you."

"You're not alone. I guess I aroused some old memories—or hatreds: Contrell, Stark, two fires. Not everyone's happy with that."

"But why your daughter? What's she got to do with this?"

"It's your city. You tell me. But it seems like there's a lot of conflict around here, a lot of hostility and hatred."

"Shit!" Stallworth slumped back in his chair as Chavez handed the photo back to Mark. "Putting a bullet hole in a young girl's head is the sorta thing I would've suspected weird Lester of until today. Beginning to look like it's crazy Bill again though, doesn't it? He's the one with a Polaroid. I used to wonder about him, the way he was always hanging around kids. I don't know why he'd call you, though. I guess we're going to have to start looking into his background. Could be more there than we thought."

"Doesn't mean Cady couldn't have taken the picture. But why would he? It's a threat. There's nothing sexual about it. Just like finding child pornography at Bill's doesn't mean it's his."

Stallworth rocked forward in his chair and gave a sarcastic laugh. "Right! Someone broke in to *rob* Bill, didn't find anything, so left a photo of your kid along with some nasty pictures instead."

"No. Someone killed Bill and left those pictures to make you believe he was the one who's been molesting kids."

"Jesus, Sherlock Holmes here." His eyes shifted suddenly and he fell silent as a thought obviously hit him.

"What?" Mark said.

Stallworth leaned forward, put his elbows on the desktop, and rested his jaw on his fingers. "I just remembered—I was the one that found Carl Stark's body after the fire; he was on the floor like he was trying to get under the smoke and crawl to the door when he passed out. Anyway, the funny thing is, Bill was out there, too. Came in while I was poking around the rubble, started yammering on about things, doing his loony-tunes act. I kicked his ass out of there." He glanced at Chavez, and seemed suddenly troubled.

Mark said, "Tell me about the molestations you've had around here."

"Who the hell told you we'd had a molester?"

Chavez shifted in his seat. "We were talking out at Bill's."

"Well, hell, Hector, don't let me get in the way. You boys finish up."

"Started before my time, Eldon. You'd remember better than me."

" 'Course I remember. Guess I don't see its relevance to anything Mr. Ritter is involved in. And a picture of a kid mutilated like the one you got is unsettling, but not exactly a police matter without some more substantial threat. I guess you don't have to worry about it anyway since the perpetrator is dead."

"Then you're convinced it was Bill?" Mark asked. He was clearly dubious.

"Like I say, we'll look into his background. But have you got a better idea?"

"The only evidence you have is those pictures. And they weren't hidden very well."

"Then Les Cady snuck in and killed Bill to make it look like he was molesting kids so we'd leave him alone? That's what you think?"

"I didn't say that. I said the only evidence you have could have been planted."

Stallworth picked up a pencil and began to tap it on the desktop. "Jesus, you sound like some fancy defense lawyer. Tell you what. Why don't you lighten up some? The person taking pictures around here and threatening your daughter is dead. So relax. As for your parents, let us worry about it, and leave the police work to the professionals."

Mark stood up. "Like those two psychopaths you've got working for you?"

Stallworth colored. "What the hell are you talking about?"

Mark told him of his run-ins with Sample and Kachen.

The chief's face reddened. "And your lady friend didn't tell you why you might be having trouble with them?"

Mark said no.

"Then maybe you better ask her. Hector, show the man out."

33

Lisa liked the smell of Janis's paints—oil paints, they were called, but they came in a tube like toothpaste and looked like colored bird-poo, all curled up like that, and didn't look like oil at all—but she was bored by Janis's painting. The woman stood in the back room wearing an overcoat that went all the way to her knees, and for some reason Lisa felt she didn't have anything on underneath it, but that was okay, she guessed. Janis was an adult, a mommy probably, and she didn't think a mommy would do anything bad. Still, it was *borrr-ing* watching her paint with her gobs of bird-poo. So Lisa wandered around the store, taking books out of the racks and looking at the pictures.

There was a whole shelf of books with photographs but she didn't like them—mostly without color, and the ones with people looked gross, ugly old people with lines on their faces, sitting in Denny's or office buildings or factories. Janis said her father made them and they cost a lot of money. Dumb, dumb, dumb.

Every time a customer came in the store Janis would come out carrying a stinky paintbrush and say, "I'm in back if you need me."

This one old man, the one that had been at the newspaper with Karen yesterday, had said, "Umm, you sure do smell good, Janis," and she laughed and said, "Burnt umber" and something about how he ought to go home and take a cold shower, which sounded dumb, too. Any shower was dumb. You stand there and let a pipe spray you in the face. If was more fun to sit in the tub and kick and roll on your tummy, and sometimes dip your head in so your hair got soap bubbles on the front and you looked like a grandma.

Lisa decided to look at one of the *Goosebumps* books though some of the words were hard for her. She plopped down on one of the old couches that smelled funny and began to read, but it was difficult with the music Janis played with that guy singing who sounded like he was being made to sing and really didn't want to. What did "blowin' in the wind" mean? Danny in her class got a citation from Miss McCloud 'cause she heard him say "pissing in the wind." Must be the same thing, kinda.

"Hi, Lisa."

"Who are you?" Some man. How come the door didn't ding when he came in? He was looking at books, and looking at her.

"I'm Pooh Bear."

"You're not Pooh Bear!" She giggled.

"Sure I am. I'm looking for Christopher Robin. Do you know where he is?"

"Are you the man who was in the bushes?"

"Sometimes bears are in bushes, and sometimes they're in your house." He put his hands on his belly and said "Ho ho ho" like Santa. That was dumb. Bears don't go ho ho ho. But bears do go in bushes. And over the mountain, to see what they can see.

"Can I sit next to you? I feel very tired." He didn't wait for an answer but plopped down on the couch next to her, instead of at the end.

She moved as far to the side as she could.

"What are you reading?" He took the book from her hands. "*Goosebumps*?" He gave an exaggerated shiver. "Is it scary?"

"I guess."

"Well, I'd *never* scare a little girl. Not one so pretty as you. I like little girls."

"I don't like it when people say I'm pretty."

Pooh Bear was surprised. "How can you not like being called pretty?"

"Because everyone does it."

"Oh my, then I'll never do it again. What shall I call you?"

"Lisa."

He put his hand out to shake. "Lisa it is. Shake."

The girl reluctantly took his big hand. It was soft and wet with sweat but she said nothing, even though it made her feel funny.

Pooh Bear rubbed his wet hands together. "I'm hungry. Do you know what I like to eat?"

"Of course. Honey."

"Honey! I love to put my finger in the honey pot, then lick it. What do you like?"

"Ice cream!" But she was getting tired of this game. This funny looking man was very definitely not Pooh Bear, no matter what he said.

"Do you like to ride horses?" he asked.

Lisa was surprised, but interested at once. "Horses? I only did it once. They weren't ponies either, like Jimmy said. They were real horses. And we did it at the park."

"Would you like to go horseback-riding again? I think you would, wouldn't you? Girls always like horses. You could ride just like a grown-up. You could ride all day."

Lisa said, "How?"

"Ask your daddy." His voice became insistent. "Tell him to take you to the ski resort. They have horses there in the summer."

She looked dubious.

"And if he doesn't want to take you," Pooh Bear said, sensing possible resistance, "hold your breath and turn blue."

"That's dumb." But she saw Chad do it once in preschool and it worked.

"All right," he said urgently. But this was very important to him and he repeated himself, trying desperately not to sound too excited. "Be sure to tell Daddy about the horses. At the resort. Okay? Horses at the resort. And don't tell him it was Pooh Bear's idea. Tell him it was *Lisa's* idea. Okay?"

"Okay." Abruptly she bounded out of the couch and bent to put the book back in its rack.

The man came hurriedly up beside her, kneeled down, and put his hand on her waist, then slipped a folded piece of paper in her rear pocket. "You're very important to me, Lisa. *Very!* And Pooh likes you very much. Will you remember that for me? Pooh Bear likes Piglet and Tigger and *Lisa* very much."

"That's for little kids."

"Oh, I thought I heard voices," Janis said, and the man pushed hurriedly to his feet.

"Janis."

She pulled back on the beads. "Come on back and I'll show you what I'm working on. You can give me your dishonest opinion." She glanced at where Lisa was pulling another book off a shelf. "Are you doing okay, hon?"

"I guess."

"Well, let me know if you need anything. I'll be in back." The beads jangled.

34

Noel Atchison said, "What in God's name are you doing?"

"Straightening up, Noel. It's a pigpen in here."

"It's always a pigpen in here." Atchison sat back and frowned as Karen Paige bustled around the city room, picking up stacks of paper, old display ads, and reams of wire-service stories no one was interested in. "Did you finish the piece on Bill?"

"Turn on your computer. It's written, formatted, and ready to go on page one with the photo as soon as it comes back from the lab. But the paper won't be ready until you finish your 'Home of the Week' puff piece. So get to it, boss."

"It's been done—" But she had disappeared toward the rear with an armload of last week's papers, heading for the black recycling bin in the alley. When she came back he said, "I don't think I like this. Not at all."

"We need a new custodial service. These people are incompetent. Look at this!" She ran her finger along the top of a desktop bookcase holding dictionaries and a battered thesaurus. "Dust! And they were in just two days ago."

"Damn it, Karen, they don't clean desks. I won't let them. Now would you please sit down for a minute so we can talk!"

Karen dropped at once into a swivel chair adjacent to Atchison's, and faced him squarely. "Okay. Talk."

"What the hell's gotten into you?"

"Not a thing."

He tilted back, shut his eyes, contemplating dropping it. Then his chair eased warily forward and his voice softened into resignation. "Don't tell me it's Ritter."

"I won't."

"But it is, isn't it?"

She smiled. "Butt out."

"Jesus."

"What does that mean?"

"It means you have terrible taste in men. If you don't mind me telling you so."

"What would you have thought if I had made derogatory comments about your wife?" Noel's wife of thirty-two years had passed away two years earlier.

"That's different."

She stood up. "It's precisely the same."

"Come on, Karen. You've seen how he hovers over his kid. And he's a widower. So you'd have two women to compete with: a dead wife and mother to his kid, and a seven-year-old who's going to look at any new female like Cinderella looked at her stepmother. You want that kind of grief?"

Karen pretended not to hear, putting her hands over her ears. "I can't understand a word you say." Suddenly she swooped down and put her face just inches from his. "So why don't you just hush up before you ruin everything?"

The front door slammed and a moment later B.J. Blake stood in the city room. "Came to see if anyone wants to go over to Vail for dinner tonight. I've got an appetite Harmony can't satisfy."

Atchison rose to his feet. "I'm going home. See if you can talk sense into this woman before she goes and screws up her life." He paused and added, "Again."

Blake looked surprised and turned to Karen. "What's he talking about?"

"Male menopause, B.J. Noel's having trouble with the changes he sees."

Atchison shook his head and went out the door. Blake's eyebrows rose. "The world's getting too complicated for me. I take it you don't want to go to Vail tonight. Hey, are you wearing lipstick? What are you doing that for? Or *who?*" He paused a minute, then sat down. "Oh, God, don't tell me. . . ."

35

"Hell, yes," Mason Hightower said, striding rapidly back and forth behind his desk. He dropped noisily into the chair, and began to fiddle with a letter opener. "Micah called me, all agitated and hyped-up. Told me you were the Contrells' kid. Just about knocked me on my ass when I heard it. I hadn't thought about the

Contrells in thirty years. When I asked him how he knew you were their kid he said he just *knew*, that's all. Said you were adopted and taken up to South Dakota by some folks called Ritter. I said, 'Micah, how do you know this?' Well, he got kinda riled like he does sometimes but I guess he knows what he's talking about." He tossed the letter opener on the desktop.

"We'll find out when we get the birth certificate and check the prints," Mark said. "But Colorado won't turn it over until I can prove who I am and I can't prove that without the prints. But an attorney can probably get it for me. I'd like to hire you."

Hightower's leather chair squeaked forward. "Shouldn't be a problem. Give me a dollar as a retainer just to make it official and I'll send a letter today. Probably take a week to clear up."

Mark took a dollar out of his wallet and laid it on the desk. "Now you're my lawyer." As Hightower slid it into his desk drawer, Mark said, "And you can tell me why the hell you said you couldn't find anything in your dad's files when he was the one who handled the adoption."

Hightower waved a hand across the desk in exasperation. "Hell! It must have been filed under Contrell, not Ritter. 'Suppose I just flipped by it. I'd plum forgot what the Contrell case was, if I ever knew. Obviously it wasn't a big deal to me." He settled back, put his hands on the rise of his belly, and raised his voice. *"Sal!* Got a minute?"

The middle-aged secretary came in at once.

"Did you ask around about the summer of 'sixty-eight like we talked about?"

She looked at Mark and shook her head in defeat. "I called everyone I could think of. No one could remember anything unusual. It was a long time ago."

"The name Contrell mean anything to you?" Hightower asked.

Her gaze edged away as she thought. "No—"

"What about a man out east of town who shot his wife thirty years ago? Then set his house on fire."

Her eyes widened at once. "And the mother worked at Donner's and the father was jealous or crazy or something! Used to drink a lot. Oh my God." She reddened with embarrassment and looked at Mark. "Was that your dad and mom?"

He flipped his hand over. "Maybe. Probably."

"Oh Lord. Ruthann Fletcher. I went to high school with her. The only girl who would talk to Les Cady. Remember? Oh my. I can't believe I forgot Ruthann. We were such good friends when we were seniors."

"Exactly what I was saying," Hightower told her. "Folks tend to forget others' problems."

"The summer of 'sixty-eight. My goodness! A lifetime ago, wasn't it, Mason? Weren't you sparkin' Caroline Bellamy back then?"

Hightower was more than mildly annoyed. "That was a couple of years earlier. I was gone to college in 'sixty-eight. You should know that."

"Well, la-de-dah," the secretary mocked. "I still remember you chasing any girl you could. A dirty young man is what you were. Never did understand why you didn't marry."

"Because my wife would keep talking about me chasing girls like you're doing now. Lord!"

The phone in the outer office rang and Sally giggled and said to Mark, "Some men live in the past. Mason tries to cover it up." She gave him a quick glance. "You can't, though, can you? It sticks like glue. It's the only thing we'll never be rid of." She hurried out to her office, shutting the door behind her.

Mark said, "Rollins only cleared up a part of the problem." He handed the photocopied story of the fire to the attorney.

"This the missing article you were talking about?"

"One of them."

"How'd you find it?"

Mark told him.

"And you don't have any idea who sent it?"

"No."

Hightower tilted back, read the article, and frowned. "I don't see what it has to do with you."

"Do you remember the fire?"

He frowned with annoyance. "Like I said, I was in college in 'sixty-eight. Worked in a plastics factory in Denver in the summer making cheap little desk sets—pen and pencil holders. Heard folks talking about the fire when I visited, of course. Guess it was a big deal. Still don't see how it involves you."

"I don't either. Except that a month later Ed Contrell killed himself and his wife. Also in a fire."

Hightower slowly rocked forward. "Don't mean nothing." He picked up the letter opener again and began to tap it on the desk.

"But this article does. Someone sent it to me. Expected me to see something."

"Does look that way." The big man hunched forward and began to read it again.

Before Hightower could finish Mark asked, "How did Walter Lowndes happen to end up with the ski resort after the fire?"

The attorney looked up abruptly. "Hell, I don't know. I wasn't in Harmony back then. I don't even remember what year he took over. Place lay fallow for a while. I remember that."

Mark stood up, walked over to the windows, and stared out. He couldn't see the resort, only the virgin mountains to the north. "What can you tell me about him?"

"Who? Lowndes? What do you want to get into that for?"

He turned around and rested his seat against the windowsill. "I want to know everything I can about Harmony in 1968. He's part of it."

"Well, I'm not the one to talk to about Lowndes. Or 1968. Talk to his daughter. Or see the man himself, if he'll talk to you. I hear he's gotten rather imperious, doesn't think he needs to deal with mere humans now that he's a legend in his own mind." He stopped abruptly. "You don't think Lowndes sent the article to you, do you?"

"How do I know what to think? That's why I want to find out as much as I can."

"How many folks knew you were looking for these newspapers?"

"Everyone I could tell."

"Not much help. Interesting, though. Has to be something in that story we don't see."

Mark pushed away from the window. "You've heard about Bill." It wasn't a question.

"Yeah, Rose over at the station told Sal. Sad thing. He'd been around here forever. Can't imagine why something like that would happen."

"Bill had a picture of my daughter from last year. It was taken from our backyard in Seattle." Mark explained about finding it.

Hightower was disbelieving. "Doesn't make sense. How could he have taken it? He didn't even know you and Lisa existed. And it's not exactly what someone with a sexual interest in the young would want, is it? Of course, he did disappear from time to time. Could have gone up to Washington, I suppose. What'd Stallworth think?"

"About what you said. Someone also left this for me after searching my room." He handed the Polaroid picture across the desk, then sat down again.

The attorney frowned and shook his head. "Sick. What's it mean?"

"Stallworth's taking the easy way out. He thinks Bill did it. Or Les Cady."

"I guess that's typical police thinking. If it's Bill, he doesn't have to do any real investigative work. I don't know much about the psychology of child molesters but neither of these pictures look like they have anything to do with sex. More like someone's trying to frighten you."

"The other photo was taken a year ago. Someone must have been watching us. Could have been watching us all year, for all I can tell. And whoever called tried to make me think he'd molested Lisa. If he's trying to frighten us, he's doing a pretty good job of it."

"You don't think he really harmed her, do you?"

"No. But I think he's scared. Of me. Scared I'm going to discover something I shouldn't."

Hightower winced and rubbed his temples. "How do you know your room was searched?"

"He wasn't subtle. Things had been moved aside. And this picture was left where I'd find it. It had to be when I was at lunch. He must have known I'd be away for a while."

"How would he know that?"

Mark stood up and stared down at the attorney. "Questions without answers! I've been in Harmony for three days. Besides that photograph, my car's been trashed, I've had a phone call threatening Lisa's life, and found a picture of her taken last year in Seattle. And someone killed Bill."

Hightower began to tap the letter opener against his thigh. "I don't suppose you'd believe me if I told you this is really a pretty friendly town."

"I don't suppose so."

The attorney suddenly sensed the absence of the main topic of their conversation. "Where is Lisa?"

"Janis Lowndes's. At her store." Mark began to wander again, stopping and staring at the wall of landscape photos the attorney had taken. The colors in most of them seemed sharpened, as though Hightower had intensified them during processing.

The other man raised his eyebrows in appreciation. "Lucky you. Magical Janis." He paused, smiling foolishly, or with embarrassment.

"Well, anyway," he said after a moment, "give me a chance to go through Daddy's files again. This time I'll look for a Contrell. Maybe I'll turn something up. Better look for something dealing with Mr. Carl Stark, also. Someone sent you that story for a reason."

"And kept a copy of it for thirty years. There's also a reason for that. And for the threats. Whatever it is, I'm beyond the point of curiosity. Now I'm ready to break someone's neck."

Hightower hunched over his desk, the article in one hand and the Polaroid photograph in the other. His eyes moved slowly from one to the other and back again. "Two different people sending you an anonymous message. It's got to be. I wonder what ties these two things together."

36

Janis Lowndes was pulling into the motel parking lot with Lisa as Mark was getting out of his car. He walked over to the passenger side of the topless Jeep Wrangler, and tried to dampen the anxiety that seemed to have become such a part of his being lately. Forcing a smile, he asked, "Were you a good girl today?"

"Of course. I'm always a good girl." Lisa jumped out of the Jeep, both feet hitting the ground at the same time, and gave her father a hug, small arms working to encompass his waist.

Janis smiled, her white teeth sparkling against magenta lips. "She was perfect. Even though I don't have a lot for kids to do. She read a *Goosebumps* book. Or looked at it. I'm not sure which. Then I let her play with a sitar."

Mark smiled at Janis while hugging Lisa. "I don't think I've ever actually seen one."

"It was made by a man who used to live here in the early seventies. He even made one for George Harrison."

"He's a Beatle," Lisa said helpfully.

"Ah," Mark said.

"The strange one," Lisa added.

"I thought that was Lennon."

"No. He's the smart one."

"Too confusing for me."

"We had time for a little cultural history," Janis explained as she eased out of the Jeep. The sun seemed to make her long red hair, bobbing against the washed-out pallor of her face, glow like the heating elements of an electric furnace. She was barefoot, wearing a white silk ankle-length dress from India and—Mark could tell as he watched the fullness of her body as she moved beneath it—nothing else. He felt a stirring, and an unexpected but wholly pleasant attraction that drew his mind from the anger and anxiety that had been consuming him. With an effort he forced his eyes from her body to her face. "Thanks for watching her. I know she must have gotten underfoot."

"Not at all." Green eyes sparkled with a gentle humor, as though she understood, and perhaps sympathized with the feelings she unintentionally aroused. She was, Mark thought, the most completely calm yet sensual person he'd ever met. Or was he merely reading Karen's snippy "artist of sex" comment into her persona? Whatever it was, being with her made his knees weak, like the first time he jumped from an airplane during jungle training.

Janis said, "The shop's never busy this time of year so I spend my time painting. It's nice to have someone there." She turned her head as she saw a blue Taurus turn into the lot. "In fact I've already invited Lisa to dinner tonight if she brings her dad along. I was going to make a vegetarian curry but I could manage bacon double cheeseburgers if that's what she prefers."

"And ice cream," Lisa added, as if it had already been discussed.

"That was kind of you," Mark said, fighting a strong desire to accept. "Maybe tomorrow. Karen's having us over to her house tonight. In fact—" He moved aside as the Taurus drew to a stop.

"Another time, then." Janis smiled easily at them both, wriggled crimson-tipped fingers at Karen, and climbed into the Jeep.

Karen put her window down as Janis headed out of the lot, the wind billowing long hair behind her like party streamers. "I'll take you to the medical center before dinner. You have blood on your arms where she sank her talons into you. And your heart rate has made your face glow like Rudolph's nose."

Mark turned toward her, started to say, "What?" but changed his mind.

"Never mind," she told him wearily. "Just follow."

Mark and Lisa trailed along in the windshield-cracked Z3 as Karen led them to her seventy-year-old single-story house in the original part of Harmony, far from the condo developments and the Resort. Huge pines dominated the front and rear yards, leaving the entire structure in shade, and a border of roses separated it from its only near neighbor. The door was unlocked. "What's to steal?" she said when Mark commented on it. "Besides—" A large dog of doubtful heritage exploded into the room, growled with unusual viciousness at the visitors, then went up on his hind legs and lapped Karen's face with his outsized tongue. "All right, get down, Remington."

When Mark raised his eyebrows at the name Karen said, "Everyone around here has a gun. I felt out of place. So this is mine. Let's go in the back. We're going to barbecue chicken. I'll even let you handle everything if you feel some instinctual male need to be in charge of the fire."

Lisa had seemed moody since returning from Janis's but lightened up as she began to play with Remington. Mark and Karen sat on lawn chairs and watched the two of them run around the yard as smoke seeped from under the hood of the barbecue. Karen said casually, "How did Lisa end up with Janis the Mankiller this afternoon?"

The little girl looked over from where she was throwing a ball to the dog, and a note of some emotion Mark couldn't identify slipped back in her voice. "I don't like her. She talks funny. And the store smells. And there are funny men in there."

Karen smiled. "Your daughter is an intuitive genius. An inherited trait? Or developed through prior experience with artful and cunning females?"

"I want to go horseback-riding!" Lisa announced before Mark could reply. She stared at the two adults with surprisingly demanding seven-year-old eyes.

Mark was startled at the unexpected request. "Horseback-riding?"

"I want to go," the girl repeated. There was a sudden whine in her voice. "I never get to."

Mark looked at Karen who said, "There's stables out at the resort. I guess I could take her tomorrow. If that's all right with you."

"Yeah, sure." He still wondered where this had come from. "Okay, hon. Tomorrow. Maybe I ought to buy one of those throw-away cameras. This might be one of those moments you want to remember."

Lisa cheered and clapped her hands. Then she started screaming and slapping at herself.

Mark jumped up. "What is it?"

"A spider!" Shrieking, she hopped up and down and swept her hands over her stomach and legs. "I hate them. I hate them. Get it off me."

Mark knelt down, his arm around her waist, and turned her around. "I don't see one. It must be gone. You probably scared it away with your screaming. Spiders don't like people who scream."

The girl was trembling, and tears covered her face. "I hate spiders. Don't let them get on me again."

Mark gave her a long hug, calming her. "I'll keep them off you, honey. Promise." Then his voice turned conspiratorial. "I think Remington wants to play keep-away with the ball."

Lisa wiped her eyes with the back of her hands, then suddenly snatched the ball from the ground and held it above her head. "Can't have it!" Her fear seemed suddenly gone.

Mark sat down next to Karen again. "She was at Janis's because I had to see Eldon Stallworth. I thought it better to do it alone. We can talk about it later."

"I'll go watch TV if you want to talk about it now," Lisa said as Remington tried to take the ball out of her hand.

"That's all right, hon. Some things are just better after dinner."

"Like ice cream."

Karen said, "I've got Häagen-Dazs—mint–chocolate chip in the freezer." Lisa whooped and threw the ball in the air where Remington neatly caught it and bounded toward the far end of the yard, enticing the girl to chase after him.

Mark watched her run away, then glanced at Karen. "I told both Stallworth and Hightower this afternoon that their hometown is one screwed-up place. Neither agreed with me."

"I wouldn't suppose so. Or it makes them look foolish for staying."

"The old guard, those who were here thirty years ago when my dad killed my mom, all treat me like a trouble-maker if I pry a little too deeply. Stallworth, Hightower, Atchison, Rollins. Your friend with the restaurant probably won't be any different."

"Caroline Bellamy? You still want to see her?"

"Sure. I'd like to see Walter Lowndes, too, but it seems to be easier to get an appointment with the Pope. Friendly Harmony, huh? I guess there aren't a lot of people in this town I'd trust right now. You excepted." He smiled uneasily, not sure how far that trust really went.

"B.J.'s okay. He was just a kid back then, so if there was something going on he wouldn't be a part of it."

Mark gave her a sidelong look. "Did he end up rich like most of the others? And I apologize if I sound a little cynical here, but it is strange, isn't it—all these middle-aged Harmony residents rolling in dough?"

"B.J.? Not a chance. That Land King stuff is just a lot of hype. Maybe it's why he and I are such good friends—we're both struggling to make ends meet. Of course, he's got to keep up the pretense like people in his field do—the nice car and the airplane, and so on."

"How about Atchison?"

"The paper makes some money. But Noel certainly isn't rich. Not like Caroline, for example. But she didn't fall into it, you know. She's a crafty businesswoman. Trees is the third restaurant she's built here. She deserves whatever success she has." Karen stood and checked the chicken, probing it with a fork, watching the juices slip between the grates and onto the charcoal where it sent up a stream of aromatic smoke. "I called a friend of mine at the *Denver Post* this afternoon. He checked the university libraries for copies of the *Courier* but no one had any. He's going to check back issues of the *Post* to see if they ran a story on the Contrells back in 1968. There might be something there. It shouldn't take long. Everything's computerized now."

Mark stood up suddenly. "Computers! Of course! Damn it, why didn't I think of that earlier? Does the *Courier* have an online retrieval source for magazines?"

"Sure. But it doesn't go back to 1968. Only 1982, I think."

"Can I get in to use it?"

She looked at him oddly. "Tonight?"

"Why not? I won't bother anyone. Do you have a key?"

"You really want to do it tonight?"

"Yes, soon as I can."

She sighed. "It's not exactly what I had planned for this evening." She pressed her lips together. "All right. I guess I could let you in if Noel says it's okay."

"I'll wait until after Lisa's asleep, then come by when I'm done and pick her up."

"Let her sleep," she said with annoyance. "I'll bring her to the motel in the morning. But what are you looking for?"

He put his hands on his hips, and suddenly felt like walking around but forced himself to stand still. "History. Harmony's. Maybe I'll concentrate on Walter Lowndes, find out what his role was in the scheme of things around here. He seems to be the village mystery man."

"Mystery man? Hardly. Everyone knows him."

He spun on her. "But every time I ask someone about him I get some sort of bullshit about his photography, or publishing, or how he built the resort, and what an important person he is. Too important to see me, evidently. But it's all smoke and mirrors, something someone heard from someone else. Everyone knows *about* Walter Lowndes, but doesn't know *him*. Or if they do, they're keeping it from me."

"But what does Lowndes have to do with the Contrells? Isn't that who you're interested in?"

Mark answered irritably. "I don't know. Maybe nothing. But he has a lot to do with Harmony. Something here made my father crack, and no one can tell me what it was. Either they have unusually bad memories or everyone's covering up something. Maybe I need to go at it backwards and learn what I can about the people who were living here then. And not just Lowndes. But I might as well start with him. He's the only one who's likely to have been written up in the national press. If I don't find what I'm after I'll go back to the *Courier* and see what I can learn about Stallworth and Rollins and anyone else from the sixties, including your boss."

"Noel?" She was incredulous. "What are you talking about? Do you think he's involved in whatever it is you're looking for?"

Again Mark's frustration showed. "I don't know! Anyone could be involved. Why not Atchison?"

She looked at him a minute as though weighing the merits of his proposal. "All right. Let me talk to Noel about getting in tonight." She smiled. "I won't tell him he's a suspect."

As she disappeared into the house, Mark used a footlong fork to turn over the chicken. Lisa looked up from playing keep-away with the dog. "I like her."

"Remington?" He was only half paying attention and the frustration he felt earlier was growing again as he anticipated getting into the publication database and rooting about in the lives of Harmony's residents. Maybe he was finally going to learn something.

Lisa frowned expressively at him. "Not Remington. Karen." She threw the ball, now drenched with saliva, and raced after it with the dog.

"Yeah, I like her too, hon," Mark said, coming back to the present. But his mind had moved on to Janis Lowndes and her tight silk dress and red hair. How much of Janis's reputation was real, he wondered, and how much someone else's fantasy? And why hadn't he discovered the so-called graffiti about her Karen had made a point of mentioning? Had her comment just been jealousy, or was there some reason she wanted Mark to distrust Walter Lowndes's daughter?

Karen came out of the house a moment later. "Noel said it'd be okay but don't stay too long. He has to pay for it by the hour." She looked at the barbecue with distress. "God, I forgot to put on any vegetables. Do you think Lisa will mind?"

Mark glanced at her as he lifted a sizzling chicken breast. "You've got a lot to learn about seven-year-olds."

They watched a video of *The Sound of Music* after dinner, then the news from Denver, until Lisa fell asleep in her chair. Mark lifted her into the spare bedroom, then returned to the living room. Karen was standing up. She came to him, putting her arms around his neck and kissing him with an urgency that surprised him. But he responded, and felt an urgency himself, a need to be with her. Smiling, he put a hand on the side of her face, let it slide to her neck, then down her back, holding her to him. "Nice. I've been out of practice but I guess it's something you don't forget how to do."

She seemed surprised. "You haven't dated since your wife died?"

"Not much." He was uncomfortable talking about it, and his voice became strained. "It never seemed right. Disloyal, I guess."

They had moved to the couch and sat, hips touching. Mark was tense as always when thinking about Beth's death and its aftermath, but wanted to get it out of the way now, as though it were some sort of personal hurdle that had to be cleared before their relationship could mature. "I went out a couple of times with women friends when Lisa was two or three. Then I'd come home, see her sleeping in her bed, twisted around on her side like Beth—her mother—slept, and suddenly I'd feel like hell. Pretty soon it was just easier not to go, not to get involved with anybody."

Karen had taken his hand and could feel the nervous pressure as he talked about it. She asked, "What did Beth die of?"

"Alcohol. That's how I think of it, anyway. She was walking back from lunch one day. It was raining—Seattle, you know—and a drunk driver spun his Dodge pickup out of control and plowed into a crowd of office workers. Nine injured, three killed. Lisa was just eight months old."

Karen's fingers tightened on his. "You and Lisa have a pretty good relationship for a father and daughter."

Mark was pleased and surprised by the comment. "I guess we do, don't we? We actually like each other."

She moved back on the couch, pulling him on top of her. Her lips moved on his, her breath warming him. "I predict we'll have a pretty good relationship too."

"Yeah?"

"My predictions always come true. Well . . . almost always. I've had a few clunkers. Especially when I was in a casino up in Cripple Creek." She held his face and kissed him, and felt his body responding as she moved her midriff against his.

She said in a low voice, "Bet I can convince you to stay here instead of going to that lonely old office and looking at a computer screen all night."

"I'd like to. But—"

She kissed him again, lingeringly, and let her legs lock behind his. "Still—"

"Nasty old computers. Dumb old Walter Lowndes. Warm, engaging, sexy Karen."

"I really need to—"

"Yeah, yeah, sure. Rejected for an online service. That's a new one for me. At least Lisa likes me. I wouldn't want to have to compete with her for her father's affection. I wouldn't have a chance."

"Lisa would love having a female to talk to. It must be pretty boring always having Dad around."

"Kids instinctively know what's best for their folks." Which seemed to remind her of something. She slid from under him and sat up. "What did the police say about that picture in your room?"

"Stallworth said it's not significant enough to be a police matter. I guess I have to wait until someone takes a shot at us."

"God!" She ran her hand through her hair. "The cops in Harmony are idiots."

"I also told him about being harassed by his officers."

Her face hardened suddenly, and she straightened. "What'd he say?"

"To ask you."

She stood abruptly, as if pulled up, then turned and crossed her arms, determined to get it out all at once.

"Paige is my maiden name. I'm married." She paused. "To Todd Kachen. You saw him when we were going to Häagen-Dazs." Her voice was flat. "We're in the process of getting a divorce. He's being hostile about it."

Mark was thinking about the ice-cream shop, the photograph someone took as they stood in front. It took a moment for her comment to register. "He's hostile because of the division of assets?"

Karen dropped her arms to her sides and laughed with derision. "What assets? The house is rented, my car's eight years old, and there's three hundred dollars in the bank. No, he's being hostile because he's an asshole. He can't believe someone would want to leave a big beautiful blond hunk like him. Believe me, it was easy."

"How long were you married?"

"Three years, two months, and one week. We split up once before for two months. This time I wouldn't go back if he held an Uzi on me. Which he has probably considered. The divorce is final in six weeks. Then the sun starts to shine again and it'll be morning in America again."

"Strong feelings."

"And well deserved. To salvage his ego he told his friends in the department how I treated him badly. He made up stories about me being what he called an habitual liar, then tried to make out I was having an affair with everyone from Walter Lowndes to the custodian at the police station."

Something uncomfortable in his mind made Mark ask, "Were you?" But he made certain he smiled.

She leaned down, put a finger on his lips, and scowled. "Fat chance. So far I'm not even having an affair with you. You'd rather look at old magazines than spend time with my scintillating and seductive personality. Why do I think Janis Lowndes would be more successful than me?"

"Has Kachen been causing you problems?"

"Not in a way that's going to get him in trouble with the department. He's more subtle than that. Just late night phone calls, nasty comments from his friends on the force, getting pulled over for speeding. With you, though, I guess it's different. He can't stand the thought that I might choose someone over him. He has to be the alpha male in any gathering."

"Well, he'll forget about it pretty soon. You can't carry that much hate forever."

She crossed her arms again. "You don't know Todd. He can carry enough hate for all of Colorado."

37

It was already after nine P.M. when Eldon Stallworth put down the thirty-year-old file he'd retrieved from the courthouse basement, leaned back in his chair, and thought, *Mighty pretty story you told Ritter, Micah. Too bad it ain't true.*

But what the hell did it mean?

Why lie to the man? You don't even know him, never saw him before yesterday. Or have you? You been hanging around Seattle in your off-time? Or had Ritter been to Harmony?

He plopped his elbows on the desk and rubbed his eyes. Micah Rollins hadn't even been involved in that fire or its aftermath. . . .

What were you doing back in '68, Micah? Kind of finding work where you could, if I remember rightly. Ran your raggedy ass in more than once for a drunk. Times have really changed, haven't they? Probably drinking twelve-year-old Scotch at home now instead of rot-gut wine out in the woods.

He pushed the file aside and looked at the Xeroxed copies of the *Courier* article and the Polaroid photo of Lisa Ritter that Chavez had made before Ritter left.

"Fire Guts Mountain Resort." Two fires within a month, now that he thought about it.

Folks hadn't given much thought to the fire at Contrell's—a little ol' cabin going up wasn't a big deal even if the murder-suicide preceding it was.

But the resort—hell, not just the resort. The whole damn mountain burned, came all the way down to Fifth Street, lapping at businesses and people's homes. Everyone in town was out cutting down trees with chainsaws and digging fire lines, even women and kids. And the Forest Service brought in tankers to drop fire repellent and water. Still took three days to put it out, and the stink lasted until the snows came.

Stallworth pushed wearily from his chair and shut the office door even though there was only one patrolman in the room beyond. Sitting down again he closed his eyes and tried to pry loose memories buried under thirty years' worth of living and policing. Old Howie Deets had been chief back then. Howie and three officers had made up the entire department. Eldon himself had been the one to find Carl Stark, or what was left of him, in the remains of the fire. *Just like the Contrells a month later.* But Stark hadn't been shot. He'd passed out from smoke inhalation, then burned to death. At least that's what the medical examiner had said, and there was no reason to doubt it.

Eldon had been poking around the rubble, still smoking and smelling like hell, the watery ashes sticking like glue to his blue uniform trousers, when Bill had come running up to him. Crazy Bill, the kids in town used to call him back then, because he was always yelling at people and throwing rocks and barking like a dog. Then some Social Services people got hold of him and Bill had been hospitalized for a couple of years, and put on medication. When he came back he wasn't crazy, just weird. Of course, when he stopped taking his medication, which he did sometimes, then he damn well *was* crazy. He'd start talking to God or squirreling away food in his pockets until Social Services put a net over him again. Then it'd be back to the hospital for a couple of weeks. Eldon figured he was one of the few people who knew where Bill actually was when that happened. Most folks thought he was off on a drunk, or visiting friends.

Of course, that fire had been in the old days, when Bill really was *wild.* Eldon had just seen to the removal of Stark's body when Bill ran up waving his long, skinny arms like he always did, and yelling about seeing someone running around on the mountain the night the fire started. But he hadn't said running around; he said running *from.* He saw someone running *from* the fire. Eldon had thought, *Shit, this is all we need, a crazy man making wild accusations and turning an accident into a murder.* So he'd chased Bill off. Of course he'd told Chief Deets about it later but they both agreed that Bill saw phantoms every day. You couldn't take *that* to court.

So maybe it wasn't a phantom, and Bill really had seen someone. Stallworth felt a hollow feeling settle in his stomach. If that was the case they'd had a killer here in town for thirty years, assuming he hadn't died in the meantime. And Bill knew it, and knew no one would believe him.

The *killer* must have known he'd been seen, though. Else why kill Bill? If that was who did kill Bill, and it wasn't some random thief. But damn it, why now, thirty years after the fact, instead of back then? What suddenly changed, making Bill's murder necessary?

Stallworth picked up the mutilated photo of Lisa and tapped it against the desk. *This changed!* Ritter and his daughter showed up and started poking around.

He studied the girl's picture. Most of her face had been obscured by the bullet hole. Still, there was something that tugged uncomfortably at the edges of his memory, some strange fact that lay buried under decades of investigations and files and arrests. Something to do with Lisa. Well, shit, not Lisa, obviously. He stared at it. *What is it, girl? What secret do you hold? And is that what made Micah lie to your dad?* He had a sudden thought. Maybe Micah wasn't lying. Maybe he believed that story was true.

Christ!

Annoyed with himself, he got up and began to pace. *Focus on those damn photos out at Bill's.* There must have been sixty or seventy pictures of nude children. But Bill, a pedophile? Sure, maybe . . . the weird way he took an interest in kids. Hell! Bill *was* a kid, probably spent his entire adult life as an overgrown eleven-year-old playing cowboy. *Not an awful lot different from Micah,* he thought with a smile, and wondered what the well-to-do Rollins would think of being compared to Harmony's favorite nutcase.

Whatever, Bill didn't exactly fit the profile of a molester. So perhaps Ritter was right, someone put those photos there, to divert our attention from . . . what?

Maybe we shouldn't be so hasty in absolving Les Cady from the molestations, then. Just because someone else had pictures of kids doesn't mean Cady is innocent. But is he also a murderer? Damn it, someone as truly weird as Cady could do anything. He was the one person Stallworth had ever met that gave him the creeps—knowing how the man thought of children. Stallworth always wanted to go home and wash after talking to him.

The chief dropped into his chair and grabbed a piece of paper. Write it out, then, see what pieces fit together.

"Carl Stark." *Dead in a fire, 1968.*

"Ed Contrell." *And* "Ruthann." *Can't forget about her. Dead in a fire, 1968.*

Which Micah lied about!

Kinda left something out, didn't you, pardner?

Did Stark have a girlfriend? *Maybe . . .* maybe . . . Too damn long ago to remember. But still . . . there was something there, tugging away, teasing, like an itch too deep to scratch.

After the fire, the resort had been put up for sale. Stallworth wrote "Resort?" What had happened to Ed Contrell's land? Forty acres, something like that. Probably sold at auction. Stallworth picked up the phone and pushed a button. "I need to see you, Lee."

Lee Huston, the officer who had been finishing up reports next door, appeared a moment later. Stallworth handed him a piece of paper with Ed Contrell's name on it. "He killed himself out at his ranch in the summer of 'sixty-eight," the chief explained. "Have someone in the tax office give you the exact location of his property, then find out who owns it now. While you're there you might as well go back and search the sales records on the resort property, too. When the sales took place, how much was paid, terms of the sale, and so forth. And one more thing. Dig me up the files on all sex cases involving children anywhere in the county for the last thirty years. Including the little girl that was murdered a few years ago."

"And then what?" the officer asked.

"Just give it to me. I'll decide what to do." *Because I'm fishing and I don't have any idea what you'll turn up. But I know I'm close to something. I damn well feel it.*

After Huston left, the chief's gaze went back to the copy of the Polaroid photograph of Lisa. Damn it, somehow this is the key. Ritter and his daughter. They arrive in town and *boom!* Suddenly old Bill dies, Micah gets involved in something that's none of his business, people start sending weird things to Ritter . . . threats, newspaper articles. His car gets torn up. And the poor guy finds a photo of his daughter at the home of a certified crazy man. That's enough to drive anyone wild. Why now, why Ritter? What's he done to cause this? Other than show up?

Shit, if Bill was right about someone being up on the mountain when Carl Stark died then it's my fault we've had a killer living here for thirty years. Up to me to do something about it.

Property transfers.

Fires.

Child molesting.

Stark.

He stood suddenly. Jesus Christ, it wasn't Stark's *death* that's

important here but what happened *after* his death. After . . . His gaze
shot to the window, to modern Harmony. All that property. All that
money.

And a little girl!

At once it started coming back to him, in a rush of memories.

After Stark's death.

And eight years before! God*damn*! It was Cheryl, wasn't it? He'd
heard rumors back then but didn't believe them. Too weird to be
true.

But maybe not.

He dropped into his chair, full of excitement. *Goddamn it, goddamn it, goddamn it!* His heart started pounding. *Should've listened
to Wild Bill. Should've paid attention thirty years ago. Well, it's up
to me now. Since I'm a few years late maybe we'll forget some of
the legal niceties here and try to speed things up a bit. Old West
style. Might even let the man help; it's his daughter that lit the fuse.*

Stallworth picked up the phone and called Mark Ritter's motel.
No answer in the room so he left a message on the voice mail for
Mark to call him first thing in the morning. Nothing was going to
happen before then.

He disconnected with his finger and thought. The first rule of
murky evidence: Push, then wait to see what pushes back.

He began to dial again. Time for a little pressure.

Damn, he hoped that girl wasn't in any danger. But even as the
thought passed through his mind he knew she was, and that Bill had
known it, too.

38

Sitting alone in the *Courier's* darkened city room, Mark flicked on
the terminal, accessing the online retrieval system. Already familiar
with a similar service at work, he immediately went to the Search
function, and then stopped. Did he really want Lowndes, or would
Micah Rollins prove a more fertile source for what he needed? It
might be, if Rollins had a public persona, but as a local builder it
was unlikely a national magazine would have been interested enough
to do a story. Lowndes, though, supposedly had a reputation.

Lowndes was known. He leaned forward, typed LOWNDES, WALTER, and waited as a prompt said there were 167 articles. He felt a spasm of surprise. A reputation indeed. Did he want to see them all? He did, and a list of cultural, literary, and business journals appeared. Articles on Lowndes's publishing venture, on his photography, on the resort. Too many to go through in two hours. So pick a few at random.

He pulled up an article from *Fortune,* July 1987. "The Two Sides of a Mogul."

To those who know him Walter Lowndes is a gentle, soft-spoken man frequently lauded as one of the few remaining defenders of "high" culture in America, a publisher of lyric and romantic poetry in the grand nineteenth-century tradition, a biographer of the German writer Thomas Mann who died in 1955, as well as being one of the world's premier fine-arts photographers, whose pictures are part of the permanent collections in museums from New York to New Delhi.

But there was a darker side to Lowndes, the article went on: a reputation as a despotic manager who ran roughshod over his employees or anyone who would stand in his way.

Walter Lowndes laughs when offered this picture of his reputation. "My mother used to say that if you find yourself baffled by the contradictions of a problem, you should get up and walk around it and view it from a different angle, like a sculptor looking at his stone. I guess what's happening here is that everyone has their own restricted point of view. They ought to get up and walk around a bit. Maybe the new vantage point will alter their perception."

The author of the article, clearly in awe of his subject, went on to document how, starting with just a burned patch of mountaintop in central Colorado, Walter Lowndes turned Eagle Point Lodge into the country's premier ski resort, "where the high and the mighty, the rich and the very rich, come to while away the cold winter months amid marvelously groomed slopes, extra-luxurious apartments, and chi-chi restaurants where the food is exquisite and the cost prodigious. . . ."

There followed an account of how Lowndes and his partners saw the natural advantage of the mountain they purchased when it was still just a barren hillside, and understood that the rich would pay dearly for the opportunity to ski in such an environment, though only if it was properly developed. So they began with the slopes, making them into a world-class adventure that any avid skier would want to experience. Only then did they turn their attention to the condominiums and restaurants and shops that the wealthy would demand.

And that reputation for authoritarian dealings with partners and subordinates?

"I have never mistreated anybody. Weak people bring on their own problems, of course, and tend to whine when the inevitable occurs. Unable to do anything on their own, they criticize those who are successful because we are a reminder that they haven't the balls to go out and do what we did! You can't go through life worrying about people like that. If you do, they've won, they've made you pay for your competence."

An estimate of Walter Lowndes's net worth followed—only an estimate since his holdings were not public. Fifty to seventy million in the ski resort, artwork (paintings and engravings by William Blake, rare books, nineteenth-century jewelry) valued at perhaps five million dollars. And his own photographs—worth, the Metropolitan Museum of Art estimated, three million dollars. "Not bad," Lowndes said, "for someone who started off with nothing more than talent and a desire to succeed."

Mark scrolled back to the beginning of the article. "Partners." The word occurred twice. Who were these partners? Why weren't they named?

Deleting the article, he went to *Forbes* from January 1992. The author, less interested in the allegedly colorful aspects of Lowndes's life, actually came to Harmony to interview those who knew the man before he built the resort. The idea, evidently, was to do a rags-to-riches story about hard work, perseverance, and wily marketing. What he found when he got to the town was either hostility toward Lowndes for changing the nature of village life from laid-back obscurity to hypertouristy activity, or an unwillingness to be interviewed for what Caroline Bellamy ("owner of a new overpriced eatery for the Concorde set") called another Lowndes hit piece. "Why are you people always looking for the negative—?"

Mark closed it off and drew up look-alike articles from half a dozen skiing magazines: Eagle Point as a "destination resort, where every skier wants to live . . . and die," the ultimate in winter vacations, bring your checkbook and credit cards. And all of this the result of the vision of a single though somewhat eccentric, if not driven, man: Walter Lowndes. The person who made Eagle Point Lodge.

There was a small article in the *New York Times* Arts and Leisure pages about the astonishing career Lowndes had enjoyed as a fine-arts photographer. He didn't even own a camera growing up in the rural and rustic Colorado Rockies, but became interested in the art when visiting the Guggenheim while attending college in the East. "A revelation," he said later. "Like a huge white light rushing at me. I merely accepted it, stepped into its marvelous glow, and have not been the same since. It was life-altering. Truly."

There couldn't be more than three or four people in the country who could make a living as "art" photographers (as opposed to doing portraits or landscapes) but Walter Lowndes was one of them, though he certainly didn't need the money.

The mention of Lowndes as artist led Mark to call up a dozen cultural magazines which he quickly scanned. All seemed to carry variations on the same theme: Walter Lowndes as a determined defender of "high culture," promoter of Thomas Mann, and lover of beauty. A *Los Angeles Times* interview was typical:

> You wrote your biography of Thomas Mann at what age?
> "It was published in 1980 so I was in my early forties. But I spent seven years on it, off and on. And probably twenty years thinking about it."
> Why Mann?
> "I read *Death in Venice* when I was fourteen. It completely changed my life. Completely!"
> What was it that grabbed you so strongly?
> Lowndes seemed at first surprised by the question, then leaned forward, his gaze intent. "The picture of this man, this marvelous middle-European intellectual of the old school, Gustav Aschenbach, losing himself and falling completely under the sway of beauty in the form of a boy—Tadzio—he catches a glimpse of on the beach. It was like being struck by lightning the way it

altered his entire being. His life could never be the same after encountering such perfection, you see." He rapped the table loudly with his knuckles. *"Beauty! Perfection!* What higher ideal can we aim for, or worship? The book has been read for its vaguely prurient aspects, of course, but it is really a disquisition on art, aesthetics, intellectualism. . . ."

And so on, article after article. Lowndes the aesthete. Lowndes the worshiper of beauty, of perfection.

Glancing at his watch, Mark saw it was getting late. Time for one more. He went to the most recent article, June 1993. *The New Republic.* "The Mind of an Autodidact." He paused a moment. Why was there nothing since 1993? Had the world suddenly lost interest in Walter Lowndes? He began to read:

> . . . educated in the wilds of Colorado only through prodigious reading chosen by his mother, he developed an aesthetic sense that burns now to such a fine, hard point the world is incapable of seeing it. And this seems to bother Lowndes not at all. It is not the love of beauty that distinguishes him but the *intensity* of this love, the way it has taken over his mind and soul, to the exclusion of virtually everything else. "My life has been driven by the search for perfection. And I have from time to time experienced it—Mahler in music, Poussin in art, Mann in literature. And the human body in life."
>
> And his favorite book? *"Death in Venice,* of course. I read it yearly. If not more often."
>
> Does it bother you that when you go back to your hometown the people there don't know you as a force in the art and literature worlds, but only as the owner of a ski resort?
>
> Lowndes laughed with an odd gurgling sound that disguised whatever emotion he felt. "Not at all. I go to Colorado to relax, not to impress people. Especially *those* people. Though I have a warm feeling for the area that first exposed me to the notion of perfection."
>
> And your reputation for being a tyrant at work?
>
> "Undeserved. Or exaggerated. Take your pick."

Feeling suddenly uneasy, Mark shut down the terminal and wondered which quote bothered him most.

IV

39

Mark was returning from a six-mile run through the city when Karen and Lisa drew into the parking lot. He waited, breathing hard through his mouth, while they got out of the Taurus, Lisa running over and hugging him tightly around the waist. "Have you had breakfast yet?" he asked as sweat dripped from his forehead onto his sleeveless shirt.

"We made omelets. With melted cheese and tomatoes and green chilies."

Karen put her hands in her back pockets. "Have you eaten?" She was unsmiling, and looked distracted or angry. Something must have happened last night.

"I'm not hungry."

"Let's go up to the room, then."

Mark looked questioningly at her.

"In the room," she said again. "We can talk after your shower."

Lisa said, "Don't forget we're going riding today. You promised."

"Later, Lisa," Karen said. "This evening."

They headed upstairs, Lisa running in front of them and pretending she was a horse, her feet thumping noisily on the metal steps, then waiting impatiently as Mark unlocked the door. She gleefully pointed to the partly finished Monopoly game on the small table. "Dad only owns two houses. I have hotels on Boardwalk and Park Place, and houses on all the red squares, and I have all four railroads. We have to finish it today, Daddy. Please!"

"I'm going to teach her chess," Mark said to Karen. "Or kick-boxing. I'm tired of losing."

Karen started to say something, changed her mind, folded her arms across her chest. "Take your shower. We'll wait."

Mark grabbed clean underwear, a pair of tan Dockers, and went into the bathroom. When he came out five minutes later Karen was sitting on his bed. As he grabbed his shoes she asked, "What did you learn about Walter Lowndes last night?"

"That he has a reputation as a big-time businessman. That he's a true rag-to-riches millionaire. That he's strange. To say the least. But not the ogre I somehow expected. And it doesn't bring me any closer to understanding why my father killed my mother."

Karen stood and began to wander around the small room. "I don't suppose he would have known Ed Contrell anyway."

"Probably not. Different worlds." He pulled a cotton shirt from the closet and put it on.

"Doesn't matter, though." She turned around to face him.

"My friend on the *Denver Post* just called. He found a story on the Contrells in their back issues. Just one story—three column inches."

"Yes?"

"Micah was right when he said Ed Contrell killed his wife and set fire to the house. But he lied to you about their child. He died in the fire."

Mark looked at her, his shirt only half-buttoned and his intestines tightening as he tried to understand what she was saying.

"He lied," she repeated, and her voice rose. "You're not a Contrell. You're back where you were when all this started."

Mark felt as if the supports holding him up all fell away at once. A surge of anger shot through him, but also relief and confusion. His father wasn't a murderer. There wasn't some genetic malfunction to worry about. He hadn't survived a killer's rage by a lucky accident. But what the hell was Rollins—

"I called Micah at home as soon as I heard. No answer. Not even the phone machine. I think he may have left town."

"Jesus Christ," Mark muttered. His head seemed suddenly light and he felt lost. "Why would he—?" He closed his eyes.

It didn't make sense.

"Who knows? But he did it for a reason. He's up to something."

"Do you think he stole the copies of the *Courier?*"

She shrugged. "I'll ask Noel if he had the opportunity. Maybe he was alone in the office one day. But I don't recall—"

The phone interrupted her. Mark snatched angrily at it.

"Noel Atchison, Mark. I've been looking for Karen. It's important. Do you know—"

"Hold on," he said, and handed her the phone; he sat on the bed, then jumped up as Karen blanched and put her hand to her chest. "Oh my God, no! Where? Of course, I'm on my way."

She put the phone down and her eyes lost their focus. "Eldon Stallworth's dead. Murdered. A drug deal, evidently. His body was just found. I have to get out there."

Mark was stunned. "I was supposed to call him this morning."

"What for?"

"I don't know. He left a message on the phone. He sounded like he had something to tell me."

Karen didn't seem interested. She grabbed her purse. "I've got to get going. Noel has to stay at the office."

"We'll come, too."

She fumbled for the keys in her purse, then glanced at Lisa.

Mark said, "She can stay in the car."

Karen hesitated only a moment. "We have to hurry. I want to get there before they remove the body."

40

Eight miles west of town Karen swung the Taurus off the highway and onto an unmarked gravel road, then pressed on the accelerator as the road rose with surprising abruptness into the mountains in what was evidently National Forest land. Pines and aspens lined the road making it impossible to see more than fifty yards on either side.

"Are there bears here?" Lisa asked.

"There are all kinds of wild animals here," Karen said tersely, then had to hit the brakes hard as she rounded a bend and almost rear-ended an ambulance that was half on, half off the road. Two black-and-white police cars and a white Cherokee Mark remembered belonging to Hector Chavez, had pulled head-first into the underbrush in front of the ambulance.

"God," Karen said, and switched off the engine. "I can't believe it. I've known Eldon since I moved here ten years ago. He'd always been friendly until . . . recently." Without looking at Mark she opened the door, stepped into cool morning sun, and gave a shudder.

Mark turned around to Lisa, "I'm afraid you'll have to stay here."

" 'Cause I'm a kid. But it doesn't matter, Dad. I've seen dead people on TV."

"Don't say ' 'cause.' And yeah, it's because you're a kid. Believe it or not, kids aren't miniature adults. They're kids."

"I can beat you at games," she said defiantly.

Mark tapped her knee. "Just wait here. You can come up front and listen to the radio if you want. Maybe later I'll ask the man in charge if you can get out." Once the body's gone, he thought.

Karen was standing with a cop Mark didn't recognize. As he approached them Todd Kachen appeared from in front of the farthest police car, and instantly flushed with anger. "Jesus Christ, what's he doing here? Is this your doing, Karen? Goddamn it—"

Hector Chavez turned from where he was kneeling next to Eldon Stallworth's body, and came to his feet at once. He looked at Karen with regret. "Damn it, Karen, why did you bring Ritter out here?"

"What's the problem, Hector? It's public land. Don't give me any crap."

"It's a fucking *crime scene*," Kachen yelled, advancing toward them. "If you and your boyfriend want to play in the woods, do it someplace else. But get him the hell out of here."

Karen took out her notebook and looked over at the body. "Who found him?"

Kachen took a step in Karen's direction but Chavez said, "Todd, you better go down to the highway and set up a roadblock until the state patrol gets here. Shouldn't be long. Don't allow any cars up here until I tell you."

"Bullshit! I've got to go, but this goddamn civilian with his kid can stay? No way!"

Chavez turned all the way around to face him but didn't raise his voice. "Officer Kachen, as the temporary chief I am giving you a direct order. Get down to the highway, set up a roadblock, and check with me before letting anyone past. Is that clear? Because if it's not I can be more explicit."

The patrolman glared at him a moment, lower lip trembling, then spun around and stomped back to his car. A moment later he left with a screeching of tires and a spray of rocks and dust.

"He used to drive home from bars that way, too," Karen said. "I guess some things never change."

Chavez shook his head. "You didn't show real good judgment bringing Ritter out here, Karen. What'd you expect? You knew Todd would be here."

"Hector, we wouldn't be having this discussion if you didn't have an out-of-control pit bull on the force. Now, what happened here?"

The man sighed and turned toward the body, lying on its side, facing away from him. Two young men in white uniforms had just finished attaching plastic bags to its hands. "Hiker found him this morning. Shot three times in the chest at close range. Must've used a forty-five from the looks of it. Evidently all three slugs exited the body. We'll search for them but we're not going to find anything."

Mark could see the three distinct entry wounds. The front of the body was covered in blood that hadn't yet dried. "Killed here or dumped here?" he asked.

Chavez gave him a withering look. Karen said, "Want me to ask, Hector?"

The man waved at the ground, the trampled grass and the blood on the rocky soil. It was obvious there had been some sort of disturbance. "Looks like he was driving up here and came upon some sort of drug deal. Remember when we found a guy hiding a half ton of marijuana back in the woods last summer? Traffickers are thicker than deer up here. They know there's seldom any cops in the forest."

He pointed to where a small yellow marker with a black "1" sat on the ground. "Found tire tracks from a truck over there. I figure Eldon stopped to see what was going on, maybe being a Good Samaritan, and the guy started blasting as soon as he saw the badge. Eldon's gun's still in its holster. The way I see it, the first shot dropped him. The slug's probably back in the woods. Then the killer walked up, put the barrel of his gun right above his heart, shot twice more, rolled the body over and dug around in the dirt for the slugs."

"Careful, wasn't he?"

"Yeah. Careful. Now we can't identify the murder weapon."

"How do you know these tire tracks are from yesterday?" Mark asked. "Might be from two weeks. Or three days. Maybe you can't find the slugs because he was killed elsewhere and dropped here."

Chavez frowned, folded his arms across his chest. His voice turned contemptuous. "Eldon called you Sherlock Holmes yesterday, Ritter.

The point he was making was you're not a cop. Why not leave the official stuff to us?"

Karen said, "Where's his car? Eldon's?"

"Killer took it."

"And also drove his truck away?"

"Two bad guys, Karen. It happens."

Mark said, "Are Stallworth's car keys with him?"

Chavez looked as though he was going to hit Mark, then glared at the two medics. "Are you about to take him?"

"Anytime."

"Get him on a stretcher. I want to go through his pockets."

The men lifted the body onto a wheeled stretcher, then stood back while Chavez went through the chief's pockets, dropping each item into a clear plastic evidence envelope: chewing gum, wallet, pocket-knife, car keys. He looked at Mark. "Doesn't mean he didn't drive out here. Maybe they didn't want to go through a dead man's pockets looking for his keys. Coulda hot-wired it in sixty seconds." He glanced over at Karen. "Don't go writing any nonsense, now. You just report the facts."

"Aren't many facts here. I think I'll just make something up. That's what reporters usually do."

"I'm having people from Denver come out and go over the scene. We're not set up for any sophisticated evidence-collecting. But I figure they'll tell us he died right here. Like I said." He looked over his shoulder at one of the uniformed cops. "You better tape this whole area off, maybe fifty yards along the road and twenty yards back."

Mark watched as the body was put in the rear of the ambulance and the doors slammed shut. The sun was already above the tallest trees and it was getting hot. Karen said, "He was a nice guy. It's a shame. Have you told Irma?"

"I called Reverend Michaels. I'll go over later. Maybe you could—"

"Sure, Hector. Give me a call at the paper. I'll come with you. It's going to be tough for her."

The ambulance backed across the narrow road and managed to turn around, heading down the hill. Mark said, "When was the last homicide in Harmony, before this week?"

Chavez shrugged. "Eight, ten years ago."

Mark waved at the Taurus and Lisa shot out at once, and began to run in his direction, all knees and elbows. He said, "Now two murders in two days. Kind of makes you think."

"What I *think*," Chavez said, "is that this was a peaceful little town until you showed up. Maybe you'd be happier back in Seattle. I know I'd be if you were."

"Was Stallworth working on anything besides Bill's death?"

"Stallworth was the chief. He didn't do investigations. I'm in charge of Bill's homicide. And I'm alive, if you're trying to imply that Bill's killer wanted Stallworth dead because he discovered something. If so, he killed the wrong person."

"Like you said—it happens."

Karen turned toward her car. "I better write my story. Let me know if anything turns up."

Chavez's jaw tightened. "Don't give Todd any trouble down at the roadblock, Karen. We've got enough problems around here without adding domestic disputes to it."

On the way down Mark said, "Not even ten o'clock in the morning and I learn that Micah Rollins lied about my parents, and someone's killed the police chief. It doesn't look like this is going to be a very good day."

She threw him a glance while navigating the narrow road. "Do you think the two things are related? You don't believe Eldon just stumbled onto something?"

"I think Chavez is right. My coming to town has upset a lot of people. And of course now I'm back to square one in the search for my parents. I need to talk to more old-timers. You mentioned a friend of yours called Caroline something."

"Bellamy. Yeah, she was born here, knows most everyone from the old days. Except for Janis's hippie pals up in the hills. Her restaurant's over near the resort, one of the few open this time of year. Do you want to see her?"

"As soon as possible. Micah Rollins, too, to find out what the hell's going on. Why did he lie to me? He must have known that story wasn't true."

"Oh-oh, there's Todd Testosterone, 'enforcing the law' and working on his pecs. Ignore him."

Only Kachen saw Lisa in the backseat stick her tongue out at him as they slowed to maneuver around his car half blocking the road.

Kachen covertly raised his middle finger at her and muttered, "Later, you little bitch."

Once they were on the highway Karen said, "I'll call you after I write up the story. It'll probably be after one. Maybe we can have a small lunch out there. Caroline usually only has bar food at lunch in the summer. Sandwiches and such."

"That's fine with me."

Karen looked back at Lisa. "It might be a hardship for you, kiddo. She doesn't have ice cream."

Lisa pretended to pout. "Then I won't eat and I'll die and you'll have to have a funeral like for Grandma, and everyone'll be sad."

Mark put his head back against the seat and squeezed the bridge of his nose. "I forgot to ask Chavez something. Maybe I'll call him later."

"What?"

"Where does that road lead?"

"There's a couple of campgrounds farther up. Mostly it's just a fire road. Off-roaders use it sometimes."

"But it doesn't go anyplace?"

She shook her head.

Mark said, "Chavez thought Stallworth might have been passing by and came across something that caused him to stop. But there's no reason for him to even be on that road."

Karen began to tap her fingertips on the steering wheel. "Good point. Looks like an angle for my story doesn't it? But I don't think Chavez is going to like it."

41

The phone was ringing as Mark was unlocking the motel door. "Mason Hightower, Mark. I need to talk to you this afternoon. It's pretty damn important. Sometime after one, say. I'm tied up in court all morning. Don't bring Karen, though. This is between you and me. I don't want a reporter around."

Mark struggled against a rising annoyance. More stories, more secrets. More Harmony. "You want to tell me what this is about?"

"No, actually, I don't. Just be here."

"All right," Mark said with a sigh, but it'd probably be about three o'clock. He and Karen were going to be talking to Caroline Bellamy later this afternoon.

"Caroline!" Hightower said, and Mark could almost see the attorney smile. "You'll like her. She's quite a gal."

Mark dropped onto the bed and rubbed his neck. "You sound like you have a crush on her."

Hightower chuckled. "Used to, used to. She was the belle of the ball in high school. But she had a thing for Walter Lowndes, like all the other girls. For all the good it did. When he finally married, it was some society gal from Denver with big boobs and a bank account to match. Well, I'll see you at three, then. But I better warn you now—you aren't going to like it. Not one bit."

Mark hesitated a moment, then decided it couldn't possibly be a secret. "Have you heard about Eldon Stallworth?"

"Heard? No, what? Has he finally decided to fire Bobby Sample?"

"Someone killed him."

"What?"

Mark explained.

"Good God," the man said. "What's happening to us?"

Mark didn't attempt an answer, though he felt that whatever it was, 'happening' wasn't the right word; what was going on now was a consequence not of something that took place in the past few days, but thirty years ago. And he and Lisa were somehow at the center of it.

"Three months from retirement," Karen said two hours later. "Can you believe that? His wife's in a daze." She pounded the brake pedal to keep from hitting a bus that had slowed in front of her. "I went over there after taking pictures of where they found him. The pastor from their church was there trying to comfort her but what do you say to a woman who's been married to the same man for thirty-eight years and suddenly he's no longer there? No warning—no nothing— she just opens the door one sunny afternoon and sees this guy in clerical garb who hasn't been in her house in twenty years. It's a wonder she didn't have a heart attack right there."

"Did the state police turn up anything after we left?"

"Yeah. A signed confession. 'Catch me before I kill again' written in blood on the ground. Funny we didn't see it, isn't it?" Her tone suddenly eased. "Oh hell, I'm sorry. I'm just upset." She slammed the brake pedal again and pulled off the street into the mostly empty parking lot of Trees restaurant, near the slopes. "Eldon was a friend of mine, always treated me okay. Even after the trouble with Todd. Seeing him killed like this makes me want to scream."

She killed the engine but didn't get out. "I probably ought to prepare you for Caroline. We've been friends since I moved here. She's another local success story—a woman who started with nothing and likes to say now she owns Harmony's only Rolls-Royce. But she's a little off the wall. And a little loud. And . . . Hell, you'll see. Come on."

A boom suddenly rocked their car. "Better wait a moment or we'll be covered in dust." They sat and watched a cloud of dirt and debris rise from the top of the mountain. "That can't be from the restaurant," Mark said. "They've already done the framing. You can see it from here." The structure was perched on stilts at the highest point of the mountain, more than two thousand feet above them, and projected precariously over the edge like an acrobat holding a rope as he tilted away from his stand high above the audience.

"They're putting in supports for a chairlift that's going to run from the main Express lift to the restaurant. It's about half a mile, I guess. Walter Lowndes doesn't want people to have to exert themselves when it comes to spending money. Caroline said we can expect five-dollar drinks, two-dollar coffees, and thirty-five-dollar steaks. And people will pay it. Believe me, Walter's researched everything and knows exactly what he can get from his customers."

A fine layer of black dust had risen from the mountaintop, dispersed, and gently settled on the ground and car and everything else around them, like ashes from a crematorium. She pushed on the door handle. "Let's go before they set off another one."

The restaurant looked more Santa Fe desert than Colorado ski country. Rounded pink stucco walls, dried flowers, New Mexico–style Mission furniture, and soft pastel paintings and wall coverings, made for a calming, relaxed atmosphere. The sort of place, Mark thought, where the *après ski* crowd—or *never ski* crowd— wouldn't mind paying outrageous prices to see and be seen.

Caroline Bellamy was waiting for them in the roped-off dining room. She rose at once from the cluttered table where she evidently had been doing paperwork while waiting for her visitors, and smiled broadly. "I hope you don't mind the deserted look," she said, indicating the large, darkened room with its dozens of empty tables with a sweep of her arm. "We put our lunch business in the bar during the summer. But I figured with the little girl—" She smiled and shook hands with Mark.

"No, this is fine," Mark said as the woman's hand held on to his. Caroline Bellamy looked to be in her early fifties, tall, and voluminous inside a tentlike muumuu, half a dozen necklaces dangling across her bosom, rings on almost every finger, and long silver earrings that shook as she talked. Her voice, loud and garrulous, filled the empty room with a sort of excited good cheer. "Sit, sit, everyone, you next to me, young lady," she said as she lowered herself to a chair like a soufflé suddenly settling.

"I've heard about you from Karen, of course. And Sal called over from Mason's office asking if I remembered anything about 1968— a baby, and maybe an adoption, she said. Good Lord, I have enough trouble remembering what day it is. How can I remember from thirty years ago? I was only four then." She laughed loudly, her whole body quaking, then snapped her fingers at somebody in the bar before turning to Lisa, her tone more motherly. "Been hearing about you, too. Folks say you're the cutest thing to hit town since somebody found that bear cub under Hadley's porch a few years ago."

Lisa squirmed and looked at her dad who said, "She thinks people around here pay too much attention to her."

Caroline laughed out loud again, leaning suddenly forward and looking to the seven-year-old like a huge bolt of fabric falling from a shelf. "Come back and tell me that in ten years." Still, her eyes fixed with interest on the child's face, and Mark and Karen exchanged a look.

Karen touched her friend's hand. "Did you hear about Eldon being killed?"

"Oh my God, no!" The woman's face paled and her entire body tensed. "When? How?"

Karen told her what they knew and Caroline seemed to dissolve in her chair. "My God, I've known Eldon all my life. I can't believe it. A drug deal? Do you believe that?"

"There's some inconsistencies in the story," Karen said carefully. "But so far that's the official line."

"Oh Lord." Caroline put her ringed fingers over her eyes as if to will away the news. "First poor old Bill, now this." She dropped her hands and stared at her friend. "You don't think they're related somehow, do you? It doesn't seem possible."

Karen shrugged just as a waiter appeared with a tray of sandwiches and hors d'oeuvres. Caroline asked what they wanted to drink and everyone settled for water. After the waiter brought bottles of Perrier, Karen said, "Mark was saying earlier there hadn't been a murder in Harmony for years. Now suddenly two people have been killed. And only one thing out of the ordinary seems to have occurred in that time."

"You came to town," Caroline said, looking instantly at Lisa, then after a moment to Mark, her dark eyes narrowing. She quickly added, "Sorry. I didn't mean it that way. But poor Eldon."

Mark felt his fingers tighten on his glass of water. "Look, I know Stallworth was a friend of yours, and I feel sorry about what happened, but it's not why I came here. I wanted Karen to introduce us because—"

"I know, I know." Caroline sank back in her chair and the expression on her face grew cold. "Your parents. It's all I've heard about for days."

Mark's voice shot out quickly as his anger flared. "I don't know what the hell's going on around here but everyone's trying to keep something from me. And it's not ignorance or bad memories. It's deception, intimidation, and outright lies." He told her about Rollins's story.

Caroline gave a humorless laugh, earrings jangling and muumuu shifting like drapes in a storm. "Poor Micah's been acting brain-dead for years. Don't know why he'd lie to you, though. Ed Contrell! God, couldn't he come up with something better than that?"

Mark leaned forward, arms braced on the tabletop. "If you'd remembered anything you would have told Hightower's secretary. Right?" He was still fighting a desire to start breaking things. "Nothing else has occurred to you? There's nothing you remember about 1968?"

"No . . . sorry." She waved a hand. "I'll work on it. I can't keep my mind straight now, though. Not after hearing about Eldon. Why did it have to be one of the nice guys? Why not a slug like Les Cady?"

Mark sank back, annoyed at her inability or unwillingness to help, as well as at the glee with which people seemed to gang up on Cady. "Why is everyone so down on him? He's never been convicted of anything, has he? Maybe he's not what you think. Jesus, maybe the guy just looks weird."

Caroline frowned at him. "Just because he hasn't been convicted doesn't mean he's not guilty."

"I think I'll talk to him," Mark said, at least partly to annoy her. Or to annoy everyone in Harmony. "He lived here in the sixties, didn't he? He might be able to help me. No one else has."

Caroline was appalled. Her huge body shifted in his direction, necklaces and earrings jangling discordantly at the sudden movement. "What good would that do? He's as crazy as Wild Bill was. Just creepier." She looked at Karen. "I remember once in high school I was opening my locker and felt something push from behind. I swung around and there was Lester the Molester with his little bearlike body, rubbing himself against me like he was going to come right there. Kids told me you could hear me scream out on the football field."

Karen shook her head. "Caroline's right, Mark. Les is . . . not just different. He's dangerous. People like that—like he is—don't seem to have the power *not* to molest."

Mark put his glass down. "What the hell am I supposed to do, then? I'm running out of people. Who *can* I ask?"

Caroline said, "Have you talked to Walter Lowndes?"

"I've tried. He won't see me."

"Why not?"

"Who knows? His secretary says he's busy. Typical businessman BS."

"Better try Micah again, then. Pin him down. Find out why he lied."

"If I can find him. *His* secretary's claiming he's out now, too. It's all part of the Friendly Harmony 'Be Nice to Visitors' program."

"Maybe there's just no information out there. Have you ever considered that possibility? Doesn't explain why Micah would lie to you, though. Of course, he might have just been confused."

Mark turned to Karen, trying to keep his tone neutral. "Why don't you take Lisa over to the bar and get her a Coke? You could show her the rest of the restaurant, too."

Karen smiled at the girl. "Sounds like fun. Want to go?"

"Is there another dead body I'm not supposed to see?"

Despite his anxiety, Mark began to laugh, and turned to face his daughter. "Give me a hug, hon. You're one in a billion."

As Karen and Lisa left, Caroline looked at Mark with what might have been envy. "You two have a close relationship, don't you? I never had any kids but if I did, I'd want to get along as well as you two do."

He shook his head as he put the Polaroid photo on the table directly in front of her. "Someone else noticed, too."

The woman's face went ashen. "My God. Who—"

"Anonymous. A threat. And a hell of a lot better than threatening me."

She shook her head in dismay. "Sick. It's definitely the sort of thing Les Cady would do, though. I remember when he was sent to some sort of institution in Denver for a few months because he skinned a cat. Actually pulled the skin off a live cat. Can you believe it? He was cooking the flesh over a campfire when someone spotted him."

Mark unfolded the newspaper article, put it next to the picture, and flattened it with his hand.

"What's this? Going to need my glasses to read it." She picked up her rhinestone—or diamond? Mark wondered—glasses and read the story. "My God. I remember when that happened. Thirty years ago. Time does fly. So why do you have it?"

He told her about the missing newspapers and someone sending him a copy of the story. "It must have something to do with my parents. Why else would someone send it to me?"

She stared toward the bar a moment. Except for a middle-aged couple sitting at a small table Karen and Lisa were the only people visible. When her gaze returned to him she seemed uneasy. "How many people know what you're doing here?"

"Dozens, hundreds. Even you knew."

"I suppose. Still, this doesn't have to have anything to do with your parents."

As Mark put the picture and story back in his pocket the muted sound of an explosion blew down from the top of the mountain. "Are you and Walter Lowndes friendly?"

"Friendly? Friendly as anyone here can be to Walter, I guess. He's responsible for this." She waved around the restaurant. "If it weren't for the resort I'd probably be a waitress at the cafe asking if you want refills on your coffee. I've done pretty well by him. A lot of people have."

"He's not universally loved, I take it."

She shook her head impatiently. "Come on, Mark. Grow up. Santa Claus isn't universally loved. When a guy's become a success people want to knock him down. Envy rules America. You know that."

"Is his new restaurant going to hurt you?"

"I don't know. It might. Then again it might bring more people to town. I figure it's a push. I'm not really doing this for the money, anyway. I could retire now and live well the rest of my life. This is just a way to keep busy."

As Karen and Lisa entered the dining room from the far end, Mark leaned in Caroline's direction and dropped his voice. "What is it about my daughter that fascinates everyone around here? And don't say you don't know."

The woman's eye's darkened behind her jeweled glasses. "Fascinates? Who are you talking about?"

"Everyone! Including you. You were staring at her earlier."

"That's ridiculous. She's an adorable girl. There aren't that many children around here. That's all it is."

42

Ashamed of myself, Micah Rollins thought sourly as he reached out with his right hand and plucked thick, juicy blackberries from one of the overgrown bushes on his sixty-acre ranch east of town. He dropped the berries into a red plastic bucket, and continued his harvesting. A dozen feet away in the corral, one of his hired hands was feeding the three yearling jumpers Micah was training. He already had a wallful of ribbons and trophies for his show horses and was planning to open his own riding school next year. If there *was* a next year. The way things were going he wasn't a hundred percent sure there would be.

If he kept on panicking like he did when Ritter got to town there's no telling what would happen. *Ashamed of myself,* he repeated silently. He'd let Caroline get him too worried, and when that happened he usually screwed up. It's one thing he'd learned about himself years ago: *Take it slow and easy, don't let people rile you. Work at your own speed. And keep talking because you can talk your way out of anything.*

He put another handful of berries in the bucket. He had enough for at least six pies already. *Might as well keep going, though. Don't want them rotting on the vines.* He could have Consuela make up some pies for the folks at work. It was little things like that people responded to. The boss bringing in blackberry pies! Amazing how willing most people are to believe the best about you once they decided you were okay. Anything not to reverse an initial opinion. *It must be vanity,* he thought—*the inability to admit that we were wrong in the first place.*

He was, he had to confess, growing a little tired of the "good ol' boy" persona he had long ago perfected, and which had made his life into a sort of parody of old Gene Autry films. It was something he'd accepted, though, as the only way out of the poverty that had been a part of the Rollins family tree as far back as anyone could trace. It was only when Micah found out by accident that he could maneuver people against their will with a little humor, a little dang-fool silliness, that he began to craft the person he had become over the years. Good ol' Micah, everyone's friend. "You could charm the birds out of the trees," his mama used to tell him. And he could! But that was definitely Micah—everyone's friend. A little goofy, maybe, especially with that cowboy hero-worship of his, but trustworthy as all get out. And, man, can he talk!

So last year when someone shot a neighbor's three dogs that had barked all damn night for two weeks in a row, no one thought it could possibly be Micah. Why, he even showed up the next day with a beautiful little golden Lab pup for the bereaved couple. Or when his second wife's (ex-wife's by then) house burned down after she married that Denver truck salesman, it was thought to be more of the random violence the capital city was becoming known for. And Micah was there before the ashes had cooled to lend his support— even offered to make them a loan (at two percent over prime) for a new home, as long as his firm could build the house. Or when another horse trainer's prize stallion died of rat poisoning no one thought to cast a glance Micah's way.

Thing is, Micah always thought things out. Always took the calm approach. Wouldn't let himself get rattled, because he knew things would work out sooner or later. *Just give it time.*

Which was why he was ashamed at letting Caroline convince him to try to get Ritter to leave town. At first glance that might have been the right decision. But as he thought about it, Ritter, or more particularly Ritter's daughter, could be seen as *tools,* not threats: *Caroline's afraid of what's going to happen to that little girl; but when you think about it, that's exactly what we* do *want. Maybe not you, Carolin-ah, but damn sure what I want. Now all I've got to do is ensure it.*

Micah let himself down onto his knees to pluck berries off the bottom of the bush. As he was reaching far back for some lunkers he caught a glimpse of spit-shined black leather moving into his field of vision. Suppressing a sigh, he said, "Howdy, Bobby," slipping into the persona as easily as into a pair of old shoes.

Sample shook his head. "Why in hell are you doing stoop labor? Don't you got some hunch-back Mexican to do that for you?"

Micah slowly straightened to his six-foot-four height and looked at the policeman. "First thing you can do for me is stop talking about my employees in that tone of voice. It shows a lack of respect and I resent it. You understand me?"

"Yes suh, Mr. Rollins, suh. I surely do."

"The second thing you can do," Rollins said, brushing dirt off his jeans, "is stop smart-mouthing me. Since I'm the man who's putting money in your greedy little pocket, the least you can do is show a little respect."

"Oh, yes massa, I's sorry. I's be showin' y'all all the 'spect you deserve. Just don' beat me no more."

Rollins threw the man a look and bit back an angry response. It annoyed the hell out of him to have to even deal with a cretin like this but he had been using Sample for two years—mostly construction-related collection and loan work—and Bobby had been invaluable in the past. As he would be in the coming week. But once that was complete, he was afraid the young man was going to have a tragic motorcycle accident. Some of these mountain roads are so damnably treacherous! He felt a little lift just thinking about it. Bobby and his bike plunging a thousand feet to the bottom of an inaccessible ravine!

Micah put his hands on his hips. "So what's Hector Chavez think about poor Stallworth? Must have him racking his brain."

"Thinks like I said he would: The chief comes up on a drug deal, gets out to investigate, and gets popped. You know how crazy these druggies are."

"Anyone ask why he was up there?"

"Hell, they're curious, sure. But it's nothing to get concerned about. He's the chief, he drives around. 'Enforcing the Law,' you know. It was his life."

"Did you leave a little weed on the ground like I told you?"

"Sure." Sample grinned his Adonis grin, thinking, *Left a little weed* ashes. *No sense wasting the good stuff.*

Micah walked over to the corral and smiled as one of his jumpers noticed him and wandered over. He said, "Hey, Bobby, grab one of them carrots out of that barrel and give it to Moonlight here."

Bobby picked up a carrot and held it gingerly over the fence. The horse snatched it so quickly and greedily that Bobby thought he was going to lose his hand. "Hey, goddamn! Fucking horse."

"Take it easy, Bobby. Horses have an instinctual understanding of human nature, you know. He probably reckoned you were going to pull that carrot back at the last minute. You were, weren't you?"

When the man said nothing Micah smiled. "Well, stay on top of the investigation. If Chavez or the state lab comes up with anything I want to know immediately."

"Yes, suh, immediately, suh."

"Don't you ever get tired of being a complete ass, Bobby? You were a jerk when you were a Cub Scout twenty years ago tying other kids' shoelaces together. Only difference now is you're bigger. Don't you think it might be time to grow up?"

"Got lots of time for that, boss. Got some partying to do first. Now how about that other ten grand you owe me?"

"Well, believe it or not I don't carry ten thousand dollars in my pockets. We're going to have to go inside for that."

Bobby glanced down at his hand as if amazed it was still connected to his wrist. "Let's do it, man. I ain't got all day."

Rollins led the way into his den and went straight to the desk where he took an envelope from the center drawer. He tossed it at Bobby before sitting down in a leather armchair. The cop opened the envelope and began counting the hundred-dollar bills.

"It's all there, Bobby. Christ sakes, I've never shortchanged you."

"Just *feeling* it," Sample said. "Getting to *know* it. Making it my friend."

Rollins sat back and crossed his legs. "Might be more where that came from. I am getting a little worried about Mr. Mark Ritter. He is beginning to get under my skin with all his meddling. If he gets too annoying you can make him disappear. In the meantime I'm going to stay away from the man. I'm afraid he's unhappy with me."

Sample straightened the money into a neat stack with two hands, then bent it in half and stuffed it into his front pocket. He took a minute to admire the bulge it made, then asked, "What the hell did you do that you needed the chief dead?"

Rollins leaned forward. "Well, if you knew that, I'd need you dead too, wouldn't I?"

Sample smiled. "Ain't no one to do that for you. You sure as hell ain't about to—" He paused suddenly, thinking about it. "Unless *that's* what this is all about! You popped someone back in the old days and now it's coming back to nip you in the ass." He started laughing. "You're probably the one that killed old Bill, too, aren't you? Jesus Christ, Micah fucking Rollins, big-time businessman, shot old pervert Bill to death. What the hell for? Was he blackmailing you? Did Bill have pictures of you and five-year-old boys? Man! What would Red Ryder say?"

For one of the few times in his life Rollins lost his temper, and his voice shot up. "Damn you, I did not kill Bill!"

"Whoo-ee," Sample said, roaring back on his heels. "I done touched a sore spot. Must've come close to something."

"Don't start playing guessing-games with me, Bobby. You don't want to bite the hand paying for your party time. We've got us a nice business relationship here—you and me. Let's keep it like that. Don't go getting nosy. It'll help both of us. You understand me?"

Sample grinned at him. "Well, my man, I didn't mind doing Stallworth for you at all. Fucker kept getting on me because I had some 'citizen complaints' in my file from folks pissing and moaning about parking tickets and such. Asshole wouldn't stand up for his own people. Always treated me like I was some kind of mistake he was trying to forget. But if you want anyone else dead it's going to cost you double. At least."

"Bobby, you are completely amoral, aren't you? You'd kill anyone if the money was right."

"If the money was right? Yes suh, I would. Even ol' massa Micah. But I'm beginning to think ol' massa's just as deadly as me. Better watch my back, don't you think, boss? Don't you think I better be real careful with my life? Before I end up dead in an accident? Maybe shoot myself with my own piece?"

Rollins shook his head in dismay. Killing Bobby Sample might be the one great deed Micah Rollins would accomplish for humanity in his lifetime. Well, no, he'd serve the world in other ways, too. Walter Lowndes, for example. But Bobby would be up there near the top.

The young patrolman was acting antsy, bouncing on the balls of his feet, probably hot to start spending his money. He said, "What's this Ritter dude done to get you so worked-up? He find out you killed someone, too?"

"Ritter's role in my life is my business, Bobby. Let's just say he's become a major thorn in my side."

"Thorn in Todd Kachen's side, too. He's dickin' Todd's wife, you know."

"So I hear. I figured you'd be moving in on that by now. It's not like you to let a good-looking gal slip away. Especially to an outsider like that."

"Got to stick by my bud," Sample said with a shake of his head. "Can't be double-crossing my oldest and bestest friend in the whole wide world. Unless she offers it to me."

"Messing around with Karen kind of makes Ritter unpopular around here, I guess. People been talking about him much?"

Bobby unconsciously massaged the role of bills in his pocket. "Hell, everyone knows he's here looking for his folks. You couldn't be the daddy he's searching for, could you?" He grinned stupidly at Rollins. "You do kinda look like him—you both got that dumb-ass look on your face like, 'What the hell's going on around here?' "

"If you keep guessing, Bobby, you're sure to strike pay dirt someday. Seems to me, though, that's the day I move your name from the Asset side of the balance sheet to the Liability side. In the meantime we are going to keep an eye on Mr. Ritter. You and me. Like I said, I need him and his kid right now. Got a job for 'em. But if the young man continues to annoy, you will take care of things for me." *As your last act on the face of the earth, you dumb fuck.*

"Happy to be of service. Gonna cost you, though. Gonna get expensive."

"Don't worry," Rollins said, getting up. "In the long run, Bobby, it won't cost me a penny."

After Sample left, Micah sat down again and started to think about Mark and Lisa Ritter. The air around him seemed newly charged with promise. *Mark and Lisa Ritter! Looks like they're going to have to stay in Harmony a couple more days for things to work out. Never should have tried to scare him away, especially with that stupid phone call. But now that it's done there's no sense crying about it. The*

*important thing at this point is to grease the skids a bit, speed every-
thing up. The girl's the bait, of course; just gotta dangle her in the
water and wait for a tug on the line. Won't take long. Can't be too
obvious about it, though.*

It reminded Micah, whose memory of high-school years was infalli-
ble, of when he'd been failing Biology as a junior. He'd snuck into
Mr. King's office when the teacher was pulling his sixth-period coach-
ing stint with the girls' tennis team. Micah found the final exam in
the file cabinet and quickly Xeroxed it, not that time was a problem.
King would spend the whole fifty minutes out there, watching the
girls reach above their heads to serve, or bending over to pick up
loose balls. But Micah was careful to get only a B-minus on the test
rather than an A. *Don't overplay your part; you have to live up to
other people's expectations, not exceed them, because that's when
they begin to wonder.*

It was the same philosophy he used when bidding on state construction work. The highway-department secretary in Denver who fed
him rival bids for $5,000 a project made it possible for Rollins
Construction to win contract after contract without lowballing the
bids too much. Still, sometimes he'd overbid just to make things look
on the up-and-up.

How things look, he'd long ago learned, was more important than
how things are. And if people buy into that easygoing, affable, hero-
worshipping cowboy persona, half the battle is won.

He relaxed back, his eyes going to the six-foot cardboard Roy
Rogers "standee" guarding a corner of the room, and began to think
about old Bill. Bobby had indeed hit a sore spot. It was bothering
the hell out of Micah that someone killed the old fart. What did Bill
mean to anyone? Damn it, who the hell else in Harmony was killing
people?

43

In the Z3 in front of Mason Hightower's office, Mark decided to
try Caroline Bellamy's advice, and used his cell phone to again call
Walter Lowndes. Sorry, his secretary said, not sounding sorry at all,
but Mr. Lowndes simply did not have time to see anyone not con-

nected to his day-to-day business activities. He was a very busy man. There would be no point in calling again, she added forcefully, because the answer would be the same.

Mark fumed as he shoved the phone in the glove compartment. Getting to see Lowndes was like trying to arrange a personal visit with the president of the United States.

Upstairs in Hightower's outer office Mark said, "I hope you don't mind that I brought Lisa along."

"No, no," the attorney said. "It was only reporters I was worried about. This won't take long. She can wait out here with Sal."

Mark said to his daughter, "Maybe you could show her how to play Hangman."

"Hangman!" the woman said. "I haven't played that in years. Let me get a piece of paper."

Mark smiled gratefully in her direction, then followed Hightower into his private office. The older man waved him to one of the four chairs in front of the desk, then dropped heavily into the one next to it. "This is not," he said with deliberateness, "a pretty story. Or one I will enjoy telling. So get comfortable and share a little misery with me."

Mark's intestines clenched as he sat. "You discovered who my parents are?"

Hightower put his palms on his thighs. "Let us approach this, if not logically, at least chronologically. First—" He brought his large hands up and massaged his eyes and forehead as if he had a headache, then dropped them heavily to his sides. "The first thing is, that story Micah told you isn't true. The part about the Contrells dying was—"

Mark waved him off. "I know. I found out this morning I'm not a Contrell. It's all bullshit."

Hightower leaned back, surprised. "You're ahead of me, then. Micah tell you why he lied?"

Mark shook his head. "We haven't been able to get hold of him. His secretary claims he's out of town."

"Oh, horse-pucky. I saw him tooling around in his big ol' Caddy right after lunch today. You got any idea why he did it?"

"Not until I talk to him. He ought to have thought up a pretty good excuse by now."

The attorney shook his head in despair. "It's a crazy world we're living in. And getting crazier by the minute. Well, let me tell you what I dug up." He leaned forward again. "I went back over Daddy's files last night, this time looking for anything involving Carl Stark, instead of Ritter or Contrell. And I found it right off, in July 1968, just like that newspaper article.

"Seems Carl left a will. From the scratchy notes in the file I guess this mightily surprised folks. He evidently wasn't what you'd call real responsible. An easygoing guy who never gave much attention to the ski area, just sort of took every day as it came. But something happened that made him start thinking about the future." He glanced at Mark. "Seems he became a father."

Mark could feel all the muscles in his body tense.

Hightower leaned forward. "Carl had a girlfriend named Cheryl McAfee. I never knew her. Remember, I was away at school at the time. Anyway, Cheryl was only fifteen when she had this child. Looks like Carl wanted to marry her but Cheryl's mom was dead set against it, and of course she was still a juvenile, and in those days they didn't have much to say about things. So Cheryl's mom and my dad had the baby adopted out when he was just one month old." He looked over at Mark. "Mr. and Mrs. Matthew Ritter of South Dakota were the adoptive parents."

Mark sat for a moment without moving, his mind flying off in a dozen different directions. "Carl Stark," he finally managed, and tried to picture what this person looked like. His father.

Hightower settled back in his chair. "I remember him, but not too well. Nothing to make him stick in the mind. Certainly not like Ed Contrell. At least you don't have to worry about being the son of a murderer. Carl was a bit wild but hell, he was at that wild age, and small towns in those days didn't offer much in the way of entertainment except partying and drag-racing. But at least now you know. I'll see if I can dredge up a birth certificate for you."

Mark stood up, a sudden bundle of energy, and began to pace. "Carl Stark. I've heard the name."

"Sure. Owned the ski area. Folks will remember him. At least you'll be able to find out what kind of man he was. Have Noel Atchison take you around to some of his friends."

"And Cheryl McAfee?"

"Well, that's a little more difficult. She was only fifteen at the time, seems to have left Harmony right after that. Don't know if folks'll recollect."

Mark began to stalk back and forth in front of the desk, his gaze on the floor. "You said Stark left a will."

Hightower leaned back. "Like I say, that kinda surprised people, I guess, but being a parent can make you start to think of the future. Certainly did for Carl. He left everything—which means the resort land—in trust for his wife. She was a juvenile, of course.

"The so-called resort never was worth much, and after the fire even less. For purposes of the estate they valued it at thirty thousand dollars. That'd be, what? A hundred thousand in today's money. Of course, the resort today—hotel, ski slopes, restaurant—is probably worth sixty or seventy million, maybe more.

"Anyway, it looks like my dad didn't trust young Cheryl's mom, and didn't think Cheryl would ever be mature enough to handle that amount of money so he drew up a purchase plan that sent the monthly payments into the trust, and then disbursed them to pay Cheryl's educational and living expenses as long as she stayed in school. You see this all the time in dealing with teenagers. The idea was to make her self-sufficient by encouraging her to get an education. I guess they sent her to some boarding school in Texas. She supposedly went on to college after that but the estate was transferred to an attorney in Austin when she was twenty-one so there's little detail.

"Whatever money was in the estate is certainly long gone now. Walter Lowndes bought the property, of course. Can't imagine where he came up with the money. I don't remember him being that well off. His folks had had some money at one time but certainly weren't rich. More 'shabby genteel.' "

Mark stopped his pacing. "And Cheryl McAfee. You don't know what happened to her?"

"I called the attorney in Texas. He died ten years ago but I spoke to one of the partners. He looked it up and called me back and said that Cheryl had left instructions that her whereabouts were not to be made known to anyone without her permission, so he called her and she said she didn't want to talk to me. Maybe she didn't like my dad. Can't blame her. He was the one that handled the adoption. Evidently giving up the baby was just between her mom and my dad. She was against it."

"Did you tell her attorney about me?"

"Nope. I just told him I wanted to talk to her. Figured it was up to you if you want to try to reenter her life at this time." He reached over to his desk and picked up a piece of paper. "This is the attorney's name. Give it a night before you call, though. As you've seen, these things can be tricky. Sometimes it's better to let sleeping dogs lie."

"Same thing Micah Rollins told me." He glanced at the paper and put it in his pocket. "Carl Stark and Cheryl McAfee. I'd like to see the birth certificate. The one with their names and my name on it." The implication being he no longer trusted what anyone told him.

"I've already sent to Denver for it. Shouldn't take too long."

Mark sank into the chair. "I thought I was this close once before."

"Don't know why in hell Micah lied to you. Give him another call this afternoon. See what he says. Or I can call him for you."

"I have a feeling he's going to be as hard to get to as Walter Lowndes. He won't talk to me, either."

Hightower's eyebrows went up. "Why do you want to see Darth Vader?"

Mark sighed and leaned back, feeling his muscles tighten with anxiety. "Why am I seeing anybody? To play 'Remember when . . .' I guess I have a better reason now since he bought his property from my dad. He ought to remember Carl and Cheryl. I'd like to fill in the family album. As well as find out what I did to become a threat to someone." There was both sarcasm and irritation in his answer. But he also felt a spark of enthusiasm now, a sense of getting to the bottom of things.

Hightower frowned at him. "Doesn't surprise me he won't see you. Walter's gotten to be too important to spend time with mere mortals now that he's a millionaire. Or so he thinks. Fancies himself the Donald Trump of Harmony, I reckon."

Mark was silent a moment, his fingers tapping the arm of the chair. Carl Stark and Cheryl McAfee. Names. But it was a place to start. And maybe as far as he would have to go. He said, "Didn't her attorney have anything else to say about Cheryl? What kind of work she does, whether she's married, anything like that?"

Hightower shook his head. "He did mention they'd paid her expenses at Baylor University but I don't know how long she went there or if she graduated."

Again Mark grew silent. Then he said, "What did you mean about this not being a pretty story?"

Hightower jabbed his legs out in front of him, and closed his eyes a moment. "Well . . . thing is, my daddy doesn't come off real well in this. It seems like the whole adoption was done very hush-hush. Or, to put it differently, outside the law. You're supposed to have a judge involved to make sure the interests of the child are being observed, and there's a passel of official forms to complete, and a social worker has to be assigned to the child, and on and on. Paperwork and bureaucracy. But none of that happened. One day you were Cheryl McAfee's baby, the next you were the Ritters'. The way it was done it was almost like baby-selling. If it'd ever gotten out, my daddy would've been disbarred. If not incarcerated."

"How did your father happen to know the Ritters?"

"I'm not sure he did. He knew an attorney up there in South Dakota, woman named Eleanor Dahlquist."

Mark looked at him a moment, holding his breath. Then he blew out a sigh. "It gets more interesting all the time."

"You know her?"

"All my life." He stood up suddenly. "Carl Stark and Cheryl McAfee. One more road to go down." He let out another sigh and glanced at the attorney. "Guess I'll ask around. I wonder why I feel so uneasy about this."

44

Back in his car in front of the Harmony Professional Building, Mark turned the ignition key then immediately shut it off. Reaching across Lisa to the glove compartment for the cell phone, he called the Austin attorney Hightower had spoken to about Cheryl McAfee. Sorry, the man told him in a soft Texas accent, but Ms. McAfee had left unambiguous orders not to give her address to anyone.

"Even her son?"

The man was unmoved. "I'll call her and tell her what you've told me. But don't expect her to contact you. She considers her past life something she does not intend to revisit. Especially anything connected with Harmony."

Mark put his finger on the phone button to break the connection, then dialed directory assistance in Texas for the Baylor University number. A moment later he was talking to the registrar's office. No, they would not give out phone numbers or addresses of graduates without their written permission. "I'm with the Interior Department," Mark told her, picking a government agency at random. "We interviewed her last year and in the meantime lost her number. We'd very much like to offer her a job."

"Even so. We must protect a person's right to privacy."

Maybe. But all universities have a vulnerable underbelly. "Alumni office," the woman's voice answered.

"This is Professor Sample in the School of Education. One of our graduates, a Ms. Cheryl McAfee, has been very generous in providing financial support over the years, and we're planning to honor her in September at a banquet here in Dallas. Somehow, though, I've lost her phone number—"

"Let me see if I can find it in my computer," the woman said at once. "We certainly don't want to lose a big donor."

"I knew I could count on you," Mark said, picturing her surrounded by a dozen other fund-raisers frantically working the phones.

A moment later he had the number. A 714 area code. He'd never heard of it. He called the operator and asked what part of the country it was. Coastal Orange County, California, she told him.

Mark hung up. *Now what do I do?* Sitting next to him Lisa was singing the Barney song—*"I love you, you love me"*—to herself, and playing with a map, trying to fold it back the way it had been.

Mark stared out the window toward the mountains rising in the distance. His intestines began to cramp, as though he needed to go to the bathroom. He started to put the phone away, then jerked it back. Quickly he punched out the number. It rang twice, then a pleasant female voice said, "Hello," and he started to say something but hung up instead. His heart was beating wildly.

Holding the phone and staring sightlessly straight ahead through the windshield, he wasn't aware of anyone nearby until a cowboy hat tilted through the open window in his direction. Mark jumped but Lisa giggled. "Well now," B.J. Blake said, "if I'd known you owned a BMW *and* a cell phone I wouldn't have let you out of my sight until you'd signed up for a condo in Yuppieville. I can still get you a good resale overlooking the slopes, if you want."

Mark forced himself to sound more cordial than he felt. "Just making a few calls. I didn't want to wait until we got back to the motel."

"Lifesavers, aren't they?" Blake said, nodding at the phone. "Other people must think so, too, since I've had three stolen from my car." His smile grew larger and took in Lisa. "Hey, it's teatime, isn't it?

How would you like it if I bought you two a big piece of blackberry pie over at the cafe?"

Mark was in no mood for Harmony chitchat but wanted to counteract the growing paranoia that made him wary of everyone he met. And since B.J. was a friend of Karen's he thought he ought to try to be pleasant. He turned to Lisa. "What do you think, honey? Want some pie?"

She clapped and said, "Yeah!"

"I guess that means she does," he told Blake.

They sat in a front booth where they could look out a window, Lisa with pie and Mark and Blake with pie and coffee. Despite it being mid-afternoon the cafe was full and three people had already stopped by to say hello to B.J. and commiserate about Stallworth, though Mark felt it was he and Lisa that were the real purpose of their visits. When they were finally alone B.J. nodded at Mark's uneaten pie. "You don't look like you're having a very good day today."

Mark started to tell him about Cheryl but couldn't. It wasn't the sort of thing he wanted to share with a stranger. Instead he took out the photocopied news story and put it on the table in front of Blake. "Someone sent this to my hotel yesterday. Does it ring any bells with you?"

Blake moved his pie aside and hunched over the article, flattening the paper with his hands and carefully reading it. "I've heard about the fire from folks over the years but I was only two in 'sixty-eight, so I don't recollect it. Never heard of this Carl Stark. Why'd someone send it to you?"

Mark shrugged. "Why did someone threaten me? Why trash my car? Why try to scare me out of town?"

Blake cast a glance at Lisa who was finishing the last bite of her pie. "Yeah, well . . . can't help you there. Wish I could. Karen said it's been bothering you a lot."

Mark looked at him, surprised.

Blake shrugged with some embarrassment. "She and I talk most every day. We've been friends for a long time. Eight years probably."

"Before Kachen."

The other man seemed uneasy and started poking at what was left of his pie. "Yeah. Before good old Todd. She told me she hadn't been real up-front with you about that. I know she feels bad about it. I hope you don't hold it against her, though. Karen's a real nice person. Todd was kind of a— I guess you'd call it an aberration in her life. I remember when she told me she was going to marry him. I couldn't believe it. *Todd Kachen?* But what do you say when a good friend is going to make a real stupid mistake like that?"

Mark poured cream in his coffee and stirred it with a spoon, watching the color lighten. "Usually you say nothing."

"Which is what I did. Took her a while to admit her mistake. Well, life goes on, doesn't it? At least they didn't have kids."

"Did you and Karen date?" He wished at once he could retrieve the words. It sounded stupidly intrusive, if not jealous.

B.J. smiled. "Sure. A couple of times, years ago. Then we decided, why screw up a nice friendship with romantic nonsense? Not that there was any real romance there. That part never happened. Weird, isn't it? I mean, with us there was nothing. An absolute zero. So how did she ever feel any tenderness toward a thug like Kachen? I knew him in high school. Football was the high point of his life. It's all been downhill since."

Mark tasted his coffee, realized he didn't want it, and put it down. "You never married?"

B.J. grinned like a five-year-old. "Gonna be pretty quick. Finally giving up a life of freedom. But hell, I'm thirty-two. I just never felt able to afford it. But I figure time's a-wasting. Getting married to a girl over in Estes Park. Works in a lodge over there. Doing it New Year's Eve. Hey, you're invited."

"Congratulations. Maybe I'll be able to make it."

"Karen and I are still friends, of course. Actually Karen, me, and Jeannie—my fiancée—are friends. Karen and Jeannie are practically sisters, known each other for years. So everything's worked out fine for all of us. Except her marriage, of course."

Lisa said, "Karen's nice. She bought me ice cream."

"Is that a hint?" Blake said.

Mark folded the news story and put it back in his pocket. "Are you sure you've never heard people around here talk about Carl Stark?"

The waitress came by and refilled Blake's cup. He said, "I believe Miss Ritter wants some ice cream."

Mark shook his head. "She's had enough junk for a while. I want her to eat dinner tonight."

The waitress glanced at Mark's uneaten pie. "Well, you're not getting out of that chair until you clean your plate, young man. House rules. Give me any trouble and I'll send you to your room."

Lisa giggled and even Mark smiled. "I'll do my best."

When the waitress moved away, Blake said, "Might have heard Stark's name, I suppose. But that's all."

Mark took a breath and decided to tell him. If B.J. was that close to Karen, he'd hear soon anyway. "He was my father. My birth father."

Lisa looked up suddenly, but said nothing.

Blake put his cup down and seemed excited. "You sure? I mean you actually found your folks? That's great. That was a one-in-a-million chance, wasn't it?"

Mark briefly told him about Cheryl McAfee and Stark.

Blake was obviously happy for him. "Well, I'm glad it turned out okay. Give your mom some time. She'll come around and talk to you. Heck, in a couple of weeks she'll probably have you out to her house for a chicken dinner. Cheryl McAfee, huh? Never heard that name before, I'm sure."

"She left town when she was fifteen. That was 'sixty-eight."

"Does that mean I have a new grandma?" Lisa said.

"Maybe so, hon. We'll see."

Lisa's smile lit up her face, and she clapped her hands.

"Seems like everything happened in 'sixty-eight, doesn't it?" Blake said. "That's the year I started walking without holding on to things. Finally got pretty good at it." He laughed at his own joke.

"Walter Lowndes was living here then, too. You seem to be one of the few people I've met who has anything nice to say about him."

The other man shrugged. "No reason not to like him. Hell, I'm in real estate. He brings people to Harmony."

"Do you know him?"

"Hardly ever talked to him. Hardly even see him anymore. He's kind of a recluse, I guess. Never liked the way people blame him for every bad thing that's happened to Harmony, though. Same for Janis. I like her a lot. I know Karen doesn't, but I think she's a nice woman. Ever see the way she stands up for poor old Les Cady? Hell, no one else will. It takes a lot of courage to do that."

"You don't think Cady's a molester?"

Blake sat back and stretched his arms out along the top of the leatherette booth. "Don't know. But that's the point. Could be. Could be folks get on him because he's a little weird. I mean he looks like the kind of guy who likes to walk around his house in soiled panties and a huge bra. But he's never been convicted of anything, so I figure leave the poor guy alone. But Janis goes out of her way to be nice to him. Of course, her dad employs him."

"I did a little research on Walter Lowndes. People back east seem to like him. They think he's quite a businessman. But I'm still having a hard time getting a feel for him. And he won't see me, for some reason."

"Why do you want to see him?" Blake evidently thought it an odd request.

"At first it was because I wanted to see what he knew about the Contrells. Now it's Cheryl McAfee and Carl Stark. The reason hasn't changed: I want to find out about my parents. What kind of people they were—or *are,* in Cheryl's case."

Blake still seemed confused. "And Lowndes won't see you?"

Mark shook his head and finally picked up his fork to attempt his pie. But his stomach was sour and he didn't know what black-berries were likely to do to it.

Blake said, "Why not have Karen set something up? She used to work for him."

Mark put his fork down. After a moment he said, "For Walter Lowndes?"

"Sure. She did PR for him until she went to the *Courier.* Had a condo at the resort. Flew around the country with him promoting Eagle Point Lodge. Funny she didn't mention it. She and Walter are pals from way back."

Mark was silent a moment before turning to Lisa. "We better go, hon."

Blake slid out of the booth. "Reckon I better get back to work, too. I've got that salesman's tingle along my spine. It's going to be a good week. Something big's about to happen. I can feel it."

45

Hector Chavez leaned back in the chair in Eldon Stallworth's office and thought, *It doesn't seem right. The man's dead less than a day and suddenly I'm taking over his office, sitting at the desk he never had the chance to clean out.* It was a strange feeling. But the mayor had appointed Chavez acting chief until the City Council met; life goes on.

As does death.

Suddenly peaceful little Harmony was beginning to look like Miami or New York. Two murders in twenty-four hours. Crazy old Bill and Eldon Stallworth. Two more different, people you couldn't expect to find.

There was no reason in hell someone would want Bill dead unless it was a retaliation for his messing around with kids. If he *was* messing around with kids. That was still a little hard to believe. Even if the man did have photos at his house.

And Stallworth? Did he really stumble across something and get killed for his curiosity? It made for a good story but it was a bit far-fetched. The chief was no dummy. He wasn't going to walk into something with his eyes closed. And he had no reason to be up in the mountains anyway.

No, something connected these two deaths. There was a tie some-where. Stallworth must have suspected something about Bill's death, tried to follow up on it, and was killed. But even that didn't ring true. The chief would have known better than to try something like that without letting Hector know what he was doing.

Chavez rocked forward and picked up the notes he'd found on top of Stallworth's desk:

Carl Stark. Dead in a fire, 1968.
Ed Contrell. And Ruthann. Dead in a fire, 1968.
Resort.
Check tax records.

A copy of the photo of Ritter's kid with her head blown away.

A copy of a thirty-year-old newspaper article.

Chavez put his elbows on the desk, propped his forehead on his hands, and stared at the papers.

A thirty-year-old death.

Four thirty-year-old deaths if you counted the three Contrells.

And yesterday a mentally defective old-timer. Followed by the chief of police.

There was no pattern here, nothing to tie them together.

But Stallworth had seen something and decided to follow up on it.

Chavez again stared at the notes.

Damn it, Eldon, what'd you see?

46

"I feel like such an idiot," Mark said bitterly. The muscles in his arm rippled as he squeezed the fork. "After all the bullshit I went through, I finally had her on the phone. And I couldn't say anything. I couldn't make the words come out. I just sat there."

"It's understandable," Karen said, pushing her plate aside. The enchiladas she had made for dinner sat half-eaten next to an undisturbed mound of brown rice and refried beans. Even Lisa's appetite had abandoned her, and she pushed her food around with a fork and seemed withdrawn or angry. Karen added, "It's got to be difficult to say hello to a mother you've never known. Especially if she doesn't want to talk to you."

Lisa looked up suddenly, frowning at the adults. "When are we going horseback-riding?"

"As soon as we're done eating," Karen said. "We already told you."

Mark drank half his beer in a gulp. "I don't know what to do. I have to talk to her. I don't care if she wants to see me or not."

"Maybe you should give it a rest for a while. Her attorney told her you're looking for her. Give her a chance to get used to the idea. Maybe she'll call you."

He put the glass down sharply. "I can't wait. She's my mother. Doesn't that mean anything to her? I'm her son, damn it. She has to talk to me."

Karen pressed her lips together and looked away, but Mark wasn't paying attention.

"I'll give her until tomorrow. If she doesn't call me by tomorrow night I'll call her. Does that make sense?"

Karen sighed, looking back at him and shaking her head. "I don't know. How can I tell you what to do? I've never been in a situation like this. I don't know what makes sense. I guess I feel strange though, almost jealous—like I just found you and I'm about to lose you to another woman." Her cheeks reddened. "Stupid, huh? Like a schoolkid."

Mark's eyes shot to her. Lisa said, "Is that lady going to be my grandma now? Or my mommy?"

Mark snatched up his beer. "I don't care if she wants to talk to me or not. I'll make her."

Suddenly annoyed, Karen pushed her plate aside. "If we're going riding, we better get moving. I had to make a reservation because there's not always someone at the stables after five."

Mark stood up, his chair scraping back on the floor. "I had a talk with B.J., this afternoon."

Something about how he said it made Karen look at him guardedly. "Talk about what?"

"You."

She sat back and looked at him, but said nothing.

Mark snatched another beer from the refrigerator and popped it open. "Why didn't you tell me you used to work for Lowndes?"

Her face seemed to ease. "It didn't seem particularly relevant."

"I've been trying to see him since I got to Harmony. Why didn't you help me?"

"Believe me, I couldn't have been any help. If I could I would have."

"You could have said something when I told you I was going to do research on the man."

"Said what? I can't help you with his life. I don't know that much about him. He was my boss, not my lover."

"Tell me about your job."

"Or what?" she snapped. "You'll beat me up?" But her mood softened all at once. "Sorry. I guess I'm just tired of being talked to like that. Blame Todd." She smiled uneasily and put her hands in her lap. "My job with Walter. Sounds like a movie, doesn't it? Well: I was just out of college with a journalism degree. Along with about fifty thousand other journalism graduates that year. Somehow Walter had heard about me. He knew I was from Harmony, of course. So he called and offered me a PR position. No one else wanted me so I snapped it up. I worked for him for three years, but it wasn't how I wanted to spend my life, so when Noel offered me a reporter's job I quit."

"You and Lowndes must have been pretty close."

"Whatever that means, huh? Well actually I didn't see him that much. He's in New York most of the year. And I spent my time traveling to vacation shows and company travel departments, telling people what a lovely place Harmony is. It wasn't very exciting."

"Did he travel with you?"

She looked at him a moment, considering and rejecting a sarcastic response. "Sometimes. We had separate rooms, if that's what you're getting at."

"And after three years you and he didn't get to be friendly enough to get me in to see him now?" Mark was finding it difficult not to show his disbelief.

"I probably haven't talked to Walter ten times since I quit, and that was six years ago. Now all his PR work is done out of New York. And in the six years I've been at the *Courier* he hasn't called me once. The only time I've even seen him was on the street where we'd say hi and move on."

Lisa got out of her chair and hugged her dad. "I want to go riding."

Mark and Karen stared at each other a moment. Finally Karen said, "What do you say, Pop? Ready to play cowboy?"

He was still annoyed, but not sure at what. Himself, maybe. He finished off his beer. "All right. I'll go out there with you but not to go riding. I want to see Lowndes. Mason said he lives at the lodge. An apartment, I suppose."

Karen shook her head. "He had the downstairs rear of the main building remodeled as his living quarters when he gave up his house last year. It's pretty fancy, I guess, but I've never been there. What makes you think he'll see you?"

"Doesn't matter. Lowndes, Micah Rollins, Cheryl—I'm not going to give them a choice anymore."

47

—Now he feels himself grow warm and tremble with desire as he watches the girl walk into the stables with Karen Paige—

(Heart beats, races.)

She hasn't changed at all, not a bit. (Soars!) Look at her. *Look, damn it!* As beautiful and delicate as a mountain wildflower. How many years has it been? Almost forty? . . . And she's back. (Sharp pain in his head. Winces. Puts hand to temple).

—Still eight years old. He knew she loved him; it hadn't been her fault she had grown (closes his eyes to the terrible thought) older, fatter, uglier—

And somehow had become unaccountably cruel. Children are like that, he knows. It's happened before. Complained, told her mother. . . . (Annie went outside, drank, smoked, pretended not to hear the sounds of love.)

He feels the rage grow.

(Pain racks his body. Pain and rage.)

The little bitch, talking behind his back! And saying she'd kill him if he ever touched her again. How dare . . .

But she was old then, and fat, and oh, so ugly. There had only been one more time and he'd been drunk or he never would have done it because he hated her then (for growing old and ugly) and he'd rushed home and cleansed himself, scrubbing and scrubbing until it hurt (flesh turning pink) trying to eradicate the filth on his body.

But now she's back! He had always known that someday she'd return, hadn't he? Unchanged. *Wanting* him.

His heart leaps. All he has to do now is separate her from that Paige woman. How hard could that be?

(Body throbs.)

(Joy.)

She *belongs* to me.

(Hurries after her.)

48

Mark watched from behind the rail fence as a stablehand brought out two horses, a regal-looking chestnut mare for Karen, and an obviously aged white pony for Lisa. The man effortlessly lifted the girl onto her mount as Karen swung onto her horse.

"What's his name?" Lisa asked the man. Her excitement was obvious even from where Mark stood.

"Her name, niña? *Snowflake!"*

Karen said something and Lisa turned and waved at her dad. "See you later."

"Be careful, hon," Mark said, and wondered if he would ever stop saying that when parting from his daughter.

With Karen in the lead, they slowly crossed out of the corral, past the stables, and disappeared toward the mountain trails. Mark watched until he couldn't see them any longer, then turned and walked toward the lodge.

The building was huge and imposing, ersatz Swiss, four and five stories tall, with a stone-and-timber facade, a huge porch running along the front and sides with chairs for a nonexistent summer crowd, and inside, a massive dark fireplace between the now-closed bar and restaurant. Mark went to the hotel's check-in counter and rang a bell. No response. He rang again and a middle-aged woman appeared from the back, clearly surprised to see someone at this time of night in the summer. "Yes sir?"

"I'd like to see Mr. Lowndes."

Another show of surprise. "Mr. Lowndes is not available. Perhaps if you come back Monday. . . . You'll need an appointment, though. Have you called his secretary?"

"Often. Just pick up the phone and tell him Mark Ritter is here to talk to him."

The woman frowned, allowing her exasperation to turn to irritation. "I can't tell him anything. He's not available." She enunciated the words slowly, as if to a child.

Mark kept his temper in rein. "He lives here."

"That may be. I don't know. You'll have to call his secretary."

Screw it. He looked around. Karen said Lowndes lived in a remodeled area at the rear of the first floor. There was a door marked Private adjacent to the bell captain's desk. He strode over and tried it. Locked. The woman behind the counter smirked at him.

Mark ignored her. *I've been pissed on for four days. Your disapproval doesn't count for much.* He walked out of the lodge, down the broad stone steps, and around to the back where there was another door, unmarked this time. Locked also. An eight-foot brick-and-stone wall enclosed an area about twenty feet by twenty feet attached to the lodge. He put his hands on top and pulled himself up far enough to look over. There was a redwood hot tub, what looked like a koi pond, a stone barbecue, and half a dozen chaise lounges. French doors appeared to lead to a living area but no one was visible.

Now what?

49

Lisa felt her heart racing like it did on Christmas morning. Her horse (it *was* a horse and not a pony!) moved along quietly behind Karen's horse as they rode higher and higher in the mountains. She put her head back and saw some white fluffy clouds, as well as two big dark ones. What did horses do when it rained? Up ahead she could see a tower, kind of like a telephone pole, that held wires for the chairs that went up the mountain. Why would anyone want to do that when they could go up on a horse instead?

Riding a horse was bumpier than she thought. And slower. On TV horses usually ran, not walked. It was smellier too, because there was horse-poo everywhere. She wondered why no one cleaned it up. In Seattle you were supposed to clean up dog-poo. Maybe you don't do that for horses.

"You doing okay?" Karen was turned around, smiling at her.

"Yeah! It's fun!"

It wasn't like riding a bike, though, because your legs had to go way out, and it was kind of uncomfortable at first. But Karen didn't seem to mind. And you don't have to pedal.

Her hands were clenched tightly on the reins because she thought she might fall off if she held them lightly like Karen told her. Without thinking about it she pulled the reins toward her, and the horse made a funny noise and kind of kicked with his feet.

Karen said, "Problems?"

"No." Now she felt foolish. She knew she wasn't supposed to pull like that.

Karen had turned to the front again. Lisa was glad Karen liked riding. Dad would never have taken her. He took her to horse *races* once but that wasn't fun. Everybody smoked and yelled, and there wasn't anything for kids to do.

Lisa was glad her daddy liked Karen, too. Well, maybe not glad.

She wasn't sure. Maybe he didn't like her, maybe he was just being nice. People ought to be nice, though. She hated it when they weren't.

Two blue butterflies darted and dived past her head, not more than an inch from each other, then flew away. Lisa gave a little yelp of happiness. How did they stay so close together like that? They must be married. It reminded her of all the butterflies she saw in that field with her dad. She didn't see many butterflies at home. Of course, it was always raining at home.

She wasn't sure Colorado was any better than Washington, though. It was pretty, and sometimes it was fun, but lots of times there was nothing to do. She didn't like not having any kids to play with. And Daddy was mad most of the time, it seemed. Anyway, people were always talking about stupid things. Like this morning, when Karen was making breakfast, she kept asking if Daddy liked that other woman, the one with the store that smelled funny. But at least Karen didn't get mad when Lisa watched cartoons. Sometimes Daddy was too grown-up to be fun.

She wondered if she could see the stables from here. Turning to look behind her she saw nothing except trees. There was nothing on any side of the trail but trees. She twisted her head around and back, and stared toward the side of the mountain. Something moved up there. She squinted her eyes and peered through the tree trunks. There was a man on a horse way back there. It was hard to tell but it looked kinda like that man she saw on the highway a few days ago. He had been in the car next to theirs, and staring at her. Why would he be here, too?

50

Feeling uncomfortably like a movie cowboy, Mark sat on the top rail of the corral fence, waiting for Karen and Lisa. A cool wind was blowing, as if it were raining nearby, and it chilled his skin, raising goosebumps on his arms. When a voice from behind said, "Docker's and Nikes aren't quite the right look for a corral," he turned abruptly to see Janis Lowndes smiling at him.

He hopped down, aware that he was surprisingly pleased to see her. "And you're modeling what this year's chic young cowgirl is wearing?" He looked over her form-fitting silk dress and sandal-clad feet. She had no makeup on but smelled expensive and French. He liked it. A lot. And realized suddenly how drawn he was to her, despite their infrequent encounters.

Janis smiled and pushed back her brick-red hair with both hands, the bodice of her dress molding itself around her breasts. "I don't much like horses. At least up close. From a distance they have an earthy appeal, I suppose, like weight lifters and bodybuilders. All that sweat and those rippling muscles. But up close they smell, and their stupidity is too blatant to ignore. Like weight lifters and bodybuilders. Although in small doses they have their uses. Again . . . like weight lifters and body-builders."

"Including Bobby Sample?" Why did he say that? Mark wondered. He sounded like a resentful teenager.

But Janis had the grace to act as though the question hadn't been asked. She gazed around the corral. "Is your daughter riding?"

Mark turned and rested his forearms on the rail fence. "She and Karen. They ought to be back soon." Jesus, what a stupid thing to say. It sounded like a warning.

Janis smiled with understanding. "Then we shouldn't do anything to arouse their jealousy, should we?"

He glanced over at her. Her tone was so open and without guile, but at the same time so strange—that odd, breathless quality to her voice—that he wasn't sure how to respond. Her eyes were fixed straight ahead, on the door that led from the corral to the stables. She glanced briefly at him. "Tell me what lies you've heard about me. How do the locals warn a stranger about Janis Lowndes?"

Mark was taken aback. "I . . . Nothing, actually. I don't think anyone's mentioned you."

She gave him a quick look, a beautiful smile. "You're kind to say so. But I know it's not true. People gossip. Especially about me."

"Why would they gossip about you?" he couldn't help but ask.

She didn't answer for a moment, then said, "This is going to sound terrible, but I have two things most people desperately want but can only dream of. And both resulted from dumb luck, not anything I've done to deserve them: looks and money. Well . . . looks now, and money later. It is not always easy."

"Quite a burden," Mark replied and instantly regretted it.

She ignored the sarcasm. "Because I'm the daughter of Walter Lowndes, people are immediately prepared to dislike me. Or play up to me. Either way it's annoying. And the looks, the red hair and the . . . Anyway, people are seldom ready to admit that I can be anything but a bimbo or an airhead. I won't ask you what Karen said, but I'm ready to bet you believed her the moment you saw me."

"Really," he said. "It's not like that." She was making him uneasy with her obvious knowledge of his secret thoughts.

She dismissed his comment with a look, then asked, "Why aren't you riding?"

"I wanted to see your father. But he's not here. Or so his handlers keep telling me."

"Oh, he's here. I was just talking to him in his office. But his comings and goings can be difficult to chart. He's gotten to the point where he spends very little time in Colorado now. All his friends are back east." She was standing so close he could smell her hair—wild raspberries—and see a light reddening at the tips of her fingers where she tightly grasped the rail. Her nails were clear, her skin soft and lightly freckled.

"He's ignoring me," Mark added, turning away, trying not to stare. "He's pretending I don't exist."

"Why would he do that?"

Mark shrugged, glanced quickly at her pale face with its questioning eyes. "You tell me. He's your dad. I've never even seen him. He's a sort of phantom, as far as I'm concerned. Or a mad feudal landowner ensconced in his mountaintop castle."

The words caught her fancy and she repeated them with a laugh. "Phantomlike. Feudal. I never thought of him like that but maybe you're right. He's certainly not your typical *Brady Bunch* dad. I'm afraid you will disapprove of him."

"And your mother?"

"Long dead. Just me and Popsie. Like you and Lisa. Such fun that can be. Of course, I live in town now and he lives here—or reigns, as you would have it—with his koi, and dreams of magic and immortality, creating a piece of the earth's surface that will live forever in people's minds, tra-la, tra-la."

"You don't like him?"

"Love him. Dear old Dad." She put her hand on his arm. "Are you doing anything tomorrow morning?"

"Why?"

"You act as though I'm going to seduce you on Main Street. See? You do believe what you've been told." She squeezed his arm gently, then released it. "Actually, I thought I'd do something even more fun and bring you together with the famous and feudal Walter Lowndes. Or would you rather be seduced? That would confirm your girlfriend's worst expectations. Of me, if not you."

"He'll see me?"

"If I tell him to. Putty in my fingers, and all that. But call first. Please. I'd better see what sort of mood he's in. I never know from day to day. Your girls are returning. I'll run off before being accused of all sorts of crimes against nature. I'm sure Walter will see you, but your expectations about that side of the family will be dealt a blow." She walked back toward the Lodge.

Mark saw Lisa's pony slip into the stables, Karen following at a distance. He jumped over the fence and crossed through the corral to the rear of the stables, and up toward the front where the pony was standing and breathing through the mouth. A man had his hands around Lisa's waist and lifted her from the saddle toward his body, then let her slowly slide until her feet hit the ground. When Mark saw that it was Les Cady he immediately exploded. *"Hey, goddamn it—"*

The older man turned, saw Mark, and his pale unshaven face reddened at once with anger.

Karen came in, leading her horse by the reins just as Mark rushed up. She looked from his sweaty face to Cady's furious expression, and finally to Lisa. "What's going on?"

"I—" Mark felt suddenly uneasy. What had Cady done, other than help Lisa off her horse? Still, he didn't want him touching his daughter; didn't want his hands on her body, didn't want him anywhere around her. "It's nothing," Mark said. "Forget it." He sounded out of breath. And felt like a fool.

Cady's tiny eyes bored into him with murderous intent. His hand brushed at the ineffectual mustache that lay beneath his nose. "Something you want to say, mister?"

"Forget it." Mark grabbed Lisa's arm, making her wince. "Let's go." He brushed past Cady, dragging his daughter with him.

"What in the world's going on?" Karen asked, handing her horse's reins to Cady and following Mark out of the stables. "What are you doing?"

"Let's get out of here."

They were striding toward Karen's Taurus. "You're hurting—" Lisa said.

Mark dropped her hand, feeling embarrassed, then angry at his insensitivity. "I saw Cady and—" He jerked his head toward Lisa. "I overreacted. Sorry."

"I'm not the one who you should be telling."

"If he's what people say, there's no way I'm apologizing. Not to someone who destroys a childhood. Not a chance in hell."

Karen took Lisa's hand, put her other hand in Mark's, and tried to bring about a lessening of tension. "Let's go back to my place, boys and girls, and try to relax. I've got a half gallon of French vanilla, a quart of whipped cream, and a pint of chocolate sauce. Do you think we can do anything with that?"

51

Thinking, Micah Rollins always felt, was more participant activity than spectator sport, and facilitated by physical exertion. So, eyes half-closed, he strode a well-worn path in his office as his mind tried to work out the implications of all that had happened in the past two days. Because it bothered the hell out of him that there were things going on around here he didn't understand. Still, if he handled everything with the proper degree of care, Walter Lowndes was going to take a tumble and no one would even suspect Micah's role in it. Which would make folks in Harmony happier than a pig in shit. The bigger they are, the harder they fall, and the louder the applause. And this one will be about 9.0 on the Richter scale.

Compared to which Caroline's plunge to earth would be like a sparrow falling from a tree. Only the gods would notice. Not that they'd give a damn.

His pace picked up and he began to strike his right hand against his leg.

The kicker in all this, of course, was the girl. Damn cute little thing. What was her name? Lisa, yes. . . .

Jesus, who'd have thought?

Well, she's here. Got to deal with it.

He plucked a tan cowboy hat off a rack on the wall, jammed it neatly on his large head, and stared into a mirror that had been framed with distressed pine and rusty barbed wire. He didn't much look like Roy or Gene or the Duke or any other cowboy hero, he had to admit. Got to be honest about it. A big man, but with puffy cheeks, wide forehead, and pinkish skin. No, Micah looked more like someone they'd cast as a banker or saloon owner. Best friend, maybe, or comic relief. To Micah, though, staring into the mirror, he looked like . . . a resort owner. Yes sir, the sole owner of a multimillion-dollar resort in the heart of the Rockies. *Exactly* what he looked like.

But my, he was getting tired of playing the hayseed. That shucks–and–by–golly line of patter was getting harder and harder to keep up. Especially since folks never appreciated what he'd accomplished in life—particularly these last two or three years. Of course, someday people would know. There wasn't any point in Walter Lowndes being Harmony's only famous resident.

And that time was drawing near. So, yeah, he could keep up the act a while longer. Well, "act" wasn't exactly the right word. Micah truly did admire much about the world of his youth. A simpler time, a calmer time. A time, people liked to say, when you knew who the good guys and bad guys were.

Unlike nowadays.

Where, for example, someone had killed poor old Bill, and as far as Micah could tell, there wasn't a damn reason for it. That truly did bother him. Because obviously there *was* a reason. Meaning something was going on around here he didn't understand. Someone Micah knew, probably a friend of his, did not mind killing a harmless old man.

You just don't know who the bad guys are anymore. Has to have something to do with Ritter and his daughter. But what? *damn it.*

Kinda makes a man watch his back.

And who the hell had kept that copy of the *Courier* for thirty damn years and sent it to Ritter? Micah thought he had gotten rid of the only copies of the paper earlier this week. Well, hell, he'd worry about it later. The immediate problem now was how to get rid of Walter Lowndes.

And—sorry to say—Caroline.

Which is where young Lisa Ritter came in. Of course, Lisa was *in* the moment she arrived in town. The girl was the fuse everyone in Harmony was holding their breath waiting to see ignite. And Micah had the match.

But first he had to take care of Cheryl McAfee.

Soon as he heard the name from Caroline, who'd heard it from Karen, he remembered her. Cheryl McAfee. *Kind of girl we called a PT in high school, prick tease. Go out with a guy and get him all hot but not let him put the fire out.*

That's what he had been told, anyway. The gal never would go out with him. Of course, Micah was a few years older but she was too stuck-up for him, anyway. *Weren't you, Cheryl? Wouldn't give me the time of day.*

Well, hey, babe. Time for you to get your comeuppance. Thirty years late, so there'll be a little compound interest to pay.

Micah sat down suddenly, dropped his feet on top of the specially-made coffee table, tipped back his cowboy hat with a flick of his thumb, and smiled happily. *Got me a lot of balls in the air right now, got to keep 'em all spinning at the same time. Going to take some planning.*

As he thought about it, he began to picture the Ice Castle, the restaurant he was building for Walter Lowndes on top of the mountain. *Damn,* he thought. *I can see where that's going to be mighty important to all of us.*

Hey, Cheryl! You're about to star in a movie. "Written and directed by Micah Rollins." You betcha.

Gotta plan your role out first.

Gonna make you a star!

But I have to find out where the hell you live first, don't I?

Reckon Mark Ritter will do that for us.

Yes sir! "Written and directed by Micah Rollins. Assistant director, Mark Ritter. Best girl, pretty young Lisa."

Roll 'em! . . .

52

Mark wandered back and forth in the kitchen, drinking a Coors Gold and nibbling absently on tortilla chips while Karen and Lisa conspired together to construct elaborate hot-fudge sundaes. He was still feeling a piercing of guilt at lashing out at Les Cady which made him edgy and angry at himself, along with a growing excitement about finally meeting Walter Lowndes in the morning. Lisa and Karen were chattering loudly, opening and closing the refrigerator, and spooning things into bowls. He glanced over at them and winced when he saw what they were doing. "Don't you want to add a little ice cream to your fudge?"

"You do it your way, we'll do it ours. Chocolate's a girl thing."

The large golden dog wandered into the kitchen and licked whipped cream from one of the bowls. "Down, Remington," Karen said, and the dog remained where he was.

"Guess I'll have another beer." He opened the refrigerator and yanked out a bottle. "Coors," he muttered to himself. "A guy thing."

"Anyway," Karen added, pushing the dog away and flicking her tongue against a quivering mound of whipped cream, "chocolate is supposed to have an aphrodisiac effect on the chemicals of the brain. I would have thought you'd be interested in testing the theory. I guess you're not, though." She stuck her tongue out at him.

"What's *disiac?*" Lisa asked as she dipped her spoon into the sundae.

Mark popped the top off the bottle. "Something to do with chemistry. And brains. Ask Karen. It's too complicated for me." He sat down at the table and watched the enjoyment on his daughter's face as she dug into her ice cream. "Simple pleasures," he muttered, and knew he sounded angry or resentful, but his mind had moved on from Walter Lowndes to Cheryl McAfee.

"Nothing simple about it," Karen told him. She smiled, determined not to be upset by his attitude. "We're dealing with very complex issues here: taste buds, neurons, chocolate. Life itself. What more could you ask for?"

Mark held the bottle up, label forward, like a TV announcer and said sourly, "Beer." He rose suddenly, and began to pace again.

Karen shook her head. "We girls choose to ignore your boorishness."

Lisa looked suddenly at her father. "I can go horseback-riding again, can't I? You're not mad at me, are you?"

Mark patted her on the shoulder. Why did he feel so terrible every time his daughter looked at him like that? "Of course I'm not mad at you, hon. I just lost my temper back there. I've got a lot on my mind."

Karen shot him a look.

He picked up on her question. "Maybe I'll try her again tomorrow.

We'll see." Then without planning he said, "What do you think of Mason Hightower?"

She looked at him as if it were the last thing she'd expected him to ask. "He's okay. I like him, I guess—"

"Do you trust him?" There was a demanding quality to his voice that made her narrow her eyes as she watched him pace back and forth.

"Sure. Don't you?"

"I don't know. There's something there that bothers me, though. So far I can't put my finger on it. But I will. What about Noel Atchison? You trust him?"

"Is your paranoia level up tonight? Perhaps you could try medication." She slid her sundae in his direction.

Mark shook his head, finished the beer, plunked the bottle down. "I guess I don't trust anyone who lived here in the sixties."

Karen smiled and sucked whipped cream off her spoon with an extended humming sound. "Does that mean you do trust nubile young Janis? I saw her working her feminine wiles on you as we rode back tonight. Men are such suckers for that red hair and those big . . . eyes."

Mark's pace increased as he strode back and forth in the kitchen. It annoyed him when Karen spoke like this, and he recalled Janis's remark about people resenting her looks and wealth. He cast a quick glance back at Karen. "She's going to do what you couldn't, and get me in to see the infamous Walter tomorrow. Your pal, ex-employer, and three-year traveling companion."

Karen looked steadily at him. "Well, good. I guess. I won't be able to watch Lisa when you're with him, though. I'll be in and out of the office all day. But what's the point of even talking to him now? You know who your father was. You know who your mother is. You know where she is. And you know she doesn't want to see you."

Mark sat down suddenly and stared into her face. "But not what she's like. Or what Carl Stark was like. Walter Lowndes is older than Cheryl but he'd have known her. This is a small town, everyone knew everyone else. He'd know my father. He bought Stark's land from the estate. He can tell me what he remembers about them."

"Now that you know who your parents were, you could probably get that information from a dozen people." She shook her head suddenly and gave a little laugh. "I'm acting like someone from an old melodrama, aren't I? I just didn't want you hanging around slinky and sexy Janis. Forget what I said. Of course you should talk to Walter. Who knows Harmony better than the man who developed it?" She reached over, held his hand, and smiled. "It's the chocolate affecting my brain. I'm not responsible for anything I say. Or do. I feel myself losing control even as we speak." She glanced at the kitchen clock, widened her eyes theatrically, and sounded like a character from *Gone with the Wind* as she dredged up a broad southern accent. "My, how late it's gotten. Don't you think you two ought to spend the night here rather than go all the way back to your drafty old motel room?"

Mark turned a questioning look on Lisa who had just finished the last spoonful of ice cream. She asked, "Can I take a bath? I haven't had one in *days!*"

Mark smiled at her, feeling one of those inexplicable piercings of parental love that seemed to slow his heartbeat to zero. "Sure you can, hon. Maybe I'll take a shower later."

Karen squeezed his hand. "I'll see to it." She went into the bathroom and started the water. "How about peach bubble bath?" she yelled, and Lisa squealed in delight as she hopped off her chair and went into the bathroom.

Later, as Lisa splashed in the tub, Mark and Karen lounged on the couch, and Karen flicked on the TV. "Background noise," she said conspiratorially, and snuggled into him, her face inches from his. "I haven't had to do that since boys came over to the house when I was fifteen and my dad would come downstairs when he heard a spring in the couch squeak." She kissed him, then playfully bit his lower lip. "Why have I felt you've been ignoring me? It makes a girl feel awfully annoyed, you know."

"It probably looks like that," Mark conceded. "I know this sounds stupid but I've had a lot on my mind. My mother—"

"Understandable." Her tongue darted against his chin, then traced a path down his neck. She undid the top button of his shirt and left a trail of heat down his chest. The southern accent returned. "Just make some room in your little ol' mind for me. Okay? If you need to push anything out of consciousness you can delete your fantasies of nasty ol' Janis Lowndes."

Mark laughed. "It's not like that."

"Liar, liar, pants on fire." She bit him on the chest.

Mark shifted on the couch so her body slipped suddenly under his, and her back sank into the soft cushions. His lips brushed against hers, and her mouth opened; the feel of his tongue was like a jolt of electricity and she jerked his midsection sharply into hers. "I feel your interest rising."

He kissed her neck, and she began to feel breathless. "I was right," she managed after a moment.

"About what?"

"Pants on fire." She smiled and held his head up so she could look into his face. "What time do seven-year-olds go to bed?"

"None too soon."

"What time do you go to bed?"

"None too soon."

"I can't wait."

Water splashed in the tub.

"I guess we'll have to," he said, lifting up, and felt stupidly guilty, like a child caught being bad.

She pulled him closer. "Let's make the time pass while Lisa's in the tub. Just remember, I haven't done this for months. I have a short fuse."

"Try what Victorian brides were told by their mothers: Turn your mind to thoughts of the Empire."

Ten minutes later they heard water flowing out of the old-fashioned cast-iron tub, and Lisa yelled, "What am I supposed to wear to bed?"

Karen stood and smoothed her blouse. "Good question. I don't have any children's clothes."

"Maybe you could borrow some from Les Cady."

"Not funny. Well . . . maybe just a little."

Mark rose also. "She can sleep in her T-shirt and panties. We'll change tomorrow morning in our room. If you have a washing machine I'm going to have to use it anyway. We've been away for a while."

After Lisa was put in the spare bedroom, Karen said, "She scared the heck out of me with a nightmare last night, screaming about something in her sleep."

"Monsters," Mark said. "Just a thing she's going through."

"Nothing to worry about?"

"I don't think so."

"How long does it usually take her to fall asleep?"

"Six to eight seconds."

"Good." She led him into the other bedroom. "Let's see who can undress the fastest."

* * *

An hour later Karen drew her knees up and smiled, "Time for your shower?"

"Not yet. I'm still testing fuses."

"Each time it gets quicker. Must be the chocolate."

"Hooray for Hersheys."

At one A.M. they showered together, a slow, soapy dance that culminated the way all their previous diversions culminated. Karen murmured, "Australia, New Zealand, Kenya, Singapore . . ."

"Hmmm?"

"The Empire. Lord, I love the English."

As the water drilled into their bodies, she added, "I think I'll call in sore tomorrow."

"A new employee benefit?"

"If Noel doesn't go for it I'll write a story about him lusting after Janis. Who you will never look at like *that* again. I saw your eyes bulging."

"Never have, never will."

"Liar . . . liar . . . liar. And it wasn't just your eyes bulging. *Ummmmmm.* Hong Kong, Cuba . . ."

"Cuba was never part of the Empire."

"Let's pretend. Estonia, Mississippi . . ."

Mark had dried off when Karen came out of the bedroom holding Lisa's pants. "I'll hang these up," she said, then felt something in the rear pocket. She pulled out a piece of paper, unfolded it, and began to shake.

"What—?" Mark asked. He took the paper from her.

Block printing on lined binder paper like a child would use at school:

I LIKE YOU LISA. I WANT TO SEE YOU AGAIN. POOH BEAR.

"That goddamn Cady!" His voice trembled. "He must have put it in her pocket when he was helping her off the horse." His mind raced, sweat broke out over his body, and the room began to sway. "I'll kill him. Goddamn it, I'll kill him."

"Take it to the police tomorrow. Let them handle it."

"Not a chance. *I'll* take care of it. He's been doing this for thirty years, for Christ's sake. Where have the police been? Everybody knows it's him. My God, he killed a girl."

"So what are you going to do? Shoot him? Be reasonable!"

He stared at her as she swam in and out of his vision, and his heart pounded uncontrollably. Hurriedly, he pulled on his underpants.

Alarm raced through her. "What are you going to do?"

"Ask Lisa. Ask her what he did to her."

"She's asleep!"

"I don't care."

"But nothing happened. He didn't *do* anything. I was with her all the time."

He glared at her with sudden fury. "Were you with her when he had his hands all over her?"

"He was helping her off the horse. She couldn't get off by herself. What did you expect him to do?"

"I expected *you* to help rather than let some child molester grab her. My God, Karen, I trusted my daughter with you." He started toward the door.

"Let her sleep, Mark. You can ask her in the morning."

But he was already in the other bedroom. "Lisa, Lisa, wake up." He dropped to his knees and shook her arm.

"Daddy . . . ?" Her eyes came open, blinked, widened when she saw his bare torso. "What?" She pushed uneasily onto her elbow.

Mark put his hand on her shoulder. "Lisa, who is Pooh Bear?"

"Pooh Bear? Winnie the Pooh." She rubbed at her eyes with her knuckles.

"Did you talk to a man named Pooh Bear at the stables?"

She shook her head in confusion. "No. I talked to Karen."

"Yes, yes, I know. But when that man helped you off the horse, did he say he was Pooh Bear?"

She again shook her head and a look of concern came over her as Karen came in the room in a white terry-cloth robe, wet hair hanging around her shoulders.

Mark's hand tightened on Lisa's bicep. "Listen to me. Did Les Cady—the man at the stables—talk to you today? Did he talk to you anywhere at all?"

The little girl looked from Karen to Mark and winced at the pressure on her arm. "No!"

"Did a man touch you?"

"No!" She was getting disturbed.

"You're scaring her," Karen said, and Mark threw her an angry look, then showed Lisa the note he found. "Have you seen this?"

She sat all the way up. " 'I like you . . .' " She read aloud, then her face broke into a smile. "Did you write it for me?"

Mark's emotion broke, like a dam suddenly giving way under pressure. "No, I didn't write it. . . . I don't know who wrote it, honey. But if anyone talks to you like this, if he says he likes you, I want you to tell me. Will you promise me that?" She did. "And if anyone touches you—"

"Like you told me?"

"Yes. Like I've told you. If anyone touches you, tell them to stop. And then what?"

"Tell you."

"Perfect!" He gave his daughter a hug. "You got an A on your test. Smartest kid in the world. Now go back to sleep."

He waited until her head was on the pillow, then bent and kissed her cheek. "How much do I love you?"

"More than a million dollars and a million years," she said automatically.

"Better than that. More than a million hot-fudge sundaes."

But she was already asleep.

Mark stood looking at her a minute, then took Karen's hand and walked back to the other bedroom. "Sorry. Sometimes I overreact, I guess."

"There's nothing to apologize for. Anyone who wouldn't overreact in a situation like that doesn't deserve to be a parent. But you need to handle this like an adult tomorrow."

"I'll see Chavez. But what the hell is he going to do? I doubt this note is a crime. Not in itself."

"But at least he can let Cady know he's being watched. Perhaps that will be enough."

"Yeah," Mark said. "Perhaps." But knew for a certainty she was wrong.

53

Janis Lowndes caught Bobby Sample admiring his nude body in the mirrored wall of her top-floor condo two miles from the resort. "Which do you like best?"

"Which what, babe?"

"Muscle, Bobby. What else is worth looking at in your world?"

"You *know* which one is best, babe. It's your favorite, too. Ready for another ride or did I wear you out?"

She closed her eyes, listened to a Vivaldi violin concerto playing in her mind, tried to fit the words of a Bob Dylan song to it, finally shook her head and sunk into a Smashing Pumpkins CD, replaying the video behind her eyes.

Sample stood up, went to the mirrored wall, flexed his biceps, squatted, tensed his legs, rose, and silently accepted the applause of the nation. Could've been a Mr. America, or Mr. Universe if he hadn't gone into police work. Could've been a star! He clasped his hands above his head and applied enough pressure to make the muscles up and down his arms bulge, then slowly rotated as though on a turntable. "Hercules," he announced. "A Greek God." He turned to Janis and smiled. "Like what you see?"

God, she thought with an inward sigh, *I must be mad. How did I ever start with Bobby?* Boredom? Loneliness? It didn't make any difference. It was time to bring this bizarre pairing to an end. But doing so without the unpredictable Bobby turning violent was going to take some tact.

"Hey," Bobby said. "I asked if you like what you see."

Janis opened her eyes for only a second. "Flaccid."

" 'Fuck's that mean?"

"Means you can't."

"Can't what?"

"Think about it for a minute, Bobby. Give it the old college try." She sat up, swung her bare legs over the side of the bed, mystical lines from William Blake weaving threads of gold through the fragments of the Smashing Pumpkins song. She put her chin in her hands and closed her perfect green eyes, the wind from an open window drying the perspiration on her thighs and breasts. Bobby was a million miles away, a dream, a fantasy that was fading quickly.

Sample looked at her without comprehension, not knowing if he should be angry or not. Just to be safe he decided he better be. "Who the hell are you to act like I'm some dumb fuck? You sit in your store all day and make what? Fifty bucks?"

She returned reluctantly to the tedium of the present. "And you, Bobby? Are you getting rich giving parking tickets to tourists? Are you the scourge of Harmony?" She pushed off the bed, walked naked to the wall, punched a button on the built-in stereo system. Gregorian chants sprung suddenly from a dozen hidden speakers, the mysterious harmonies instantly soothing.

"Turn that fuckin' boogie music off. It gives me the creeps."

"It would touch your soul if you had one, Bobby. It's almost a thousand years old."

"The only thing I want touched is between my legs. And stop actin' like I'm such a dumbshit. I made more money in the last two weeks than you made in six months."

"Did you really, Bobby? Then I take it all back." She put her palm on his sweaty chest. "My hero! My own Ionic Donald Trump. Such a wily devil you are." She grabbed a handful of chest hair and pulled.

He grimaced, and seized her wrist, twisting painfully. "Don't fuck with me, Janis."

"Or what, Bobby? Tell me the 'or what' part. Tell me about blood, broken bones, and dreams destroyed. Tell me how my life will be ruined!"

He flung her on the bed. "I ain't kiddin' you, Janis. Don't mess with me. I ain't just some dumb local cop anymore. Got me a new job."

Her eyes closed and she rolled onto her stomach. "Doing what, my hero?"

"Doing what no one else around here has the balls to do."

Janis turned over at once and clapped her hands gleefully. "You get to tell my dad off! Good for you! Such courage!"

Sample looked at her with disgust, then cast around for his clothes. He grabbed his trousers and climbed into them without underwear.

"But Bobby, I won't be able to tell what you have the balls for if you cover up like that. I know! I'll do a comparison. Bobby's courageous and valiant balls against—oh, I don't know. The eighth grade at the middle school."

"You already started with Ritter, didn't you? Seen you hanging around him, acting all sexy. I know you was with him last night when I called, Janis. Heard him laughing in the background."

She got up suddenly, went to the mirror, stared at her one hundred and eight pounds a moment, then struck a pose, flexing her biceps like Sample as her bright red hair fell almost to her butt. "But it wasn't. I was with Todd Kachen. He's been such a lonely boy since Karen kicked him out. But so eager, so hard, and full of energy!"

Sample looked at her hatefully. "Someday you'll be sorry you treated me like this, Janis. I'm more important than you think I am."

But Janis was lost again in music, this time "Quartet for End of Time" by Messiaen, and Dylan's "Sad Eyed Lady of the Low-lands." She lay on her back, eyes closed, moving slowly to the music. Bobby pulled his pants off, came over to the bed, and crawled between her legs. Her eyes were still closed, and her body tense, when he entered her, and she saw for the briefest instant in her mind not Bobby Sample, but Mark Ritter, then a mélange of faces as the music again took over, and she drifted through a dozen centuries, and realities.

54

Karen awoke on top of the covers, her hand on Mark's chest, and her head on his arm. She sat up suddenly, heart pounding, and looked at the digital clock next to the bed. "Oh my God, no," she whispered to herself. "No! Please!"

Mark sat up. "What?"

"Don't say anything. Please! Not a word." She grabbed his wrist and squeezed. "Promise me."

"What—?"

"Someone's at the door." She was jumping out of bed, hurriedly getting into a robe.

Mark could hear it now, a door opening and closing. Before he could say anything she whispered, "Todd."

Mark sank back. Then he started to get up.

"Please." She came back to the bed, pleading. "Don't say a word. Don't get out of bed. Just lay here. I'll get rid of him. Whatever you do, don't go in there!"

Before he could say anything she was gone, quietly shutting the door behind her.

Voices from the living room. A light switched on, bled under the door.

Mark sat hurriedly in the darkness. Where was his underwear?

More voices. Angry. Sounds—like a piece of furniture bumped into or moved.

Mark stood up, felt on the floor for his underpants, slipped them on.

Karen said something and Kachen grunted.

Mark went to the door and listened.

". . . out of here, Todd. I'll call Chavez if you don't. I mean it."

"Fuck you, Karen. This is my house too. I can do what I fucking well want, and what I want is you. You're still my wife."

"Todd—"

"You want to do it in the bedroom or here on the floor? You used to like it here. Remember?"

"You're drunk."

"You're a bitch. Does that make us even?"

"I warned you."

"Warned me what? You been too busy dickin' that dumb fuck Ritter to pay attention to anything. I hear you don't hardly come to work no more, you're all the time with him. What's the deal? You think he's going to take you out of Harmony, maybe to Seattle? She-it! You're just something for him to do while he's here, like reading the paper or playing solitaire. He don't like you no more than you like Walter Lowndes."

"Or Bobby Sample? He's been coming on to me every day, you know. Keeps asking me to go over to his place for the night. He's not the great friend you think he is, Todd. Bobby's out for himself. Like all you cops."

"No good, Karen. Bobby wouldn't fuck me over. But you would. Fact is, you're going to do your wifely duties right now."

"Dream on—"

The sound of a crash, a bell, Karen's muted shriek as the phone hit the floor.

Mark stepped through the door. Karen seemed to shrink. Todd Kachen, in uniform, looked surprised, then laughed. "Holy shit, look at the dude from Seattle. No wonder you didn't want to tumble, Karen. The stockbroker here done wore you out. Never did take long, did it? You was always good for about five minutes then it was roll over and go to sleep."

"Go home, Todd. You're drunk. You can hardly walk."

"Shut the fuck up, Karen. Never could stand to hear you whine."

Karen picked up the phone and quickly dialed a number but Todd pulled the cord, yanking it out of her hands.

Mark took a step forward but Karen said, "No, please. He'll kill you."

Kachen lost interest in Karen and advanced unsteadily toward Mark. "Hey, don't pay her no attention, dude. You and me can decide this ourselves. Who gets the pretty lady? Just like the Old West. Showdown!"

Karen raised her voice. "Todd, you're drunk. Go home. I'm calling Chavez right now."

"Hang on, girl. You and me got things to do yet tonight. Let me take care of the city dude first."

Kachen took several steps toward Mark who didn't move. Then he lunged forward, his fist raised, and Mark hit him with the side of the hand in the Adam's apple. The man dropped at once to the floor, gasping for breath. Mark watched as he writhed and moaned. His face was turning red.

"What did you do?" Karen screamed in alarm. "He can't breathe. Look at him."

Mark said, "What do you want to do with him?"

"Do with him?" She sounded hysterical. "Is he going to die?"

"I don't know. Depends how hard I hit him. He's still breathing. Sort of."

Kachen's feet were moving but his face was purple. He couldn't seem to get air in his lungs. Mark dropped to one knee and felt the man's neck. "I don't think it's serious. But if the Adam's apple is driven too far back it can cut off his air. I thought it better than the Old West showdown he wanted. Quicker, anyway."

"Where did you learn that?"

"Survival training. Never had to do it for real, though. Of course, him being drunk made it easy."

Kachen moaned, was able to get his hands to his neck.

Mark said, "Did you call Chavez?"

She shook her head. "How would I know his number? I dialed Domino's."

"Is Todd's car outside?"

She glanced out the window. "It's his personal car. I guess he was getting off shift and stopped at Bobby's or someplace to drink. Typically stupid thing to do in uniform."

"Let's get him home. Grab his feet."

"And just drop him at his house?"

"You got a better idea?"

"The emergency room."

Mark used his foot to roll Kachen on his stomach. "I don't think he needs it. He'd be in a coma by now if it was that serious. Tomorrow he'll have a red neck, which is poetic justice, and feel as if he was struck in the Adam's apple by a hammer. Probably won't want to eat much for a few days. But he'll get over it. You better tell Chavez, though, or you'll have to deal with him again."

She shook her head. "I thought you were a stockbroker."

"We're a fearsome bunch. Especially in a bear market. Grab his feet."

Mark opened the front door. "I hope your neighbors aren't watching. I'm not dressed for formal introductions."

She looked at his underpants. "You're not dressed for anything. Well . . . a few things."

They carried Todd in the darkness to his car. He was beginning to come around. "You bastard. . . . Cheap fucking shot." He could barely speak, and began to cough.

"Not so, Todd. Very good shot." They laid him in the backseat. Mark asked, "How far to his house?"

"He's renting a condo about a mile away. I'll show you."

"No. I'll follow. You drive your car. Lock the front door, though. Lisa's asleep."

They left Kachen in his car, in the condo parking space. Mark said to him, "You might want to let a doctor look at that tomorrow."

Kachen swore at him in guttural tones.

Mark got in next to Karen and she headed back to her house. "Tomorrow," she said, "Todd will be telling people he stopped five burglars trying to break into a supermarket, and they got away after holding him down and kicking him in the throat."

"I was thinking of what you said about us being better off not needing the cops. Other than Hector Chavez, I don't think there's a one who'd lift a finger to help us."

She said, "I wouldn't even trust Chavez anymore. We're on our own now, pal."

V

55

As Les Cady's note, with its perfect third-grade printing, stared up at him from the coffee table, Mark dialed directory assistance while Karen made breakfast for Lisa. "I'm afraid all I have is Pop Tarts or Raisin Bran."

"Oh, I *love* Pop Tarts. Dad won't buy them."

Karen pushed down the toaster tab. "Evil man. He probably doesn't supply your daily dose of Häagen-Dazs, either. Tell him girls need to keep their calcium up."

Mark didn't hear her as he jotted down the number and immediately began dialing. "Harmony Police Department."

"I'd like to talk to Chief Chavez." His eyes went again to the note—*I LIKE YOU LISA*—and his fingers tightened on the receiver.

"*Acting* Chief Chavez. He isn't in yet. It's only seven-thirty. You wanna leave your name and number?"

Mark felt a moment of rage. *My daughter's being threatened by a sexual predator and you want me to wait for a return call?* But it would be useless to ask for Chavez's home number. He forced his voice into a semblance of normalcy. "Mark Ritter." He read off the number on the phone and there was a long silence.

"That ain't your number, asshole. It's Todd's."

"Just give it to Chavez. And tell him it's important."

"Yeah? Maybe I will. And maybe I'll tell Todd to stop by his house and see you instead. He's got a right to come in his own house and toss out an asshole intruder. Right?"

"I don't know. Why don't you ask him? And make sure *Chief* Chavez gets the number as soon as he comes in." He hung up and looked over to the kitchen. "I just chatted with a friend of Todd's. Seemed like a civil fellow, polite and friendly. Like most Harmony cops."

"If he's on the front desk at seven-thirty in the morning it means he screwed up. Probably called his boss a wetback."

"He thought Todd might want to visit later. Maybe he'll bring some ice cream. It's supposed to be good for sore throats."

"Actually," she said, "I have a court order keeping him a thousand feet away from me."

"Didn't help last night. Is the house on the court order?"

"I didn't think about it."

"Words meant for a tombstone." He pinched the bridge of his nose and brooded a moment. "I guess I'm going to miss my run this morning."

"You got your exercise last night. With Todd. With me, too, come to think of it."

"Not the same thing." He stood up, sat down at once, and made a decision. Or voiced a decision made last night as he lay next to Karen, staring into the darkness. "I'm going to call my mother again."

"It's only six-thirty in California." There seemed to be a slight catch in her voice, as though she was surprised, or didn't want him to make the call.

"I want to be sure I get her."

"You want Lisa or me to go into the other room?"

"Stick around. I need some moral support. I don't want to hang up again." He dialed the number while Karen watched from the kitchen. Even Lisa turned from the television.

As it started to ring he felt a line of sweat break out on his back and ribs. He swiveled away from his two onlookers and faced the window. On the fourth ring a recorded voice answered with the phone number, no name. His mother's voice. He started to hang up, then pulled the phone back and, speaking quickly, said, "This is Mark Ritter. I don't want to cause trouble for you. I only want to talk. Please." He paused, then added, "I have a seven-year-old daughter. We'd both like to talk to you." There had to be something else to say but suddenly he couldn't think clearly. He added Karen's number and the motel number, then hung up and sat back, exhausted. Why had that been so difficult for him to do? But it was, and he was sweating profusely.

"Now we wait," Karen said evenly and, as though talking to a business acquaintance, asked, "Do you want some coffee?"

"I'm too wired for caffeine. Toast maybe." He leaned forward, grabbed the phone again, and tried directory assistance for a home number for Micah Rollins but there was none. Strike three with the phone for this morning. "Guess I'll have to go out there."

"Why?"

"To find out why the hell he lied to me. Why the big cock-and-bull story about a fire and the Contrells? Why does he give a damn what I think?"

"Maybe Cheryl can tell you."

"Maybe." He stood up suddenly, nervous and unsettled. "What are your plans today?"

"Work. Remember that? Noel sure does. He's getting snippy about the time I've spent out of the office."

"God!" He winced and shook his head as he remembered. "I should check in with my work, too. It's been awhile." How long? he wondered. Two weeks? He picked up the phone again and dialed his office number.

It would have been better to have remained out of touch. Where the hell had he been? his boss wanted to know. What were his customers supposed to think? They relied on him for investment advice and he can't be found. These were some of the most important people in Seattle. Big accounts. Merrill Lynch wasn't about to leave them high and dry. No, of course not, Mark told him, but he couldn't return right away. He had family matters to clear up. A major emergency. *When?* A week, Mark guessed. But his boss was having none of it. "Today's Thursday, Ritter. Be at your desk Monday morning or you're out of here."

And so much for winning the sales contest. He hung up feeling nothing. The job was suddenly meaningless. He was going to talk to his mother, find out what led her to give him up without a fight. Or had there been a fight? And why hadn't she tried to find him? Wasn't she curious even once in the past thirty years?

And—he felt the anger rising again—he was going to find out why the hell Micah lied to him. Maybe Cheryl could—

The phone rang. "That you, Mark? I called the motel and couldn't find you. Thought maybe Karen would know where you're hiding out."

"Mason?"

"Pretty early for a lawyer, ain't it? But I couldn't sleep well last night. Conscience, I guess. Guilt. I know, another alien concept for attorneys, but there it is. Anyway, I need to talk to you. First thing this morning if that's all right with you?"

"Sure. Nine o'clock?"

"That'd be dandy. Well, 'dandy' ain't the word. What the hell, see you at nine."

Lisa waited in the outer office with Sally as Mason paced an agitated path on his thick carpet. "Coulda told you before but decided not to. Makes Daddy look kinda bad—well, real bad, I guess. And Eleanor Dahlquist. And Cheryl's mom and . . ." He sat down across from Mark, a pained look on his face.

"Thing is, there was some money changed hands when you did. Cheryl gave up her baby—you—and, like I said, being just a kid herself, legally, didn't have any say in things in those days. Her mom made the decision for her. And collected three thousand dollars from the Ritters."

"Child-selling?" Mark was disbelieving. "That's why I was given up? Because somebody *sold* me?"

"And my daddy collected one thousand dollars, as did Eleanor Dahlquist."

"Jesus."

"Illegal as hell, of course, the way it was handled. And probably why the Ritters kept it a secret. Could have been big trouble for everyone. Even if it did turn out okay for everyone involved."

"Okay?" Mark bolted to his feet. "For God's sake, I was sold like a goddamn bar of soap or a used car. That's *Okay?* Kick the tires, pay your money, and take a kid? No wonder my mother doesn't want to see me. She goddamn sold me. Who wants to be confronted with a used car he sold years ago?"

"Don't go blaming Cheryl, now. Like I say, she probably didn't have a say in any of this. It was *her* mom."

But Mark wasn't paying attention. "Three thousand dollars! What'd my sweet old grandmum do with it? Take a vacation? Buy some clothes?"

"Don't know what she spent it on. That was a lot of money in those days. Three or four months' salary for most folks. Seems to me the mom moved away about the time Cheryl was shipped off to boarding school. Sometime that summer anyway."

Mark was striding around the room. "Babies for sale! Who came up with that idea? Your dad?" He kicked an oak magazine rack, spilling the contents on the floor.

Mason was trying to rein in his own discomfort. "Can't say. From some notes I found in the file it looked like Eleanor Dahlquist had done this before. A number of times, I guess."

"Good old Eleanor. Jesus Christ!" He was yelling now. "A little thousand-dollar finder's fee and she'll round up a baby for you. Is she still in the business? How does she find buyers and sellers? Does she have a Web page, or advertise in the *Denver Post?*"

Hightower shrugged. "I wasn't about to ask her. She could get disbarred over this, of course. Or go to jail. It's still not legal, not the way she did it."

Mark flung himself in the chair and covered his eyes with the palms of his hands. "No wonder she didn't want me looking into things. I guess she was right. I should have left well enough alone."

"I reckon ninety percent of the people who start on a quest like yours say the same thing. Secrets are secret for a reason." He sat down on the couch.

Mark felt wrung out. He ran a hand through his sweaty hair. "I wasn't doing it only for me. It was for Lisa, too. She doesn't have any grandparents, no relatives at all except me. I wanted her to have a grandmother, someone to spoil her and love her and give her things—" He stood up abruptly as he remembered, and reached in his rear pocket. His hand was shaking. "I found this in Lisa's pocket last night. She says she doesn't know how it got there."

Hightower read it at a glance. "Les Cady?"

"He helped her off a pony at the resort last night. He must have put it in her pocket then. He had his hands all over her."

" 'Pooh Bear'? Does that mean anything to her?"

"Seems not to. I guess he was going to try to make contact with her later. He's had enough experience with this sort of thing. He'd know how to make a child trust him. And all kids love Winnie the Pooh."

Hightower was thoughtful. "Is there anyone but Cady who could have given it to her?"

"He was the only one besides Karen who was with her at the stables."

"What about before? Was she wearing the same clothes all day?"

"Sure." He paused. "We were a few places before then—out where Stallworth was killed, here, at the cafe."

"Who found the note? You or Lisa?"

"Karen. She picked the shorts off the bathroom floor and was about to hang them up."

Hightower started to say something, then changed his mind. He shook his head. "Well, don't let the girl out of your sight. Someone's been getting close to her."

"Exactly." He began pacing around the room again.

"Have you told Chavez about it?"

"Not yet. I might need your help there." He told the attorney about the continuing problem with Karen's husband. "It's not just Kachen, though. It's Bobby Sample and most of the department. They're going to give me trouble every time I try to see Chavez."

Hightower folded the note and put it in his pocket. "I'll talk to Chavez this morning. Something's going to have to be done about Cady."

"How about shooting him? Child molesters can't be 'reformed.' They're compulsive, they can't control themselves. Goddamn it, if he touches Lisa again I'll take care of it myself. I mean it. I don't care what happens to me." He glanced at his watch. "I better get going. I have to check in with Janis and see what time to come out to the resort. I'm meeting Walter Lowndes this morning."

Hightower grunted. "Finally got the legend of Harmony to agree to see you, huh? Ought to be interesting, you two, the mood you're in. Kinda wish I was there to watch."

56

Using the car phone Mark called Janis to see if the meeting with her father was still on. She didn't sound as positive as last night. "It'll be okay, I guess. But wait until at least ten-thirty. And keep it to twenty minutes or so. He's not feeling his best right now."

"Do I bow when entering and leaving?"

"Try to be civil. I'm taking a chance with this. Don't make me wish I hadn't."

* * *

With an hour to kill he stopped by the *Courier*. Karen was looking for something in the back so he sat down at the online terminal while Lisa amused herself with paper and scissors. A few minutes later B.J. Blake bustled in with a newspaper-sized cardboard portfolio. Noel Atchison looked up from his desk and said, "About time, B.J. We were about to go to press without you."

Blake plopped his portfolio down on a vacant desk, flipped it open, and took out a photo-ready full-page advertisement for Century 21–Harmony. "Yeah, sure, Noel, like you'd put out an issue with a blank last page." He held it up admiringly. "This is why folks buy your paper. Want to see what their land's worth. Ain't no news to speak of. Shoot, you don't even print comics. Oh, hi, Lisa. Learning how to be a reporter like Lois Lane?"

"Waiting for Dad," she said, sliding off her chair and looking bored.

Blake turned to see Mark getting up from the terminal. "Still checking up on old Rottweiler? Karen said you were obsessing."

Karen came in from the storage room. "I didn't say 'obsessing,' B.J. I said 'fascinated.'" She gave him a peck on the cheek. "There's a difference."

"I learned enough last time," Mark told him. "It got pretty repetitive after the twentieth article on the genius of Harmony."

Blake sat down and smiled at Karen. "Can't imagine there's anything magazine writers would know about him that you don't know. Didn't you make up most of his lies for him?"

"I did not make up lies! Maybe repeated some—"

B.J. was already into his impersonation. "Yes," he said, sounding vaguely Middle European, "I used to stand naked in ze voods and recite poetry to ze vermin. In German. And speak Greek at the creek to the sheep. Ze pigs, of course, speak Latin."

"I don't think it's a lie, B.J. I think he used to do things like that. Didn't he, Noel?"

Atchison took Blake's advertisement. "That's what folks were saying back then. Nature-boy Walter communing with the cosmos. Never saw it myself, though. Anyway, I've got to get to the printers. See you all later."

Mark came over and took a chair next to Karen. Blake said, "You don't look in the best of moods today. Still having mom problems?"

"Problems?" Mark asked. He arched his head back and closed his eyes. "Yeah, I guess you could say that. I just found out my mother put me up for sale when I was a baby. That's kind of a problem, isn't it? How much do you think a baby went for in 'sixty-eight?"

Blake looked at Karen, then back at Mark. "Couldn't tell you."

"Three thousand dollars, if he had all his fingers and toes. I guess that would have bought about thirty acres of prime land, from what you said earlier."

"Yeah. Guess so. That was a lifetime ago, though. Thirty acres in Harmony, if there were thirty vacant acres, would go for fifteen to twenty million now."

Mark opened his eyes. "Half a million an acre? Quite a jump."

"Well, we're surrounded on three sides by National Forest. And most of the land around the resort is already built on. Good parcels are at a premium. Got to go east of town to find something affordable. That's the main reason business is so shitty for Realtors here, unless they're into high-end resales, which I'm not. Not enough land to sell in town, and not enough folks who want to live out of town. All the yuppies want ski-in condos with heated walkways and home-delivered meals from three-star restaurants, not ranch or forest property."

"Still, a lot of people have gotten rich here."

"Oh, hell yeah. Old-timers mostly, though." He reached over and patted Karen's hand. "You ever notice that? It's the *old* old-timers. Not young 'uns like me and you. We struggle by and hope the same thing happens to us someday."

Mark said, "But none as rich as Lowndes?"

"Oh Lordy, no."

They were suddenly interrupted by a muted blast from the mountaintop. Karen shook her head. "That seems to be going on forever, doesn't it?"

B.J. glanced toward the window. "Having structural problems, from what I hear. Micah's construction company's doing the work, you know. Guess he's not real happy with the added expenses he's running into. But nobody's hung a building off a peak like Eagle Point before. It's got to be a pain. No access roads, either. Had to bring everything up by helicopter. Been nothing but trouble for a year."

"Couldn't happen to a more deserving man." Mark winced and

rubbed his neck as a headache began to build. *Tension,* he thought. From finally getting to see Lowndes, or from learning his mother sold him to the Ritters? Take your pick.

"Oh, I don't know about that," Blake replied. "I've known Micah all my life. Always liked him."

"B.J.," Karen said, getting up, "you like everyone. It's part of your appeal. Or part of your salesman's line of patter." She moved behind Mark and began to rub his shoulders and neck.

The comment seemed to cause him to think. "Well, I do like everybody. Everybody I know. Some folks I haven't met yet—Saddam Hussein, Charles Manson . . ."

"Which reminds me," Mark said, looking at the wall clock. "Time to see Harmony's own Maximum Leader, Generous Father, and famous, if reclusive, cultural icon. Why do I suddenly think it's not going to turn out the way I hoped?"

57

Janis was waiting in the resort parking lot, this time without her retro-hippie outfit but in white shorts, a loose green blouse without a bra, and leather sandals. She seemed nervous but put her arm through Mark's, pressing against his biceps, and began leading Lisa and him toward the lodge. "I'm doing this because you wanted me to. I'm not convinced it's a good idea. Bearding the lion in his own den. Isn't that what it's called? The important thing is never to show fear. Lions thrive on it, you know. Look him straight in his evil eye and make him back away." She squeezed his arm but when he looked at her face there was no expression; then she smiled so suddenly but so enigmatically he couldn't tell what to think. "I'm kidding. I guess. No need to be afraid of Walter. But people are. Sometimes he's a little erratic. Hell, why am I making excuses? You'll see."

She turned abruptly to Lisa and took the child's hand. "Did you enjoy your pony ride yesterday?"

"It was a horse. I want to do it again. But I want to go fast."

"Then you better wear a helmet. Horses can be dangerous, you know."

A sharp sound, as though metal slamming on metal, came towards them from the top of the mountain.

"It never seems to end, does it? Idiots in the state bureaucracy are afraid the whole restaurant could come tumbling down in a big snowstorm. Or earthquake. It's all delays and paper work and added cost, of course. None of which makes Dad happy. But then, little does anymore."

They mounted the broad steps to the main lodge building and went into the deserted and semidarkened reception hall, with its huge stone fireplace and unattended front desk. Janis took a ring of keys from her pocket, discovered the correct one, and used it to unlock the door Mark had tried earlier. "His office," she explained as she pulled it open. An extremely long corridor led toward the rear of the building. As they began to traverse it a voice boomed from the room beyond. *"That you, Janis?"*

She glanced into Mark's eyes, her own face suddenly drawn. "Whatever you think about him, you're wrong. Everyone is. But I suppose the truth could be worse. It depends on how you look at it."

"Time to walk around to the other side of the statue?"

She smiled uneasily. "Father's one maxim. You've been checking up on him. He won't like that."

Mark glanced down at Lisa who seemed unruffled by the strange talk or the loud voice continuing to explode like artillery fire down the long hallway—*"Janis . . . Goddamn it, Janis!"*—that seemed to take forever to traverse.

And then they were in the room, and Mark gasped silently as Walter Lowndes stood in front of him, a gangly, bent-over man of perhaps sixty, though he looked eighty, propped up on two canes strapped to his forearms, one of the canes waving angrily in the air as his guests appeared, his daughter in the lead. "Damn it, girl, I was yelling at you." Only the right side of his facial muscles moved as he spoke, the other side evidently paralyzed by a stroke, and as unyielding as granite.

"I'm sorry, Dad, I didn't hear. You'll have to learn to speak up. Perhaps assertiveness training would help."

Lowndes brought his cane down with an angry thud and his eyes went to Mark, then to Lisa where they lingered too long, before shooting back to Mark with an aggressive insistence. "You're the one making so damn much trouble in Harmony. Ritter!"

Mark stared in fascination at this man he had heard so much—and read so much—about. He was probably six-three or six-four if standing erect, and one hundred eighty pounds, but his body was bent, and horribly weakened by disease or disability. His huge head, rolling uneasily on narrow shoulders, reminded him of one of those strange abandoned statues on Easter Island—a massive brow slanting in a straight line onto a long nose, gaunt, outthrust jaw, and lips that could not smile.

"Mark and Lisa Ritter," Janis said, making the introductions. "My father can't shake hands when those canes are strapped to his arms, but he probably wouldn't anyway. Well . . ." She gazed around, tense and expectant. "Shall we sit? Or stand and glare at each other for an hour?"

Lowndes shot an angry look at his daughter, then stomped over to a huge carved mahogany desk, and dropped down with a thud on a padded chair. Mark, still trying to get his bearings, slowly lowered himself to a leather couch next to Lisa, and glanced around at the room. It was traditional Colorado chic—pine walls, overlarge stone fireplace, exposed rafters, fake Navajo rugs on the wood floor. Or maybe not fake. The pottery and Kachina dolls looked authentic, quite old, and valuable. He turned his attention to Walter Lowndes, keeping his tone neutral. "How have I been making trouble for you?"

The older man glared at him from his granite face as the fingers of his right hand began tapping non stop on the almost bare desktop. "Our little town is completely dependent on tourism. Anything that gives the area a bad name is going to hurt all of us. Since you arrived"—he leaned over the desk, his torso flopping loosely like a marionette with too much slack, and jabbed one lengthy crooked finger after another in Mark's direction—"our local crazy man has been murdered, which fact was featured on the Denver television news. The very next day Eldon Stallworth was killed, a story which made network newscasts all over the country, as well as, I am told, the local news in New York City because of my connection to both areas. You also managed to get into some sort of tussle with Micah Rollins, one of Harmony's most respected citizens, as well as a friend of mine. And half the policemen in the department want to throw you in jail for—you'll pardon the crudism—shacking up with the wife of one of their colleagues. Seems like a lot for, what? Five days in Harmony? Another week and you'll have the whole town burning to the ground."

Mark was unmoved by the hostility. "I'm looking for my mother—"

"I know who you're looking for!" The guttural voice rasped like sandpaper scraped on tender flesh.

"I found her."

Lowndes pushed back in his chair, only mildly interested. "And who might this be?"

"Cheryl McAfee."

The half-paralyzed face showed obvious disbelief. "Not possible. I know her. Can't be."

Know her? How could Lowndes possibly know Cheryl McAfee? Mark said, "It is. She is."

"No."

"I've called her."

Lowndes's voice rose demandingly. "And?"

"She wouldn't talk to me. But she's my mother."

The older man's eyes drifted to the ceiling, fingers clenching as his mind struggled to work it out. "Cheryl McAfee . . ." He turned to Janis, who helped. "A long time ago, Dad. When you were young."

"Don't patronize me, damn it. I told you, I remember. Cheryl . . . McAfee. I never would have guessed it. She was the town tramp. I would have expected her to kill herself with drugs or drink by now. If not more dramatically—a bullet in the temple after a maudlin note about the cruel, cruel world."

Mark felt himself grow warm. He had an urge to grab this man's huge, ascetic monk's-head and slam it into the fancy polished desktop. Instead he handed Lowndes the photocopied news story about the fire at the resort. The older man glanced quickly at it, then pushed it aside. "I am not on the Pulitzer committee this year. What am I intended to do with this?"

"Before he died, Carl Stark owned this place."

"Hah! Get your facts straight, boy. The feckless Stark owned a decaying tow rope on a barren hillside in an obscure and unvisited area of a little-populated state. *I* built Eagle Point Lodge. *Me!* Not Stark, or anyone else. Whatever you may hear from itinerant journalists or envious townspeople."

"Carl Stark was my father."

"*Now I remember!*" The old man's eyes flashed and his face arranged itself in what was evidently a look of triumph; in his excitement he raised one of the canes and brought it down with a crash on the desk-top, lifting a paper several inches in the air. "Now it comes back. Stark left his land to that little tramp and her bastard child. Of course! And that's you?" He half laughed, half jeered, clearly amused by this turn of events. "My God! Carl Stark for a father and Cheryl McAfee for a mother. What a heritage that is, what a *remarkable* gene pool to choose your inheritance from. Tell me, do you have a strong longing for cheap beer and country music? Do you find yourself sitting around waiting for money to fall from the sky into your greedy and talentless hands? If so, you are truly the child of those unfit and shiftless adolescents."

Lisa, on the couch next to Mark, began to squirm. "I want to go outside." Ignored by everyone, she slipped from her chair and began to wander around the large room.

Mark held his temper in check as he looked at Lowndes. He was fascinated, as well as repelled, by the aging figure staring at him over the desk. "You're older than Stark and Cheryl were. How did you know them?"

"Older than the pubescent and desirable Cheryl, but who wasn't? Every man on the mountain was trying to get into that from the time she was twelve years old. And finding it quite unchallenging. Not unlike my daughter here. How old were you dear, when you offered up your virginity to a passing stranger?"

Janis had retreated into her own mind and said nothing. Lowndes threw her a disgusted look, then continued:

"I was Stark's age, maybe a year older. He must have been twenty-five, twenty-six when he died. Never did marry his little inamorata. She *wouldn't* get married, the way I heard it. Wanted to have more fun squirming under the local studs before putting on an apron. Anyway, Carl wouldn't have been happy with her. He liked them young and she was getting up in years. Fifteen, something like that."

Without taking his eyes from Lowndes, Mark reached over and retrieved the news story from the desk. "Someone sent this to me. Any idea why?"

The old man slipped the canes from his arms and dropped them to the floor. His mood seemed suddenly to have darkened. "Why the hell should I care?"

"He—or she—wants to tell me something about the fire. And my father's death."

"Then why not just *tell* you?" He stared at Mark with blatant dislike.

"I don't know why. But I think you do."

"I do what? Know about the fire? I helped put it out. Half the town did."

"And then you bought the land."

"That sounds almost like an accusation, doesn't it? Are you implying I killed Stark and burned the place down so I could buy it from the aggrieved mother of his child? How bizarre. Janis, dear, tell your friend how bizarre that is."

"Did you?" Mark asked.

Lowndes hunched over the desk. "What is the appropriate response here? Yelling at you? Hitting you with my cane? Suing you for slander? Or calling the egregious Bobby Sample over to toss you in jail for being a public nuisance? If he's not too tired after his all-nighter with my daughter. What do you think, Janis? Is he up to it?"

His daughter's head—pale, pale, like alabaster—moved slightly but her eyes were closed, and her lips moved to some interior melody.

Lisa's excited voice burst unexpectedly from the courtyard outside. "Daddy, Daddy, look!" She ran into the room and then disappeared outside again.

Lowndes swung on his daughter with a sudden fury that startled Mark. "Get that girl out of there."

Janis rose at once from her trance, hurrying to the walled court-yard. Mark followed, finding Lisa on her knees peering into the beautifully landscaped pond.

"Look at these fish," the girl said loudly. It was the most animated he'd seen her in months. "Look at that one, the gold-and-brown one. He kissed my finger." She jumped up, pulled on Mark's hand, then dropped again to her knees.

"Father's koi pond," Janis said. "He takes immense pride in it. More than anything else nowadays. He's constantly worried that someone—his 'enemies' as he says—might pollute the water, or kill the fish, or somehow upset the delicate environment he's created here. It's all very expensive, though money is certainly not the issue."

"The fish are the only living things that love him," Mark guessed, and Janis glanced in his eyes but said nothing, reaching down for Lisa's hand.

"Can't I stay out here?" the girl asked.

"I'm afraid not. My father won't let anyone play with the fish. Not even me."

Janis led Lisa inside. Mark hesitated, drawn to the pond where a dozen bizarrely but beautifully colored koi slowly maneuvered amid rocks and grass and lily pads, before he returned to Walter Lowndes's office.

The old man seethed with fury as Mark took his chair. "Keep that child away from my fish. No one is permitted—"

Mark bristled at Lowndes's imperiousness. On one level he sought information, but on another he saw himself and Lowndes, like two ten-year-olds on the playground, egging each other on for no purpose other than to see who was the meanest kid in the school. His tone became demanding, almost sarcastic. "We were talking about murder, not goldfish. You managed not to answer my question. Did you kill my father?"

The old man's voice turned savage, and his upper body again jerked forward. "Go back to your helpmate in all this, boy. You are being advised by Mason Hightower, aren't you? That in itself beggars understanding. But if you actually trust the unworthy counselor, have him dig into the details of the property sale for your edification. You will discover that the land transfer dates from three years after Stark's death, a period during which I was in the East, creating Lowndes Press. I returned to Harmony in the fall of 1971 and put together a partnership to purchase land that anyone else could have bought in the meantime. Ergo, no motive. So get on your high horse and trot out of here. Pronto. I have work to do."

Janis rose at once to escort Mark out but he didn't move. While a part of him, the adult part, he sensed, wanted to storm out, another part felt the need to get in the final schoolyard jab. "I did some research on you. Old magazine articles. You have quite a reputation. But I'm sure you know that."

Lowndes appeared to have dismissed Mark from his consciousness.

"You ate it up, didn't you? The way those big-city writers fawned over you? You probably saved everything in a scrapbook, like a child would." Lowndes's indifference spurred Mark on as much as if the old man had slapped him. His fingers began to grip the arm of the couch. "You're supposed to be some sort of intellectual. Say something intelligent."

Janis said sharply, "Mark, let's go," and took Lisa's hand.

But Mark had lost whatever self-control he possessed when he entered the room. He settled back in the chair and crossed his legs. "How would you sum up your career? Pseudo-intellectual, phony artist, third-rate poet? General all-around asshole? Help me out. Choose a term."

Lowndes's eyes swung suddenly in Mark's direction and he began rapping his knuckles on the mahogany desktop. *"Builder!* I created something from nothing, and leave it to the world. You've done . . . what?" More rapping of knuckles. "What?" he demanded again, his voice filling the room. "What have you accomplished with your life? What has been its purpose?"

For at least a minute only the sharp, repetitive crack of knuckles on wood sounded in the room. Mark stared at the half-paralyzed old man and didn't know what to say, torn between derision and a sudden compassion as he saw Lowndes struggle against some internal turmoil that twisted the pliant half of his face into a mask of pain, whether real or imagined. "This partnership of yours," he finally asked, making his voice more insistent than he felt. "The people who bought the resort—who was involved besides you?"

Rap, rap, rap with bony knuckles. Faster and faster, harder and harder, as though bones would shatter. Voice racing, raging, eyes drilling into Mark's, Lowndes shot back at once. "I am the majority and managing partner. It is *my* resort, no matter what Micah or Caroline tell you. *I* make all the decisions. And before you ask, there is no role for you or your daughter in any of this. I know what you're up to. You're trying to take it away from me but you won't be able to. The sale was completely aboveboard, even if your conception, birth, and adoption clearly were not. Now if you'll remove yourself from my office I can get on to my pseudo-intellectual work."

Mark was shaking with rage, and maybe disgust with himself, as they strode down the long corridor. His fingers opened and closed into sweaty fists. He faced Janis, his voice demanding. "What's wrong with him?"

She had her hand on his arm, the fingers digging unconsciously into his flesh. "Physically?" Her words rushed out. "He had a massive stroke five years ago. He's had three smaller strokes since. As you saw, he's partially paralyzed on the upper left side. It destroyed much of his memory also, especially short-term memory. Sometimes, like today, he's pretty good. At other times he can't read a menu and tell you what it said. But he can tell you about a movie he watched forty years ago."

Mark's fury wasn't diminished. "And mentally?"

She hesitated a moment, wondering whether to go on. "The stroke changed him," she finally said. Her fingers tightened on his arm. "It's more than just a memory problem. He distrusts people, loses his temper. You have to understand that his brain was damaged. It was bound to affect him. But he can be managed if he keeps on his medication. Actually, he was fine until—"

"I got to town." Mark was sick of hearing the same response to all of Harmony's problems.

"He's not taking his medicine now. I can tell, though he insists he is. It's not the first time. It's always been after some sort of trauma— for instance, when a close friend of his died. This time I think it was you, something you did. At first I didn't want you to meet him, then I thought he might say something, tell us what it is that set him off."

"And he still manages to live alone here?"

"There's an RN who lives in a suite on the top floor. When I'm not here she spends all day with him, then checks in from time to time during the night. And he can call her by pushing a buzzer on the desk."

Mark shook his head. It didn't seem possible. The legendary Walter Lowndes. Only sixty years old. "How does he run this place?"

Janis let go of his arm. "He doesn't. Not since the stroke. Micah and I make the decisions."

"Micah!"

"Look, Mark, I don't know why he lied to you about your parents. I'll talk to him about it. But that's between you two. Micah's been a partner with Caroline and my dad for years. We've always gotten along fine. But it was my dad who built this place, and he ran it by himself until three or four years ago. He made it what it is today. We can't afford to let it get out that Walter Lowndes is no longer in charge. We need the goodwill of the financial community as well as the media to maintain our success. So please keep what you've learned here to yourself."

"If he can't function what does he do at that desk all day?"

"Makes decisions, gives orders, fires people. And then usually has no memory of any of it. But he has periods of lucidity, also. Lucid, but not necessarily rational. Then the three of us sit down and talk more or less calmly, and decide what to do. That restaurant we're building was completely his idea. He did all the initial conceptualizing. We took care of the details."

"Is Caroline Bellamy part of this subterfuge, too?"

"I'm not sure how much Caroline knows about his mental state. But she's an investor, she doesn't want to be involved in day-to-day decision-making."

They could hear Lowndes's furious voice booming from his office. "I'd better get back," Janis said.

"He doesn't sound too incapacitated to me."

"In some ways he's not. Most of the time he can drive a car or ride a horse or order dinner. And as long as he takes his medication, the mood swings are less severe. But the memory loss is not going to be corrected." Another burst of yelling rolled like bowling balls down the narrow corridor to them. "I really have to get going," Janis said, quickly adding, "Don't judge my father too harshly. Please! He's not responsible for everything he does. You and I are."

But as Janis ran off Mark's thoughts had already shifted from Lowndes to his partners. *Micah Rollins and Caroline Bellamy.* What in God's name did that mean? He didn't know, but it bothered the hell out of him.

As he jammed his thumb on the remote to unlock his car, he could again hear Lowndes yelling furiously at his daughter, and from the other direction explosions from the top of the mountain, lifting clouds of black dust that soon descended on the town like a layer of guilt.

58

Angry with himself for getting into a shouting match with Lowndes, Mark sat with Lisa in his car in the Resort parking lot, wondering what to do next. For days he had been trying to see the old man and when he finally managed to it had deteriorated into a squabble between two unruly children before he could learn anything of value.

Why such instant hostility on the part of the man? *Cheryl McAfee. . . . She was the town tramp.* So what? Why should Lowndes care about people he hadn't seen in decades? *Carl Stark for a father and Cheryl McAfee for a mother. What a heritage that is, what a remarkable gene pool to choose your inheritance from.*

And what a pathetic character the famous Walter Lowndes had

become. Watched over by a daughter who probably feels more responsibility than affection, and spending thousands of dollars on a koi pond so he can find at least an approximation of love. If not people, fish. This is what he has to show after sixty plus years of life. *"I created something from nothing, and leave it to the world. You've done . . . what?"*

Suddenly he snatched the cell phone from the glove compartment. *It all starts with me,* he thought with another rising of irritation. *Isn't that what everyone keeps saying? I'm the spark that set Lowndes off on one of his weird irrational mood swings. I'm the one whose arrival somehow resulted in two deaths.*

Taking the phone number from his wallet he dialed Cheryl McAfee in California and realized, as it rang, she wouldn't *be* a McAfee today. He didn't know her married name. *"Cheryl McAfee. . . ."* She was the town tramp. After four rings the answering machine came on. *Damn it!* He clicked off the phone and slammed it down on the seat.

"Can we put the top down?"

"What?"

"The top."

"Wait a minute."

He turned the phone on again, called directory assistance in South Dakota, and got Eleanor Dahlquist's office number. Again no answer. Now what?

"What a remarkable gene pool to choose your inheritance from."

He dialed the *Courier* and Noel Atchison picked it up. No, Karen wasn't there; she was out taking pictures for a story. Any message? Mark told him there wasn't, then called her home phone and waited for the machine to come on: "Lisa and I are going to California. We'll be back in a day or so." He started to say, "I love you," but decided he wasn't at that point yet, probably never would be, and said a hurried "Good-bye" instead.

"California?" Lisa said excitedly. "That's where Barbie's from."

"Barbie who?"

"The doll."

He called for the number of Midwest Express. "How do you know?" he asked her as he was connected to the airline. "I didn't know she was from anywhere. She's just there. Everywhere. Since the beginning of time."

"California Barbie! Everyone knows that. And Beach Barbie!"

Lisa squealed as he made reservations for an afternoon flight to Orange County.

"Don't get excited, hon. I'm afraid neither Barbie nor the beach are on our agenda."

Half an hour later Mark was throwing clothes into a suitcase at the motel when he heard a knock at the door. Reaching over with one hand, he flung it open, saw Janis Lowndes, and went back to his packing, leaving her standing on the landing.

"I don't think I did a very good job explaining about my father," she said, stepping into the room. "I wanted to try again." She pulled the door shut behind her.

"Yeah?" Mark went into the bathroom, grabbed his electric razor, and came back, throwing it into the suitcase on the bed. "Did you get your toothbrush?" he asked Lisa, who replied, "Yessss!" in a peevish voice.

Janis seemed to finally sense what they were doing. "Are you leaving Harmony?" Her eyes widened in surprise, or concern.

"Seeing my mother." He pulled a shirt out of the closet, the bottom half of the theftproof hanger clattering noisily to the floor. "In California."

Janis looked around as if she wanted to sit, but remained standing as Mark shoved the shirt in the suitcase without folding it.

"I think you got the wrong impression of my father back there," she finally said, adding, "and maybe of me, too. We're not as bad as we appear."

Mark looked up suddenly, his face blank but his eyes challenging. "No? How bad are you?"

She stepped forward, as though she wanted to touch him, then at the last minute decided not to. "Like I told you, my dad has not been well for a long time. The reason I came back to Harmony was to take care of him when he's out here. And to help run things. You saw how he is—"

"Crazy."

"That's not fair, Mark. He's ill. He has been for a long time. I guess I didn't see it at first, either. Or maybe I didn't want to see it. After all, he's my *father,* this famous, vital mover-and-shaker, suddenly deteriorating mentally and physically right in front of me. For a long time I thought it was just eccentricity, more of the 'colorful' personality he'd constructed for the press so people would pay attention to him and Eagle Point."

Mark said to his daughter, "Are you sure you've got everything?"

"You asked that already." Annoyed that the television was off she began to bounce on her bed.

This time Janis put her hand on Mark's arm. "Just listen to me for a minute. I want you to know what he's like."

He stopped what he was doing. "Why?"

The question surprised her and she faltered for a moment. "So you won't judge him too harshly. Or me. You went away mad this afternoon. It upset me. I want to set things right."

Mark started to say something flippant, then stopped himself. "I have a plane to catch."

"I won't keep you. Five minutes. Okay?"

He snapped the suitcase shut, then hesitated before dropping down on the bed and staring at her without emotion. "Five minutes."

Janis sat opposite him at once. "I told you about the paranoia. It's not just an offhand expression, it's real, it's part of his behavior, his worldview. He distrusts people, everyone, even me. He's always been that way, I guess. I know when I was a kid I'd hear him yelling at people who worked for him, even poor Les Cady, accusing them of all sorts of wild things. He fired most of his bookkeepers over the years, convinced they were stealing from him. He used to scream at my mom, accusing her of having an affair. He'd scream at me for trying to hurt him by not doing well in school. It was all just fantasy, though, a reason to blow up."

"You mean he's been like this for twenty years?"

"Not 'like' this, getting like this. Every year it's been worse, I guess. Until the stroke he was just difficult, hard to get along with. Ever since, he's seldom been rational but at least he's been easier to be around as long as he takes his medication. But sometimes he forgets, or decides he doesn't need it anymore, or gets angry and stubborn. Then we'll have a bad patch. That's what we're in the middle of now. But he's not like this all the time. And when he treats people rudely, like today, it's the illness talking. You can't take it personally."

"It sounded very personal to me."

She put her hand on his, and her voice became pleading. "Please. I'm trying to be your friend. Don't reject me because of my father. I've already lost my family because people refuse to understand."

"What are you talking about?"

"My mother's side of the family won't have anything to do with Walter. Or me since I stick by him. They blame him for my mother's death. Everyone on my father's side has been dead since I was a child. So it's just him and me now."

"How did your mother die?"

"A brain aneurysm. But her parents insist it came on because Dad had been yelling at her for weeks about having an affair. I know it upset her but I tried to tell them you can't have a blood vessel break in your head because someone's yelling at you. Maybe in cartoons but not in real life. They won't listen, though. Even Mason Hightower believes it!"

"Mason?"

She waved her hand impatiently. "That's who Dad thought she was having an affair with. It's not true, of course. They were just friends. I think they had known each other since attending CU back in the sixties. But suddenly Dad blew it all into something entirely different."

Mark felt a strange feeling move within him as his intestines suddenly tightened. "Your mother and Hightower?"

"That's why he doesn't handle any of the resort's business. When Dad found out Mason and my mother used to go together—"

"You said they were just friends."

"They were friends later on. But they were going together when she met Dad at a charity dinner in Denver. I don't think there was ever any resentment on Mason's part that she and Dad got married, if that's what you're thinking. But Mason was always ready to think the worst of Dad after that."

Mark shook his head, trying to make sense of this. But he was already too disturbed to think clearly. He didn't care about these people, anyway. He was finally going to talk to his mother—that's all that mattered now. He stood suddenly, anxious, annoyed, wanting to leave. "Why won't your dad talk to me about the fire or the old days in Harmony? Why all the hostility when I bring it up?"

She looked defeated. "I can't tell you. He never talks to me about the past, either. I always assumed it was because he lived in the present and never worried about what's happened. It always seemed a pretty healthy attitude."

Mark turned suddenly to Lisa. "You ready to go?"

She jumped off the bed. "Yep."

"Go to the bathroom first."

When Lisa closed the bathroom door, Mark turned abruptly back to Janis. "What the hell's going on in this town? Ever since we got here people hesitate around Lisa, stare at her, move away, or say how pretty she is and want to touch her. And don't say you haven't noticed it."

"Who do you mean? Are you talking about Les Cady? Because he was in my store?"

"I mean everyone. Except you. You hardly know she's there."

Janis shook her head. "I don't know what you're talking about. I never paid any attention. Honestly."

"You didn't see your dad stare at her?"

She became uneasy. "I didn't notice."

"Sure you did. Crazy old Walter. Did you also see that he hardly read that article I showed him? Do you think he's the one who sent it to me?"

"Why would he do that?"

"Why would anyone? But he was familiar with it, wasn't he? He didn't have to read it."

She shook her head, not willing to think about it.

"I want to search his office." Mark surprised himself with the statement. He hadn't given it any thought until this instant.

"You want to do what?" Panic suddenly entered her eyes.

"Old paranoid Walter is hiding something from me. You know it and I know it. I'm going to find whatever it is. Maybe he's even *expecting* me. He sent the article to me to prod me into finding out what the hell is going on."

Janis's eyes had gone wide and her long hair swayed as she shook her head back and forth. "Well, he's sure as hell not going to let you search his office!"

"No. But you might."

"Let you go through his personal belongings? Are you crazy?"

"I think I'm exactly as crazy as Walter Lowndes."

Janis seemed to shrink within her clothes. "No. No way. I can't do that. He's my father!" She came to her feet and put a hand on Mark's arm. "Look, even if my dad's had some problems in the past that doesn't mean there's something for you to worry about now. He's harmless. He doesn't even run the resort anymore. He's practically an invalid sometimes. I'm not going to do anything to set him off. Especially poke around in his office. As long as we can keep him stabilized on his medication he's actually quite kind." She stepped closer, and Mark could see a sheen of perspiration on her upper lip. He found himself reacting to her closeness, his anger turning to confusion, and his pulse quickening. He had a sudden desire to reach out and take her in his arms, but the bathroom door banged loudly open and Lisa came out. The impulse vanished; *only a fantasy,* he told himself, and then also told himself: *There's something not quite real about Janis, something as disturbing as it is attracting.*

"Ready," Lisa announced, anxious to get going.

"Anyway," Janis added with a smile, "Don't forget that the sins of the father, whatever they are, aren't the sins of the daughter." As her fingers tightened on his biceps Mark looked into her face and she blushed, an emotion that startled him with its openness, but also eased his mind somewhat; maybe she wasn't the hard, calculating woman she sometimes seemed. Then she dropped his arm and tried to lighten her tone. "So don't take anything out on me. Okay? I'm just a girl trying to help her pa. If I can't convince you he's really a nice guy at least try to separate us in your mind. Walter, period. Janis, period. Two different people. Okay?"

Mark hesitated a long moment. "Okay."

She smiled, leaned suddenly forward. "Thanks." And kissed him briefly on the cheek. "I want us to be friends. I mean it. More than friends, if possible. But I don't want to interfere with you and Karen, either. So I'll let you decide."

He looked at her, and before he could stop himself, asked, "What would Bobby Sample say to that?"

Janis's face froze, and she hesitated a moment. "There aren't a lot of men my age in Harmony. Bobby and I were never serious, not even close to it. I hope people aren't going to hold that against me all my life. Anyway, it would be different with you. With Bobby it was just physical. With us it'd be more than that, deeper." She looked into his eyes. "I know you feel it, too—something special between us."

Her tone suddenly changed and she looked over at Lisa. "Gosh, going to California. Sounds like fun. Do you guys want a ride to the airport?"

Mark told her they didn't, and turned at once to his daughter. "Come on, hon, we've got to hurry." He snatched up his suitcase, and by the time he locked the door Janis was receding from his mind. In a few hours he'd be seeing his mother, whether she wanted to or not. What kind of person was this woman who sold her child for three thousand dollars? What would she have to say to him after thirty years?

59

Ninety minutes later, striding rapidly through the concourse at Denver International Airport, Mark glanced anxiously at his watch. Another hour until takeoff. Maybe he'd buy a newspaper to pass the time. But nothing was going to make time pass more quickly now. Not until he talked to his mother.

Lisa yanked on his hand. "Isn't that the man who bought us pie?"

"Who are you talking about?"

"Over there. The man with the cowboy hat."

There were half a dozen men with cowboy hats but Mark noticed B.J. Blake at once. Mark was in no mood for pleasantries but Blake didn't seem to be, either, stalking in their direction with his head down. Maybe he wouldn't see them. But when he was twenty feet away Lisa said, "Hi!" and Blake looked up and smiled almost at once.

The two men shook hands and Lisa said excitedly, "We're going to California."

"Oh! Lucky you." He glanced at Mark's carry-on. "Not staying long?"

"Probably not. Are you on your way somewhere?"

"No. Picking up some out-of-town clients. Leastwise, I thought I was. They didn't show. Happens all the time. Now I've got to sit around for two or three hours in case they come in on a later flight." He frowned, took off his hat and wiped a line of sweat from his forehead. "Hell, it's not like I'm losing sales by not being in Harmony. It's the boredom. I *hate* waiting in airports. Hey! You folks got time for a piece of pie or a cheeseburger? It beats sitting in the waiting area staring at folks reading newspapers."

Mark was about to tell him no, but Lisa's instant "Can we?" overruled him.

They settled for an eating area in front of a half dozen small restaurants and shops. Mark had coffee while B.J. and Lisa had pieces of blackberry pie with vanilla ice cream.

While Lisa used her spoon to spread ice cream over her piece of pie, B.J. said, "Happy to see you and Karen get together like you did. She's had some hard times recently. Because of Todd."

"We're just seeing each other, B.J. It's not like we're getting married."

Lisa looked up abruptly and frowned.

"Well, you never know," Blake said. "Couldn't do better than Karen. Maybe she doesn't exactly look like Janis Lowndes but she'd give you the shirt off her back." He chuckled to himself. "Well, Janis might, too. Shirt off her front, actually. If you get my drift."

Lisa looked at her dad. "What did you say about getting married?"

"Nothing, hon."

Blake cut into his pie. "Karen saved my business a couple of years back. I was hangin' on by a thread when she got the idea to do a special issue of the *Courier* on real-estate opportunities for landowners in the central Rockies. They'd print up a few thousand extra copies and send them to people on the coasts, using mailing lists from local hotels. She wanted to do stories on folks getting rich on Colorado property over the years, and then, of course, interview the Land King for expert opinion, and so on. She thought it'd drive a lot of business my way.

"But Noel didn't want to do it, said it'd look like they were using the newspaper for commercial purposes. Hell, the *purpose* of the paper is to sell advertising, not give people news. And they do a special Pioneer Days issue every year, and a Christmas issue. Anyway, Noel and Karen got in an argument over it and she ended up getting fired.

"They finally compromised a few days later and agreed to do an issue on 'business opportunities' in Harmony, and not just real estate. I still got a big spread, though. And Karen even talked Noel into flying her back east to shmooze with newspaper editors and chat up Harmony as a place to do business. Had a small software firm move here because of it, and it probably convinced a telemarketer to move in. I figure I sold about two million dollars' worth of property in a piss-poor market. I couldn't have done any of it without Karen. And she didn't get anything out of it, except a trip back east."

"I like her because she likes riding," Lisa said. "And going to malls."

Mark raised his eyebrows. "How do you know she likes to go to malls?"

Lisa took a bite of her pie, now completely hidden behind a blanket of white ice cream. "She just does."

Blake finished his pie and pushed his chair back from the table. "Wish those folks would show up. It's not a big sale, one of those thirty-five-acre 'ranchettes' for city folk who want to play cowboy. But it's going to be tough paying the two women in the office without it. Land sales are the pits."

"Why not specialize in big-ticket items—commercial real estate and high-end condos?"

Blake gave a sarcastic laugh and flicked a finger, cowboy style, against his ten-gallon hat. "Yeah, right! Can you see me sitting around and talking intelligently to bankers about capital budgeting or amortization schedules? Might as well talk poetry with Walter Lowndes. The last poem I learned was 'Rock-a-bye Baby.' You think he knows it?"

Lisa began to sing, *"In the tree top . . ."*

The mention of the resort owner revived a memory. "Did you know Lowndes's wife?"

"Lord, no. She died when I was a kid."

"Do you remember how she died?"

"No. Why?"

"Janis told me it was a brain aneurysm but that her mother's family blames Lowndes for it."

"Why not? He's blamed for everything else that goes bad around here."

"Janis's mother used to date Mason Hightower in college. Lowndes seemed to think they were having an affair about the time she died."

"Is that what Janis told you?"

Mark nodded.

"Why's she diggin' out the family laundry for you? You two aren't getting involved, are you?"

"Of course not," Mark told him with more certainty than he felt. "We were just talking." He didn't feel comfortable sharing information about Lowndes's mental health with B.J., and instead said, "I guess what bothers me about this is that Mason Hightower never mentioned it to me."

"You're upset because Mason didn't tell you he and the missus used to date? Why should he? You want a list of girls I used to go out with?"

"This is different. Number one, because he's my lawyer; number two, because he lied to me. He said he doesn't handle any resort business because Lowndes and Mason's dad didn't get along."

Blake chuckled. "So a lawyer lied to you. You're a little old to be surprised, aren't you?"

A boarding call for Mark's flight came over the PA system.

"Normally, they don't lie to their own clients." *Or maybe they do,* he thought, remembering Eleanor Dahlquist. He stood up, anxious to board. "Hurry up and finish your pie, Lisa. We've got to go."

Blake slowly came to his feet also. "I reckon I'm going to have a long, lonely wait here in the airport. Sometimes I think I shoulda taken up bank-robbing rather than real estate. It's more stable. Anyway, you folks take it easy and have fun in California."

Thinking about finally confronting his mother, Mark snatched up his carry-on bag and gave B.J. a look. "Whatever this trip is, it's not going to be fun."

60

This was going to be fun.

Bobby Sample had row 22 of the half-empty 737 to himself. He relaxed back, propped the *Penthouse* magazine he had bought in the airport shop on the seat-back tray, and finished off his second beer of the short flight. A Sam Adams Cream Stout this time. Damn, he loved that stuff. Better than Coors. Expensive, though. Ten rows in front he could see the rear of Mark Ritter's head moving back and forth. Dumb fuck had a little curly-cue of hair on the back of his head that wouldn't stay combed. Kinda like the Beav on that old TV show. Made it easier to watch him but, sheez, the guy didn't even turn around to see if someone might be following. *Hey, you don't know how important you are, do you, buddy?* Fat ol' Micah knows, though. He figured the best way to find out where the hell the McAfee woman lived was to follow her kid. Hell, it was sure-fire.

When Bobby had phoned Micah and said Ritter was headed for

Orange County, California, Rollins was elated. *"Whoop-dee-doo,"* the man had said, about the closest Bobby had heard him come to swearing, and quick-like, reserved a rental car at the Orange County airport; it would be sitting in the lot, all paid for, with the keys in the ignition. Just drive out onto the street and wait for Ritter to come by on the way to the freeway. Piece of cake.

Micah said the freeway was two blocks west. The 405 freeway, he called it, and Bobby wondered if they'd started numbering their freeways with "1." Whole place must be covered with cement, then. What am I supposed to do when I find out where the gal lives? Bobby asked. Call me, Micah had told him, using that real calm tone Bobby didn't like, then we'll decide.

Yeah, sure. Bobby knew what the answer had to be. Which meant another twenty thousand dollars. Too bad he couldn't tell Janis. Then maybe she'd stop making fun of him. Yes sir, this was going to be a kick.

He stopped a passing flight attendant. "Say, hon, could I get another beer and a couple bags of those tasty peanuts? All this heavy reading gives a man an appetite."

Of course the only reading Bobby did was the captions under the photos. He leaned back, glanced out the window and noticed that when the sun was just right he could see his reflection in the plastic. Cool.

61

"Thing is, Les," Hector Chavez was saying, "I could've had one of the regulars question you down at the station. I thought it'd be a lot less embarrassing if I did it, and did it here at your house. That way it's just between me and you. Nothing official, no report. No one ever knows about it."

Les Cady looked miserable. Wearing an old T-shirt, he sat sprawled at his small Formica-topped kitchen table and moaned unintelligibly as his mongrel dog sat in the corner and eyed Chavez with distrust. A photocopy of the Pooh Bear note sat between them. "I didn't do it, man! I never even touched that girl except to help her off her pony. Then her old man comes runnin' over like I just raped her. It ain't fair. It just ain't fair." He wiped a stubby hand across his pale, almost invisible mustache, and his puffy eyes looked as if he was going to cry.

"I'm not accusing you of anything, Les. Look at it the other way. I'm trying to clear you."

Cady bolted up angrily. His round stomach was barely constrained by the T-shirt, and a patch of curly black hair stuck out above his belt. "Yeah, sure. Like Stallworth tried to *clear me* every time some jackass bothered a kid. You know how many times I've been drug into the police station? I lost count. Even had me down to Denver twice. Had to take lie detectors, talk to damn psychiatrists, have social workers come out here to talk to me, had my house searched ten times. You know what they did at that hospital in Denver? Had wires attached to my penis, then they showed me pictures of little girls and said, 'Hey, look at this one!' How'd you like to be treated like that?" He dropped down, defeated. "Got a problem, pick on Les. Lester the Molester, that's what you guys call me. I know it. Even the kids yell it at me. You come out here instead of going after the real molesters."

Chavez tried to keep his expression neutral. He had never questioned a sexual predator who admitted to doing anything wrong. Either they were unfairly persecuted, or admitted what they'd done but were convinced there was nothing wrong with it—except that a hypocritical public had decided it was illegal. Cady, he was certain, was the first type. You could threaten him with death and he'd never admit an interest in children. He said, "They made you stay in the state hospital for a while, didn't they?"

Cady shot him a hateful look. "You know they did."

"What was it for?"

"To rest. I was tired. That's what they told me."

"Your body was tired? Or your head? I don't understand."

"I wasn't thinking real good. Focus, they called it. Couldn't focus."

"But you're okay now?"

"Yeah." He paused a moment, looking at his dog and thinking. "I take medicine. It helps me think. That's why I couldn't graduate from high school. Hard to focus."

Chavez was interested but didn't want to start taking notes because it might cause Cady to clam up. "What kind of medicine is that?"

"Ritalin."

"Helps you relax, helps you sort things out?"

Cady nodded, then thought of something. "If you think I wrote that note, why not look at my handwriting like on TV? It don't look nothing like that."

"No one's handwriting looks like that. It was done with a ruler so we couldn't match it up to the writer. I saw in your file, though, that you used to write poetry. When was that, junior high?"

Cady rubbed a hand over his face, and smiled slightly. "Yeah. Eighth grade. Had a real nice teacher. Miss McClatchy. She liked my poems. They wanted me to write some in the hospital but when I did, the shrinks would make me talk about them. So I just stopped."

"Were you working for Walter Lowndes when you went to the hospital?"

Cady stood up and began to walk around the cluttered cabin. Chavez could see that the sink was full of dirty dishes that looked as if they had been there a long time. The dog's head came up and two moist black eyes followed Cady as he moved. "Was working for him two or three years."

"And he saved your job for you? That was mighty nice."

Cady whirled on him from ten feet away. "Folks make fun of Mr. Lowndes, too, just like they do to me. Call him names, act like he's mean. He's the only one around here that treats me nice. Him and Janis."

"Mr. Lowndes is always nice to you?"

"Has his moods. Screams some. Mostly nice, though. Janis, too."

"Old Bill and you used to be friends, too, didn't you?"

Cady looked at him suspiciously. "You going to say I kilt him?"

"Of course not. But maybe you could help us find out who did. You were with Bill a couple of days before he died, weren't you?"

"Saw him that afternoon. He was walking toward that cabin of his. All shook up. Wouldn't talk to me. Said he was in a hurry."

"He say why?"

"Said he saw a ghost." Cady laughed uneasily. "Maybe the ghost kilt him."

Chavez glanced at the TV a dozen feet away. There were three videos on top of a VCR. He couldn't read the titles. "I don't think it was a ghost, Les. If I tell you something, can you keep a secret?"

The man looked at him with distrust. "Yeah . . . Sure." He stayed where he was, his bowl-shaped body sagging, looking like a surly adolescent about to be disciplined. The dog, a spaniel of some sort, eased onto its feet and came over to get scratched.

Chavez said, "We found some dirty pictures out at Bill's. Pictures of kids."

Cady colored. "And you think I gave them to him?"

"Not at all, Les. Just wondering why your fingerprints were on the envelope the pictures were in."

The man jumped up. "Were not. That's a lie."

"Well, actually they were." Chavez had just gotten the report from Denver, and had not been at all surprised.

Cady looked confused. He sat down. "Don't make sense."

"Why? Did you wipe the envelope?"

The man's beady eyes drilled into him. "Didn't do it. Never saw those pictures."

Try going at it from the other way, Chavez told himself. "Did Bill ever tell you about his interest in kids? Like when he got a few too many beers in him and started talking?"

"No sir! Never did. Never talked dirty around me. Talked nonsense about his granddaddy or the old days in Harmony or how he used to be a cowboy on a ranch in Wyoming. Never paid him much mind. Just the alkie talking. But never did talk dirty, not even about adult women."

"I suppose Bill could have taken that envelope from your house. What do you think?"

Cady didn't answer.

"Where do you think those pictures came from?"

"Don't know where they came from! You want to search this place? That what this is all about?"

"No, Les, I'm not interested in searching your house." Not without a warrant, anyway. He probably should have done that already but the fingerprint report didn't come in until he was ready to come out here. "It's just that there's been a lot of strange things going on. Bill dying, then Chief Stallworth—"

"Deserved to die. Always blaming things on me. Glad he's dead."

Cady was getting worked up again. Chavez thought he better get to the crux of the issue while he could. "Have you got any ideas on Bill's or Stallworth's deaths?"

"No!" The word was thrown at him like a knife.

"How about those dirty pictures?"

"No!"

"No point in bothering you anymore, then." He came to his feet. "Nice-looking dog. What's his name?"

"McDuff."

"Who's he named after?"

"No one." He looked at Chavez as if the question were inane. "It's just his name."

Chavez pretended to gaze around, trying to read the titles of the videos sitting on the VCR. One was *The Sexpert*. He could only see one word on the other: *Lickers*. He turned back to Cady. "You get cable here?"

"Yeah. Sure. Whole resort gets it."

"Get the Disney Channel?"

"Yeah."

"They got this show on in the afternoon called *Winnie-the-Pooh*. My kids love it. All these cute voices, you know. You ever seen it?"

"I work in the afternoon."

Chavez pushed open the door. It was getting dark already, and a light breeze was blowing. When he was outside the dog scooted out too, and Cady came out to retrieve him. As Cady was heading back inside, Chavez said, "Before you went to the hospital, did you like playing with kids? You know, playing doctor, stuff like that?"

"You don't believe me, do you? Don't matter what I tell you, you still don't believe me."

"It could be the medicine they gave you that made you change, Les. Coulda made you forget things you used to do. It's why they use medicines like that. Are you supposed to check with them to make sure you're still taking it?"

"Why don't you call them, see what they say?" He went back inside and slammed the door.

Chavez said, "I'll do that, Les. Yes I will."

62

Janis Lowndes, barefoot and wearing a white sheath dress with Indian embroidery along the hem and side, stood in the middle of her father's office, and said hopefully, "You're walking much better since dinner."

His voice rasped out, but not unkindly. "It comes and goes. Like much else in life." He moved in short jerky steps to his desk without the use of a cane, and picked up a package from the coffee table. "Just look at this," he said, cautiously moving the wrapping paper aside. "It arrived this afternoon. I was almost afraid to open it. But of course I did."

His daughter stepped forward. "Another book." One of the old man's obsessions. He did nothing halfway. Normally she would have had little interest but this time she looked at it gratefully; a new book usually meant he would be in a good, if not always rational mood, at least until morning. And there were some things she needed to find out, things she didn't expect Micah could, or would, help with. "William Blake or Thomas Mann?" And silently thought, *Please let it be Blake.*

"Can't you tell from the binding?" His voice boomed with impatience. "A first-edition *Death in Venice,* signed by both Mann and the binder. Look—" He reverently opened the ornate leather cover and tilted the book so she could see the scratchy sepia signature of the author. "Marvelous."

She was silent a moment, then to say something, asked, "How much did you pay for it?"

The half of his face that worked shifted suddenly into a smile. "Thinking of your inheritance disappearing into the pocketbooks of avaricious European booksellers, my dear? Perhaps it is, from your standpoint at least. Did I tell you I recently willed my collection to the Getty Museum in Los Angeles? Mann lived on the Coast, of course, during the forties. They estimate my library's worth in excess of two million dollars. But there should be something left for you."

"You know I don't care about that, Father." *Death in Venice,* she thought with a shudder.

"Then you're a fool, Janis. Not too surprising, though. You haven't shown any signs of intelligence in the conduct of your private life."

"And you have?" she asked, and at once regretted it. Her father was no longer responsible for his behavior, and it was needlessly cruel to criticize him.

His mind slipped, like a coin falling between cracks, to some earlier time, long before the first stroke. "If you people understood anything I have been saying for the past twenty years, you would realize that moral law, what you would call the Ten Commandments, is propagated only to keep the masses in line. William Blake understood this. People of my stature, or Thomas Mann's, or, of course, Blake himself, or *anyone* of genius, is relieved from worrying about such *niceties!* We make our own law."

"Then maybe there is nothing wrong in my own behavior," she couldn't help but say.

"You have yet to prove your genius." Still holding the book he sat behind his desk. "Or are likely to, despite inheriting half your genes from me. Nonetheless, my child, I love you." He began to flip through the exquisite blue-and-gold volume, searching out favorite passages long since committed to memory.

Janis took a breath and forced herself to ask, "How have you been feeling lately?"

His head snapped up at once. "That sounds like a question you have asked before. And always with dubious intent."

She proceeded cautiously. "It seems like you're having one of your down periods. As you said, it comes and goes."

"And?" He stared at her with sudden feeling, and his fingers began tapping on the desktop. "And? And? There is always an *and*."

"I think you ought to go back to New York and see your doctors," she said with forced cheeriness.

"Absolute nonsense. I feel fine."

"Are you taking your medicine?"

"Do you wish to count the pills, perhaps tick them off on the calendar, or maybe check my mouth after each one as they did in the hospital to ensure that I didn't hide them in my cheek and spit them out later? Or worse, save them up for an embarrassing suicide attempt?"

"Yes." She smiled beautifully, hoping to disarm him. "That would be fine. Can I? We can start with your Prozac. Where's the bottle?"

"You are an idiot."

"But you love me nonetheless." She took a silent breath and moved on to what she really wanted to know. "Why did you have Les Cady put that odd lock on your den door? Are you hiding something from me again?"

"Of course I am. It is full of the medicine I have not taken. It covers the floor up to my ankles." He gave a guttural laugh but his mouth remained in a frown, and his hand kept tapping on the desktop.

"You've redecorated it, haven't you? Can I go inside? I'd like to see what you've done. You've always had a better eye than I."

"Of course I have a better eye. Your aesthetic sense began and terminated with Rossetti and Millais in art, and that poor sap Dickens in literature. You're as common as milk."

"No Mann for the little girl?" she said slyly.

"No sense for the little girl, no discernment, no true taste. Regrettably, you do have artistic talent, of a magazine illustrator's sort."

"You're too kind, as always. Now, about your den—"

His eyes drilled spots of heat into her face. "It is my room, Janis. Surely you wouldn't want me to barge into your private rooms. One of your policeman friends might lose his erection forever."

She smiled, trying to relax him, as well as to relax herself. "Why were you so rude to Mark Ritter and his daughter this afternoon? He's only trying to find out what his parents were like."

Lowndes half rose then fell to his chair; his right hand flattened on the desk, then clenched, then again flattened, over and over, as if he couldn't make a fist, and couldn't stop trying. "Is *that* what this is all about? My rudeness? How extraordinary! It has never bothered you before."

"It has bothered me for twenty-seven years. I am asking specifically about today, though."

"I explained myself adequately at the time." With sudden flawed energy he rose and came around the desk, facing Janis, half of his face working itself into a paroxysm of anger. "That man hates us. Couldn't you see that? He hates all of us, and he's making Harmony look bad to the world. We can't allow it. We depend on the goodwill of the skiing population. What would happen if people stopped coming to my resort?"

"You know very well he did nothing wrong. He just happened to be here when Harmony made itself look bad."

"That, as your policemen friends would say, ain't nothin' but bullshit, little darlin'." He paused a moment, his mind working. "You're after him, aren't you? That's what this is really about. You don't want me to screw things up for you."

"I don't know what you mean."

"Of course you do. Don't treat me like an idiot. Ritter! Not your usual type, is he? That, I suppose, signifies something. Have you decided finally to put away your childish things?"

Janis stared at him a moment, not certain how far to take this. Finally she said simply, "I like him."

"That in itself is a change of monumental proportions. *Liking* never seemed to be an issue in your past relationships."

She said nothing.

Her father was growing angry. "No more policemen? No more weight lifters? No more cowboys? Are you giving up all your amusements in some vain attempt at normalcy?"

"Are you?" she shot back.

He glared at her a moment as if deciding whether or not to get upset. Then he let loose a sound meant to be a half-laugh, and began to stalk toward the walled courtyard, still without his canes.

Janis hadn't moved. With her father in one of his rare lucid moods, she didn't want to irritate him, and couldn't risk pushing too hard. But there were things she was desperate to know—paramount among them what was in the room he recently locked up, and why Mark's appearance in Harmony upset him so. Keeping her tone casual— "walking on eggs," she had long ago termed it to herself—she said, "I'm surprised you told Mark about Micah and Caroline."

Lowndes turned back to her, looking confused as the memory of what he said struggled to return. "I did tell him that, didn't I? I wonder what I was thinking. Perhaps to throw a spanner in whatever fantasies he's constructing about his mother."

"You must really hate her."

"The McAfee woman?" He laughed and continued outside. "I can tell you with complete honesty that I had not given that vile young woman a second's thought in thirty years. It was only when this noxious son of hers, whose birth I do remember well—another bastard in the backwoods—showed up that she roared reluctantly back into memory. No, I do not hate her. Hating the insignificant is so time-wasting when one can instead hate the vital and the powerful." He disappeared into the courtyard.

Janis followed, looking like a specter in the twilight as the evening breeze lifted strands of hair and gently blew them around her face. She put her hand to her head to keep the hair from her eyes. "I can tell when you're not doing as well as the doctors would like, Father. You begin to perseverate on Thomas Mann. Or on Beauty. Or *Death in Venice*. It's like a signal."

Lowndes laboriously maneuvered his body to the ground so he could kneel next to his beloved koi pond. " 'Perseverate'! Wherever did you unearth that loathsome word? From some social-science textbook? It has the aura of the approaching, and one hopes final, millennium about it."

"From Dr. Howell."

"Ah! The famous Dr. Howell, with his fancy pharmacopoeia of colorful mind-altering drugs for the old, the bizarre, and the untamable. Does he have you watching me? Are you keeping me on a leash for the good doctor? Is he the one who told you to monitor my Prozac consumption?"

"He asked me to watch out for you. It's not the same thing." In fact, Lowndes's doctor had told her exactly what the old man had guessed: Along with the nurse she was to ensure that he didn't, as so many in his condition do, self-diagnose a cure, and decide that he no longer needed his medication.

Lowndes twisted suddenly in her direction. "Why, you little shit. I should have known. So Howell thinks I'm about to go cuckoo. Is that it? Is he going to try to hospitalize me again? Given his bill last time I don't doubt it. Perhaps he needs a new Porsche."

"You know very well that since the stroke you sometimes have bad days. They don't just happen—they grow gradually." *Like now,* she didn't say. But the signs were obvious and escalating. She tried to sound helpful. "And usually it's because you don't keep up on your medication."

"I take my medication when I need it. At the moment I am doing quite fine."

"I want to see what you've put in your den, Father. I want you to let me in. Now."

The old man bent forward, easing a finger in the pond, with its lily pads, grass, and rocks. At once a fish came over to gently nibble it. "Ah, Seaeagle quite understands me. This is what your odious and interfering Dr. Howell would call unconditional love. See how he sucks at my finger? He is showing me his devotion and loyalty. And he naturally has mine as long as he maintains his beauty."

Janis stepped forward, peering into the clear water. The fish was beautiful almost beyond description; an electric, surreal splotching of bright orange and white, eighteen inches long, it had cost her father six thousand dollars, and was the pride and joy of his collection. He would sometimes come out here and sit for hours staring into the clear water, relaxing, and thinking—she often wondered—about what? What went through his diseased mind as he stared endlessly into the shallow water?

Janis kneeled next to him, keeping her tone friendly. "Let me make the plane reservations for tomorrow. Then we can see the doctors Monday."

"You are not paying attention. I think you were like that as a child. Willful, just like your mother. It became more pronounced after she died, didn't it?" Lowndes had his whole hand in the water now. He slipped it slowly forward, touching the fish lovingly, caressing its sides, then hooking his first two fingers under its gills. Suddenly he yanked the fish out of the water with a triumphant grunt, and twisted around until it was trembling from his fingers under Janis's nose. "As much as I love you, child, I will not put up with your interference in my life. *Any* aspect of my life. You and Micah may think you're running things now but I'm still the head of our little organization. Do you understand?" He flipped his hand over and the fish landed at her feet and began to flop in the dirt as air rushed into its gills, sucking its life away.

"Put it back, Father. Please."

"It annoys me. As you and Micah are. This is *my* resort. Not yours."

"You're being melodramatic. It's not like you. You hate melodrama. Put the fish back in the water."

"Why? Are you afraid to watch it die?"

"I'm going to make the plane reservations." She rose. "You have to see Dr. Howell."

Lowndes grunted with exertion as he reached over and grasped the fish by the tail. "Listen to me." He began unexpectedly to scream, his fingers tightly squeezing the carp. *"Listen!* I will not have people dictate to me. I won't have it. I built this resort, this company, even this pond. I will do with it as I please." He raised his arm and brought it down viciously, striking the fish's head against a rock, and splattering Janis with a spray of blood and brains and tiny bits of bone.

His daughter stood frozen, looking at her dress as blood dripped along the white fabric to the ground. Lowndes stared at his hand holding the remains of the fish, then threw it angrily into the pond. "You did this," he shouted, his lizardlike flesh growing moist and red. *"You* did!"

Janis turned toward the door.

Walking out to her Jeep after cleaning her dress as best she could, Janis watched as headlights hurtled toward her across the empty parking lot. A moment later Karen Paige pulled her Taurus next to

Janis's car and stepped out. "I was hoping to see your father. Is he here?" She glanced up at the darkened building.

Janis fought off a surge of resentment at Karen's sudden interest in her family's affairs. "I'm afraid he's not feeling well right now. Is it anything I can help you with?"

Karen's eyes went to the wet marks on Janis's dress, then shifted to her face. "Mark left for California after seeing your dad. I didn't get a chance to talk to him before he left. I wandered what he learned about his parents."

"I'm afraid my father didn't have much to say. I guess he didn't like Mark's mother very well. But he doesn't like most people."

"Too bad. I was hoping there was some big revelation. Something made him leave for California on the spur of the moment."

"Then he knows where his mother lives?" Janis was surprised, and happy for Mark, though for some reason she felt her father would be upset. And the thought went fleetingly through her mind that Mark's relief at finding his mother was suddenly more important to her than her father's irritation.

"He has her phone number. I guess he called her."

"Interesting. But I think I won't tell Dad. He's already pretty upset about something." She thought for a moment, then made a decision. They weren't going to be able to keep her father's condition a secret forever, and it might be better to let some people learn of it now. "He hasn't been well since he had a stroke several years ago. Sometimes he can be difficult to deal with. Micah and I have had to take over the day-to-day operation of the resort."

Karen's eyes clouded over. "I'm sorry," she said, meaning it. "I didn't know." But it explained why Lowndes had been seen so seldom in the past few years.

"Mark will tell you my dad treated him badly today. He did. He got pretty nasty about Mark's mother. But I hope Mark doesn't stay upset about it. It's not personal. When Dad gets like this it's how he treats everyone. Including me."

"It must be difficult for you."

Janis frowned, her irritation at Karen unaccountably returning. "You don't know."

VI

63

The Holiday Surf Hotel was sandwiched between a Jaguar dealer and a French restaurant on Pacific Coast Highway in Newport Beach. At eight o'clock Friday morning while Lisa brushed her teeth in the bathroom, Mark sat on the bed, took a deep breath, and dialed his mother's number. It rang three times, and when she answered he said, "Don't hang up. We're going to talk."

There was a pause where he could hear nothing but the blood pounding in his ears, then, softly, "What do you want?"

"I'm in Newport Beach. I just want to talk. Face-to-face. That's it. Then I'll leave forever if that's what you want. But I have to talk to you."

Her voice dropped to a whisper. "Please don't do this to me. I have a family. A husband . . . and two boys, twins, twelve years old. They don't know about . . . anything from before. No one does."

Mark heard someone say, "Who is it?" and Cheryl's muffled, "Ellen. She wants to have lunch this afternoon."

Mark could feel his nerves tighten. "Look, I'm not trying to cause trouble but I have to see you. You're my *mother*—"

"Don't," she said at once, and sounded as though she was going to begin crying. "Please. Don't say that. You don't know."

His voice hardened. "I'm going to see you one way or the other. Either we meet someplace—today—or I'll come over to your house and see all of you—you, your husband, your kids."

"No, my God, no. Don't come over here. Oh God—"

"Then tell me where. Hurry."

"Seaview Park. Ten o'clock. It's off Pacific Coast Highway in

Corona Del Mar. Sit on one of the benches. It's a small park. I'll find you. My God," she added, and paused a second, "you're thirty. Thirty years—"

64

Caroline Bellamy jammed her huge Rolls-Royce to a sudden stop at the rear of the lodge, and marched straight to the unmarked door next to the eight-foot wall. Buoyed by the three bourbons she had consumed before coming over, she pounded on the door with her fists until it opened and a middle-aged woman said, "What—?" and immediately put up her arm to bar the way. But Caroline pushed around the woman and stormed up to the ornate mahogany desk where Walter Lowndes sat with nothing but a cup of coffee. His voice was devoid of emotion, but his eyes dark. "Caroline. What do you want?"

She seated herself in a leather chair in front of the desk, her multicolored muumuu falling around her like a tent. To the side of Lowndes the French doors were open to the enclosed courtyard with its spa, koi pond, and patio furniture, and sunlight drifted in with a mild Rocky Mountain breeze. Caroline leaned suddenly forward. "Get rid of your keeper."

The other woman came near the desk. "Mr. Lowndes, I don't think you—"

The man glared at her. "Leave."

She started to protest but Lowndes's skin flared red, and he scowled with the right side of his face. *"Now!"*

Her expression hardly changed. "I'm going to call your daughter."

When the door closed behind her, Caroline said, "She acts like a nurse," and began at once to have suspicions of what was wrong. Her eyes fixed on Lowndes's face and she began replaying her past few visits to the man, always at long intervals, always with Janis or Micah present, always after waiting to be told it would be okay to come over.

Lowndes glared across the desk. "I repeat: What the hell do you want?"

"Want?" Startled, Caroline came back to the present. "Walter,

I'm your partner. I *want* to talk to you. Do you think you can handle that?"

With an effort, he pushed back in his chair but said nothing, staring at her with glassy eyes.

She fixed him with a tremulous gaze. "Why have you been ignoring me? Why is it every time I try to see you Janis or Micah tells me you're busy, or not feeling well, or on your way to New York? The only time I get in to see you is when they say it's all right. What in God's name is going on around here? Are you sick? Or have they got you on some kind of leash?"

The planes and valleys of Lowndes's face seemed to tighten suddenly as he stared at her. His right hand swept across the vacant desktop as though clearing it of debris. Then it stopped abruptly and one by one his fingers closed into a fist. Still he said nothing.

Caroline sighed and ran a heavily-ringed hand through her short hair. "My God, I don't know what to say. What's come over you? You didn't used to be like this. At least you could be civil. Come on, Walter, we're friends. We've known each other all our lives. Have you forgotten that?" Through the open door to the courtyard she caught a glimpse of Les Cady adding chemicals to the spa and trying to listen to their conversation. The pear-shaped man threw her a look of pure hatred, then slipped out of view.

Caroline shook her head and sank back in her chair. "Why in the world do you keep that vile man around, Walter? No, don't answer. I know: he's the goat you tie your sins to each year and drive out of the encampment."

"Caroline, what is it you *want?*" Lowndes's fingers found the blue ceramic coffee mug with EAGLE POINT emblazoned on its side, and moved it closer.

Caroline drew a breath. *Bourbon, do your thing.* "I want you to go back to New York."

He stared at her a moment, as though confused.

"I spend July here every year. You know that, surely."

Goddamn it, Caroline, stop pussy-footing. "Walter, go back to New York. If you stay here there'll be nothing but trouble. Do it tomorrow. Have Janis take you. Or I'll take you. Or go by yourself. Just leave."

His body trembled as he stared fiercely at her. "Get the hell out of here."

Make your point, damn it. What can he do to you? This time she didn't take a breath, and the words rushed out as though attached to one another. "I don't want you anywhere near Mark or Lisa Ritter. They're nice people. I know what you're thinking and I don't want you to do it. Leave them alone. And no more notes to the girl, Walter. Never again!"

"*Notes?*" He seemed confused and his eyes lost their focus as his head shook back and forth. Was there something there he'd forgotten?

"Walter, go away. Now. Leave Harmony. You don't need to be here to run the business. We can do it. Micah and I. Stay in New York with your friends. I'm serious. I don't want you around here. Ever again. Just get out!"

Lowndes's body shook terribly as he tried to work out her meaning. She couldn't mean leave, leave now? What right had she—?

Suddenly his control vanished. With a trembling arm he lifted the coffee mug, holding it for a full second above his head, then crashed it down on the polished desktop, sending coffee and broken pieces of ceramic flying across the desk toward Caroline. "*Get out of my office!*"

The woman sat frozen, the quivering of her earrings for a moment the only movement in the room. Spots of coffee appeared on her face and dress. A tiny piece of blue ceramic, no larger than a marble, had fallen on her shoulder; as she sat it rolled off and came to a precarious rest on her wide lap. Unable to compel her body to move, she stared at it intently, as if its very existence were impossible, a piece of Venus that had plunged through the atmosphere to materialize suddenly on her stomach.

Lowndes was on his feet, bending over the desk. He seemed unaware of what he had done. "I know what you're planning, Caroline. But you won't be able to get away with it. Get out of here, now! Do you understand? Get out!"

My God, she thought, still not moving: *Walter, what's happened to you? What's happened to your mind?* And far back in the most distant recesses of her consciousness, still affecting her emotions as well as her behavior, was the memory of her and Walter forty years ago, and the fun times they had, and the certainty she had clung to for so long that they would one day marry. The smartest person she ever knew, she used to think. And the nicest. My God . . .

Les Cady appeared suddenly in the doorway leading to the courtyard. He frowned from Lowndes to Caroline. "Everything okay, Mr. Lowndes?"

Caroline stood up suddenly, the piece of ceramic flying to the floor at her feet. Lowndes's hand, she could see now, was bleeding onto the desk, and he still held a broken piece of the handle gripped tightly in his fist. A pool of coffee undulated on the desktop in front of him, merging with the dripping blood. His eyes were open but he no longer seemed to know anybody was there.

Caroline met Janis racing toward her in the hallway. She grabbed the younger woman by the arm and almost threw her against the wall. "What the hell's the matter with him? And no bullshit this time."

"Hold on, please, Caroline. Let me check with him. Wait here. Please!" Janis went quickly into her father's office, and a minute later the nurse Caroline had seen earlier came hurrying down to join her. Janis left them and rejoined Caroline, quickly leading the other woman toward the hotel lobby. "It's not his fault, it's the stroke. Didn't Micah tell you how bad he is?"

"No, he didn't tell me! I knew about the stroke, of course, but nothing like this. All Micah ever said was, Walter didn't want to see me most of the times I called. The last time I saw him without you or Micah chaperoning must have been three years ago."

Janis's lips narrowed into a frown. "Micah told me you didn't *want* to see him, that you weren't concerned about making decisions about the lodge anymore. You just wanted to be a silent partner."

"That's crazy," the older woman shouted. She balled her beringed fingers into meaty fists. "What the hell is Micah up to? As far as I knew Walter had been acting a little eccentric lately, not—"

Janis took Caroline by the hand. "He has terrible mood swings, especially if he's not on his medication. He gets depressed and paranoid, and strikes out at whoever's near by. I try to keep people away then because I don't know what he'll do or say. I thought you were aware of all this."

Caroline's mouth was so dry she could hardly speak as they went through the door to the lobby. "You mean he's mentally ill?" She shook her head. "My God, I've got to sit down."

The two women seated themselves on a mission-style couch by the empty fireplace, the thirty-foot stone chimney dwarfing them.

Janis said, "He's not crazy, if that's what you think, Caroline. He has his periods, his ups and downs. Sometimes he's pretty good. He was this month until—"

"Mark Ritter came to town! Goddamn it, I knew it." She whirled on the young woman. "How much do you know?"

"About the old days? Please, Caroline, I don't want to know. He's my father."

The older woman considered a moment. "It's the girl. Lisa Ritter. You've got to get Walter out of town. Get him back to New York. Anywhere!"

"I tried. Last night. He blew up at me. Like he did to you."

"Then get Micah to help. Does he listen to Micah?"

"In this mood he doesn't listen to anyone. . . . Actually, the only person who can get along with him is Les."

Caroline shuddered. "Jesus, what a pair." She smiled suddenly at Janis. "Did you know Walter and I were lovers once? I thought he was a Greek god, someone on a different plane from the rest of us. Then he ran off and married some sweetie from Denver with a trust fund. Oh Lord, sorry. Your mother. No offense, just a jilted girlfriend talking."

Janis reached out and grasped Caroline by the hand. "He never told me about you two. But I knew. I just knew. I'm sorry it didn't work out."

"Oh, hell, I'm not. I wouldn't have wanted to live the sort of life he took up in New York and London. I'm a Colorado girl. Anyway, if I had married him you wouldn't be here, would you?"

"I guess not." She smiled uneasily.

Caroline felt herself calming down, rationality slowly returning. "I'm going to talk to Micah. He's got to get rid of Walter for a while, at least until we can get the Ritters out of town." Her voice softened. "Someone told me you were growing kinda close to Mark."

"Someone?" Janis said playfully. "Karen, maybe? How would people like it if Mark and I married? Then you'd never get rid of him. Or his daughter."

Caroline looked so distressed Janis laughed. "You worry too much. Now, about my father?"

"Micah!" Caroline said, standing up abruptly. "I'll call him. But he doesn't much listen to me anymore. You better try to get hold of him, too. We've got to get your dad out of here. Now!"

65

The morning fog was just beginning to burn off as Mark parked his rented Chrysler on the street adjacent to the small park. Below him on the beach dozens of perfect tanned and toned young bodies, Barbie and Ken clones, relaxed on towels while black-clad surfers emerged from the water like sea creatures as the morning waves declined, and the Pacific slowly took on a glossy flat sheen, like a plate of blue-gray glass.

"Can I go in the water?" Lisa asked excitedly.

"Later. We have something to do first." Nine forty-five. Hands gripping the steering wheel he quickly scanned the park. Two young mothers with toddlers. An older woman with a grandchild and a German shepherd sitting on a bench. A boy bouncing a tennis ball. The dull normalcy of the scene irritated him.

"Too early," he said to himself.

"What?"

He wasn't listening to Lisa. "Come on."

Mark led her to a wooden bench, then sat down and tried to calm his nerves.

"I want to play on the swings."

"Go ahead. Just stay where I can see you."

He drew a deep breath and stared out toward the sea. What would she look like? Tall like him? Dark brown hair like he had, or light brown like Lisa's? What would she tell him about the last thirty years? "I tried to find you but couldn't?" That was bullshit. She didn't want to be found even now, didn't want to meet her son. *Christ, what kind of a mother are you? You don't care what I look like, what kind of person I am? You don't care about your grandchildren?*

He began to feel agitated, felt like jumping up and running but crossed his legs and tried to make himself sit still. How could she turn her back on her own child, just draw a line across her life and say, "Everything before this time no longer exists?" *Goddamn it, I'm part of you, you can't pretend I'm not alive, not here!*

Five after ten. He came to his feet. The sky was clear now, and the morning sun hot on his skin. A half dozen sailboats, white against the unexpected perfect blue of the sea and sky, blew north in the breeze. Farther out a fishing boat headed up the coast.

Lisa was playing with a little girl whose mother sat at the edge of the sandy play area and read a paperback. The girls squealed, jumped up, sat, ran to the slide, squealed again. Still few people around. A man lying on the grass at the other end of the park, reading a magazine. A teenage girl with a deck chair walking by.

Where are you, Cheryl?

He sat down.

An airliner from John Wayne Airport passed overhead as it took off, banking steeply as it headed west toward Catalina.

You're not coming, are you? You lied to me.

And then he saw her walking in his direction, long, purposeful strides like someone on a mission. Short brown hair whipping in the breeze, large dark glasses to hide her face, white shorts and a flowered blouse. His heart pounded as she stopped in front of him. She didn't smile. There was something hard about her face, the part not covered by the dark glasses. Finally she said, " 'Hi' seems pretty inconsequential at this point, doesn't it?"

He rose, started to reach for her, then caught himself and motioned toward the bench. "Please."

She hesitated, looked suddenly nervous, then sat quickly, the space between them thirty years wide.

"Thank you for coming," Mark said, and wondered if he sounded as insipid to her as he did to himself. *I'm your long-lost son. Thank you for finally taking the time to see me.*

"I didn't want you at the house. I don't want my husband involved in this. He knows nothing about my past life. I don't want him ever to know."

Suddenly she took off her dark glasses and stared at Mark. *Brown eyes,* he thought instinctively, and began at once to tick off the salient features: light complexion, high cheekbones, full red lips . . . She said, "You look like I imagined you would. Maybe a little . . . I don't know, softer. My eyes and forehead, though. What do you do for a living?" Still no smile, no loosening of the facial muscles, emotions wound like an old clock.

"I'm a stockbroker."

"A wheeler-dealer. Makes sense."

"You don't look old enough to be my mother." Immediately Mark regretted the words. "I mean—"

"I know what you mean. I was fifteen. I *was* too young. You don't have to tell me. I heard it for months. Strange how that worked out. I got married when I was twenty-three but couldn't get pregnant again until I was thirty-two. Seventeen years between kids. Then I got a double-dip—twins." She smiled, and when the tension disappeared it took ten years off her age. Her skin, he could see, was as soft and flawless as a teenager's, her eyes clear and bold. "My twins are twelve. Did I tell you that? Boys. Aaron and Alan."

"Half-brothers of mine."

She turned abruptly toward the sea and the sailboats, looking frail and inconsequential against the hugeness of the Pacific. "I guess they are. I hadn't thought of that." She whirled back, her voice sharp, fingers clenched. "How did you find me?"

"It wasn't easy. After my mother—" He stumbled over the words, wanted to withdraw them, and felt a sting of embarrassment.

"It's all right. She *was* your mother. I never even knew her name. They didn't let me see her. Afraid I was going to make a scene. I did anyway."

"Ritter. They lived in Dexter, South Dakota."

She nodded but said nothing.

"After she died I found a death certificate in my name—Mark Ritter. Her child by birth, I guess. I started backtracking and ended up in Harmony. Mason Hightower—"

"Hightower. The attorney. I remember him. Is he still alive?" She began to rub her fingers over the metal clasp of her purse.

"That was Julian, Mason's father. Mason found some information in the files about Carl Stark, and the estate, and you. And me. He said after you gave me up you went off to boarding school."

"Dallas, Texas. Two years of Catholic discipline. I hated it. But it was good for me. At least, that's what I tell myself."

"And then college?"

"Five years at Baylor. Got a teaching degree. Came to California. Taught in Garden Grove for years. I quit last month."

He looked questioningly at her.

"I got fed up with California schools. Everyone does sooner or later. And we don't need the money. My husband's an engineering professor at UCI. He's also the associate dean. I decided to take some time off and figure out what to do with the rest of my life. You're getting thirty years of history all at once, aren't you?" She turned on him suddenly, knuckles white as she squeezed her purse. "It wasn't my idea to give you up, you know. Please don't blame me. They made me do it—Hightower and my mother. I wanted to keep you. Carl—Carl Stark—and I were going to get married. But they wouldn't let me."

"What happened to your mother?"

"She died when I was still in boarding school. Like half the women in town she had some stupid idea Walter Lowndes was going to marry her, but of course he didn't. I heard he married some socialite from Denver."

"She's dead, too."

"Doesn't surprise me." Her lower lip began to tremble. "What did he do, rip her heart out or feed her arsenic? He is a complete bastard, the most evil man I ever knew. He's the reason I never went back to Harmony."

"He's built Stark's resort into something pretty impressive."

She stood up suddenly, her body tense and face flushed. "Yes, I know all about that. The big-time Eagle Point Lodge operator. The King of the Hill in American skiing."

"Did you know that Caroline Bellamy and Micah Rollins were partners of his?"

Her head jerked abruptly in his direction. "Caroline? No, I didn't know. I'm surprised. We were friends. I don't remember Micah Rollins, only the name." Her face darkened as she thought about it. "I don't know why Caroline would do that. Go into business with Lowndes, I mean."

"Why does it surprise you?"

"Because we were friends, damn it, even though she was a few years older than me."

Mark still didn't understand. "But why shouldn't she be involved in the resort?"

Cheryl was wound to the point of breaking. Her voice shot up. "Because Walter Lowndes killed Carl! He killed the man I was going to marry, the only man I'd even dated until I met Richard. When Walter couldn't persuade Carl to sell his property he killed him."

"But Stark died in a fire."

"Who do you think set it?" She was standing facing him now, yelling, drawing the attention of the others at the park. "He killed Carl and set the resort on fire to cover himself. Then bought it a month or two later from the estate for half what it was worth."

"He told me he didn't buy it until three years later."

Her hands clenched. "How do you think I paid for boarding school? Walter Lowndes bought the resort while I was still living in Harmony. The money from that paid for my education. And to get me out of town. When I was in college the attorney handling the estate told me Lowndes restructured the partnership later, but he got his hands on the resort in 1968."

"Why would he lie to me about it?"

"Because he would lie about anything." She flung herself back onto the bench. "I told you, he's completely evil. That's a word you don't hear anymore, do you? But it's the perfect description of Walter Lowndes. Evil!"

"His daughter told me, whatever you think about him, you're wrong. It was almost as if he has a public and a private persona."

Her head jerked disbelievingly. "He has a daughter? People like that shouldn't be allowed to have children. Especially when good people can't."

"Like the Ritters?"

She turned to him with concern. "Were they good people? I hope so. God, you have to believe me: I never wanted to give you up. Carl and I were going to marry when I was eighteen, and raise you. It was my mother—"

"The Ritters were wonderful. But it would have been nice to have my real mother, too."

She reached out suddenly and grabbed his hand. Tears welled behind her eyes but didn't come. "I've thought of you every day for thirty years. Do you believe that? Every day. And I've never told anyone. Not a soul. All this time . . ." She dropped his hand and began rubbing her fingers along the hem of her shorts.

Mark stared away, watching the fishing boat as it came to a halt offshore. Finally he said, "Did you have any proof Lowndes might have been responsible for Carl's death?"

She laughed shortly. "Proof! I know! Okay? I just know."

"You never mentioned it to the police?"

"You mean did I tell that fat slob we had for a chief that I was certain our upstanding and brainy young Walter Lowndes was a murderer? No, I didn't do that. My fiancé was dead, my baby was being stolen from me, my mother was pushing me out of town . . . No, I just kept quiet and cried for three months."

"Your mother was paid three thousand dollars by the Ritters. Did you know that?"

Cheryl put her head in her hands. "Not until she called me in Texas one night, drunk. She bought a new Camero, she said. A convertible. Blue, with a white stripe on the hood. She was so happy. That makes me a baby-seller, too, doesn't it? I've thought about that every day for thirty years, also."

Mark put his hand on hers but she shook it off. "Why did you have to come back? Why couldn't you stay lost? Why do I have to keep going through all this? It's been *thirty years!*" She began to tremble with sobs.

Mark took a piece of paper from his shirt pocket and tried to hand it to Cheryl but she wouldn't stop crying and wouldn't take it. He snapped open her purse and dropped it inside. "My phone number in Seattle, and the motel in Harmony. If you ever want to talk."

He eased back on the bench and waited as she regained her composure. As she took a Kleenex from her purse he said, "The girl in shorts playing in the sand over there—she's your granddaughter. Lisa Ritter."

When Cheryl looked at Lisa, she went pale. "Oh my God, no." She bolted up, the Kleenex falling to the ground. "Please, no . . ."

Alarmed, Mark jumped to his feet. "What's wrong?"

But Cheryl wasn't paying any attention to him. She began to run, racing back the way she had come from, her purse slapping against her bare leg. Mark started to follow but stopped when he realized he couldn't leave Lisa.

A hundred yards away Bobby Sample had dropped his *Penthouse* and leapt to his feet. *Stay with Ritter or follow the mom?* Hurriedly making up his mind he headed after Cheryl. " 'Fuck's going on around here?" Too many crazy folk, screaming and yelling. Bobby didn't like that.

66

When Micah Rollins walked into the Rocky Mountain Cafe Karen was the first to see him, but she dropped her eyes and her face closed up.

Uppity bitch, he thought. *Don't matter none; like it or not you're the one I came to see. Need to find out exactly how much you folks know, and how much you suspect.* He made his face brighten with a smile. *Lighten up, Karen, fifteen minutes from now you and me will be buddies again. I guarantee it. Twenty minutes and I could have you in bed, pointing your toes at the ceiling.*

Noel Atchison, sitting across from Karen in the booth, didn't notice Micah until the man feigned pleasant surprise and said, "Hey folks, mind if I join you?" and dropped down next to Karen, who moved at once to the edge of the booth.

"Hot out there, ain't it?" Micah said. "Makes a body want something cold. How about you?" He smiled at Karen, thinking, *You're about the coldest thing I know right now; maybe I ought to warm you up.* It'd be doing Ritter a favor, give him one final night of pleasure.

Atchison said, "Been out of town? Haven't seen you for a couple of days."

Rollins nodded enthusiastically. "Had to go to Denver to meet with the Boy Scouts. I'm volunteering my company for construction work at one of their camps. Lost Valley, they call it. Gonna airlift a John Deere earthmover and some materials to build latrines. Also got my people to pledge fifty thousand dollars for the Scout food drive this October. Winter hits the homeless pretty hard in Colorado. We always like to help out any way we can."

The waitress came over and Micah ordered pot roast and coffee. He turned to Karen. "When I got back to my office there must've been fifty messages on my desk to call Mark Ritter. Guess I know what that's about."

She fixed him with a hostile stare. "Oh?"

"I found out that story I told him about his family was a little off-base. I guess it's just age. Sometimes I get facts messed up in my mind. Happens to all of us sooner or later, don't it, Noel?"

Atchison pushed the remains of his steak sandwich aside. "Can't say it does, Micah. I'm a newspaperman. I don't make mistakes, I only point them out."

Rollins chuckled. "Well, anyway, I feel real bad about misleading Ritter. Been trying to call him but he always seems to be out."

"Gone to California," Atchison said, and made a face when Karen frowned at him.

Micah directed a questioning look at her and she spread her hands on the table. "I don't think he wants everyone to know where he is."

Micah said, "Well, I reckon I can figure it out. Soon as I got back to town I heard about Cheryl McAfee." He laughed lightly and touched Karen's hand. "The local rumor mill is faster than your paper, hon. Folks are saying Cheryl is Mark's mom. Coulda knocked me over with a feather. I hadn't thought of her in years. But I got out my old yearbook—"

"What do you mean, got it out?" Atchison said. "Christ, Micah you *live* in the 1960s. I figure you have that old yearbook on a table next to the bed, probably take it on business trips with you."

"Not true," Rollins laughed. "I live in the *1950s*—Roy and Gene, white hats and black hats, six-shooters that never ran out of bullets. The sixties were the beginning of the end."

Karen was curious about what he'd said. "What do you remember about her?"

Rollins patted her hand again. "Nice gal, real nice gal. Always liked her. Had a rough time of it because she didn't have much money but, hell, none of us did back then. You remember that, Noel! We all do."

"That's not how Walter Lowndes remembers her," Karen said evenly.

"Oh?" Micah was suddenly interested. "How do you know that?"

"Janis told me. Mark and her dad had a chat yesterday."

"Didn't know that." He paused longer than he intended and his voice sounded strained. "What exactly did Walter have to say? Something interesting?"

"Janis didn't say. But evidently Walter didn't think much of Mark's mother."

"Well, shoot, what would Walter know about her? She was behind me in school by seven years. I looked it up. Walter must be at least fifteen years older than her. Isn't that right, Noel? I don't think he'd know Cheryl McAfee from a posthole digger."

The other man sat back and thought about it. "Well, let me see. I'm five or six years older than Walter. So . . . yeah, I'd say he was maybe fifteen, sixteen years older than she'd be."

Micah smiled warmly at Karen. "So don't let that old fart tell any stories about Cheryl. She was a real nice girl. Everyone liked her. We all felt sorry for her having such a ditzy mom but we can't choose that, can we? Gotta play the hand we've been dealt. So Mark's gone to visit her? That's nice. Boy, I'll bet he's excited."

"I'm sure he is."

"What part of California does she live in?"

"He didn't tell me."

"Well, if you talk to him on the phone you tell him I remember his mom, and she was a nice gal, no matter what old Walter told him. Tell him I'm sorry about that Contrell story, too. I like the man. Truly do. Don't want any bad blood between us. Things just got mixed up in my mind. I didn't remember that baby dying, only the murder and fire. Well hell, when he gets back I'll tell him myself. Feel like a fool, I can tell you. But it ain't the first time, won't be the last, either."

"Can I quote you on that in the *Courier?*" Atchison asked, pretending to write the words on a napkin.

Rollins laughed and dropped his hands on the tabletop. "Tell you what, Noel. If you get your paper to cosponsor that food drive the Scouts are putting on I'll let you run a picture of me wearing donkey ears and eating crow." Still smiling, he turned to Karen. "You shouldn't put too much faith in what Janis says, either. She's always in her own weird little world, isn't she? Someone was telling me she had her hooks out for Ritter but he wasn't interested. Good thinking on his part. Janis has the brains of a butterfly."

Atchison said, "That isn't fair, Micah. That poor girl takes a lot of heat for being Walter Lowndes's daughter. And for looking like Helen of Troy. I don't like it when people pick on her."

Karen smiled beautifully. "Oh, please, Noel. Let people pick!"

Her boss grunted. "Just because you and Ritter—"

Micah interrupted. "Are you and Ritter getting serious? Hey, that's great. Really! Glad to hear it." He sat back in the booth, and sighed. "Boy, now I really do have to apologize, don't I? Hate to lose you as a friend because of what I told him about the Contrells. It was just a mistake. Maybe I'm the one with butterfly brains."

"Don't worry about it, Micah. And I don't know if we're serious or not. We just met. Give us some time."

"Yeah, I can see where time is what you need. You and Todd still aren't legally kaput, are you? Takes too damn long for the legalities and the lawyers. I know about that. Believe me." He leaned confidentially across the table toward Atchison whose mind suddenly seemed to be elsewhere. "Mention of Todd reminds me: I was talking to Hector Chavez this morning. This isn't for the newspaper, Noel. Okay? It's just preliminary now. But I've been trying to convince Hector to get rid of Bobby Sample. Man's a menace, a crazy with a gun. Can't have that around here. Someone's going to get killed someday and then the city will get sued, and we won't be able to *afford* a police department."

Karen was about to suggest that Todd be grouped with Sample, but decided it would look too much like sour grapes and kept silent.

Atchison absently nodded his head. "I suppose I could do another editorial on professionalism in the department. Karen already talked to me about it."

"Without mentioning names," she reminded him. "I don't want this to look personal."

The food came for Rollins. He poked the mashed potatoes with his fork. "Good thinking. It'll make it easier for Hector when the time comes. It ain't easy to fire a cop. Speaking of cops, has there been any progress in finding Stallworth's killer?"

"Nothing we've heard," Atchison said.

Rollins shook his head. "It's a damn shame, a fine man like that being murdered. No sense of morals in this country anymore."

"You won't get any argument there, Micah." Atchison pushed to his feet. "Karen and I have to get back to work. I think the editorial is a good idea, though. We'll work on it." But his mind had moved beyond newspaper work; all this talk of the old days had gotten him thinking, and there were a few things he wanted to check in the *Courier*'s back issues this afternoon.

Rollins slid out so Karen could leave. When she was out, his voice became concerned. "I sure hope we cleared up any little misunderstanding between us. You tell Mark I didn't lie to him, I was just confused."

Karen patted his arm. "Don't worry about it, Micah. He'll understand."

Rollins smiled and sat down to his pot roast. *Worrying is exactly what I'm* not *doing. You on the other hand—*

67

Cheryl Davidson (the name McAfee something she hadn't thought of for years) sat bent over on her couch, elbows on knees, and hands clenched angrily next to her cheeks. *I won't cry,* she told herself for the hundredth time. *I will . . . not . . . cry. Goddamn it, I won't!*

But her face was red and wet and her eyes swollen almost shut as she jumped to her feet and began to stalk around her upscale Newport Beach living room. Why did he have to show up? Why couldn't he leave well-enough alone, leave *her* alone?

But she'd known for two days he wouldn't stay vanished. Somehow he'd get her phone number; that's what his dad would have done, sweet-talk someone into divulging it even though they knew they weren't supposed to. Then come out to see her no matter what she wanted.

She put her palms to her eyes and pressed. It had been like someone rushing up from behind and pushing her into a whirlpool; and at once she began to drown.

". . . He claims he's your son. Should we give him your phone number?"

"No, God, no, not under any circumstances."

But as soon as she'd heard his voice she knew. Slammed the phone down. And began, not very slowly, to fall apart, like a doll picked to pieces by a child.

Her eyes went to the antique clock over the mantel. Almost three o'clock. The kids would be home any minute. Three hours until Richard. Dinner. She started to tremble. How in God's name was she supposed to make dinner with this hanging over her?

She should have told Richard years ago, before they got married. *Oh, by the way, hon, I had a kid when I was fifteen, a beautiful baby boy. Where is he? We sold him, got enough so my mom could buy a new car, a convertible. Hey, anytime you want a car just let me know. That's what I'm here for.*

"Hi, mom."

"Hi, mom."

Cheryl gritted her teeth, didn't turn around, didn't want them to see she had been crying.

"What's to eat?" Alan asked.

Cheryl's voice shot out peevishly. "I don't know. Look in the refrigerator."

"Something wrong?" Aaron, the more perceptive of the two, came up near her.

"I said look in the damn refrigerator!"

The boys exchanged a glance. She still had her back to them.

"Okay if we have a Coke?"

"Jesus, do what you want." She spun around. "I'm going for a walk. I'll be back later."

The twins stood there, alarm growing in their faces as she stomped away, slamming the door behind her. This wasn't like her; something was very, very wrong.

See what you did, goddamn you! she screamed inwardly the moment she was outside. *You made me yell at the two most wonderful children in the world. Goddamn you, Eric!*

Where had the name Mark come from? She had named him Eric though they put Baby McAfee on the birth certificate. Why did those people have to rename him? Baby Eric. . . . She and Carl had looked through a book of names and chose Eric because no one in Harmony was called that, and because it sounded so nice. Eric if a boy, Kathleen if a girl. Oh, what a pretty name that was. . . .

She held her arms stiffly at her side as she stomped down the street. The surest way to be alone in Orange County, she thought, was go for a walk. It could be a month before you saw another adult not in a car.

She came to a corner, caught a glimpse of the sea, and turned inland instead, up a hill. Her temples began to throb, and her eyes momentarily squeezed shut as if someone had slapped her. Mark's face filled her inner vision; the moment she'd entered the park she knew. The hairline, the cheeks, the mouth. God, it was all she could do not to run up, wrap her arms around him, kiss him. She had missed him so much, for so many years. But she couldn't, couldn't! And would never be able to.

Where was his wife? He hadn't said anything about that, had he? Divorced? Or had she followed family tradition, given up her baby and taken off? That would be ironic, wouldn't it? *Jesus, don't be such an ass!*

Cheryl spun suddenly around, feeling warm, sweat beading on her forehead, and headed quickly down the hill toward the beach. At Pacific Coast Highway she hurried across six lanes between racing teenagers in sports cars, and strode between two rows of houses until the ocean appeared as a vast undulating blue plane rising and falling sensuously in front of her. Still in her low leather flats she crossed the beach to where the sand was wet from the tide, and sank down, kicking off her shoes and letting the water rush up to her toes. Surfers were out on boards two hundred yards distant, waiting for a wave, but she didn't see them, her eyes filling instead with the summer of 1968, the horror . . .

. . . the noise, Cheryl screaming, flailing her arms, her mother, seeming so large as she loomed over her, yelling like a crazy woman, grabbing her hair and pulling at Cheryl and shaking her like a dog tearing apart a toy. And fifteen-year-old Cheryl sobbing, begging. *Please, please, please, I won't give up my baby, I won't do it.* It was this terrible noise she remembered most, and her mother's red sweaty face, glowing in the overhead light of the house trailer, and the *greed* that emanated from every pore of her body as she said, "You don't have anything to say about it. I already made the arrangements. You're going to get rid of it." *It, it, it!* It, the baby, screaming from his bassinet while she and her mother raged at each other. *What an introduction to the world, Eric, your mother and grandmother fighting over who had the right to decide your fate.*

But Cheryl was only fifteen, a juvenile, and no match for a thirty-two-year-old conspiring with an attorney who had a profitable little business going, selling babies from teenagers to couples who couldn't have one or who had just lost a baby.

So Cheryl that night stole a car from a gas station downtown and took off, with Eric in the bassinet on the seat beside her. She didn't even tell Carl because there was nothing he could do; unmarried fathers, underage mothers, what were they against the weight of the legal establishment? Julian Hightower let Carl know if he gave them any trouble he'd be arrested for statutory rape and do ten years in prison. *Hard time,* he'd promised, rapping his fat red knuckles on the desk. *Hard fucking time, boy. You're a rapist. You know what they do to rapists in prison?* So Cheryl panicked, grabbed the baby, and ran as fast as she could. She had five dollars in her purse, and it was gone when she was arrested a day later at a truck stop in Kansas trying to beg money.

Back in Harmony they put her in jail for two nights, made sure she understood she now had a police record, then gave her an option: Shut up about the baby, or do time for car theft and have the state take the child, instead of the family who wanted it. No telling who'd end up with it then, probably some welfare couple acting as foster parents so they'd get more state aid. Chief Deets seemed honestly perplexed by it all. *Why wouldn't you want to give him up? You're only fifteen, for heaven's sake. You've got your whole life in front of you.*

Over in Julian Hightower's office, Cheryl had whirled on her mother. "How much do you get out of this?" Immediately she saw it was true, not just her mother, but Hightower. Her mom, in a rage, slapped her hard, but Hightower said, "Now, now," like she was a child who had stubbed her toe, not a mother forced to sell her baby against her will.

For thirty years she had tried to force all this from her mind. But it had been impossible. All she could do was pretend it wasn't there, not allow it to bubble to the surface. But it *was* there, affecting everything that happened after that day, causing her to hold her temper with the twins, never argue with Richard, because she couldn't bear to lose someone, anyone, again, even if it was only emotionally. They had taken away the one she had loved most in the world, and then took away Carl. It would never happen again.

She opened her eyes to the anxious roiling of the sea as waves broke in front of her with a crashing sound. As swells too small for a ride rose and fell surfers in shiny black wet suits bobbed above the line of the horizon, looking like children on a seesaw. Finally a good-sized wave began to move in their direction and, as if someone had blown a whistle, a hundred black shapes levitated to their boards, catching the crest and rushing toward her on the shore, most falling gracelessly as the wave broke, only a handful upright as they swept in, serpentine fashion, near shore. There was an unusual elegance and beauty to it but Cheryl wouldn't let her boys surf. Too dangerous. Too many broken necks. She couldn't tell them the real fear, of course: *I've already lost one child, I'm not going to lose another.*

So many decisions over the years had been affected by that, by the experience, as real as if it were happening right now, of standing fearfully in Julian Hightower's office while the other couple, the *buyers,* waited in another room so the two sides wouldn't have to share the embarrassment of each other's company. How had they paid? *Will this be cash or check?* And Cheryl at the last minute saying, "I'm not going to do it!" Her mother exploding, howling, tearing the screaming baby from Cheryl's arms. Hightower had to restrain Cheryl, grabbing her from behind and putting his hand over her mouth, then screaming in pain when she bit him. Finally she had sunk onto the floor in a corner and cried until it was just her and her mother left in the room, while behind the locked door next to her the buyers took possession. *Did they check you for damage, sores, a busted antenna or bad tires? Did they ask to see the maintenance record?*

She recalled watching her mother walk away from the lawyer's office with her new boyfriend, a waiter at Steers, later that night. Mom's night to party: Look at all the money she had. While Cheryl sat on the sidewalk outside the cafe, her face red and wet, her heart breaking; she never felt such hatred in her life before or since. But hatred can heal too, because she made it through two years of boarding school by lying on her bunk at night while the other three girls in her room slept, and thinking of nothing but getting back at the people who did this to her . . . until the hatred was gone, replaced by a bottomless hole that had held nothing for years.

A month after she had been forced to give up her baby Carl died. And they had expected her to believe it was an accident. *Hell,* she could imagine them saying, *she's a stupid fifteen-year-old with a half-crazy mother. You think she's going to suspect anything?* The "they" here was different than before but the result was the same. Carl's will had been a shock, hadn't it, guys? No one suspected that. Even Cheryl hadn't expected it. But Carl had been planning ahead.

Still, it made up for nothing. Within a month she had lost her fiancé, her baby, and was rushed out of town. It was the last time she had seen anyone from Harmony.

Until today.

What now, Eric?

Tears trickled down her cheeks. *God, he's mine, he's my child. I want him! I want him to be a part of my family. I can't lose him again.*

But how do I bring my son into my life without telling Richard—and the twins—of my past? It can't be done.

What will he say, this man who lives such a protected life studying solar-powered engines, traveling the five miles back and forth from home to the university, day after day? He knows so little of the real world, and deplores what he does know. *Will I lose you, too, Richard, and my children, as I lost Eric? Can you accept us—the two of us, Mark and myself, as he is, and I really am? Can Aaron and Alan accept us?*

I'm a grandmother now! "God, can you believe that?" she said aloud, and a laugh escaped with a sob. A grandmother! Chilly seawater ran suddenly between her toes, then flowed away, leaving little squiggly indentations in the sand, like the nail marks of a many-fingered hand. Overhead, seagulls shrieked, swooping low, looking for food.

Cheryl dropped her head to her chest. What her family—her new family—thought about it was irrelevant, she knew.

She had to find Mark.

She had to tell him the danger he was in. Or more accurately, the danger his daughter was in.

There was no way he could realize it.

But she started weeping again, as the seagulls chattered and dived in an eons-old ritual, and the icy sea rushed in to cover her feet. *It's happening all over,* she thought, and recalled once more sitting that night on the sidewalk outside the cafe, her face red and wet, her heart breaking, and at the same time so full of hatred that thirty years couldn't dispel it.

Goddamn, Bobby Sample thought. *Is she going to walk out to sea and drown herself or not?* It'd simplify his life if she did. But that didn't seem likely as Cheryl picked up her shoes and walked barefoot back toward Pacific Coast Highway. Well, hell, didn't matter none. He had her address. He could do her in a minute once Rollins gave the word. Kinda liked the look of the woman, though. Liked how her blouse wrapped around her breasts when the breeze was just right. And the soft curve of her butt when she bent over to grab her shoes. Maybe he'd enjoy himself before doing her, let her go out with a smile on her face.

He followed her across the highway, and back to the house.

68

Karen had already left work for the day when Noel Atchison put down the large bound volume of 1968 *Couriers* he had been reading and tilted back in his chair. *The thing is,* he mused, *Walter Lowndes lied about something that could be easily checked.* That didn't make much sense. If you're going to lie, do it about something you can't be called on.

All this was assuming that Karen got the story right when Ritter called her this afternoon. Which she always did. According to what

Walter Lowndes told Ritter, he didn't buy the resort until 1971, three years after the fire. But that, as Cheryl McAfee told Mark, was bull. Noel remembered when the property was sold because it enabled the girl to leave town. Folks were pretty happy about that because they figured her alcoholic mom would leave, too. That had to be 1968. And he'd found the sale briefly mentioned in a *Courier* article on local real-estate prices. So why the hell lie about it? That must be what was in the other missing issue, though—a major story about the sale of the resort to Lowndes.

Atchison swiveled around far enough to stare out the window at the sky. Maybe he wasn't a newspaperman by training but he knew enough to begin wondering when Harmony's leading citizen felt sufficiently threatened to lie to a complete stranger who was doing nothing more than looking for his mother.

Not that Lowndes was some moral paragon incapable of deviousness and dishonesty. He was, as Caroline Bellamy once mentioned to him apropos of nothing, a complete bastard, a petty tyrant who lorded it over everyone as though he was some sort of feudal baron who was due the respect and obedience of his subjects. If he really did suffer a stroke it must have been divine retribution, God finally having enough and reminding Walter that he was, after all, only a mortal, and not a very nice one at that.

But there was a story here, somewhere. Or more than a story—this was getting into the realm of real interesting legal issues. He rocked forward in his chair, grabbed a pen, and began to list the old timers: Micah Rollins, Walter Lowndes, Caroline Bellamy, old Bill, Eldon Stallworth, Cheryl McAfee . . .

Hadn't thought of Cheryl for three decades until lunch today. But then it started coming back in a rush. Real pretty girl with a real crazy mom. Got herself knocked up by Carl Stark, almost married him till her mother intervened. That's kind of what got events moving thirty years later though, wasn't it? Who would have thought three decades ago that when most of those involved were in their fifties and sixties, and the rest of the world was awaiting the new millennium, all the actors were going to be called back onstage once again? Jesus, what a thing to look forward to. But if Cheryl had married Carl and not given up their baby none of this would be going on. So it's the *baby!* And maybe the baby's baby. The spark that lit the fuse. Now *that's* interesting.

If Cheryl and Carl had gotten married, Walter probably wouldn't own the resort. Of course, Carl wouldn't have done diddly with it, never did have a lick of business sense.

He wrote "Cheryl's baby—Mark Ritter," then wrote "Lisa." Look at that: three generations of McAfees. And the oldest only forty-five. He looked again at his list of names. Two of those people are suddenly dead. Wild Bill and Eldon Stallworth. Probably the two most dissimilar people in Harmony.

Ritter got to town when? Monday? And then these two old-timers, who hardly ever spoke or met, die within days of each other. A coincidence? What would Sherlock Holmes have said? Not fucking likely, Watson.

But all Ritter had done was ask a few questions. The man was looking for his mom.

And found her!

Or Mason found her for him. *Oh-oh,* Atchison thought. *I've forgotten him, haven't I? He's about the same age as the other players on our stage.* He neatly printed: "Mason Hightower." *The attorney kind of sits in his office over there and pulls Mark's strings, doesn't he? "Go here, go there, see Walter, talk to Cheryl." I wonder what his purpose is. And if he ever knew Cheryl.*

Cheryl. Odd how Mark found her—because it was really *Mason* who had dug her up. But not until it suited his purposes. Whatever *they* were. He drew a box around her name and thought about it: Cheryl was just a kid back then. Had a child out of wedlock—a big deal in those days—and left town in shame. That's what usually happened. The resort had been sold almost at once. To Walter Lowndes. Though Lowndes now denied it, claimed it was three years later. *Bullshit, Walter, you are fibbing to us little folk.*

Okay, put that aside a minute and go back to Ritter. Everything happened after Ritter came to town. *Because* Ritter came to town. *If he hadn't, we'd be having another sleepy summer, and two people who'd lived here all their lives would still be alive.*

Atchison closed his eyes a moment and moved it around in his mind. Then suddenly sat up straight.

Maybe it wasn't Ritter's arrival that set everything off, but his kid's. *Not* the dad—

Taking a blank piece of paper he wrote "LISA RITTER, AGE 7" in large block letters right in the middle, then hunched his body forward and stared down at the words.

Lisa . . . Ritter.

Think, damn it!

His eyes focused on the name.

Lisa Ritter.

Not the dad. The daughter.

Maybe none of this would have happened if Ritter had showed up in town without the kid. *Jesus, for want of a baby-sitter . . . two people would be alive now instead of murdered.*

He drew a box around her name and began to darken it in.

Not *the daughter . . . the granddaughter. Cheryl's granddaughter. There's something there, damn it, something in that relationship. Cheryl . . . Mark . . . Lisa. Three generations. Got to be something about that. Something that caused two people to die.*

Noel couldn't remember much about Cheryl; she had been too young. But he knew her mother, had gone to school with her for one year. Annie something. Then she married McAfee, had a kid, or vice versa; got divorced soon after. Or maybe McAfee just took off. That was worth looking into. But Annie was what people here used to call white trash. Worked in the theater as a ticket-taker, lived in an old trailer, had what folks referred to as loose morals. *More like no morals,* Noel thought, then jerked his head up.

Four *generations, then, with Annie. . . .*

Atchison rubbed his temples. *Jesus, what a town this is. Okay, go back four generations, then.*

Walter Lowndes started hanging out with Annie McAfee when he was high-school age. The original odd couple—Annie two or three years older than him, with a baby, and living in a filthy trailer. Walter, the town intellectual, reciting poetry and painting pictures, or acting high and mighty in his Bohemian, phony-cultured way. The odd couple. But everyone knew why he was over there every night— Annie was an easy make in a town where girls made a point of proclaiming they were going to march to the altar as virgins, if not die that way. And Annie was always able to get hold of booze— Walter was a Jack Daniel's fan even then. Hell, he'd get looped and pick fights and spout poetry all in the same night. So, yeah—an odd couple, but both parties getting what they wanted: sex and booze for Walter, sex and a little respect—and maybe even a little money— for Annie. Then Walter went away to college. When he came back four years later he took up with Annie again. It was a little harder to see what he was getting out of it this time. And it didn't last more than a year or so. But this was long before the resort was sold, *years* before.

Still . . . there was something there.

He focused on the child's name again, now surrounded by a huge black box, and drew his pencil back and forth, back and forth, as he thought.

Lisa . . . Lisa . . . Lisa.

Then the pencil dropped from his hand.

He stood up suddenly. Where could he get a photo from the early sixties? The schools, maybe—class pictures—but they wouldn't be open until Monday. *Who else?*

Micah! Micah saved everything from his childhood. Probably still had old lunches he hadn't eaten. He'd sure as hell have photos.

He grabbed the phone, excitement beating in his chest. *Christ, Micah, you aren't going to believe this. Damn well aren't going to believe it.*

69

Janis Lowndes held the cordless phone to her ear as she paced back and forth in her penthouse apartment. "You're the only one he'll listen to, Micah. I tried to convince him last night but he started screaming at me. Now it's up to you."

Micah relaxed back on the couch in his den and sipped from a Waterford tumbler with two inches of Johnny Walker over ice. "Come on, Janis. What do you expect me to do? If he doesn't want to go back east there's nothing we can do about it."

"Maybe you can lease a plane in Denver. We could take him ourselves."

"What? Sedate him, then put him in a sack and carry him on board? Be realistic, girl. If he doesn't want to go there's nothing we can do about it. Anyway, I talked to him recently. He seemed okay to me."

"Micah, he is not okay. He blew up at me last night and at Caroline this morning. He's convinced everyone's out to get him."

"Well shoot, they are, aren't they? I mean, I'd get a little paranoid too if my family and friends were trying to hijack me to New York."

Janis came to a stop. "Micah, why didn't you tell Caroline how bad my father is? She had no idea."

"Oh, horse-pucky! I told Caroline more than once that Walter just isn't capable of rational decision-making anymore. She knew exactly what he was like. Don't let her try to make out I'm the bad guy here. If she thought Walter was going to talk calmly with her it's her damn fault. You know how she's been drinking lately, anyway. She was probably half-drunk when she showed up out there. It's too bad, she used to be more sensible than that."

"He talked to Mark Ritter yesterday. Did you know that?"

Micah paused. "So I heard. Have a nice chat, did they?"

"Dad's not taking his Prozac, Micah. What kind of talk do you think they had?"

"None too good, I'd guess. Exactly what happened?"

"They insulted each other like a couple of schoolboys out to prove something. Then Dad told Mark that his mother had been the town tramp. He also indicated you and Caroline were partners in the resort. It just sort of spurted out, I don't think he intended to do it."

Micah sighed to himself. "What sort of reaction did that get?"

"Curiosity. Interest. What did you expect?"

When Micah didn't reply Janis added, "He's talking about *Death in Venice* again, too. It's obsessed him. And he's doing something with his den."

"What do you mean, doing something?"

"I don't know. He's had a lock put on the door and won't let me in."

Micah paused, not sure he wanted to go on. Finally he said, "You ever been in there?"

"Yes." The word was said in such a way as to cut off further inquiries.

"Must be something extra-nasty if he's locking it up." Micah found himself trying not to think about it.

Janis didn't reply.

Brooding now, Micah unexpectedly took the conversation in a new direction. "You know anything about this newspaper story someone sent Ritter?" It had been on his mind for days, and was increasingly worrisome.

"Why should I know anything about it? I've never even seen it."

"I'm kinda curious who's sending him things. Just like it'd be nice to know who killed Bill, wouldn't it?"

"Micah—" Exasperation. "What are you getting at?"

"You're screwing Ritter, aren't you? I just thought you gave him that article."

"And shot Bill? Micah, you are really something."

"All right, girl. Don't get all lathered. I'm just trying to figure some things out. I'm confused right now and I don't like being confused." He paused a moment and picked his glass up. "You say Walter's not taking his medication?"

"He wouldn't be acting like he has if he were."

"All right, Janis." He let out another sigh, upset at the way things were going. "I guess you're right. We're going to have to do something. Leave it to me."

"You'll take him to New York?"

"I guess that's the only alternative now, isn't it? But don't tell the nurse, or anyone back east. Let me take care of it."

After he hung up, Micah slammed his glass down on the coffee table, spilling scotch on his hand. He didn't like this. Not one damn bit. Besides not knowing who killed Bill, and who (else?) was tipping off Ritter about events from thirty years ago, Walter Lowndes was out of control. In other times this might not have been a big deal, but Micah couldn't risk it right now. On the other hand he damn well couldn't let Walter out of Harmony, either. Maybe he'd have to hurry things along some. It worried him, though. *You're more likely to screw up when you rush things,* and he very much didn't want to screw up because everything was already a little too fine-tuned for his taste. But there didn't seem to be any choice.

VII

70

Walking rapidly down the skyway ramp from the early-morning flight, Mark and Lisa crossed through the mostly vacant waiting area with its sea of seats, to a long silver-and-gray corridor leading to the train that would take them to the baggage terminal.

"Can we have breakfast here?"

"No, I want to get back to Harmony. We'll eat in town."

They passed a fast-food restaurant, a closed bar, and a series of hotel advertisements framed like artwork behind glass. Mark caught a glimpse of himself reflected in the glare of one of the ads, gave a start, and turned his head slightly toward the rear.

"I changed my mind. We're going to eat here. Let's see what's up ahead."

It was a small nondescript restaurant with two dozen blond-wood tables and no customers. The waitress was on them at once.

"I want pancakes," Lisa told her very precisely. "And chocolate milk. And orange juice."

Mark ordered eggs and coffee. "I'm going to go to the bathroom, hon. I want you to stay here. Okay? Don't leave, no matter what. Even if someone asks you." He paused, then said, "Unless it's a policeman," and tried to smile.

Lisa grinned. "Sure. And don't talk to strangers."

"You got it, Kiddo."

Ignoring the bathroom at the restaurant, Mark walked down the corridor leading to the moving sidewalk. What did they teach in survival training? *Stealth, Speed, and Surprise.* Anyway, he'd never met a big-time weight lifter who could fight. Or recite the alphabet.

He turned suddenly at the restroom sign, stood in the small vestibule, and when Bobby Sample tried to walk past, grabbed him from behind and slammed him face-first into the wall.

"Hey, what the fuck do you think you're doing?"

Holding Sample from the back Mark shoved him through the restroom doors, then rammed his body against a waist-high sink. "What the hell are you doing following me?"

"Fuck you, cowboy. You just got yourself an assault charge."

Mark grabbed the cop by the back of the neck and slammed his Adonis-head into the mirror, breaking the glass. "Seven years' bad luck, Bobby."

The man howled in pain and almost lost consciousness as blood ran down his cheek. Mark ran a hand along his body and didn't find a gun but did discover a plastic restraint balled up in Bobby's back pocket. "What's this, Bobby? A sex toy for a police deviant?" He strapped the restraint around Bobby's wrists, pulled it tight, then spun the man around. "Why are you following me?"

Bobby swung his square head back and forth, trying to clear his muddled thoughts. Blood flew from a cut on his forehead to his shirtfront. "I don't answer to you, asshole."

"Okay, how about I call Chavez and ask him why you followed me? It must be official police work. You're not allowed to freelance, are you?"

"Who says I did? I just came to the airport to see my aunt Tilly off and suddenly you grab me from behind when I'm walking back to my car. Fucking chickenshit move, Ritter."

Mark jerked an airline ticket out of Bobby's shirt pocket and scanned it. "*Charles Bronson?* Weird fantasy, Bobby. He's old enough to be your parole agent."

"You planted it. Prove I was on that plane."

"Somehow I think you'd do something to draw attention to yourself. You're not exactly subtle, are you, pal? You can't even tail someone without getting your face bloody."

"Yeah? Who are you, fucking Columbo? What'd you do when that chick ran off from you at the park? Sat there with your finger up your ass."

"And you followed her home?" The thought that Sample knew where his mother lived made his anger explode, and he wanted nothing now but to hurt the man.

"Figure it out, Sherlock."

Mark seized him by the shoulders. "Why? Who paid you? Lowndes?"

Sample said nothing but bulled his body forward, shaking his shoulders, and trying to kick Mark in the shins.

Mark shoved him sharply back against the sink. *"Why are you interested in my mother?"* He was shouting and his voice echoed off the hard enameled walls. *"Why did you follow me?"*

Sample spit in his face.

"Stupid move for a man who's cuffed, Bobby." Mark grabbed him by the shoulders just as a middle-aged Japanese tourist with a camera dangling from his neck, walked in, looked at them, and paled. Mark hesitated a moment, said, "Hi," and smiled stupidly.

The man stared at him, and seemed rooted to the floor. But his lower lip began to tremble.

Mark muttered "Fuck it," and pantomimed a gun, aiming it at the man who turned at once and rushed out.

Sample was pulling on the restraints, trying to get free. Mark spun him around, pushed him into a toilet stall, then shoved furiously on the man's back so he lurched over, his feet flying out from under him and his head bouncing off the toilet seat. With his foot, Mark rammed Sample's face into the water, then released him.

The cop jerked his head up, sputtering. "I'll fucking kill you, Ritter. I mean it."

This time Mark held his head under water for thirty seconds. "I'll take the restraints off after you drown. The police will think it's some weird new method of suicide. Something Charles Bronson would do."

"Goddamn you . . ." The toilet water was red with blood.

"You're no fun, Bobby. All you do is scream. Does Janis know that about you?" He reached down, pulled off the man's shoes, then removed his pants. "No underpants? Always ready for action, I guess. Is that Charles Bronson's slogan? Or something you decided for yourself?"

Holding Sample's clothes, he kicked him in the butt, sending him sprawling toward the toilet tank again. "Don't go running out in the terminal. Someone might think you're some kind of sex-crazed maniac. Especially since your wallet and ID are about to disappear. But if you hang on here, someone's bound to come in sooner or later."

On the way out Mark grabbed a CLOSED sign from the inside handle and dropped it on the outside of the door.

Back in the restaurant he put ten dollars on the table and said, "Let's go."

"Aren't you going to eat?"

"I don't think so, hon. I want to get back to Harmony."

And after seeing Chavez about his out-of-control cop, try to find out what caused my mother to take off.

But to accomplish that, he knew he was going to have to talk Karen into doing something she definitely wouldn't want to do.

71

"I just stood there like an idiot staring at her," Mark said, striding back and forth in Karen's living room while his daughter ate a second breakfast in the kitchen. "I started to run, then remembered Lisa. I couldn't leave her. So we went back to the motel. I called her at least twenty times but the phone was unplugged."

"You must have some idea why she ran away."

"But I don't!" He halted and threw both clenched hands in the air as if warding off a blow. "She just snapped. She fell apart, started bawling, and ran off as though someone were chasing her." He stomped back to where Karen was sitting on the couch and dropped down next to her. It was only her and Lisa's presence that kept him from screaming.

Karen said, "What were you talking about when she started crying?"

Mark put his head in his hands. "We weren't *talking* about anything. I pointed out Lisa. She was playing with another little girl."

"And Cheryl didn't say anything?"

"She freaked. She screamed, went into her hysteric act."

Karen took his hand. "It obviously must have something to do with Lisa, then."

Mark jerked his hand away and rubbed his face as though scrubbing it with soap. " 'Something'! For God's sake, if there's *something* about Lisa to set her off she should have *told* me. Cheryl's my mother, Lisa's her granddaughter. It's time to stop treating us like strangers."

"Didn't she tell you anything?"

Mark sank back against the cushions and thrust his legs out in front of him. "Lowndes. She told me about Walter Lowndes."

Karen straightened. "Lowndes? What about him?"

"This isn't a news story, Karen. It's family stuff. *My* family. It's not for the *Courier*."

"I'm not writing a story. I'm trying to help you."

"Hell, I'm sorry." He took her hand and squeezed. "I didn't want to tell you on the phone. It sounds crazy. She thinks Lowndes killed my fa— Carl Stark."

"What?" Karen looked at him incredulously. *"Walter Lowndes* killed Carl Stark? Why, for God's sake?"

"Stark wouldn't sell the resort land. Lowndes wanted it."

Karen shook her head. "No, no, no. I don't believe it. It's too fantastic. Walter Lowndes? He might be a bastard, but a cold-blooded killer? I don't think so, not unless he was a completely different person thirty years ago."

Mark tried to drop her hand but she wouldn't let him. She said, "Your mother's believed this for thirty years, carried it with her for thirty years, and done nothing about it? Does that sound right to you?"

"What could she do?"

"Go to the police. That's what people do when they have evidence of a murder."

"She doesn't *have* any evidence. Other than her knowledge of Lowndes. And the fact that Stark wouldn't sell. And that Lowndes ended up owning it anyway."

"That's not very damning."

"Doesn't mean it's not true."

"Then we've harbored a killer in this town for thirty years? And I *worked* for him? I don't believe it."

"You've harbored a child molester for thirty years! I saw him this morning bouncing around on a horse out in the meadow when we were coming in from the airport."

"That's different."

"Why?"

"It just is." She dropped his hand and brushed hair back from her forehead. "Les Cady's . . . I don't know, mentally deranged. He's like an unmanageable kid. He probably isn't responsible for what he does. But Walter is different. When I worked for him I thought he was the most completely in-control person I'd ever met. He was not the sort to risk his future by killing someone. Not a chance."

"Why? Because it was motivated by money? Was that too common, too tawdry for Harmony's famous intellectual?"

From the kitchen Lisa said, "Can I get more milk?"

Karen said, "Sure, hon. It's in the refrigerator."

Mark jammed his hands in his pockets. "I didn't even get a chance to talk to Cheryl about Carl Stark." He sighed deeply. "This is frustrating as hell to me. Why can't I find anything out about my father? I don't know a damn thing about him except that he was a lousy businessman. But what kind of person was he? What did he think of being a dad?" He jerked suddenly to his feet. "Screw it. If she won't tell me I'll ask people around here. What about Caroline Bellamy? She must have known Stark. Maybe she remembers something—"

The phone rang. Karen picked it up, then handed it to Mark. "Mason."

"Got your birth certificate," the attorney said, sounding cheery. "The fax just came in from Denver. Did your neighbor ever send the one from South Dakota?"

"I don't know, I haven't talked to Chavez recently."

"I showed him that Pooh Bear note of yours, by the way. He sent it to Denver for lab analysis but after the way it's been handled it isn't likely they'll come up with anything. Unless Cady left body fluids on it. You never can tell with perverts. I'll call Chavez, see if the other birth certificate arrived. You'll need to get printed so we can compare you to the official certificate. No name on this one, by the way, just 'Baby McAfee.' Why don't you stop by this afternoon?"

"All right. What exactly does it say? Read it to me. Word for word."

"Baby McAfee. Boy, born June 9, 1968. Seven pounds, eleven ounces. Mother Cheryl Lynn McAfee, father Carl Roger Stark."

"June 9. My folks, the Ritters, told me it was June 1."

"So you're younger than you thought. Lucky you. See you this afternoon."

"Hold on," Mark said. Quickly, he told the attorney about his run-in with Sample, while Karen looked at him with an open mouth. Hightower said, "Jeez, boy, you're making yourself mighty well-known in town, aren't you?"

"Kind of looks like it," Mark agreed.

When he hung up he glared at Karen. "I didn't ask for this. He followed me. He's obviously working for someone. Lowndes, probably. It's his town. And he's not going to be happy with Cheryl coming out of the woodwork after thirty-plus years."

"Or he's keeping an eye on you for Todd. That'd be my bet."

"Could be." He held her gaze, tired of talking about it.

She stared at him a moment, then shook her head. "Mark Ritter, the policeman's friend. You're not going to be able to drive a block without getting a ticket for speeding."

But Mark's mind had reverted again to Cheryl. "Goddamn it, I don't care how crazy she acts, I believe her. I think Lowndes killed my father."

Karen was still dubious. "Because Cheryl said so?"

"Because my mother said so."

She threw up her arms.

"I'm going to break into his house."

"What?"

"I want to see his secrets."

" 'His secrets'? What in God's name are you talking about?" She looked at him as if he had lost his senses.

"Everyone has secrets, Karen. You, me, everyone. I want to see Walter Lowndes's. He's a businessman, he's successful, he's famous in the cultural world. I'm betting he's conscientious enough and egocentric enough to keep records of every deal he's been involved with. For legal reasons if for nothing else. Hell, he's probably expecting biographies after he dies. I think he'd keep information—records, files, computer disks, something—on any business or photography or publishing effort he's put money into. It might be hidden away, it might even be in some sort of code, but I'm going to look. It can't be that hard; I know what dates I'm looking for: July 'sixty-eight when my father died and August or September 'sixty-eight when Cheryl said Lowndes bought the resort."

"What do you expect to find? A videotape of him killing Carl Stark? A handwritten confession?"

He looked at her coldly, dismissing the sarcasm. "I'm going to need your help."

Lisa walked in from the kitchen and looked at the two adults standing and staring at each other like prizefighters waiting for the bell. Karen said, "I'll get my stun-grenades and plastic explosives."

"It won't be that dramatic. Just get him out of the office."

"What am I supposed to do? Sweet-talk him into coming over here for an afternoon of fun and games?"

Lisa said, "What are you fighting for?"

He said, "After I saw Lowndes yesterday I talked to Janis about him. You're not supposed to know what I'm about to tell you, so put away your reporter's hat for a minute."

She looked like she wanted to hit him. "Okay, it's away."

"He's no longer capable of running the resort. He's lost most of his near-term memory from a stroke, and he's emotionally unstable. He has a full-time nurse to help him when he needs it. You'll probably have to go through her. When I saw him yesterday he seemed just barely under control. He could be worse today."

"Janis told me some of this yesterday. So how am I supposed to get him here? He sounds like he ought to be institutionalized."

"Tell him you're doing an article on the early days of the resort. Tell him you expect it to be picked up by newspapers all over the West—how a lone visionary created a multimillion dollar Shangri-la where everyone else saw only dirt and trees, blah, blah, blah. He's your pal, you'll know what to do. Play into his ego. It seems to be the only part of his mind that's intact. Tell him you want some up-to-date quotes to counteract the bad publicity the town's received. But tell him you have to do the interview at the *Courier* because you'll be the only person in the office."

Her arms hung limply at her sides. "When do you want me to do this?"

"Now. Today. I want to get in his office this afternoon."

"This is stupid. Walter Lowndes is not a murderer."

"Please, Karen."

She shook her head. "There's no point. It's your mother's thirty-year fantasy! Don't play into it."

He folded his arms and tried to speak calmly. "What's the problem? It won't even be a lie. You can actually write the story. And it might help me learn something about Cheryl McAfee and Carl Stark. My parents."

She sighed and ran a hand through her hair. After a moment she asked, "What time?"

"Two or three o'clock."

Karen picked up the phone. Mark said to his daughter, "Go in the bathroom and brush your teeth."

"I don't have my toothbrush here."

"There's one in the cabinet below the sink," Karen said absently. She sat in a chair and picked up the phone while Mark went into the kitchen and made himself some toast. All he had had on the early-morning flight to Denver was a glass of orange juice. When he came out Karen had gotten past Lowndes's secretary-nurse and was arguing with the man himself.

"But it's publicity—" She threw Mark a hostile glance. "The focus of the story will be on your unusual ability to see the future—"

Mark checked the bathroom where Lisa was just finishing her teeth. "I have to go potty."

"All right, hon." He shut the door and went back in the living room.

A moment later Karen was off the phone. She shook her head wearily. "One o'clock. But he's not thrilled by it. I guess he just assumes the world recognizes his genius already."

"Try to keep him for two hours or so. I'll carry my cell phone. As soon as he leaves, call me and I'll get out of there."

"What are we going to do with Lisa when I'm interviewing Lowndes and you're at his office?"

Just then the girl came out of the bathroom.

"She can watch television in the city room while you're talking to him."

Lisa said, "I want to go horseback-riding instead."

Karen smiled uneasily at her. "Tell you what, hon. We'll go horseback riding later. I promise you." And then to Mark: "Okay. It'll work if Walter doesn't have a fit. He has a temper, you know."

Mark was only half listening to her. He had something to accomplish before searching Lowndes's office. "Have you got time to go out to Caroline Bellamy's with me? I want to ask her about Carl Stark and Cheryl."

"I don't have to go into work today. It's Saturday."

Mark jerked his head back. "It is, isn't it? I've been losing track of time. Let's go. I think your friend Caroline knows a hell of a lot more than she's let on."

72

As they had a few days ago, Mark, Lisa, and Karen sat with Caroline Bellamy in the empty dining room of Trees, while in the adjacent bar a man operated a floor polisher, slowly weaving away from them toward the sunlight bursting through an open door in the distance, then turning and coming laboriously back the other way. Mark had already told Caroline about Cheryl McAfee.

"Of course I remember her," the woman said with her usual exuberance. "She was about ten years younger than me. Actually, I remember her mother better. She was a sort of—" Her face tightened with embarrassment, an emotion that seemed unusual if not alien to her, and her body shifted uneasily within the loose dress.

Mark tried to encourage her. "Cheryl seemed to have some hostility toward her mother."

Caroline glanced at Lisa who was drawing with a pen on the back of an order form. "I don't even remember her name. She lived in an old trailer and was raising her daughter by herself. Worked at the Rio Theater downtown. Friendly to men, if you get my meaning. If she'd worn beads and made candles people would have called her a hippie. Instead they thought of her as a tramp."

Mark leaned forward, his forearms braced on the tabletop. "You must be able to tell me *something* about Cheryl, the kind of person she was—"

"But *you've* talked to her!"

"For five minutes. She wasn't very communicative. She wants Harmony out of her life for good."

"Well, I can understand that," Caroline told him. "All Harmony meant to her was poverty and an unwanted pregnancy—" She flushed a blood-red. "Oh, Lord, I did it again, didn't I? You wouldn't think a foot this big would fit in a mouth so easily. Well, I'm sorry. It was a stupid thing to say. How do I know it was unwanted?"

"Unwanted enough to give away," Mark said evenly.

"Damn it, that's not fair," Karen said unexpectedly. She seemed quick to take Cheryl's side in all of this. "Put yourself in her shoes.

She was fifteen, in high school, everyone telling her to give the baby up. What did you expect her to do?"

Mark struggled against a surge of rage. He wanted to scream: *I expected her to keep me, for Christ's sake! And love me. Not sell me to the highest bidder.* Instead he said to Caroline, "You must remember Carl Stark, too. I don't know anything at all about him. He would have been about your age."

She eased her large body back in the chair and smiled. "Of course. Carl was a nice kid. A little rowdy in high school but most kids in these mountain villages are. Nothing to do but drive fast and party. He did both. So did I."

"Was he in trouble with the law?"

"Nothing like that. In those days if you were driving drunk the cops would take you home. Now they book you, put your name in the paper, try to make you look like a fool."

Tired of all the adult talk, Lisa slipped from her seat and began to wander around the huge, mostly darkened room with its dozens of tables, all with chairs resting upside-down on the tabletops. It looked very strange to her, a silly thing for adults to do.

Caroline said, "Folks were surprised when Carl left his land to Cheryl. I do remember that. It never occurred to anyone he'd even have a will."

"Especially Walter Lowndes?" Mark asked, and watched her expression. She didn't know he was aware of her business relationship with Lowndes.

Caroline seemed uneasy. "What do you mean?"

"Lowndes was the only person to benefit from my father's death. Isn't that right? I got shipped off to South Dakota, Cheryl was sent to boarding school, and Lowndes ended up with the resort. Or am I missing someone here?"

"He didn't *end up* with the resort. He bought it. And it was nothing but a piece of bare land."

"With the best natural slopes in America."

Karen got up and went after Lisa who had pushed open the door to the kitchen.

Mark snatched the pen Lisa had been playing with and began to tap it on the table. "My mother thinks Lowndes killed Carl."

"*What?*" The word burst out just as the floor polisher shut off in the bar. In the sudden silence Caroline stared at Mark in obvious shock. "She thinks *Walter*—" She sank back and shook her head as

Karen and Lisa came back to the table. In a whiny voice Lisa said, "I want to go outside."

Caroline was clearly upset, but also disbelieving. "Your father died in a fire, Mark. I was there. I remember this all very clearly. No one killed him. Has she forgotten that? It's been thirty years. God knows what sort of fantasies she's dreamed up, but *murder?* She was only fifteen, her boyfriend had died, her baby was taken from her, her mother rejected her. It's only natural she'd look around for some-one to blame for her troubles but believe me, no one killed your father. He died in a fire started by a bad electrical connection." She leaned across the table, her huge earrings swinging at her cheeks. "Do you want me to talk to her? I'd be happy to. But this is crazy. She's got to get this idea out of her mind before someone ends up getting hurt."

Mark shook his head. "She doesn't want any contact with Har-mony."

"Where does she live?"

He shook his head again.

Caroline's face turned angry. "Then you talk to her. Convince her she's on the wrong trail here. My God, what a thing to carry around for thirty years." She swung angrily on Karen who was trying to keep Lisa from squirming from her chair again. "Did you know about this?"

"Just since this morning. I don't believe it, either, Caroline. Maybe someone did kill Carl but I just can't see Walter—"

"No one killed Carl Stark!" She hit her fist on the table. "The police investigated! They even had an arson squad from Denver come in. It was an accident!"

Lisa was getting cranky with all this adult disharmony. "I want to go horseback-riding. I don't like it here."

Even Karen was getting edgy. "I said I'd take you later. Just try to sit quietly for a minute. Can you do that?"

Mark said to Karen, "Try to take her someplace besides the resort this time. Lowndes might be there."

Caroline Bellamy was stunned. Her body sank back against the chair, and her ringed fingers fell with a dull thud on the table top. "And he would do what? Kill you people? My God, Mark, you've lost your senses. Even if something did happen involving Carl Stark, that was thirty years ago. What do you think is going to happen now? Do you think Walter has gone on killing people all this time?

Or has some blood feud against your family? Jesus!" She pushed her chair back and looked as if she were going to stomp away.

Angered, Mark said, "Lowndes told me you and Micah Rollins were partners of his in the resort. Is that why you're so worked-up? You don't want anyone probing into your business dealings?"

Caroline's mouth dropped open. "Walter told you that?"

Mark stared at her as she tried to regain her composure. She put her hands in her lap, made her voice and face go neutral. "Walter didn't have enough money to buy the property outright. He asked us to go in with him. We've always been silent partners—just investors. We don't involve ourselves with running the resort. That's all Walter's doing. Of course, we've both made some money off land purchases and our own work, too. My restaurants and Micah's construction business. Walter likes people to think he owns the resort outright, though. He runs things, he makes all the decisions." She paused a moment, frowning. "I'm surprised he told you."

Mark said nothing about Janis's assertion that she and Micah were running the resort now. But he felt more confidence in Janis's reliability than in Caroline's—or anyone else's.

"How did you and Rollins happen to have enough money to buy in?"

Caroline hesitated only a second, then, like a skydiver, once the first step was taken it was easy. "It was Micah's mostly. His folks had a lumber business and a couple of pieces of property in Denver with a little equity. He sold them to come up with the money."

"And you?"

"I sold my car and mortgaged the house I inherited from an uncle. And we were married. Micah and me."

Karen said, "No!"

Caroline smiled uneasily at her. "True. Three years. I finally got tired of living with a little boy, and I guess he got tired of having a mother around. So we split. All friendly-like. That was 1971. We had to redo the partnership agreement then, but we kept it the way it had been—equal shares, and Walter the managing partner."

Three years after the initial sale, Mark noted. So Lowndes could only be accused of a partial lie. Assuming Caroline was telling the truth.

Karen smiled and shook her head in disbelief. "I'm sorry, Caroline. I just can't see you married to the Lone Ranger."

The other woman laughed. "Well, it was interesting. Especially when he wore his mask and spurs to bed."

"Get along, little dogie," Karen laughed.

Mark said, "Look, this is all very amusing but I came here to find out about my father. Come on, Caroline. There's got to be something you can tell me besides the fact that he was a nice guy who liked to party."

The woman gave him a look of patience coming to an end. "I told you what I remember. Carl Stark was just another guy. Nothing special. Don't you think your mother is the person to ask about him?"

Not trying to hide his irritation, Mark rose. "Come on, Lisa." He glanced at Karen. "Let's go. I've got someone else to see." He nodded curtly at Caroline. "Thanks for your time."

Karen gave Caroline an apologetic look. "I'll call you."

But Mark and Lisa were halfway out of the restaurant by then.

73

Mark jammed the key in the ignition of Karen's Taurus. "There's someone I need to talk to. You want to come along or not?"

"In the mood you're in? I don't know. Who is it?"

"Caroline Bellamy's ex." He slammed the car in gear and it shot forward like a drag-racer. "Marvelous Micah. Harmony's magical cowboy. The man with the fertile imagination."

She sank back in the seat and closed her eyes. "He had lunch with Noel and me yesterday. He said he wanted to apologize to you for getting the story about the Contrells wrong. Just an innocent mistake."

Mark pressed down on the accelerator as they rose onto the highway and headed west. "Right. Like bombing Pearl Harbor was an innocent mistake. You coming or not?"

Karen sighed with resignation. "Why not? I'll see him in a whole new light after talking to Caroline. I hope you're not going to get on him like you did to her, though. I have to keep what friends I have left here. You don't."

"Up to him, I guess. So far we haven't exactly been pals." They drove through town to the western outskirts where Rollins's construction firm sat in its parklike setting, framed on three sides by towering pines and blue spruce. Micah's green Cadillac sparkled in the parking lot out front. Mark killed the engine. "You can wait in the car with Lisa if you want."

Her voice was tentative. "What exactly are you going to do?"

"Set him on fire."

"Jesus, Mark—"

"How do I know what I'm going to do? I'll know when I do it."

She hesitated. "I've been trying not to, but I might as well ask: How did you bang up your knuckles? They look like they've been bleeding."

"I scraped them on a toilet stall in Denver."

Karen sighed again and turned to Lisa in the backseat. "Hang on, honey. We'll be back soon."

"And then we'll go riding?"

"Pretty quick."

"She's becoming obsessed with horses," Mark said as they strode inside.

"It's a stage. Boys come next. Then shopping."

Rollins's secretary recognized Mark. "Hi. He's—"

Mark walked past her and yanked open the door.

Rollins, in a white Nike warm-up suit, was vigorously treading on a cross-country exercise machine, sweat pouring from his face. His eyes went wide with confusion, then narrowed in anger, but he managed not to say anything.

Bobby Sample, his forehead bandaged, was more impulsive. "What the fuck is this?" He jumped to his feet from a leather chair, his hands already clenched into fists.

"Morning, Micah," Mark said. "Always happy to see a man keep in shape." He smiled at Sample. "What about you, Mr. Bronson? Like to see a guy stay sharp, ready for any emergency? Like losing his pants?"

As Sample took a step forward Mark motioned Karen to a chair and took the one beside her. "Let's chat about my parents, Micah."

"Listen, fuckhead," Sample shouted, moving in his direction, "you just dug your own grave."

Mark ignored the policeman and said, "You can judge a man by his friends. Isn't that what people say, Micah? Doesn't say much for you, does it?"

Rollins ground to a stop and reached for a towel hanging from the front of the exercise machine. "Bobby, sit down."

The secretary appeared suddenly in the open doorway, tottering on her hastily slipped-on high heels. "I'm sorry, Mr. Rollins. They didn't listen."

Rollins mopped his face. "Gloria, shut the damn door and go back to whatever it is you do all day."

Rollins waited until the door closed, then walked over to his desk and sat down, still holding the towel. He plopped his elbows on the desktop and pressed the towel to his head like an ice bag. "What in hell do you two think you're doing?"

Bobby Sample seemed to go suddenly from outrage to audacity, and pulled his chair close to Karen. "Hey, Todd sends his greetings, babe. Got any message for him?"

With more bravado than she felt, Karen looked him straight in the eye. "Fuck off, Bobby."

Rollins's eyebrows went up as he stared from Mark to Karen. "Why don't the two of you get out of my office before I let loose this here junkyard dog on y'all?"

Mark crossed his legs and smiled. "Let's start with the story you told me about my parents. Very creative. But not an 'innocent mistake.' So why'd you do it?"

For the first time Rollins's face lost some of its aggressive flush, and he tilted back in his swivel chair with a chuckle. "Is that what this is about? Pretty good story, wasn't it? Had you going for a while, anyway. Poor, itty-bitty baby saved from the horrible fire after Daddy done Mommy with the family forty-five. I could tell the part about being the son of a murderer probably didn't set too well, though. That why you're all riled up?"

Mark held his temper. "Why'd you lie to me?"

Rollins laughed, thoroughly relaxed now, and dropped his towel on the desk. "Don't need a reason! Maybe I believed it was true. Maybe not. So what? It was a better story than the real one, wasn't it? So you're the kid of some teenage tramp who was humping half the guys in town. You like that better? Guess your daddy liked 'em inexperienced. Used to be a rumor about that. Old Carl, they said, did not like pubic hair. Made him all antsy, broke out in hives and couldn't perform." He winked at Karen. "Your boyfriend comes from weird stock, hon. Hope you're taking birth-control pills. And buckets of penicillin because there's no telling where he's been dipping his stick. Think maybe I seen him over at that sheep ranch east of town, making the ewes happy." He smiled, picked up a coffee cup that had THE BOSS printed on it, and took a sip, enjoying himself.

Mark could feel the pulse beating in his neck as blood rushed to his head. "You did it as a *joke?*"

"You're not tracking very well today, boy. I said it don't matter why I did it."

Bobby leaned toward Karen and whispered, "Let's go over to the locker room while these dudes argue. Todd said you like to do it in the shower. I'll lather you up, get you all slippery, then go for a ride."

Karen pretended he didn't exist.

Mark's gaze locked on Rollins. "I've been talking to Caroline Bellamy."

"Fine woman. Putting on weight, but hell, she works in a restaurant all day. She's got a right, I guess."

"She said you two used to be married."

Bobby Sample almost gagged. "Say what?" He suddenly lost interest in Karen.

Rollins threw him a look, then settled his attention on Mark. "My, my. All the old secrets are starting to slither out, aren't they? Like worms from under a rock. Harmony exposed. Have *Hard Copy* and the *Enquirer* here next. Well, she's right. It didn't last long, though. Sort of a starter marriage. On my third now." He indicated the picture on his desk. "The new one looks like Michelle Pfeiffer, don't she? Probably good for another three or four years, then I'll cut her loose. Got me a rule, though: Never marry anyone under eighteen. Unlike your daddy."

"I also know you and Caroline are partners in the resort with Walter Lowndes."

Bobby Sample again seemed surprised, and suddenly very interested.

Rollins's thin lips disappeared in his pinkish round face as he asked sharply, "Something wrong with that?"

"My father used to own the resort. We always come back to that."

Rollins braced his arms on the desktop and nodded to himself as though finally understanding. "So that's what this is about. You think old Walter gypped your daddy out of the resort property. I guess you figure that ought to be you sitting in the catbird seat over at the lodge, counting your money instead of working for a living."

"My mother thinks Lowndes killed my father. She's sure of it."

Rollins said nothing but the cords in his neck became visible as his facial muscles suddenly tightened. He leaned back and tried unsuccessfully to appear calm. "That is not the sort of thing you go around accusing people of." He turned to Sample. "That sound like the sort of thing you go around accusing people of?"

"No sir, Mr. Rollins. Sounds pretty bad to me. Ought to be a law against it. Probably is one."

Mark turned to the policeman, his tone calm and a little concerned. "You're looking green, Bobby. Been drinking out of the toilet again? I had a dog like that once. Had to have him put down. He was brain-damaged from the chemicals in the water."

"Fuck you, Ritter."

Mark shook his head. "That the best you can do?—'Fuck you, Ritter'."

Micah Rollins's hand closed on his towel, though he didn't pick it up. "Your mama got some proof of this? You are talking about Cheryl McAfee, right? Little Cheryl-the-slut got some proof, or is she just thinking out loud?"

"She didn't say."

"Then maybe you better not make accusations you can't back up. Sounds a lot like slander, doesn't it?"

"If Walter Lowndes killed my father to acquire the resort, it'd put a little hitch in your partnership, wouldn't it? Especially if the property was acquired fraudulently. In that case it might even revert to the previous owner. Or at least there would be a civil suit over wrongfully depriving a child of his inheritance."

Rollins leaned back and put his hands on his belly. This time he did relax, the conversation heading off in a direction he understood. "Thought I saw where this was going. How much do you want to go away?"

"How about all of it? The whole Eagle Point Resort."

Rollins blinked, then gave a chuckle while glancing at Sample. "You are one dumb fuck, Ritter. Just like your daddy was." He wiped his forehead with the towel, then dropped it on the desk. "You think you can come in here and threaten me and I'll just roll over for you? You've been working in an office, moving pieces of paper around too long, Ritter. You don't know how the real world works. You sure as hell don't know how Harmony works. I don't get pushed around. You hear? *I* do the pushing. And you have become the pushee."

Karen said softly, "Let's go, Mark."

Mark didn't move, his eyes riveted on Rollins's wide, fleshy face. "When I told you Lowndes might have killed my dad, you were mad. But not surprised. Interesting."

"Is it?"

"I talked to Lowndes a couple of days ago. We even chatted about you. We're chums now, me and Walter."

"Heard about your meeting. But you didn't talk about me. I've known Walter all my life. He doesn't confide in people off the street. It just don't happen."

"He did with me, told me about his medical problems, said you'd been keeping him on a pretty hefty dose of Prozac so you could run things. He finally figured out what you're doing, though. It's going to make things tough for you in the future. Walter's no dummy."

Rollins glanced over at Sample, then back at Mark. "Exactly what else did he tell you?"

"He said you and him were real close. But he doesn't think much of your intelligence. Thinks you're dumb. *Real* dumb. It depresses him having to work with someone like you. But heck, Walter's an intellectual—a poet and artist—and you're a . . . What is it you are, Micah? A carpenter? Of course, for a hammer-and-nails guy, you've done pretty well for yourself, riding on his coattails. But Walter figures he doesn't need you any longer. Carpenters are a dime a dozen out here."

Rollins's eyes drilled into Mark's, but it took a moment before he could make himself speak. "You just walked up to the edge of the world, Ritter. Doesn't seem very bright, does it? Because now you're staring down into the fires of hell." He stared into Mark's eyes. "You understand me? You know what I'm telling you?"

"Mark—" Karen rose to her feet.

Mark didn't move. He'd taken a chance and hit a nerve. He wanted to see where it would lead if he kept worrying it.

Rollins tilted back in his chair, his eyes drifting to the large floor-to-ceiling windows next to his desk. He craned his neck to look out. "That your piece-of-shit car out there, Karen? Christ, must have a million miles on it."

Karen said, "I'm going."

Rollins's eyes moved from the car to Mark. "That must be your little girl out there in the car. Pretty thing, isn't she? Damn pretty. I saw a girl like that splattered on the highway last year. She'd been in her folks' piece-of-shit car when the brakes failed. Dad, the girl-friend, the kid—all dead. Remember that, Bobby?"

"Hell, yeah. I scraped the bodies up, put 'em in little sandwich bags for the coroner."

Mark stood, facing Rollins as he relaxed behind his huge desk. "We'll be in touch."

Rollins rocked forward, putting his coffee down with a bang. "No you won't. *I'll* be in touch. You are not calling the shots around here, Ritter. Never have been. You're the ball. Harmony's the bat. Understand what I'm saying? It's been a game with us. But I think it might get nasty now. I think suddenly you're in some real deep shit."

Karen was at the door. Rollins gripped the towel, still staring at Mark. "Officer Sample, I have a couple of fuckups in my office. What do you think we should do with them?"

Sample grinned. "Already know what I'm going to do to Karen. Been thinking about it for a long time."

Mark picked the cup off Micah's desk. There was only a half inch of coffee in it. He turned to Bobby and said, "Second time today. I'd think you'd learn."

As Bobby looked at him with a blank face Mark poured the coffee in his lap, dropping the cup after it. When the policeman exploded off the chair Mark hit him as hard as he could just below the breastbone. Sample *whoosh*ed aloud as the breath shot from his lungs, and staggered forward. Mark clasped his hands together and brought them down on the back of Sample's neck, driving him to the floor.

Micah Rollins seemed appreciative. "Air Force survival training, huh? Tae kwon do, something like that? Someone said you were pretty good. Must not've been Bobby who told me."

Mark turned toward the door where Karen stood. Sample was moaning on the floor. Micah said, "Well now, I guess it's up to me to decide what to do with you. Tell you what, Mark. I gotta give this some real deep thinking. But I'll get back to you on it pretty quick. Okay?"

Mark turned the key in the ignition. "Sorry about that. We never should have gone in there."

Karen mopped sweat from her brow. "You didn't have to do that for me." Her heart was pounding, and she wiped her hands on her jeans.

"Maybe not."

"I don't mind telling you how Bobby scares me, though. That's not a tough-guy act of his. Todd used to tell me how crazy he was. Now I believe it."

Mark had already pushed Sample out of his mind. Putting the car in gear, he said, "I'll drop you and Lisa at the *Courier*. When Lowndes gets there, call me, then keep him as long as you can. Two hours if possible. As soon as he leaves, call me again so I can get out before he returns. I don't want to end my burglary career the same day I begin it."

In Micah's office Bobby Sample sat in a chair and rubbed his neck. "Second time that chickenshit son of a bitch hit me when I wasn't expecting it. I'm gonna tear his fuckin' heart out."

"Okay by me, Bobby, but after we take care of business. You understand?"

Sample put his elbow on his knee and held his forehead, catching his breath. "Was that McAfee bitch telling the truth? Did old Walter really kill Ritter's dad?"

Rollins hunched forward, worried, but not about Ritter or Lowndes. There were more important problems to deal with. "It doesn't matter, Bobby. Point is, we would have been better off if she'd stayed buried in California. Now she is causing me some mighty big problems. I'm not about to risk giving up everything I've made here. Going to have to take care of her."

Sample glanced at him. "Didn't know you and Lowndes were partners. Looks like my price is going up."

"Make it look like an accident. And don't go sticking your head in a toilet this time. Makes you look dumb. Don't like my people looking dumb." But already he was thinking, *That only takes care of Cheryl. The bigger problem is Walter Lowndes and that little girl.* Maybe it was time to start forgetting about subtlety and start thinking in terms of results. Which meant speeding things up. *It's going to have to be today, then.* Can't afford to wait any longer, the way things are starting to race out of control. Shouldn't be a problem, though. He could handle it.

He was reminded of that high-priced management consultant he hired last year to study his construction business. What was that term he used for a new way of thinking? A "paradigm shift"! Micah smiled to himself. He liked that. A paradigm shift. A new way of thinking.

He set himself to rethink seven-year-old Lisa Ritter.

And Walter Lowndes, the man who couldn't keep his hands off her.

Time to let the old man have her. Give him a couple hours of fun before he dies.

It was the least Micah could do for the old fart.

74

Caroline Bellamy sat behind her desk in the cluttered restaurant office with the door closed while the skeleton kitchen crew prepared for lunch on the other side of the wall. "Damn it, Micah," she said into the phone, "why didn't you tell me how crazy Walter is? He ought to be locked up somewhere."

"Well, now Caroline, it's not that bad—"

"Don't tell me how bad it is. I tried to talk to him yesterday but he went batso and started screaming and banging his coffee cup on the desk. He's nuts, pure nuts, and you and Janis knew it all the time. Why the hell didn't you tell me?"

"He is *not* that bad, believe me. It comes and goes, Caroline. Sometimes he's as rational and calm as you or me."

"What really bothers me, Micah, is how stupid you must think I am. That man is beyond rational. And if you don't believe it, you're as bad as he is. My God! Why in God's name weren't you honest about it? You must have known I'd find out. What did you think I'd do? Go over there with mental-health workers and have him committed?"

"Didn't want you worrying—"

" 'Worrying'?"

"Like you are now, Caroline. You start getting upset and next thing you know I'm getting weird phone calls like this one. Or you start talking to people you shouldn't be talking to. Thought it best if you just stayed on the sidelines a bit and let me and Janis handle things."

"Or is it Janis you *are* handling? Oh, never mind, I got no claim on you now. Wouldn't want to. Janis told me you're going to take Walter back to New York. When are you leaving?"

"Well, I can't exactly leave right now. And Janis can't convince him to go anyway. So unless we kidnap him it looks like we're stuck here awhile."

Caroline sighed, and didn't say anything for a moment as she pressed a hand to her aching forehead. Finally she said, "It's blowing up all around us, Micah. I knew it would someday. I *knew* it!"

"Now, Caroline—"

"Don't try sweet-talking me, Micah. I'm getting real tired of this hillbilly act of yours. You're as calculating as a Philadelphia lawyer, so cut the crap. You heard what Ritter said about Walter. It's gotten away from us. There's no telling where it'll stop now."

Rollins's tone changed. "Why in hell did you tell him we was married once? No need for him to know that."

"What? You ashamed of it? Maybe I don't look like that trophy wife you got now, but I'm twice as smart as your other wives put together. It was me who convinced you to go into partnership with Walter. You were afraid of losing everything you had. You're not timid like that anymore, are you? You're a regular John Wayne now. Maybe that's what being married to me did—made you stand up and fight."

Rollins chuckled affectionately. "Can't argue with you there. But the reason I didn't want to go in with Walter was I figured you was sweet on him, hon. Didn't see any point in drawing you two closer together."

" 'Sweet' " isn't the word, Micah. Head over heels in love was more like it. But he always figured he was too good for me. The bastard. What's happened to him serves him right, the way he treated people around here for so long."

"Did you tell Ritter about us being partners in the resort?"

"That was crazy Walter's doing, Micah. It sure as hell won't be a secret any longer, not with Karen knowing. Which means Noel Atchison knows, which means it'll probably be in the paper next week. That's not what I'm worried about. It's Cheryl McAfee. She's going to bring us down, hon. I feel it. She's bad news. Always was."

"Well now, Caroline, you just stop frettin'. I've taken care of things."

Caroline felt her spine grow cold. "What does that mean?"

"That means don't worry. It's all taken care of."

Just got to make me a phone call, he thought as he hung up. *And rely on a girl's love of horses.*

75

——A putrid tubercular-infected Venetian mist swirled about Walter Lowndes's mind and body as he strode unsteadily—eight up, fourteen back—in his small walled courtyard, the leather-bound volume held at eye level in his left hand while his right clutched the cane he didn't need at the moment. Effortlessly translating from German to English, he was caught in the grip of an idea so long-held and so powerful that only periodically did his mind flash reminders, like sudden fierce strobes of light from a tower, that he was not the character in the book he was now reading, and had in fact read at least once a year for forty years, and daily this past week—

Walter knew—at least in one of the manifold levels that his consciousness repeatedly traversed —*knew* he was not Gustav Aschenbach, of course; that would be madness, and mad Walter Lowndes was not. He knew he was not strolling on a sultry, diseased beach in Venice—that, too, would be madness, surely. But he *was* sharing the experience Thomas Mann had so exquisitely and knowingly expressed—was reliving, as he had been meant to, Aschenbach's enthralldom to the highest and most *pure* of all desires, the perfection of the human form.

Yes, yes, yes—those blinding laserlike flashes of light again, annoying reminders of sanity of a sort—yes, he was *not* Aschenbach, *was* Walter Lowndes, was walking (eight large up, fourteen small back) in his Colorado courtyard. But how often is it given to us in life to come across a book in which the author has so captured the spirit of our inner being that we feel our soul, our fine, ethereal nonbeing *being,* absorbed into the hard reality of the experience we are reading, becoming a *part* of the written word?

As *here* . . .

—He read, and hurriedly flipped the page, his mind now Thomas Mann's fevered mind, racing, racing—

and *here* . . .

He moved more quickly now, excited, thrilled.

—Read again, turned the page—hurry!—anticipating, and had his soul shot through with sudden blinding light, felt his heart pound with pure aesthetic joy at Mann's words as the famous philosopher first notices young Tadzio in the hotel dining room:

> With astonishment Aschenbach noted that the boy possessed perfect beauty. His face, pale and reserved, framed with honey-colored locks, the straight sloping nose, the lovely mouth, the expression of sweet and godlike seriousness, recalled Greek sculpture of the noblest period. . . .

Greek sculpture of the noblest period! That had been it, the life-changing moment in all of their lives—Aschenbach's, Lowndes's, Mann's, Tadzio's, the girl's—never to be repeated, when *perfect beauty* appeared suddenly, spontaneously. Life-changing, life-enhancing for Lowndes, life-ending for Aschenbach, but ending as it should, mind and soul focused wholly on the inexpressible beauty of the youthful human body.

Walter Lowndes, mortal being, whose poor mind glowed now, suddenly halted, closed his excited sixty-year-old eyes, mentally skipped ahead five pages to where

> Aschenbach was again astonished, terrified even, by the really godlike beauty of this human child.

Eyes still closed against the physical world, Walter rocked back on his heels, face pointed to the sky (as William Blake did two centuries ago, and saw angels descend on moonbeams, though Lowndes saw only Lisa Ritter). *Terrified* was indeed the word, chosen out of an infinity of alternatives. Mann, of course, would have to have lived this himself in order to apply just *that* nuance, that precise feeling, to this encounter. It was not fiction, not creativity, but *reporting* on an experience he and Mann had shared—an experience vouchsafed to but an insignificant handful of individuals in the long course of history: to understand and worship the supreme *perfection* the human form was capable of attaining.

Eight up, fourteen. Stride, stride. Again his mind, feverish, jumped ahead to Mann's words, the excited epiphany of his wonderfully tragic experience:

> To be at rest in the face of perfection is the hunger of everyone who is aiming at excellence . . .

Gustav Aschenbach, made mindless and mind-*full* by the transcendent beauty of this perfect child, and who, like a smitten adolescent, followed him everywhere, putting himself in the family's way, taking the same excursions they took, sitting near them on the beach—anything, anything—to see, to make eye contact, to view, to be a part of, to smile. To love.

Love. . . .

Not easy. Not easy at all.

Aschenbach knew: Everything great in life comes into being *in spite* of something.

Of course, Lowndes mused: *My life is a perfect example of that as the world conspired to keep beauty away from me.* But the aesthetic life, here at the tag end of the twentieth and final civilized century, had become like that. To love simple beauty and not flash or noise or excitement, was to willingly exile oneself to the untenable narrow margins of modern existence.

The small book went up again in front of his eyes. Reason and understanding became numbed, he read, the hard, granitelike words rising unexpectedly from his memory now rather than the novel. . . . Nature shivers with ecstasy when the spirit bows before beauty.

—*"Shivers with ecstasy"*—

And she had come back to him. What more could he want?

But he had to go to her now.

Lisa.

He was trembling. Go to her room; then he'd promised to see Karen Paige. Why had he done that? He had so little time.

Go to her room.

Hurry.

Experience. . . .

76

Parking the Taurus on the road so it wouldn't be noticed and remembered later at the resort, Mark jogged the half mile to the empty parking lot, then slowed to a walk as he crossed to the main lodge building. As he was passing the front entrance, his cell phone rang.

"He's out front," Karen said.

"Thanks. Hang on to him as long as you can."

Going at once to the rear of the building, he tried Lowndes's private door. Locked, naturally. He looked around to see if anyone was watching, then grasped the top of the wall and pulled himself up far enough to glance over. The redwood spa was bubbling, chlorine-scented steam rising into the air, but no one was in it, no one visible anywhere. Using his feet for leverage on the bricks, he pulled himself over and dropped down.

One of the French doors was open to the courtyard, a screen door in place to keep out insects. He turned the handle and it opened. Stepping into Lowndes's private office, he let the door quietly latch behind him. The lights were out, the door to the hallway open. He hurriedly crossed the plush carpet, shut the door, shut another which probably led to living quarters, and dropped down on a chair to catch his breath. He was surprised to find his torso covered with sweat. *I'd never make a good burglar,* he thought; *too damn nervous.*

How much time did he have? An hour? Two, if Karen could keep Lowndes occupied.

Where to start?

His nervousness grew. He didn't even know what he was looking for. Something to do with Lowndes's—and his partners—purchase of the resort property from Carl Stark. His father! Or something to do with Stark's death. Or 1968.

Why hadn't the death been investigated before? It was too damn convenient, too coincidental not to arouse suspicions. Lowndes tries to buy the property, Stark refuses, Stark dies in a fire, and Lowndes ends up the owner. No, it was too pat. His mother was right: Walter Lowndes killed his father to get the resort.

But suddenly it was more than Lowndes, wasn't it? Maybe he should be searching Micah's house, too. Or Caroline's. The question of murder for profit was no longer as simple as it had seemed.

Micah and Caroline, though, were unlikely to have kept records from three decades ago. But if Lowndes was as careful as Mark thought, there would be something, maybe not a smoking gun but *something,* in this room. His eyes went to the four-drawer file cabinet. Too obvious? Probably. So try the desk first.

He lowered himself to Lowndes's padded swivel chair and pulled open the center drawer. Pens, pencils, a fistful of architectural drawings of the restaurant being constructed at the top of the slopes, miscellaneous junk. Whatever he was looking for wouldn't be in so open a place anyway. He heard a bang from somewhere close by and his heart leapt. Jesus, it sounded right next door. He froze, listened, tried to still his pulse. Nothing.

Okay, Get on with it. Hurry!

Top left drawer. Computer manuals, blank paper. Middle drawer, pamphlets from restaurant suppliers. Bottom drawer locked. He yanked sharply on it several times but it wouldn't open. *Okay, come back to it later.*

What time was it? Ten after one. Top right drawer, stationery, memo pads, more pens. Other two drawers, spreadsheets, cost analyses, letters from his auditing firm, checkbook. And a handful of loose capsules. Medication of some kind. The Prozac he wasn't taking?

The file cabinet, then. He hurried over to it, yanked open the top drawer. At least a hundred personnel files. He started to flip past them, one by one, then took a handful out at random and glanced inside. Salary information, job descriptions, termination notices, sickness reports . . .

The phone in his pocket rang. *No, Jesus, no—Lowndes can't be coming back already.* Seventeen minutes after one. *Damn it!* He hit the ON button and whispered frantically, "What?"

"He's on his way. I couldn't keep him. He lost his temper, started screaming at me. I guess he didn't believe I was really doing a story."

"When did he leave?"

"One minute ago. I'm sorry—"

"That gives me five minutes at the most. Christ!"

She said, "Are you coming back here?"

"I don't know," he whispered. "Maybe I'll stop in and see Chavez. It depends on what I find." He clicked off the phone and hurriedly yanked open the second drawer. It was crammed with financial data filed year by year, going back to 1968. Damn it, there wasn't time to look at it. His heart was pounding. Pulled open the third drawer. Mostly empty. A small enamel jar with a screw top. An old adding machine. Rolls of tickets to something. Fourth drawer, more files, financial data, and miscellaneous junk. Then his eyes lit upon a file with the word RITTER on its tab. He yanked it out. There was nothing inside. *Why would Lowndes have a file on me? I'd never even heard of the man.*

Goddamn it, I can't worry about it now, I've got to get out of here. He felt an overflow of emotion, felt like hitting something, and slammed the drawer shut. Without planning to, he went back to the third drawer, twisted the top off the enamel jar, and saw a key.

Maybe! But hurry!

He crossed to the desk, tried the key in the bottom drawer, and felt it give. Heart pounding, he yanked it open and almost gagged as he saw at once what it contained—hundreds of photographs of nude children, some alone, some posing suggestively for the camera, some in sex acts with adults. Just like the ones at Bill's.

Mark felt as though he had been kicked in the stomach. He sank back on the chair. *My God . . .* There must be several hundred. His head ached, and his body trembled with outrage. So many children!

Again he heard a noise from beyond the wall. He looked at his watch: one twenty-five. Jesus, Lowndes was going to be here any minute. Hurrying to the file cabinet, he put the key back in the jar, then returned to the desk. He rifled quickly through the photographs. In the back of the drawer he found a two-page computer listing of at least a hundred names with e-mail addresses, probably other pedophiles Lowndes exchanged photographs with. There was also a list of half a dozen Web sites. He tried to memorize the addresses but his heart was beating so rapidly he didn't think he'd be able to retain anything.

Get some proof or nobody will believe it! Hurriedly, he grabbed a handful of photos. Boys, girls, none over eight or nine years old, some only two or three. All nude. He started to put them in his shirt pocket when his heart stopped and he died, or thought he did as his body went icy cold and his hand froze in mid-air. A half dozen pictures of Lisa lying nude on a bed, her legs spread for the camera. He heard himself mutter softly, "Noooo . . ."

And from the door which he didn't hear open, Janis Lowndes

said, "Bobby Sample told me he's going to California again. I think he's going to kill someone." She was nude, carrying a towel, and her eyes seemed unfocused, as though she was sleep-walking.

Mark pushed unsteadily to his feet. His head was spinning. "Your father—"

"—will kill you if he sees you here."

Mark trembled with rage, shoved a handful of photos in his pocket, steadied himself against the desk.

Her eyes went to the open drawer. "Things are not always what they seem. And this isn't the time. Or the place."

He slammed the drawer shut with his foot. The sound reverberated all around them. "Do you know what he is? Do you know your father is a pedophile?"

Janis was dispassionate. "He just drove up. He'll be here any second. Please, you have to leave. He can't find you here. Go through the courtyard. Hurry."

Mark couldn't stop his body from trembling. His stomach hurt so much he thought he was going to vomit. "I'll kill him." He was talking to himself, not Janis, and moved quickly toward the door.

She stepped in front of him and put a hand on his arm. "This isn't the place to confront him. Go to the police if you think he's done something other than collect pictures. As far as I know that's all he's done. He likes to play with them in his photo lab. It's his hobby."

"Hobby?" Mark fumbled in his pocket, showed her the picture of Lisa. *"How the hell did he get this?"* His arm shook as he held the photograph out. The blood drained from Janis's face but otherwise she was stoic. She started to answer, but a door slammed and she said hurriedly, "It's too late. Put the picture away."

Mark looked as if he was going to hit her.

"In your pocket," she said calmly, and directed his hand downward. Then put her arms around him and pressed her body against his as she kissed him.

Walter Lowndes's angry voice filled the room with fury. "What the hell are you doing in here?" He lurched forward from the waist, propped on his cane, and stared furiously at the two of them.

Janis pulled back from Mark and smiled easily. "Oh, hi, Daddy. We were on our way to the spa. There are so many people at my building, and we wanted some privacy. I just got a little anxious and stopped for a minute. You know me. Don't mind us, though. We'll get out of your way." She undid Mark's belt and began to pull him by the loose end toward the courtyard.

Mark resisted, his eyes fixed on Lowndes, his mind a storm of emotion.

"*Get out!*" Lowndes shouted, and his body trembled. "*Now!*" Janis tried a little-girl voice, pouty and angry. "I guess we'll have to use the spa later. See if we care!" She began to pull Mark toward the corridor door. As Lowndes again yelled at them she whispered, "Please. Go!" and led Mark into the hallway and along to the door leading to the lodge. "*Please,*" she repeated with urgency. "This is not the place to confront him."

"Where did those pictures come from? Why does he have a file on me?" He was trembling with rage.

Janis said, "Not now. Later!"

Mark felt himself being dragged away, then blinked as he saw that he was standing in the hotel reception area. The clerk behind the counter was staring at him. He thought, *The police. I've got to get to the police.*

He began to run.

Janis picked up her towel from the floor and gave her father a look of transcendent calm as she stepped toward the courtyard and the spa. She was humming a song by the Grateful Dead, and Jerry Garcia's face floated before her eyes.

Walter Lowndes was shaking so furiously he had difficulty maintaining his balance with his cane. His voice trembled and raged at her. "What were you two doing in here?"

She stopped and turned toward him. "We made love. On your floor." She pointed to the spot.

The man's large, granitelike head quaked as he stared at her. Janis came back, stood in front of him and made a pouty face. "Is my popsie upset? I'm so very sorry. I won't do it again. Ever, ever, ever. Now, is everything okay?"

A vein on Lowndes's right cheek throbbed. He looked briefly at his desk, then back at his daughter standing nude in front of him. "I asked you what you were doing. Answer me!" He disentangled himself from his cane, threw it on the floor, and slapped her as hard as he could.

Janis's eyes closed as one side of her face reddened with welts.

Lowndes hit her again, making her head snap backwards. "Why is that man intruding upon my affairs? What is going on?"

Janis dropped the towel. "I don't think I'll go in the spa after all."

As she walked away Lowndes yelled, "Tell me, damn it! Why is this man after me?"

She didn't turn around. "Why don't you ask Bobby Sample?"

Lowndes was beside himself. "*Sample?* What the hell does he have to do with anything?"

77

Hector Chavez leaned his butt against the desk and said, "If you don't calm down I'll put you in a cell. I am not kidding."

Sweat beaded across Mark's forehead and he felt as if he was going to explode. "That's my daughter, damn it! I want him arrested."

Chavez flicked another glance at the picture, one of a dozen Mark had given him, then turned away in embarrassment. The door to his office was open and in the background they could hear phones ringing and the static-filled squelch of police radios.

"The first thing you've got to consider is that it might not be real. Lowndes is a photo expert, an artist. I've seen some of his stuff for sale at his daughter's place. Looked crappy to me, but I'm not exactly a connoisseur. Some of what he does, I guess, is just cut-and-paste and call it art. So that might be what he did here—your little girl's face on another kid's body."

Mark bolted to his feet. "*I know my own child.*"

"The hair's different, isn't it? Doesn't look like Lisa's."

Mark sank into his chair and snatched the picture off the desk. "Somebody put it in pigtails. The sun hat's not hers, either. It's all part of the fantasy, the innocent little girl waiting for the man. Anyway, goddamn it, he had *hundreds* of pictures. Hundreds!"

"So did Bill."

"But Bill couldn't have put that note in her pocket. He was dead!"

"So you think Walter Lowndes is Pooh Bear? And he's been following you and your kid around?"

"Isn't it obvious?"

"And when could he have given her that note?"

Mark was too upset to reason it out. "Lowndes did it! No one else could have."

Chavez folded his arms across his chest. "You say there was a *list* of pedophiles in the desk drawer?"

"What else could it have been? It wasn't real names, though—screen names, e-mail addresses. Along with some Web sites. I only remember one." He recited it to Chavez who wrote it down, then sighed with resignation.

"All right," the policeman said, coming to a decision. "I'll take these pictures to the DA and try to get a warrant. Then we'll see what Mr. Lowndes has to say."

"A warrant!" It was all Mark could do not to launch himself at the man. "You can't wait for that! He'll destroy everything by then. You have to get out there now. That's why I came here."

"Look, Ritter, you're smart enough to know if we go in without a warrant, any evidence we discover will be thrown out. We're going to do this right. Shouldn't take more than a day. Anyway, most folks don't realize e-mail can be traced. If Lowndes has been communicating with a group of pedophiles we'll be able to trace every one of them. It's one of the few advantages of the computer age." He added cautiously, "Still hard for me to believe Walter Lowndes would do something like this, though. Seems more like Les Cady."

"I know where I found those pictures."

"But do they *belong* to him? See what I mean? Say, for example, you shot someone and I find out about it and take the gun away from you. Then the FBI rushes in and catches me with it. Doesn't mean I'm the killer. Like Janis said, things aren't always what they seem."

Mark shot out of his chair at the mention of Janis's name. "I tracked down my mother."

"Yeah?" Chavez moved around his desk and sat down. "Congratulations. I know it was a worry to you."

"Janis thinks my mother's life is in danger."

" 'Janis thinks'? What are you talking about?"

"She lives in California. I went out to see her a couple of days ago. Where do you think Bobby Sample was during that time?"

The chief leaned forward, not happy with where this was going. "What the hell are you trying to say?"

"Sample followed me to California. Janis told me he's leaving for there again. She's sure he's going to kill someone. That someone sounds like my mother. You have to do something before he tries it."

Chavez's face reddened. "That's crazy! Bobby Sample might be a little pushy but he's not a killer."

"You know better than that. Sample's crazier than your worst dream of Les Cady. He ought to be locked up somewhere and permanently medicated."

Chavez bolted up, sending his chair crashing against the wall. "Listen, Ritter. You've come in here and accused Walter Lowndes of being a child molester because of a handful of pictures, and one of my officers of being a potential killer on the basis of some druggie's fantasy tale. Seems to me like you and Karen are kinda after Todd and his friends for personal reasons. Maybe you ought to go back to your room and cool off a bit before you end up being sued for slander."

"Where was Sample the last two days?" Mark asked at once.

"Right here in town."

"Wrong. He was in California. He was on my plane coming back this morning."

"Bullshit!" But there was little force in Chavez's manner.

"Ask him how he got his face banged up. It looks like someone shoved his head in a toilet."

"Look, Ritter, you gotta expect Todd's friends aren't going to be too friendly to you. But to try to imply that one of them's a killer— that's nuts!"

"You've got a lot to learn about your force, Chief. The whole department's out of control. And you know it. Are you going to bring Sample in, or let him take off for California to kill my mother?"

"Why the hell would he want to kill your mother?"

"If we knew that we'd know why everyone's been jerking me around since I came to Harmony."

"Shit! So I'm supposed to bring him in on your word? Or Janis Lowndes's? Fat chance."

Mark spun around and headed for the door. "Then *I'll* take care of it myself. You might want to start looking for a replacement. Sample's not coming back."

78

Upset from her encounter with Walter Lowndes, Karen sat at her desk in the city room, breathing heavily through the mouth, while at the other end of the room Lisa played with a word processor. Karen leaned back, drew air deeply into her lungs, and closed her eyes. Lowndes had been distrustful from the moment he'd entered the building and saw the girl.

"What's she doing here?" he demanded even before sitting down. The knuckles of his right hand, looking like chips of white marble, reddened in the veins as the fingers that held the cane squeezed closed.

Karen had been nonplussed by the obvious hostility. Why should Walter Lowndes care about Lisa being there? "I'm just watching her for a bit. She won't get in the way."

The old man glared at Karen, his mind working as some sort of fury seemed to be building up. She noticed that the single cane he carried wasn't needed for walking today, and he seemed mentally alert. So much so that she felt buried under the terrible weight of his gaze. The dark eyebrows jerked together, lines deepening in his forehead.

"Where's her father?"

She lied easily: "He had to talk to Mason Hightower about something."

The man stared at her. "My daughter tells me you and Ritter have become close. Sleeping together, obviously. She's a bit jealous, I imagine, though she shouldn't be."

Karen let the comment fly past, as though of no consequence. She wasn't going to be distracted by the man's familiar rudeness. She indicated the chair he continued to hover over. "Please sit. We can get started. I'm interested in how you first got the idea for Eagle Point when there was nothing here but empty land."

But it had gone badly from the first. Ten more minutes and Lowndes was pushing to his feet, angrily cutting off any more questions. "Everything you've asked is something you are more than familiar with. You probably know more about Eagle Point than anyone but me. So tell me what the real purpose of this alleged interview is."

"Please, Mr. Lowndes—"

His eyes went again to Lisa. This time they locked, and didn't move away. His voice dropped. "The girl shouldn't be here. This place is filthy. In a multitude of ways."

"We hope to publicize the resort to—"

"Get the girl out of here!"

"What?"

"Get her out of here! This place is disgusting." He stood unsteadily in front of Karen, swaying slightly. Their eyes met and his mind shifted with arbitrary abruptness. Years seemed to intervene, and confusion darkened his gaze. "My daughter is after your boyfriend," he said finally. "She's prettier than you. And far more unyielding and remorseless. It is a family trait." And he was gone, but not before slamming the door like a five-year-old.

Karen had gone to the front window and stared out as Lowndes argued with the nurse who had been waiting behind the wheel of his red Jaguar. Finally the woman moved to the passenger seat, allowing the old man—he wasn't that old, she suddenly recalled, only in his early sixties—to drive home. The car exploded away from the curb with a screech of tires, as though Lowndes was in a hurry to get somewhere.

She sat again at her desk and called Mark, to warn him of Lowndes's impending return. When she hung up, Lisa came over. "You said if I was quiet you'd take me horseback-riding."

Karen looked at the little girl, and the earnestness of the child's seven-year-old face drew a smile from her. *Was I ever that sweet?* she wondered. *Maybe so. But, Lord, how the years change us. And never for the better.* She took Lisa's hand. "I've already made the reservations, hon."

"Can we go now?"

She felt a surge of warmth toward the child and gave her a hug. As Lisa hugged her back with obvious affection Karen's mood eased, the concern over Walter draining away. "I'll tell you what, young lady. Let's get a big sloppy hamburger and a milkshake first. How about a peanut butter–chocolate shake? Then we'll go riding. Sound okay?"

Lisa squealed and clapped her hands.

As she stood the phone rang. Janis Lowndes said, "Is my dad there, Karen?"

A sudden despair settled again on Karen's shoulders. "He left a minute ago. Upset."

Janis paused. "I just found out he had gone over there. If I had known earlier I would have stopped him. I don't want him under any extra stress. As I told you, he's not been well."

"I could see that." The understatement of the year.

"Micah just called me. He's decided to take my dad to New York later today. He's going to try to charter a Lear jet from Denver International."

"What will happen to him in New York?"

"He'll be evaluated and put on a medication schedule again. They'll probably keep him two weeks or so. It's not the first time."

"I hope it works," Karen said honestly.

Again Janis paused. "What happened between you and Micah this morning? He seemed upset about it but wouldn't tell me. Embarrassed, I guess."

Karen didn't feel like going into it. "He was extremely rude, Janis. I've never seen him like that. Maybe it was because Bobby Sample was with him. They practically threatened us. I've known Micah for years. I thought we were friends. I guess not."

"Well, I know he feels bad about it, Karen. He's having Noel and a few other people out later this afternoon for a tour of the Ice Castle. They're all going to ride up in the lift, take a look at how the building's coming along, and have a little meal with catered food from town. I think he's trying to get Noel to stop being so negative about the restaurant in the newspaper. Anyway, he wanted me to invite you and Mark and Lisa, if you're not going riding."

"I'm afraid Lisa's heart is set on horses. Anyway, it might be better if Micah and I stay away from each other for a while. It'll let us cool down a bit. And there's no way in the world Mark's going to want to go out there. Not after today."

She could hear Janis sigh. "I kind of figured that. I'll let Micah know you'll be riding instead. I think he'll be done at the restaurant by the time you're finished riding anyway. I know he wants to get Dad to the airport as soon as he can. At least you won't run into Walter at the resort. That ought to be reassuring, the way he's been lately."

"Will you be helping to take your dad to Denver?"

"Micah doesn't want me anywhere around here when they leave. He thinks Dad will be harder to handle if I am. I guess he's given a lot of thought to this. Is Mark there? I need to talk to him about something."

Karen's voice was uneasy. "No, he's not. I don't know where he is."

"Well, tell him to call me at once. It's about Bobby Sample. It's pretty important."

When Karen was heading out the door with Lisa she wondered momentarily how Micah knew they might be going riding today; she didn't recall mentioning it to anyone. Then it slipped from her mind as more-troublesome worries filled her thoughts.

At the same time Karen and Lisa were leaving for the resort Micah was saying into the phone, "You're *sure* they'll be out at the stables, then?" Trying desperately not to show too much interest.

Janis said, "Lisa's set on it. You know how girls are with horses. I guess you'll have to make up with them later."

Micah hung up and thought: *Perfect!* He sat back, relaxed now, and let out a sigh.

Perfect!

But, then, he knew it would be.

When Janis, standing at the reception desk, had put the phone down she suddenly realized where Mark was, and began to hurry toward her father's office. But she knew she was too late.

79

As the combination lock clicks for the second time today behind Walter Lowndes, a gray fog rises in his mind, and the years shift with an arbitrary abruptness, as they did when talking to Karen Paige in the *Courier* office. Like stage scenery being randomly pulled up and down, first it is 1968, then 1961, then 1998, as the past collides, merges with, then destroys the present, only to reemerge again—

—Heart pounding, his joy boundless, he checks the window—yes, yes, drapes pulled shut—totally dark now. Feeling on the wall for the switch, he flicks on the artist spotlights, then drops into the wide, soft leather couch that is the only piece of furniture in the entire room—

—Laying the Mann volume down next to him, his heartbeat grows larger as his mind fills with thought-pictures. . . . He remembers, more than remembers, experiences—and feels a stirring deep within his soul, a palpable rising and hardening of emotion that spells true happiness—

—So many years it's been—has it been years?—his fingertips tingle with electricity as he recalls the soft feel of skin, so pale and yielding, like molding a cloud with one's hands. *That* memory lingers most of all, though this room excites him, too; it is like a thousand years unexpectedly added to his life. And he did it all for her. Isn't that the greatest gift of all? To make a momentous effort like this, not for oneself but for one's other self.

As his eyes focus on the wall, his fingers tracing the tactile-rich tooled leather cover of the book, his thoughts narrow like the tip of a laser, and fix intently on Gustav Aschenbach, so recently returned to Venice (as Walter has just returned to Harmony, both expecting a holiday), where suddenly he (both *hes*) encounters the surpassing beauty of young (Tadzio/Cheryl). And of course, enthralled and trapped by the viselike imperatives of the ineffable, Gustav—the philosopher, the aesthete, the lover of perfection—stays long past the time he must leave to save himself and, falling victim to the influenza outbreak, dies amid the squalid and terrifying beauty of this most stately of cities.

Critics (Lowndes feels a terrible rising of anger, a rushing of blood in his ears) couldn't understand what Mann was explicating, laying out in black-and-white for everyone. We are meant to experience not the pathos of Gustav's death (the tragedy was only in the nonconsummation of love) but to feel, to actually *feel,* the excitement of this single life-altering encounter with perfect beauty, and the sacrifice made for it. Death is prosaic, a million-times-a-day experience. But the truly limitless beauty of Tadzio was *extra*ordinary and, at that, passed over by all but Gustav. Even the child's family failed to appreciate it, leaving the old man and Tadzio alone with their secret, and secret smiles, and the unfulfilled love that made both of them soar so.

Thomas Mann understood, of course, what Walter Lowndes understood and now experienced: It is not the recognition of perfect beauty that expanded Aschenbach's (and Walter's) consciousness, that made his heart beat so, but the addition of it as a new and fifth dimension to their minds, to their *being,* that altered them, allowed them to walk with joy amid the rapidly expanding ugliness of the world.

Lowndes sighs—age—and forces himself to his feet as his drab conscious mind—that tedious quotidian repository of dull facts and experiences and interpretations—wrestles with the deeper, more primitive (snakelike) seat of emotion hidden beneath the mammalian outer brain, to reach—not understanding, that is too facile—but being-ness with the pure and the perfect.

Lowndes falters suddenly as he feels his mind racing—can almost see it—feels his respiration increase, *feels* (Molding her flesh, like a cloud.)

begins to walk rapidly now about the room (Hurry!)

the purity of her form becoming him becoming her

(Hurry, Walter, hurry!)

reaches up, pulls the drapes open six inches. And sees her, *sees her,* with Karen Paige, *(Damn* the woman!) walking from the car to the stables as he knew they would, talking together, giggling.

Walter turns, rushes to the door.

Now!

(She's yours; take her!)

Now!

80

*M*an alive, old *Walter is one nutty dude,* Micah Rollins reflected as he headed out to the parking lot after making sure Janis had gone back to her own home for the evening. He wished he could take care of the Noel Atchison problem right now, but he'd better wait until weird Les Cady was gone. Anyway, Karen and Lisa had finally shown up. Walter had obviously seen them, too, because a minute later he came hurrying from the rear of his living quarters and out onto the asphalt. Exactly as planned. Nutty, but as predictable as an eclipse.

Jesus, look at him, hobbling outside with his cane. The dumb fuck! *What sort of weirdness is going on in that looney tunes mind of yours, Walter?* Must be like a dormant volcano doing nothing for years, then suddenly spewing hot shit all over the place for two minutes before shutting down again. *Wouldn't your East Coast friends like to see you now?*

My Lord, his whole body's shaking. Looks like he's got Parkinson's disease. It ain't that, though, is it? It's the sex-crazies. Mr. Intellectual's got a lot of loose connections upstairs. Especially when little girls are around. Trying to patch everything together with medications didn't work out too well, did it? Kinda like using electrical tape to tie two power lines together when they're both shooting sparks all over the place. *No sir, the man doesn't even know what decade it is.*

Well, I've lived here all my life, Walter. Just like you. And all my life you acted like I was some kind of dumbshit that couldn't hold a candle to the big-time thinker who gets his picture in the New York papers. Always treated me like some sort of retard that needed to be led by the hand when the discussion got too difficult.

Jesus, how many times have I had to sit through your damn Death in Venice *speech? Took all my energy not to start screaming, or drown you in your fucking koi pond. Christ sakes, all your beauty and ecstasy isn't worth diddly against a big ol' Caterpillar Model 950 earthmover. I've got six or seven parked behind my office right now. Any one of them could smash you and sexy young Tadzio all to shit before you knew what was happening.*

On the other hand, you might appreciate what's going down tonight. It's kinda like a ballet, Walter, and everyone's got his little dance to do. You even get to have the girl for a couple of hours. You should like that. Hell, enjoy it, do with her as you will. The only person who might be a problem now is her papa. Man's a little hard to predict. Got a temper on him. So I can't tell exactly how it's all going to play out. Only what the end result will be.

Plan A or Plan B?

Micah raised his fist at Lowndes's backside: *Hey, Walter. It starts now, let's see what happens when the hick-town construction worker pushes the East Coast thinker over the edge. You ready? Damn it,*

I'm giving you the girl. It's what you've been waiting for most of your life.

Micah got in his car. *Going to have to go back to the office while Karen and Lisa are out riding.* Didn't want Walter or Les Cady finding him out here. He'd check back in a bit and see if Lowndes did his part, or would need any help. Not likely though; Micah had told him the girl was going to be here. It was all the push Walter needed. And in his state Karen wasn't going to be a problem at all.

Later Micah would call Ritter. He was supposed to be at Karen's. *Hey, guess what old Walter's doing to your little kid right now?*

That should get things hopping.

81

What the hell was that all about? B.J. Blake wondered, watching Micah Rollins shake his fist at old Walter Lowndes. B.J. had been checking out a small condo he was going to advertise—"2 BR, 2 BA, near slopes, low down. Won't last!"—when he noticed Rollins start to get in his glow-in-the-dark Caddy, then suddenly stop and stare.

Staring at Lowndes. B.J. could see the whole thing from the front seat of his five-year-old Ford Explorer. So what the hell was going on? He knew from Karen and Mark that Micah had been up to no good lately, lying to Mark about his folks. Also, someone had been threatening Mark, trying to get him to leave town. Knowing something of Micah's business practices, B.J. had suspected him but finally decided it must be Todd Kachen.

But now that he saw Micah standing there and shaking his fist at Walter he had to wonder. The man didn't even have the guts to do it to Lowndes's face. That's the kind of guy who would make anonymous phone calls to scare someone.

B.J. pushed the cowboy hat back on his head. Maybe he'd watch this a little more, see how it unfolded.

82

If Chavez wasn't going to do anything about Bobby Sample, Mark would have to.

He felt the pain in his fingers as his hands tightened on the steering wheel. Goddamn hick-town police department. He swerved suddenly to miss an oncoming motorcycle, and realized he was driving in the middle of the street. He shook his head, trying to clear it as blood roared in his ears. The police here were not only inept, they were never going to turn on one of their own.

His flesh grew cold as he wondered where Sample was right now. *Damn it, why'd I leave my mother's number back at the motel? I should have kept it with me.*

He'd call Cheryl, tell her what Janis said about Bobby. Then . . .

He gagged as he thought of Walter Lowndes, and the picture of Lisa in his desk.

He didn't give a damn about probable cause or warrants or the other niceties of law that kept monsters like that out of jail. This was his daughter the man was after, not some hypothetical victim. The moment he finished with his mother he was going out to the lodge, and not leaving until he found out once and for all time what Lowndes had done to her.

He began to breathe hard, gulping like a runner at the end of a race, his chest heaving over and over as air wouldn't stay in his lungs. *Stop it, stop it . . . you're going to hyperventilate. You need to be in control.*

Less than half a mile to the motel. He was doing sixty along the city street when he jerked his foot from the accelerator as the other photograph, the one he had discovered at Bill's, leapt into his mind: Lisa alone in their Seattle backyard. It had been taken at least a year ago. Had Lowndes been stalking her that long? *A year? And I never noticed it? I'm her father. How could I not have seen something?*

Perhaps one of Lowndes's pedophile pals in Seattle had taken it, and now it was circulating over the Internet, being enjoyed this very minute by perverts the world over.

*   *   *

Leaving the motel door open, he went straight to the dresser, rummaged on top until he found the scrap of paper with Cheryl's phone
number. Fingers shaking so badly he could barely control them, he
dialed the number, squeezed the receiver and walked in a tight circle
as he listened to the electronic *ring, ring, ring* . . . no answering
machine, nothing. She wasn't there. Or didn't want to talk to him.
God, now what? Call the Newport Beach police? He began to pace,
thinking it out.

What would the police do if he called? Maybe drive by her house
once or twice. A lot of good that would do. *But at least they could
get word to her.*

He bent toward the phone, was about to pick it up when it rang
and his heart jumped. "Yes?"

"Is this Mark Ritter?"

He recognized his mother's voice at once. "My God, where have
you been? I've been trying to call you."

She sounded on the edge of panic. "I'm at the Denver airport. I
need to see you. Right now! I have a return flight in two hours. I
need to get back before my husband finds out. How long will it take
you to get here?"

His mind was rushing. The Denver airport. "An hour. Less. Tell
me where to meet you."

"The Midwest departure lounge, gate A37. Do you know where
that is?"

"I'll find it."

A minute later he was racing down the stairs toward the parking
lot when he realized he had to tell Karen about the pictures he had
found at Lowndes's. He started back toward his room when he
thought, *Damn it, I haven't got time; call from the car.*

Once on the highway heading east he held the cellular phone
and steering wheel with his left hand while he punched out Karen's
number. It rang four times, then the machine came on.

Goddamn it, where are you?

He listened to her cheery recorded greeting, then, speaking rapidly,
said, "I'm going to Denver to meet my mother. I'll be back by seven
or so. Karen, don't go out to the resort, don't go anywhere near
Lowndes or Les Cady. Do you understand? Stay away from both of

them, Lowndes especially. I'll explain when I get back." Then he added, "I love you," and accelerated at once to ninety.

83

Karen waited for Lisa's pony to catch up and then move ahead of her on the trail. "Remember not to pull too tight on the reins, the horse won't know what to do. Just hold them loosely like this." She held up her hand and demonstrated.

"How can I make her go faster?"

"I don't think she wants to go faster. This isn't like an amusement-park ride that tries to scare you. Both you and the horse are supposed to enjoy it."

"Can we go someplace different from last time?"

"Maybe. We'll take a look at the trails as we get higher. Sometimes the horses don't want to take them."

"Why couldn't Daddy come?"

"He's busy." *Probably talking to Chavez about Walter Lowndes. Maybe not, though.* He couldn't have found anything in the short time he'd been in Lowndes's office. "We'll have dinner with him later, hon. He'll be waiting for us at my house." She felt a sudden shiver on the back of her neck as though someone had grabbed her with an icy hand. *What was that for?*

Lisa said, "Do I get to be in front?" as her pony headed up the hill. But Karen wasn't listening. She was wondering if that was Micah she had caught a glimpse of, watching her and Lisa leave from the stables. Micah was supposed to be taking Noel and others up to the restaurant, wasn't he? Why would he be down here? She abruptly urged her horse forward. "Wait for me, honey."

Walter Lowndes stood impatiently in the middle of the barn as Les Cady finished pitching hay into an empty stall. "Go on, go home, Les. I'm closing everything up tonight. You're the only one still here."

Cady felt a surge of gratitude at this unexpected order. "Thank you, Mr. Lowndes. Been a long day. Got two more folks out, though. Karen Paige and the Ritter kid." Cady was always careful in his speech never to show any interest in children, thus "the Ritter kid."

Lowndes supported himself against the wall of the stall. "Yes, yes. I know. But it will be all right. Karen can put the horses away. You can go. Now. Hurry."

"Are you sure?" Les had no desire to stay though he didn't want to appear too eager to leave, either. But at home there was a frozen pizza he had saved for his Saturday-night meal, and he'd been thinking about it all day. And a video he wanted to watch; been thinking of that all day, too.

"She knows how to take care of horses, Les. Go home. Now!"

An odd breathlessness in his employer's voice made Les glance at him. "Yes, sir. I will."

"And leave the tackroom unlocked. I have some work to do." As an afterthought he added, "We have some rope in there, don't we? Rope?"

Cady walked across the parking lot to his home at the base of the slopes, leaving the older man alone in the barn. Lowndes's heart raced with four decades of accumulated joy as his mind pictured the future with a bright, crystalline clarity, the inevitable pairing of him and the girl, to the point where beingness was infinite and identical for both of them.

Nature . . . shivers with ecstasy when the spirit bows in homage before beauty.

He hurried into the tackroom and looked for the rope. He was sweating. He couldn't remember sweating in forty-five years.

At the edge of the parking lot, just where the county road met the resort property, B.J. Blake sat in his Explorer and tried to put the pieces together. Karen and Lisa Ritter off on horses. Micah pulling out of the parking lot after shaking his fist at Rottweiler. The resort dark. Cady trudging home. Old Lowndes waiting by himself in the barn.

The only way the pieces could fit together was to force them a little bit. B.J. didn't mind that: Kinda push this one into that one and it started to form a picture, though he wasn't sure of what. But if Karen and the girl were riding, they'd be gone for a couple of hours.

Maybe he'd follow Micah a bit. Something wasn't right here. And Micah sure as heck was involved.

Might as well ask him.

84

Bobby Sample, a ticket to Orange County sticking up out of his shirt pocket, sat in a small bar at the Denver airport, nursing a Samuel Adams while reading *Guns and Ammo*. He'd already caught a glance of his reflection in the glass wall of the bar. The swelling around his eyes was going down and, with a little of Janis's makeup, didn't look too bad. The cut on his forehead was covered with a Band-Aid. Damn well better not leave a scar. Hey, that might be okay. Tell folks he got it taking out a crazed Hell's Angel with a switchblade. Curly black hair still looked nice, of course: real nice. Like one of them old Greek statues. But that fucking Ritter was going to pay mightily for sucker-punching him.

He glanced at his watch. Another hour until the plane took off. *Hell, it doesn't matter. Just sit here, put my feet on a chair, suck up a few brews, and think what I'm going to do with the twenty thousand dollars I'm pocketing for doing ol' Cheryl McAfee.*

He'd already decided not to worry about making it look like an accident. Fuck you, Micah-bird. That was too much trouble for twenty grand. Instead, Bobby decided, he'd just go over to her place tomorrow morning, make sure the kiddies were at school, and pop her. He could hear the sound of the automatic in his head: *ffft, ffft, ffft,* and she's dead. Then jimmy the rear door, take a few goodies, and disappear. Ain't no way anyone could tie it to him. He'd have to drop the Glock down a sewer but hell, he'd be able to afford a lot of guns pretty soon. Maybe he'd have Rollins help out—like with another ten grand. Time for Micah to open up a little here. Especially now that Bobby knew the old cowboy was a partner in the resort. And used to be married to Caroline Bellamy. Micah and Mountain Woman. *She-it, all sorts of secrets oozing to the surface now, like maggots on a dead body.*

He signaled the waitress for another beer. Hell, twenty grand really wasn't enough for the professional-type job he was doing. Make a down payment on a Chevy Suburban, though. Already had one picked out at Fancy Dan's Chevrolet in Denver. White as October snow, a big ol' V8 that probably got two miles a gallon, and enough room inside for a soccer team. He was going to have a TV and VCR fitted in that space between the two front seats, and a mattress put in back. Then he could drive up in the woods at night with some local ladies, put a kinky porno film in the VCR, and let the girls do what the girls did so well. As long as Janis didn't find out. He'd like to make *that* arrangement legal so when they did break up there'd be some big alimony bucks for the sad and suddenly impoverished hubby.

Bobby went back to his magazine and lusted over the ads. A Browning twelve-gauge side-by-side, a nasty-looking Ruger revolver that'd blow a hole through a tank, surplus M-16s that you could illegally convert to automatic in about fifteen minutes . . . then almost spit out a mouthful of Sam Adams as he saw Cheryl McAfee walk by not six feet away.

Jesus H. Christ, what in hell is this? He bolted up, leaving the magazine open on the table, the beer glass half-full, and hurried out onto the concourse. She was heading away from him, almost running, upset about something, carrying only her purse. He stood in utter disbelief—*She's been here all this time?*—as she turned into the waiting area of gate A37. Bobby pulled out his ticket and read the clerk's notation: *Gate A37.*

Goddamn! he thought. *Goddamn!*

He laughed out loud, not really sure what this meant but certain it was going to add some interest to the day.

Still chuckling, he went back to his table, picked up his beer, and gave this new development some thought. *Shit, maybe I'll save myself a flight and do her right here. Wait till she goes into the restroom and pop her a couple of times while she's on the can. Or do it in the parking structure at the Orange County Airport before she heads home.* That was a place made for a homicide if anyplace was.

Well, shit, he had time to think about it. *Relax! have another beer, Bobby.* Something told him today was going to be fun.

85

B.J. Blake pulled his Explorer over to the side of the road when
Micah stopped at his office at the edge of town. Maybe confronting Rollins wasn't the wisest thing to do right now. The man was
obviously pissed about something, the way he shook his arm at
Lowndes and then got in his Caddy and drove out here.

B.J. had just gotten a glance at Rollins's headquarters building as
he shot past on the highway but there didn't appear to be any lights
on. So why did the man stop?

Something was wrong, though. Something was going on that
involved both Micah and Walter Lowndes. And perhaps Karen and
Lisa, whom he had caught a glimpse of riding into the woods.

Maybe if Rollins hadn't been such an important figure in Harmony,
B.J. would have headed on over and ask him what the heck this was
all about. But there was no point in annoying someone who could
be crucial to his future success in real estate. No one ever got rich
making enemies.

Still, it might be worth keeping an eye on things for a while. Karen
had told him about Micah's threatening her and Mark earlier in the
day. And now he was hanging around the resort when she and Lisa
headed off into the hills.

B.J. pulled the car around so he could see when Micah left. He'd
keep an eye on things for Karen. At least until she got back from
riding. She was a friend of his. Come to think of it, so were Mark
and Lisa.

86

The Denver airport was modern life gone mad, vast parking areas
with thousands of cars set down in the middle of the prairie,
weirdly-shaped postmodern terminals, what seemed to be every airline in the world landing and taking off at all hours. Mark followed

the signs to the Midwest terminal, parked as near as he could, and hurried across the street. For an hour his mind had filled with his mother's words. *"I need to see you. I don't want my husband to know."* . . . Know what, for Christ's sake? But he couldn't think, couldn't conceive of what she needed to tell him. And why she hadn't told him in California.

The constant, noisy bustle in the terminal—the crush of people moving back and forth, pulling luggage, swinging briefcases, talking on cell phones, shouting, waving, hugging—unnerved him. Running, he pushed through the crowd and up an escalator, then hurried along a concourse to a barrier of security people and metal detectors. He stood in line, waiting anxiously as an elderly man went through three times, each time setting off alarms, before being waved on by annoyed attendants.

Finally through the security check, he began to run again, past gates A30, 31, 32 . . . A plane had just disembarked its passengers, and two hundred noisy people streamed in his direction. He weaved through them and looked around. Where was she? Damn it, she wasn't here! He began to panic, then heard Cheryl say, "Sorry. I had to go to the bathroom. I can't keep anything down."

Mark's heart was beating wildly. He reached out and grabbed her by the arms—the first time in thirty years he had held his mother—and she fell against him, let him wrap his arms around her. A low choking noise escaped her mouth and she said defiantly, "I told myself I'm not going to cry and I'm not. Don't let me." Her hands were on the back of his shoulders, fingernails digging into his flesh. "What time is it?" she asked suddenly.

Mark disengaged himself and looked at his watch. "Five-twenty."

Her face tightened with tension. "God, we've only got half an hour." She looked around hurriedly, finding an empty waiting area across the way. "Over there."

Walking quickly, they crossed to the vacant airline counter, Mark vaguely thinking he should be holding on to his mother's hand as Lisa held on to his in unfamiliar places. Cheryl took a seat in the farthest row, facing the wall of windows, Mark next to her. She didn't look at him, put her hands in her lap, clutching her purse.

"Richard's going to wonder why I'm late for dinner."

He looked a question at her.

"Richard." She wiped a strand of hair from her eyes. "My husband.

He's teaching a summer class in engineering. He'll get home before I do."

"I don't even know your last name," Mark said.

She smiled uneasily, evidently debating whether or not to go ahead. Then she laid a hand on his. "Davidson. Cheryl Davidson. Your brothers are Aaron and Alan. I told you that yesterday, didn't I? They don't look a lot like you."

She tried a smile but it didn't stay, and her hand jerked back and tightened on her purse.

Mark wanted desperately to ask why she had to see him, but clamped his mouth shut. His anxiety was at the limits but he could see Cheryl also was about to break down. He risked a glance at his watch and she said, "I know, I know. Just let me pull myself together."

She snapped open her purse, jerked out a tissue, and wiped her cheeks. "Your daughter's so beautiful," she finally said with a small voice, and gave him a smile. "My granddaughter. Imagine, I've been a granny for seven years. No wonder I feel old. I didn't want a girl myself. I guess God was listening. Three boys." She balled the tissue in her hand. "Tell me about your wife."

Mark sat back. "We met while I was in the Air Force. She was an RN. A friend introduced us and we were married six months later. Lisa was born a year after that. Beth was killed in an automobile accident. Almost seven years ago."

"You've raised Lisa by yourself."

He nodded.

"Good for you." She patted his hand with her balled fist. "It's not easy. And it doesn't get any better as they grow up. Believe me."

She turned to the window and watched as three planes maneuvered slowly toward terminals. "This is a busy airport, isn't it? Where can all these people be going?" A man in a suit sat down near them, but Cheryl looked at him so fiercely he picked up his briefcase and left.

Mark said nothing and watched as she seemed to be mustering her will. Her head swiveled suddenly in his direction but her eyes were downcast. "I'm sorry I ran away the other day. I just couldn't—" Her hands twisted in her lap and she forced herself to go on. "It was your daughter. Lisa." Her tone suddenly changed. "How long have you been in Harmony?"

"Just a few days." The public-address system blared a recorded message about keeping an eye on your luggage.

"She looks a lot like me. Lisa does. Have you ever seen a picture of me at that age?"

He shook his head no.

"That's what made me run away. When I saw her. It was like seeing myself at age eight. It brought back everything I don't want to remember. But seeing her— I haven't been able to get it out of my mind. I don't think I've slept more than a couple hours since. Jesus!"

She stood up suddenly. "You've heard people talk about repressed memories from their childhood: Repressed, hell! I haven't gone a day without thinking about this for almost forty years. Not one damn day. I wish I *could* repress it. Then seeing you, seeing Lisa—"

She turned her back to Mark and stared again out the window. Her voice was harsh. "I am not going to break down. I will not start crying. Because if I do I will go stark raving mad. I will end up institutionalized. I am going to hold on to whatever sanity I have left with at least one little finger."

She spun around, facing him, hands grasping the purse in front of her, eyes dry, speaking rapidly, getting it all out at once.

"I was molested. That's the nice word. From the age of eight until about nine and a half. Two or three times a week I was raped, sodomized, played with, manipulated like some sort of sex toy, tinkered with, inspected, licked, bit, fingered, fondled—" Her voice had risen to a fury, and people walking by stared and frowned until she dropped into a chair again and put her hands to her face.

"I will not cry. I will not lose my grasp on sanity, that one tiny finger gripping reality." Her voice remained steady, but her cheeks were red, and sweat plastered stray strands of hair to her forehead.

Mark was frozen next to her, the airport noise suddenly gone, breathing hard but not knowing how to help. He wanted to reach out and grasp her to him but he sensed that that would be the worst thing he could do right now. A minute passed, then two, before he said tentatively, "Cady?" But thought, *No. Not Cady.*

Cheryl swung on him furiously. "Les Cady? Of course not! *Lowndes,* goddamn it! Walter Lowndes. Eagle Point's creator, the man who killed Carl Stark. He's the most completely evil person I've ever met. He has absolutely no sense of right and wrong, of morals, or common decency. He saw nothing at all wrong in what he did to me. I was *his,* he owned me, he had the right to do *anything* to me. And he did."

"But how—"

She grabbed his hand in both of hers. *"Because my mother let him!"*

Mark sank back in the chair, stunned. "Your mother *let* him?"

"Helped him! She'd make sure I was home when he came over to the trailer we lived in. The two of them would sit and drink or smoke dope. Sometimes he'd go home. But mostly he'd take me into her bedroom and my mother would leave. Or she'd watch television, the sound turned up loud so she didn't have to hear. She'd be five feet away, laughing, while Walter Lowndes was lowering his body on mine."

Mark's head spun. "But why?" His mouth was so dry he could barely form the words. "Why would your mother—"

"Because she loved him. Isn't that why we do all the stupid things we do? She thought this *big shot,* this actual honest-to-God college graduate would marry her if she let him do whatever he wanted to her daughter."

She hunched forward, her arms dangling between her knees, dry-eyed but muscles tensed like a boxer, and her voice raspy with hatred. "She was as evil as he was. But stupid. Lowndes would never have married trailer trash like her when he could have his pick of Denver debs. Which, I later learned, he did."

Mark said nothing. He was dazed, and inexpressibly sad at what his mother's childhood must have been like. He rose to his feet, steadied himself against the vacant airline counter. A plane was drawing up to gate A37, the skyway passage being extended in its direction. In a few moments Cheryl would have to leave. He turned from the window. "Why did he finally stop? Did your mother make him?"

Cheryl's jaw jutted out and her mouth curled down in disgust. "Because I got to be too *old.* I was losing my baby fat and whatever else it was that Lowndes needed for a satisfactory sex life. I suppose he found someone else. But when he was with me he was crazy, talking about 'beauty' and 'perfection,' and God knows what else. I couldn't listen, I couldn't do anything. I was frozen with fear."

"How did your mother justify all this to you?"

"Justify? She told me it's what girls did, and not to be upset about it. Girls and men, she said. And told me that if I ever told anyone about it she'd cut me open with a knife and take my heart out. She even showed me the knife, jabbing it so hard into the table in front of me, it vibrated. It looked about two feet long to my eyes."

"Jesus." Mark sank into the chair.

"But old Mom never gave up hope Lowndes would marry her. She probably died with that thought in her mind."

Mark's head began to throb. He rubbed his neck, stared at the tile floor.

Cheryl turned on him, her voice so trembling and insistent that he had to look at her. "That's why I ran when I saw your daughter. She looks exactly like me at that age. *Exactly!* I saw it happening all over again, everything he did to me for over a year, I saw it happening again. Do you understand what I'm telling you?"

Mark stared at her as he tried to make his mind work. "I found a nude photo of Lisa in Lowndes's den. . . . I think. The police chief thinks it might be a composite—Lisa's face on another body."

"Do you have it with you?"

It was in his shirt pocket. He hesitated, then showed it to her.

Her eyes closed for a long moment. Then they opened. "It's not a composite." When his head snapped up she said, "It's me. He took hundreds of photographs of me, thousands maybe. He said it was for a shrine. A shrine for Cheryl."

She held his gaze. "It almost sounds as though he loved me. He loved me so much he wanted me around all the time. So he took these pictures. Cheryl without her clothes on. Cheryl in the bath. Cheryl on the bed. Cheryl playing with her friends.

"But he never loved anyone. He is an evil, loathsome, disgusting man, and if I had been braver or stronger or smarter I would have killed him. It's the one thing that kept me going while I was at boarding school—thinking of Walter Lowndes, planning out how I would do it. It would be slow, over a period of a year, a little each day. And painful. Like he killed me inside. I should have come back to Harmony and done it. I've thought about it for years. How many children suffered because I didn't have the courage to do it?"

Mark's voice was soft. "The police knew there was a pedophile in the area. A girl was killed a few years ago; at least one other girl attacked. They assumed it was Les Cady." As soon as the words were out he wished he hadn't said it; he had no desire to add to Cheryl's burden of guilt.

But his mother wasn't paying attention. She stood up, walked to the window, her back to him. "He traded those pictures. He had 'friends' all over the country—sick, sick men who had to have sex with children or they couldn't have sex at all. He told me how wealthy and important these men were. Important people. Sometimes they'd have parties back in Chicago and there'd be all these children there— a lot of them were immigrants from third-world countries. These men would sponsor them in this country or act as foster parents. There were seven- and eight-year old girls and boys from China and the Philippines, and Mexico. These people were sponsoring them out of kindness, everyone felt, out of charity. But the whole point was sex. Nothing else mattered to them.

"He never took me to one of those parties, though. He used to tell me how he didn't want to share me, how I was his alone. 'The perfection of the human form,' he said over and over, and told me that such beauty terrified him. He'd lie next to me in my mother's bed, whisper in my ear over and over, 'You're mine, Cheryl, mine alone. I own you.'

"He's kept these pictures of me because that was who he was in love with—eight-year-old Cheryl. When I grew older he hated me. If I saw him on the street he would sneer at me, or call me a slut. I felt like dirt by the time I was ten. My own mother hated me, Lowndes was disgusted every time he looked at me. For years I hated myself. Until Carl. . . . He was the only person in the world who loved me during the first twenty-three years of my life. And he died just months after we first . . ."

She sat down and put her head in her hands. "Carl and I had to sneak around to see each other. My mother didn't want anything to do with him. She knew he and Lowndes were feuding and she still had this wild fantasy of becoming Mrs. Walter Lowndes, mistress of Harmony. Fat chance."

"Are you sure Lowndes killed my father?"

Her head jerked abruptly and her face tightened with some furious emotion he couldn't identify. Rage? Grief? Madness? For a moment it looked like she wanted to hit him, then it passed. "Why do you say that?"

"The police are convinced it was an accident, an electrical fire."

"The police! If it was murder they'd have to take on the town benefactor. Even in those days Walter Lowndes was the most power- ful man in Harmony."

A boarding call for Cheryl's flight came over the PA. She clutched her purse tighter.

Mark said hurriedly, "Did Lowndes ever call himself Pooh Bear?"

"Pooh Bear? No. Why do you ask?"

"I found a note in Lisa's pocket. Someone put it there. It said, 'I like you,' and was signed 'Pooh Bear.' "

"Lowndes. It has to be."

Another boarding call came over the public-address system.

"I had to warn you," Cheryl began, and stared out at the airplane on the other side of the window. She turned and put a hand on his arm. Impulsively she jerked forward, kissing his cheek. "Seeing your daughter . . . seeing Lisa—it knocked the breath out of me." She stood suddenly. "Because I knew Walter Lowndes wouldn't be able to keep his hands off her. You have to understand his fixation with me—with the eight-year-old me. It was a madness with him, a sick, single-minded obsession. It consumed him. That's why he's kept those pictures for forty years."

She seized his wrist. "Don't you see? He's going to go after Lisa. He won't be able to help himself. He'll have to have her. She's *me*—Cheryl—all over again. He'll do anything to have her. Even kill you."

Of course, Mark thought. That was it, the fascination for his daughter. Others must have seen Cheryl's face in Lisa also, and thus the strange interest they took in her. His head shook back and forth but he couldn't think things out. Where was Lisa right now? Where did Karen say she was taking her?

The first hint of tears collected in Cheryl's eyes. "I wasn't able to sleep at all last night. I lay there in bed next to my husband and heard Walter Lowndes whisper in my ear, 'Your daddy loves you. You know that Cheryl. Daddy loves you.' "

Mark stood up. His head ached, and his stomach tightened with nausea.

The final boarding call came over the PA.

Cheryl looked as if she wanted to leave but held back.

She put arms around Mark and hugged him, kissed his cheek again. Her face was wet with tears. "Mark, listen, listen to me!"

His eyes were unfocused.

She grabbed both of his arms roughly, fingers biting into his flesh, and forced him to look at her.

"Walter Lowndes hated me for growing up. He despised me, took every opportunity to insult me, make me feel like dirt. One night when I was in high school I was walking home from a friend's house and I cut through a field next to the school. Lowndes was out there with some woman, drinking whiskey and laughing. She noticed me first and said something. Lowndes spun around and saw me and started calling me a slut. He was drunk and could hardly stand. He called me a whore and started coming at me. I screamed and tried to run but he caught me and hit me and called me names and told me how ugly I was, and all the time he was tearing off my clothes. He threw me down, kicked me, took off his pants, and fell on me. And while he was raping me he said over and over, 'You're ugly, ugly, look at you.' And I believed him, and I was. Because this was happening to me, and because he only loved eight-year-old Cheryl.

"That was nine months before you were born. I never told Carl about it. The first time he and I made love was the next week. I thought— I don't know, maybe I thought if I had sex with Carl it would cancel out anything Lowndes did. But it didn't. I knew. All the time I was pregnant I knew. Walter Lowndes is your father. And now he wants your daughter. And he'll figure out a way to do it because he's Walter Lowndes and he always gets what he wants. Always."

87

Furious at leaving his cell phone in the car, Mark grabbed a pay phone on the wall and dialed Karen's number. The answering machine came on again. Goddamn it! Goddamn it! *Goddamn it!* He slammed the receiver down. Where the hell could they be? Not horseback-riding! He began to feel sick. He'd warned her about Lowndes. She wouldn't have—

Control, he told himself. *Control, not panic.*

Maybe she left a message on the machine. What was her code? It was her birthdate, wasn't it? 417 or 517. He tried 417, and as the machine slowly rewound he turned to see his mother disappear down the skyway to her plane. Then he heard, "Hi, Mark. Lisa and I decided to go riding. Or Lisa decided. I really don't have a choice here. Believe me. Seven-year-olds can be crankier than I remember. Don't worry about old Walter. He won't be there. And, *yes,* I'll keep Lisa away from weird old Lester Cady. I'll even help her off her horse myself. 'Bye."

But Lowndes *would* be hanging around. He'd be waiting for them.

"Now he wants your daughter. And he'll have her because he's Walter Lowndes."

The police department! Mark shoved coins in the phone. He'd called it enough to remember the number. He punched it out, held the receiver with a death grip as a voice he didn't recognize answered.

"This is Mark Ritter." He clenched his teeth to keep from screaming. "Karen Paige and my daughter are horseback-riding at the Eagle Point Resort. I need someone to go out and get them and take them to her house. They're in danger out there."

There was a hesitation on the other end, then, "Danger? What are you talking about?"

"Walter Lowndes is after my daughter. He's a child molester—"

"He's what? Walter Lowndes? Are you nuts?"

"Listen to me. Lowndes has been molesting kids for forty years. He's mentally ill. He molested my mother and now he's after my daughter."

"Ritter, you're crazy. Your mother?" The man made a sound like a laugh, then turned to someone and said, "Hey, pick up line five and listen to this."

Mark bit down his anger and tried to keep his tone reasonable. "All I want you to do is send someone out there to escort them back to Karen Paige's house. It won't take more than a few minutes. Please! I'll explain later."

"Ritter, this is a *police department*. Not an escort service." The hostility in the man's voice was obvious. "We don't run errands for people. Even big-city people like you."

"Please listen," Mark begged, feeling himself beginning to lose control. "Walter Lowndes is a murderer. He killed Carl Stark thirty years ago. He molested my mother when she was a little girl and he's after my daughter now. If you don't get out there there's no telling what he might do."

Another cop's voice came on the line. "You've got proof of all this, I'm sure. We wouldn't want to make a false arrest, would we? Especially someone like Walter Lowndes."

"I'm not asking you to make an arrest. I'm asking you to save my little girl."

"Your *proof?*" the voice insisted.

"My mother told me!" he screamed into the phone. A half dozen people walking nearby turned to stare. A security guard halted twenty feet away and watched as Mark twisted around toward the waiting area, then back to the wall. "My mother told me how he molested her, and now he has this fixation—"

"Come on, Ritter," the first man said. "That's not proof. Even in Seattle."

"Let me talk to Chavez."

"He ain't here. It's Saturday. He's home making menudo. Maybe you should talk to Bobby Sample. I understand he's got something to say to you. Or how about Todd Kachen?"

"Give me Chavez's number."

"You know better than that."

He took a breath, gritted his teeth. "Are you going to go out to the resort?"

"You give us some probable cause, some reason, then maybe we'll send a car by. If we got time. Like I said, it's Saturday night. The bars are filling up. Folks'll start shooting each other in another hour or so. Busy time for us."

"Goddamn it, I'm telling you Lowndes is going to harm my daughter. He might kill Karen. You don't know how someone like him might react."

"Hey, seems like Karen can take care of herself. That's what Todd says. Got a temper on her. And a pretty good right hook. Seen a black eye Todd had last year."

"Lowndes is going to—"

The line went dead.

Mark slammed the phone down and fumbled in his pocket for more change as Bobby Sample, a hundred feet away, handed his boarding pass to a smiling reservation clerk, and sang softly, "California, here I come. . . ."

No more change. Mark took out a credit card and went to another phone. He got the number for Trees from the operator and called Caroline Bellamy. When he told her about the threat to Lisa she began to panic. "Oh, my God. Of course I'll go out there."

"Get hold of Chavez first. If you can't, try to convince whoever's on the desk at the station to send someone out. We don't know what sort of mental state Lowndes will be in."

"Of course." She hesitated. "You're convinced Walter killed your father too, aren't you?"

Mark couldn't tell her what he had learned about his parentage. He said, "Lowndes killed Carl Stark. He molested my mother as a child. There's no telling how many children he's harmed. Or killed."

Caroline said at once, "I'll call the police."

Mark dropped the phone without hanging up and ran for his car.

88

Instead of the police Caroline called Micah Rollins.

"I'm telling you, he's off the deep end. He's completely snapped."

"And you say Ritter called you from Denver?" Micah hadn't anticipated Ritter being out of town. What the hell was he doing in Denver? That meant it would be at least another hour until he got to Harmony. Damn! He'd had a feeling this was all too fine-tuned to work out properly. So, Plan B, then. Anyway, Ritter knew his daughter was at the resort. He'd be there soon enough.

Caroline was still going on about Walter. "I told you this was going to happen, Micah. As soon as I saw that little girl I knew what he would do. You know what he's like."

"Micah's heavy sigh rolled down the line. Just get her to shut up. "All *right,* Caroline. Tell me what you want."

"They're supposed to be riding horses. You get out there and find them and bring them back to Karen's. Then you and me are going to have a heart-to-heart with Janis."

Micah's voice hardened. "What kind of heart-to-heart are you talking about?" Meeting with Janis wasn't in Plan A or B. Wasn't in no plan.

"Either she gets Walter into a hospital and stops him from running after little girls, or we turn him in."

"Don't know about that, Caroline. Don't know at all. Seems to me we're kind of over a barrel here. We can't exactly waltz into a police station since there's a murder charge hanging over our heads, too."

"I don't care. Let them try to prove it. I'm not going to sit around any longer while he's out molesting children."

"Don't go blaming Walter for every sin of the last half century, Caroline. Les Cady's been out there wagging his jasper at little girls, too."

"I don't know what Lester's done or not done. But I do know what Walter's responsible for. I'd hoped he had it under control but

I guess not. At least not where this girl is concerned. It's up to us to get him to stop."

"I don't know, Caroline—"

"Micah. Stop talking nonsense and get out to the resort. You get Karen and Lisa out of there. I'll meet you."

Caroline hung up, then went straight to the bedroom and opened the nightstand drawer. She hadn't touched that .38 revolver in years. She picked it up, checked to see if it was actually loaded.

Should have done this a long time ago, she thought. *Should have done it decades ago.*

Meanwhile Micah was trying to slow his heartbeat. *Relax. Don't rush into anything. This is getting a mite complicated. Have a drink and think it out.* He stood up and poured himself a Scotch. Ritter was suddenly a bigger problem than Walter. Fact was, the problem of Walter was solved since he was out at the resort right now amusing himself with the little girl. But what the hell did her dad go to Denver for?

Well, it didn't matter. This was going to be a bit riskier than the original plan. But it was cleaner, too. Because it got that meddlesome ex-wife of his out of the way once and for all. Been waiting a long time for that.

It might be best to speed Ritter up a bit, though. *Why not?* Micah thought. *It'd give me a chance to have a little fun, too.*

He put the glass down and stood up.

"Let's do it."

89

"Whew!" Bobby Sample said, shaking his head with relief. "Hope y'all don't mind me movin' up here. The air-conditioning doo-hickey's broke back there. Hotter than the dickens."

Cheryl Davidson glanced at the man, then turned to the window as the half-empty plane settled into its flight path for the trip to Orange County.

"Bet you're happy to be goin' to California, ain't you? Get out of dusty old Colorado and back to the land of surf and sun. I'm just assuming you're not from Colorado. You got that California-girl look. Healthy and snappy-looking."

Cheryl hadn't turned from the window but Bobby couldn't stop talking. Must've been the eight beers he'd had at the bar. "Love that airport you folks got out there. *John Wayne!* Yes sir! That's what we ought to do in Colorado—name airports after movie stars and cowboys. What've we got? Denver ... International ... Airport! Could've been Charles Bronson Airport. Or Chuck Norris, the kickboxing airport." He paused a moment, enjoying the fantasy. "I do love it when folks say, 'Hey, Bobby, where y'all going?' And I say, 'John Wayne. I'm going to John Wayne.'

"And they got that statue of the Duke out there, must be eight feet of bronze, wearing his six-shooters and spurs. A real man. I gotta good friend kinda adores him—all cowboys actually. Well, he's not actually a friend. An employer. Kind of a dork, if you want to know the truth."

Bobby slapped his forehead and leaned across the empty seat. "Hey, where's my manners? I didn't introduce myself. Bobby Sample. I'm a po-liceman. An 'enforcer of the law,' we call it. Sort of like John Wayne. From the fine town of Harmony. You ever been there? Great place to live."

Cheryl's head spun in his direction. Her eyes were red and her makeup smeared—looked like hell, actually—and she stared angrily at Bobby's guileless face for several seconds. He thought she was going to say something but she turned abruptly to the window as if he weren't worth talking to. *Uppity bitch*.

A flight attendant leaned in their direction. "Would you two like anything to drink?"

Bobby relaxed back and smiled at the young woman in a way that he knew communicated what he *really* wanted, and was confident in his knowledge that she reciprocated the notion. Probably tearing his clothes off in her mind right now. "Well, shoot, doll, I guess I'll have one of them import beers. How about a Heineken?" Hell, he was going to have twenty thousand dollars real soon. May as well spend some of it.

"And the lady?"

Bobby turned toward Cheryl. "Hey, hon, what y'all want to drink? Little white wine, maybe?"

Cheryl spun on him. "If you don't leave me alone I'll have you arrested for assault."

The flight attendant's eyes went suddenly wide. "Ma'am?"

"Leave me alone! Both of you!" She turned again to the window, and stared out furiously, her shoulders heaving.

Bobby smiled apologetically to the young woman, and whispered, "She gets a wee bit tense about flying. You know how it is."

"Of course." She patted Bobby on the shoulder. "I'll be right back with your beer."

Bobby unstrapped his seat belt and sighed loudly as he tilted the chair as far back as it would go. "Yes sir," he said and closed his eyes. "California. Newport Beach. The sand, the sea, boobs hangin' out of bikinis everywhere you look, just like on *Baywatch*. Imagine someone going from little ol' Harmony to Newport Beach. America's a great country, ain't it?"

Bobby almost fell asleep, sitting there contemplating the greatness of America while sucking on his beer, and once in a while thinking about that twenty grand he was going to get for doing old Cheryl here. *Like finding money under a rock*, he told himself. *Didn't even have to raise a sweat. Yes sir, this is indeed the Land of Opportunity.*

90

A light breeze from a nearby summer squall rustled Walter Lowndes's coarse gray hair as he stood in the open doorway of the stables and watched Lisa Ritter stare around uncertainly while perched on the back of her pony. He leaned forward, both large hands gripping the polished handle of his cane. "I'm sorry I can't help you off the horse, my dear. I'm not as strong as you remember. You'll have to get off yourself."

"I can do it," the girl said with a mix of defiance and bravado. But she didn't move. "Where's Karen? Sometimes she helps me."

"Karen just went to my home. She asked me to bring you there. She wants to see you. But you must hurry. Get off your horse. Quickly!" There was a catch to his voice, a breathlessness, that made Lisa uncomfortable, though she didn't know why. It could not be Walter, though. She had seen and talked to him before, and Karen had spoken to him as if he was a nice man. Not like the Pooh Bear man Dad was talking about. *He* was fat and had a red face and talked stupid. Her expression serious, she swung her right leg over the pony's back while trying to disentangle her other foot from the stirrup. The tip of her shoe got caught, however, and she stumbled as she hit the ground.

"I'm sorry," she said needlessly as she fell to her knees at Lowndes's booted feet. The air smelled of manure, and there was no sound anywhere except their voices.

"No worry, Cheryl. No worry at all. Tie the pony up so we can go. Hurry, tie him." The words spilled out quickly, as if time were of the essence, though Lisa noticed nothing to cause her worry. She took the aged pony's reins and led him to a stall.

But Lowndes didn't want to wait. "Tie him to that post. Hurry. We have to hurry."

The girl turned suddenly as a memory returned. "Were you the man at the park?"

"Yes," he said at once. "At the park. I told you about my ice cream."

"You wanted to lick it off," she said in an accusing tone as she secured the pony to the post.

"Yes!" The breath caught in his throat, but he was smiling with half his face. This had all gone so *perfectly,* just as he expected. After Karen and the girl left on their ride, and Les Cady had been sent home, it was merely a matter of some simple preparations. Then he set himself to wait. An hour later the two barn-sour mounts made their way back to the stables, galloping a bit faster than they should, but anxious to be fed. Lowndes had heard Lisa's excited laughter and Karen's shouted admonitions to *hang on, hang on, don't let go,* and was waiting, stern-faced and brooding, in front of the barn as they rode up.

"Got to show you something in the tackroom, Karen. I came across some troubling pictures today." His face was grave and his voice worried.

"Pictures?" Karen seemed concerned though confused.

"From Les Cady, I'm sorry to say. Found them on my desk. Not the sort of thing the girl needs to see. But you've got to— Well, come on in. You'll understand what I'm talking about. The child can wait."

Karen looked at him standing—tall, thin, vague—in the broad, early-evening shadows, propped up by a cane. His fingertips tingled with pinpricks of fire as he watched her come to a decision, then hop off her horse. "Just stay here, Lisa. Don't let Snowflake inside yet."

"Hurry," Lowndes said again, knowing he sounded strange but unable to help himself. Almost forty years he had been waiting for this. Forty years! My God, it was natural to be anxious, but oh, how his heart beat. So hard! So quickly! "Please!"

Using his cane . . . *clomp, clomp, clomp* on the wooden floor, the smell of manure and hay and horse sweat everywhere. . . . Lowndes had led the way through the barn to the far end where a locked door led to the small tackroom. He fumbled with a set of keys, dropping them, and bending painfully to pick them up from amid the straw on the floor.

"Natural to be nervous, isn't it, dear? You would be too, after forty years."

Karen eyed him strangely as he managed to unlock the padlock, then pushed the creaking door open. "Here," he said, and there was an urgent, compelling, hurrying tone to his voice as he added, "You first. Go, go, I'll show you." And as she passed him into the room he lifted his metal cane and crashed it down violently on the back of her neck.

Karen shot at once to her knees, a moan falling from her lips; then she opened her mouth and tried to shout but Lowndes hit her again and she lurched forward as though kicked. Blood oozed from the back of her head into her hair, and her left hand twitched, then closed with some kind of reflex action.

Don't take a chance!

He hit her with the cane again. And again.

Then hurriedly grabbing the rope he'd had ready, he dropped to the floor. Forcing his weakened muscles to work he spun the rope around Karen's ankles then, yanking her arms behind her back, he pulled her legs up and bound her wrists to her feet. Just like a calf. Using a rag he gagged her, grabbed his cane and forced himself upright.

Later tonight he would come back and dispose of her but he couldn't wait now. *First*—his body was quivering so with anticipation—*first, Cheryl! She's come back to me.* He felt Gustav Aschenbach's terrible, terrible weakness when faced with Tadzio's flawless beauty. It was a curse, he knew, a monstrous curse, to worship only perfection.

But now he had her. The quest was over. She was his. Alone.

* * *

Walter Lowndes's heart beat hugely as Lisa finished tying the pony to the post and came over to him. He grabbed her wrist with his free hand, and at that instant an odd image came to him of Micah Rollins telling him something about the girl going riding today. The man had repeated it over and over, as if Walter hadn't understood. *Micah's a fool,* Lowndes thought, his pulse pounding with indignation. He never should have had anything to do with a cretin like that. Tomorrow he'd see about settling with Rollins once and for all. "Come," he whispered. "Come. We have to go to my home. Hurry."

Lisa resisted unexpectedly. "You're hurting." A horrible fear began to grow in her mind, as though huge cracks were opening up in the earth all around her.

He yanked her arm even harder. "Don't argue with me, Cheryl. You know what I do when you argue with me."

Lisa began to whimper. "My name's not Cheryl."

But Lowndes's fury was mounting out of control. His voice, seeming to come from only one side of his face, rasped loudly. "I'll teach you to talk back. I've warned you a thousand times, haven't I? Haven't I? Damn you, damn you! Move!"

91

Not wanting to take the time to put the top up on his car, Mark shivered in the early-evening chill as he raced along Interstate 70 from Denver to Harmony. Reaching across to the passenger seat, he grabbed the cell phone and, holding the steering wheel and dialing at the same time, he tried Karen again. The answering machine. *Goddamn it!*

He punched out the number for Caroline's restaurant and someone he didn't recognize answered. No, Ms. Bellamy was not there; she had left in a hurry and he didn't know where she was. *Janis,* he thought, then a strange feeling moved within him. *My sister. Half-sister.* . . . He had no idea what her number was. He tried directory assistance. No listing.

An eighteen-wheeler, evidently empty, swerved suddenly into the left lane in front of him to pass another truck. Mark slammed his brakes, swore loudly in the darkness, and felt the phone drop to the floor as he grabbed the wheel with both hands. At once he punched down on the accelerator, drew onto the unpaved left shoulder, and sped past the truck which honked its horn and blinked its lights repeatedly as Mark pulled in front of it.

He paid no attention, feeling on the floor for the phone and finding it. He remembered Lowndes's private number and dialed it as the truck angrily roared up behind him, illuminating the tiny car in its high beams and loudly blowing its air horn without interruption. The phone rang and rang. No answer. Where was Lowndes? Where was Lisa?

92

Except for the nurse who lived on the top floor, the skimpy Saturday-night staff had been sent home for the evening so Walter Lowndes had no concern about being seen as he dragged Lisa from the stables to the rear of the lodge building. The door leading to his living quarters was unlocked, and he pushed it open.

"In here, my dear, hurry, quickly." He yanked the girl along the long corridor to the room that served as his office, kicked the door shut, then carefully locked it.

"Where's Karen?" Lisa asked, frightened and angry at being pulled about by this strange ugly man who reminded her of a huge reptile. When he hoarsely whispered, "We'll see her later, later," her stomach knotted as a primitive warning system came alive somewhere deep inside her brain, screaming, *Run, Lisa, run!* But why? Karen liked Walter. And Karen was here. She'd see her in a minute. Lisa had always trusted adults anyway, had never met one that really scared her. Of course, she knew bad people existed. Her teachers had said so, and the policeman who came to school, and her father had warned her about Pooh Bear.

Lowndes let loose of Lisa and she moved into the center of the room, not quite running because it might look rude. The old man hobbled after her, saying nothing. She looked around, eyes darting, remembered being here before, and said in a tiny voice, "I think I want my daddy."

"Your daddy, whoever he is, has long been gone from Harmony. Didn't your mother explain all that to you?"

Lisa instinctively remained several feet from him. She hadn't liked the way he had grabbed her wrist, the hard, scabrous feel of his skin, like touching a snake or old sandpaper.

Lowndes rested on his cane, breathing heavily and watching the fear in the girl's face with growing perplexity. He had never understood this, this resistance, this senseless struggle she always wanted to mount. His voice breathless and hard with desire, rose, sped up, rose again, the words tumbling confusedly into one another. "There is no reason to defy me. Your mother said it is okay. Don't you remember? She said you were to do whatever I want. Whatever!"

Lisa's face went wild as some not-yet-formed part of her mind sensed what he was after. Fear sprang to her eyes, her cheeks flushed hot, and began to swim with sweat. She could feel her heart beating as it never beat before, feel blood pounding in her fingers and chest and head. She covered her eyes with her hands. "My mother's dead. I don't have a mother!" She began to move backwards, running from a blackness that was rushing forward to engulf her.

Lowndes stared at her frightened face. "I should be angry with you but I'm not. You made me wait a long time, Cheryl. Years, wasn't it? Or has it been weeks?" His eyes unexpectedly squeezed shut, confusion in his memory now, making him uneasy. *What was happening here?* There was a welling of emotion from somewhere, and a Novocaine-like numbness deep in his mind, so deep that the darkness was only occasionally lit with those bright strobelike flashes of light that warned him of . . . of what? He couldn't remember. Slowly his eyes opened wide, and with an effort he concentrated on what he wanted to say, forcing the words from his mouth, each one carefully enunciated but fierce with determination. "I was very upset with you. But since you've come back . . . I've decided you needn't be punished too severely."

He faltered, and his eyes closed as confusion began to rise; like a malfunctioning carnival ride, thoughts began rocketing forward and back, banging into each other, and he saw faces staring at him— Cheryl, Annie McAfee, Carl Stark. Micah? Was Micah there? Such a fool the man was. Then his eyes opened and fixed on the child, and everything began to slow down, resolve, come into a reassuring focus as his pulse returned to normal. *Yes,* he realized, *yes . . . everything is all right. No need to get upset.* She was here, and his.

Perfection. . . . So rare.

So rare!

Tadzio!

He straightened suddenly and smiled and knew it must have been the biggest smile he'd ever had, though only Lisa could see it was restricted to the right side of his face, making him look even more frightening than ever. "I have a surprise for you." He lifted the cane straight up and brought it down on the hardwood floor with an explosive crack. "A *surprise.* Children love surprises. Let me show you."

Still smiling with half his face, the other half twisted with an ugliness he couldn't imagine, he advanced on the girl, reaching out for her hand. But in her mind Lisa saw only the forked tongue slither from his serpent's mouth, moist snake-eyes glaring at her, a hissing sound come from his lips. She gasped and backed away at once, her eyes dark with panic. She began to breathe rapidly, hyperventilating. *Run, Lisa. Run.* But her legs wouldn't move.

Lowndes looked at her with genuine surprise. "You can't be afraid, can you? I'm not going to hurt you. This is for you."

Lisa was terrified now in a way she never had been before, fearful that in some strange manner she didn't understand this man was going to harm her, and no one would be able to stop him. Whatever it was he wanted to do, it was wrong, she was absolutely certain. It was wrong in the way that the policeman at school and her daddy had told her some men are bad and hurt children. ("Did he touch you? Like I said?") She needed her daddy now very much, and the thought made her sob as her heart pounded and the breath rushed noisily and rapidly in and out of her lungs, in and out . . .

Lowndes was at first uncomprehending. How could Cheryl be upset about *this?* "Your daddy isn't here. He's gone." Then he was furious. His huge hand clamped on to her wrist like the jaws of a giant viper. "Here, damn it, come with me. Let me show you."

Dragging the sobbing girl as though she were a cloth doll, he moved down a dark hallway toward his bedroom at the other end. Two-thirds of the way there, however, he halted at a door with a built in combination lock. Fingers shaking he tapped in the code, heard a click, and smiled.

"For you," he said with genuine pride, turning the handle. He pushed the door with his foot, and pulled the girl inside. Another kick shut and locked it behind them.

He let her hand slip from his, and his voice hissed with excitement. "Cheryl, look, *look*—"

Lisa's mind filled with a seven-year-old's wild terror. She wanted to run, but where? She stared around. One window. Covered with black drapes. Bright white lights overhead, the hissing of this man's venomous tongue . . .

"So beautiful it is," Lowndes told himself as he felt the excited throbbing of his body. Using his cane he began to maneuver around the edges of the room. "So beautiful. Tell me you love it, child. Tell me."

But Lisa was too frightened to talk. All she could do was cry, and she put her hands to her face and began to shriek, but Lowndes didn't hear her because she was his again, and in love.

93

Caroline Bellamy slammed her car to a stop in front of the lodge. Micah's Cadillac was nowhere to be seen. Damn it, he should have been here by now. What the hell was he doing? Then she realized that the only cars anywhere in the lot were Walter's red Jaguar, gleaming like some obscene jewel in the midst of seven acres of black asphalt, and Karen's aging Taurus.

Grabbing her purse, she raced up the steps to the main entrance and tried the door. Locked. Of course, it was Saturday night, they're never open on Saturday night in the summer. But Walter *was* here. His private entrance, then!

Breathing deeply, she began to run toward the rear of the building as the last light of evening slipped away and the pines behind the building disappeared in the darkness. No cars in back, either. All the employees were gone. Everyone! Jesus, what was Walter doing in there? But she knew what he was doing, and the thought of it made her sick.

The private door next to the walled courtyard didn't budge. She began to bang on it with her fists. "Walter, open up. It's Caroline,

Walter. Open up." *Goddamn it, you sick bastard, open the damn, door!*

Nothing.

Now what?

Maybe the courtyard entrance was open. Hope returned in a rush: The French doors were usually unlocked because they were protected by an eight-foot wall. But how to get over it? She dropped her purse, grasped the top of the wall and tried to pull herself up. No way, she just wasn't strong enough.

A ladder! Damn it, where would a ladder be? Spinning around, her eyes flew from the building to the chairlift to . . . the stables!

She began to run, her sandals clapping loudly on the asphalt. God, it must be a quarter mile across the parking lot. She wasn't cut out for this. Too old, too heavy, too out-of-shape.

Weak with exhaustion, she pulled up outside the corral as she noticed a horse with a saddle noisily pawing the ground and blowing out angry puffs of breath through his nose. Not a good sign! "Les! Walter!" No one around. The horse neighed with growing fury; he wanted the saddle off and to be taken inside to feed. *Sorry, pal, I haven't got time.* She hurried into the stables through the side door. "Les!" Still no one. Damn it, where's a ladder? There must be one somewhere. She raced the length of the building, all the way through the far entrance, and found herself outside in the evening darkness again. Jesus, the tackroom, maybe. She was about to go back inside when she saw an ancient eight-foot wooden ladder leaning against the wall. Hurrying over, she tried to lift it. Not too bad, twenty or thirty pounds. She could do it.

Holding the ladder horizontal to the ground she hurried back to the rear of the lodge. Where in God's name was Micah? Maybe he'd gone looking for Janis. But, damn it, she didn't want to have to face Walter by herself.

Not waiting to catch her breath, she slammed the ladder against the wall. Short by about a foot but it would have to do. Snatching up her purse she mounted to the second rung from the end, then swung her leg up and straddled the flat top of the wall. *I must look like Humpty Dumpty,* she thought, *this oval-shaped woman in a flowered muumuu perched on top of a wall.* Taking a breath she pulled her other leg over, and dropped into the courtyard. God, I hope I'm not too late.

94

Lisa can't stop screaming, and her body's shaking so much with fear her bones feel like they're going to break. What is this man doing? Where's her daddy? Why did he allow this to happen to her? It isn't fair!

Walter had grabbed her when he unlocked the door, and shoved her inside this room. When Lisa couldn't stop crying he got mad, yelled at her and hit her, hit her hard in the face with his hand, the first time any adult had ever hit her. Then Lisa started screaming but he seemed not to care. Adults weren't supposed to make kids scream. They were supposed to be nice, like teachers. It wasn't fair to be mean because kids are so small.

And Walter's old, like a grandpa, but grandpas were nice. Walter wasn't nice at all. He was mean, and slapped her when she refused to call him "Daddy" like he wanted.

Cowering against the wall, her body trembles uncontrollably. When is this going to stop? *Soon, please, soon!* Walter turns his ugly snake's-head to look at her and she presses back on the wall, closes her eyes and tries to become invisible. She understands none of what's happening, and thinks only: *No, no, no.*

The old man takes a staggered step in her direction, grabs her by the wrist, but she breaks free and tries to disappear into the floor, pounding with her fists on the carpet. Seizing her arm, he drags her up, and loses his temper again. "Damn you, damn you!"

Pulling her to the couch he shoves her down and his voice trembles. "Look at what I've done for you. Look!"

Lisa won't look, pounds her fists into her eyes and screams for her daddy or Karen, but Mark is fifty miles away, Karen tied up in the tackroom, and Walter Lowndes is alone with her after waiting almost forty years. Losing what control he has over himself, he grabs her with his two hands. *"Look—"*

95

The cell phone rang and Mark grabbed it at once off the passenger seat. "Yes—"

"Remember me?"

A chill went through to his bones. The man who had threatened Lisa the first morning they were in town. It was a moment before he could speak, and then his voice was so low it could hardly be heard. "Who are you? What do you want?"

A bus labored noisily in the right lane while a 4x4 Land Rover in the left acted as if it didn't have enough horsepower to pass it. Mark blinked his lights and came up sharply behind it.

"I want to help you."

Mark swore and honked at the Land Rover. The car's brake lights flashed on and it slowed deliberately. The bus on the right was having trouble with the upgrade, and the median strip was cut with ravines, making it impossible to drive on. "Who are you?" Mark repeated as he tried to figure how to get past the 4x4.

"A friend. I was at the Eagle Point Resort earlier tonight. I thought you might be interested in what I saw. It involves your lovely daughter."

"Goddamn it!" Mark muttered to himself. He pounded the horn with the hand holding the phone. The interior light came on in the Land Rover and the driver, a young man in a reversed baseball cap, raised his arm and gave Mark the finger. Then he slowed to thirty miles an hour, the same speed as the bus. There was nowhere for Mark to go.

Mark put the phone back to his ear, wanting, but not wanting, to know. "What the hell are you talking about?"

"I saw Walter Lowndes and Les Cady dragging your little girl over to the lodge building. She was screaming her head off. Gave me the chills, listening to her, watching her trying to get away. There's no one around tonight but Cady and Lowndes. Looks to me like they've got a party planned. You better do something while she's still alive. Old Walter killed a girl a few years ago, you know. It's some kind of weird sex thing he has, likes to watch kids suffer."

"Goddamn you!" Mark didn't know what to say, didn't know if he should believe it or not. He tried desperately not to, but the man knew Lisa was at the resort. And knew about Lowndes's obsession with her.

"Where are you?" the voice, frightening in its deliberate calmness, asked.

"A half hour east of town. A little more, maybe."

"A half hour! No good. Lowndes has already had her for an hour. What do you think he's doing? What's happening to her right now, this very instant? Try to imagine." He paused, then added, "Maybe you better hurry."

"Goddamn you—" Mark screamed but he heard only a dial tone, and the groaning of the Land Rover in front of him.

96

Caroline sprinted toward the French door, praying that it wasn't locked, and almost shrieked as it opened into Lowndes's office. The lights were on. "Walter?"

The phone rang.

"Walter! Damn it, Walter, where are you?"

The phone rang again.

This time she raised her voice. "Walter! Where are you?"

Damn, damn, damn!

She hurried into the darkened hallway, saw the door open to his bedroom, and thought, *Oh God, no.*

Her purse swinging at her side, she ran to the end of the hallway, into the bedroom, and stopped. Empty. The bed undisturbed.

Back into the hallway. Tried a door. Bathroom. Empty.

Another door. Small bedroom. Empty. *Goddamn you, Walter!*

Another. Locked. What the hell kind of lock was that? Push buttons! What's in there that he has to keep everyone out? Is this some sort of fantasy room, a dungeon, perhaps? Why would he have that kind of lock unless he didn't want anyone to pick it and get inside?

She tried to rattle the handle but it didn't move. *"Walter!"* Nothing. Clenching her fists, she began to bang on the door. "Damn it, Walter, open up. I know you're in there. Open the damn door."

A sound like a . . . a what, a scream? escaped from under the door. Or was she letting her imagination run away from her? Then she heard it again.

"Jesus, Walter, open the goddamn door or I'm going to burn it down!"

Scraping noises. Angry clicks. The door opened, and the breath caught in Caroline's throat.

Walter Lowndes, pale as death, sweat streaming from his half-paralyzed face, his coarse sparse hair stiff with perspiration and standing out from his bony scalp, stood in front of her, breathing heavily, as if his metabolism was out of control. Dark eyes narrowed with rage, and his voice became urgent and breathless as he pushed into the hallway, holding the door with one hand, his cane with the other. "What the hell are you doing here? Go away!" The part of his mouth that worked formed into a scowl as he raised the cane, an instinctive animal-like threat, and seemed to expect her to retreat at once.

"Walter—"

The sound of a tiny sob seeped from inside, then rose, became a terrible scream that engulfed them.

"My God, Walter. What are you doing in there? Have you gone completely over the edge?"

"Get out of here!" Lowndes knew but didn't know who she was— Caroline, yes, yes, but out of time and place. *I don't know her at this age for years and years.* But . . . he recognized her as a danger, someone that had to leave. He allowed the door to slam shut behind him with a thud, then advanced menacingly on her, his body trembling with emotion.

Caroline's intestines clenched as she sensed what was going on in that room. She put a hand on the wall to support herself. "Please, Walter, let her out. You don't know what you're doing. You're sick. Please, let me go in there and get the girl. Please!"

When she put a hand out to touch him, he swung his cane at her leg. "Don't touch me. Leave us. Now!" His voice filled the hallway, quaking with out-of-control emotion.

"Walter, she's just a little girl!"

Again he advanced, swinging the cane, catching Caroline on the ankle, knocking her off balance. She put her hand out and braced against the wall. "Walter, if you don't let her out of there I'll go to the police. I'll tell them you killed Carl Stark thirty years ago. I mean it, Walter. I'll tell the police! You'll go to prison for the rest of your life."

Lowndes straightened, looked at her with confusion as the odd words moved about his consciousness, then slowly his mind pushed the pieces together, arranged them into a coherent thought. "Carl Stark?" His eyes suddenly brightened like tiny lights in a doll's head. "Will you tell them you also helped to kill him?"

She sighed with the weight of thirty years' worth of guilt and regret. "No, Walter, I didn't. I thought you were going to burn his cabin. I didn't know you were going to kill him. I never would have gone along with it if I'd known."

Lowndes shook his head. "You can't back away now. If you go to the police you and Micah go to jail, too."

Caroline's huge body seemed to sink with despair. "Walter, please let that poor girl go. Don't hurt her. Please. I'm begging you."

His body quivered as he took a step forward and roared. "I've waited forty years for her, Caroline. Forty years! And she waited for me. Look—"

He grabbed the handle of the door and tried to turn it. Mumbling angrily he pushed the buttons that would release the lock, then held the door as Lisa's screams rushed out, filling the hallway. "Look, damn you!"

Torn between fear of entering the room and the need to rescue Lisa, Caroline edged forward. When she was in front of the door Lowndes suddenly pushed her, quickly following as the door swung shut and locked them all inside. At the same instant Caroline stared around the room in disbelief. "Oh God, Walter. No—"

97

B.J. Blake was about to give it up and go home when Micah's green Caddy shot up the access road from his headquarters building and took off in the direction of the resort.

Well, hell, he thought. . . . *Might as well play this out to the end, see where it ends up.* Still, he didn't want to piss off an important person like Micah without a reason. A salesman can't have too many friends or too few enemies.

Blake hung back so he wouldn't be seen. No need to follow. He knew where the man was heading.

Five minutes later he pulled his Explorer off the highway, through the roundabout, and over toward the main lodge. When he got near the parking lot he killed his lights.

I'm beginning to feel like one of those TV detectives, he thought with an embarrassed chuckle. Still, he didn't want to be seen snooping around. He headed around back where he could park on a service road about twenty feet above the lot, and be able to see anyone coming into or leaving the resort, if it wasn't too dark. Maybe he'd stay until Karen and Lisa left, then drop over to her house and see what the heck was going on.

He killed the engine just as a flash of light burst from inside Micah's Cadillac. He watched as the man stepped out and hurried over to Walter Lowndes's private door. Another light appeared momentarily as Micah went inside, then the door closed.

Karen's car was still here. And Caroline Bellamy's damn Rolls-Royce. But there weren't any lights on inside the resort.

That struck him as mighty odd.

98

It was more than a half hour after Micah let himself in Walter Lowndes's private entrance that Mark spun the Z3 off the highway and onto the road that led to the resort. But instead of the welcoming lights and signs of the hotel there was nothing but emptiness and desolation. The parking lot stretched for half a mile in front of him, a vast dead sea of darkened light standards thrusting up from the asphalt like the trunks of limbless trees. He sped through the lot, past the resort entrance to Lowndes's quarters in the rear, and killed the engine. No police cars. Had they left already? Surely Caroline could have persuaded them to show up. Somebody should be here. Somebody! Maybe Karen was already back at her house. Reaching to the passenger seat for the cell phone, he punched in her home number. The answering machine again, with its maddenly cheery message. Goddamn it, where was *anybody*?

Pushing out of the car, he stood for a moment in the terrible calm.

Black stormclouds were moving in from the north, obscuring the few stars out. *What the hell's going on?* The whole place looked abandoned, like a ghost town.

It doesn't matter. Find Lowndes! He's here! Someplace—

Hurrying to the lodge building, he tried the private entrance, expecting to find it locked, and almost fainted with relief when the handle turned. Pushing on the door, he stared into the narrow windowless darkness in front of him as the long hallway stretched into nothingness. As his eyes adjusted to the gloom he made out a vague hint of light, no larger than a length of thread, seeping from beneath a door thirty feet distant.

His heart filling with dread he raced down to the room, vaguely noticed the odd lock, turned the handle, and stepped back as the door opened into a brightly lit area about fifteen feet square, with bare blue walls, a midnight blue carpet, a single leather couch, black drapes drawn tight over a lone window. And Walter Lowndes, sprawled on a yellow canvas tarp on the floor, as though someone was getting ready to drag him away. Blood covered his chest and half his forehead had been blown away.

The shock caused Mark to lose his breath. He froze, unable to move for half a minute, then finally took a step inside.

My father.

No need to test for a pulse.

He felt a rush of air from his lungs, a weakness in his legs. And a surge of relief that Lowndes couldn't hurt anyone else.

My father!

But where were Lisa and Karen? He put his hand on the door jam to steady himself. Then jumped when he heard a sound behind him. Micah Rollins, wearing a cowboy hat, looked around and said, "Holy smokes, boy, you do this?"

Mark could feel blood pounding in his forehead. "I just found—" Whose strange voice was speaking? His throat thickened and sweat broke out over his torso as Micah looked at him oddly. "I'm looking for Lisa and Karen. I came in and—" Dizziness rose and his knees felt weak.

Micah stepped inside, bent down, and put a hand to Lowndes's neck. "Deader than tax relief. You sure you didn't—?" He looked over his shoulder at Mark. "I know you didn't much like him—"

"Of course I didn't kill him! Look at him, for Christ's sake! He's been dead for an hour at least, probably more." He turned, started to leave. "I've got to find my daughter."

Micah rose with a sigh and a grunt. "What the devil's going on? What's your kid got to do with anything?"

Mark felt a surge of impatience and anger. He didn't want to get into all of this again. "Lowndes was obsessed with her," he said hurriedly. "He thought she was Cheryl McAfee, a girl he raped forty years ago. His mind was gone. He was going to take her and—"

"I see where you're heading. All the more reason for you to kill old Walter, of course. Not that I believe it, but the police might."

"The police!" He had completely forgotten. "I told Caroline to call them. Where are they?"

"Coulda come out and not found anything and left. I came in the back way to talk to Walter."

Mark was beyond worrying about it. "I've got to find Lisa." He spun around and started to leave.

"Thought I heard a kid crying when I was wandering around outside an hour or so ago. Then it stopped. Figured I was imagining things."

"An hour? And she was crying?" He remembered the phone call in the car: *"She was screaming her head off."* . . .

"Sounded like it. What were Karen and Lisa doing out here, anyway?"

Mark was already heading for the door. "Horseback-riding. And Karen said she might take Lisa for a hike."

Micah brightened. "That must be why I heard the chairlift operating. She probably took Lisa up to the top of the mountain. They got a lot of hiking trails up there. Mountain bikers use them in the summer—seven bucks to ride up, another five to take your bike."

"Chairlift? Everything's shut down. It's dark."

"Well, I heard one of them operating. The Express, I think. The one that zips you right to the top. And I could tell folks had been out at the stables tonight. Must be someone around. Maybe Karen got Les Cady to start it up so they could go hiking. Ain't nothing to it but turn a switch in the motor room. Like I say, Walter kept the chairs operational all year to bring in hikers and bikers."

"But why would they go hiking after someone killed Lowndes?" He was shouting at the other man. "It doesn't make sense. You don't go for a hike while a body's lying in a pool of blood!"

Micah looked at Mark as though he wasn't thinking very clearly. "Now how in blazes would they know Walter's dead in here?"

"I don't know! I—" He stopped suddenly as the thought hit him. "Then who did this? If Karen wasn't protecting herself or Lisa, who killed Lowndes?"

"Good question. Ain't no one around here tonight except spooky ol' Les Cady."

"And Cady took them to the top of the mountain?" Another wave of panic hit him.

"Don't know if he went with them or not. But I didn't see him anywhere around here. Yeah, he's probably up on top, too. You worried he might take an interest in your little girl? Is that it? I can see where he might. Jesus, first Walter, then Cady! Poor kid. And if Cady's already killed Walter—"

"Can we get up there?"

"Sure. Chairlift's still operating."

"Any other way up?"

"Nope. It's more remote than Neptune. You go in the chair or not at all. Can't even land a helicopter anymore with all the construction equipment we got there."

"Jesus Christ!" Mark started running.

"Hold on, son. I'll come with you. You're going to need some help. I'm just the man."

99

Running as fast as he could in the darkness, Mark headed toward the chairlift, Micah Rollins trying to keep up with him.

"Hey, slow down. You're going to need my help."

Mark kept on running. He could hear it now, a low buzz and rumble somewhere in the distance. Rollins caught up to him as they passed a fenced yard where four snowmobiles used by the rescue squad waited for winter. The darkness was almost complete now, even the stars hidden behind a layer of clouds as a summer thunderstorm moved in. There was another hundred yards to go.

Breathing heavily, Rollins said, "Are you sure Walter was some sort of danger to your kid? Aren't you mixing him up with Lester the Molester?"

Mark could make out the chairlift now, a series of black bench-seats, no more than vague outlines, jerking up and down the mountain in the darkness. Rollins said, "Looks like whoever done it shot the wrong person, don't it? I mean, old Walter was weird as hell the last few years but he sure didn't molest little girls."

Mark glanced at him but didn't slow down. "He molested my mother. Forty years ago."

Micah was wheezing. "No, I don't believe it. Walter?"

Mark halted on the landing under the motor room where the chairs turned around from their downward journey and began to make their way up the mountain. He jumped onboard one, Rollins quickly getting in next to him.

"Pull the bar down," the older man said. "You don't want to fall. No snow down there to cushion the drop. And it looks like we got some weather brewing. Could shake this chair pretty good if it starts blowing."

Mark's frustration boiled over as he tried to fathom what Karen was up to. "Why would they be up here in the dark. It doesn't make sense. If the chairlift is operating they could have come down anytime."

"Probably took a picnic basket up there, then decided to do some stargazing. We got a local astronomy club here in town that's got a lot of people hyped up about outer space, and learning all about stars and planets. They come up here all the time in the summer for lectures and so on. I know Karen's done stories about it. I guess she just wanted to give your girl a little education. Lookie up there. It's not completely dark. See those lights? The construction crew leaves a few on at night."

"Goddamn it, can't this thing go faster?"

"Relax. We'll be there in a bit. It's fourteen minutes up, fourteen down. Can't change the laws of physics. This here's a top-pull lift, in case you're interested. There's top-pulls and bottom-pulls. This lift's only a year old. Hate to tell you what it cost. There's no hurry getting up there, anyway. They'll be okay. I think Caroline might be with them."

"Caroline? I talked to her on the phone after Karen left."

"Well, hell, maybe she's not, then." Micah was getting annoyed. *Don't matter what you think anyway, you dumb fuck; this is all sewed up tighter than last year's elections.* Trying not to sound like he knew the answer, he asked, "Who do you figure shot Lowndes?"

Mark almost shouted at him, "How the hell should I know?" Damn it, why didn't Rollins shut up? His constant chattering was putting Mark over the edge.

"Probably old Lester," Micah said confidently. "Or maybe Bobby Sample."

Mark's head snapped toward him in the darkness. "Sample? Why do you think that?"

"Oh, I don't know. Guy's a loose cannon, though. Got a real temper. Guess you found that out."

Suddenly a part of Mark's mind cleared, and he recalled sitting in Rollins's office earlier that morning, Bobby Sample looking on with a grin as Rollins threatened Mark's life. *You're the ball. Harmony's the bat.* Mark tried not to shiver but it felt as though someone had dragged a fingernail along his spine.

Micah seemed to sense what Mark was thinking because he smiled and patted his arm comfortingly. "Hope you don't hold this morning against me, son. Guess I was kind of rude to you. Just surprised me, the way you burst into my office. You were sort of rude, too, come to think of it."

Mark glanced at him, then turned away. "How much farther is it?" He leaned forward but couldn't tell how close they were to the top of the mountain.

"Five minutes or so. You got a gun?"

Mark turned back toward Rollins. "No. Why do you ask?"

"Might need one. Don't worry. I got one."

"You always carry a gun?" He continued to look at the older man.

Rollins chuckled. "No, not always. With all the killings lately it just seemed a good idea. You ever seen the restaurant we're building up here? Going to be a beauty, bring people from all over the country. Something to be proud of. People are going to talk about this for years."

But Mark had already lost interest in Rollins. Where was Lisa? What was happening to her?

100

Les Cady began to wonder about all the activity at the lodge. From his small cabin at the far edge of the parking lot he could see cars coming, staying, then leaving. Must have gone on for about thirty or forty minutes. One of them was Micah Rollins's car, he knew. He'd been seeing Micah around here forever, it seemed. Had a Cadillac to show folks how rich he was. Also a huge old English car, the one that belonged to the restaurant woman. Then both of them disappeared and one of those fancy little sports cars showed up.

This was all bothering to Les. Wasn't supposed to be anybody here. The boss had closed up the place like he did every Saturday night in the summer, even told Les to go home. Les had tried again to talk him out of it because there was still two people out riding, that reporter and the little girl everyone made googoo eyes at. Mr. Lowndes said, "Yes, yes, I know. I'll take care of them." Sounding funny, like he was all out-of-breath.

"You sure you're up to it? Those horses can get mighty nasty. Especially this time of night."

But the boss just yelled at him and told him to go home; having one of his bad days, he could see. Been more and more of them lately.

That had to have been a couple of hours ago. So what the heck was going on now over there? He could hear a horse neighing so he probably hadn't been fed. Then someone must have taken that reporter's Taurus away because it disappeared just before the English car was moved. But the sports car was still here. And Rollins's Cadillac was back again.

Something was fishy here. Maybe he ought to have a look. Even if the boss had told him to stay home.

Cady turned to his hound. "Come on, McDuff. Let's see what's up."

It was exactly five hundred and thirty steps from Cady's front door to the front of the lodge, and another seventy-two to the boss's private entrance in the rear. Les had taken this walk enough times in thirty years to know how far it was to the lodge or anyplace else on the resort property, and it was comforting to confirm his measurements each time he made the trip. He fingered a large brass ring of keys as he strolled in the darkness with the dog at his side. "Gloomy out, ain't it? Too many clouds for the moon to light things up. Probably rain tonight." And with the lights out at the main building it was even spookier, but no sense frightening the dog. Suddenly he stopped and tilted his head. That couldn't be the chairlift he heard, could it? McDuff was whining and moving around at his feet. "Shut up, dog," Cady snapped, and tried to listen again. He could see one lift from here, and it was not moving. The Express was a half mile away. Couldn't be running, though. That was nuts. He did hear a low faint rumble of thunder; must be some miles off. Going to storm soon; that's for sure.

Then he saw someone moving around in the darkness at the edge of the parking lot. Or thought he did. He stood still and peered in that direction for at least a minute but saw nothing else. "Good thing we don't believe in ghosts, ain't it, McDuff?"

He stopped in front of Lowndes's door. "Well, let's tell the old man we're here." Cady began to bang on the door. "Hey, Mr. Lowndes! You in there? You okay?"

Nothing happened. He turned around and stared into the night once again. "Don't like this, McDuff. Don't like it at all."

He fingered his keys, finding the right one by feel, and inserted it into the lock. Slowly turning the handle, he allowed the door to swing in.

He took a breath. "Hey, Mr. Lowndes! You home? You in there? It's me, Les Cady."

There was nothing but darkness in front of him and behind him. He hesitated. "Well, hell, got to do it." Cady took a step into the hallway and tried once more. "It's me, Mr. Lowndes. You okay? I'm kinda worried. Actually I'm kinda scared outta my pants right now." He reached up to where he knew a wall switch was and flipped it. The corridor lit up in a flash, looking as bleak as it always did, without a painting or decoration of any kind. It reminded him of pictures you'd see of a hallway leading to an operating room, or maybe the electric chair. "Come on, you useless mutt. Let's see what's happening."

The two of them walked down the passage, Cady deliberately talking in case someone was there. He didn't want to surprise anybody and maybe get shot. "Hello! It's Les. Where is anyone?"

The door at the end, the old man's bedroom, was open. Cady flipped on the light. No one there. The bed hadn't been slept in but it was still early. He turned around and retraced his steps. Might as well try the other rooms. "Hey, anybody, I'm going to be opening all these doors." *So get your clothes on, or get off the pot, or wherever you are.*

He tried a door that opened into a spare bedroom. Flicked on the light. Nothing. No one in the bathroom or the other spare room. That left the office and the den, the one with the weird lock Mr. Lowndes made him install, with that combination you punched out. Didn't matter none, Les remembered the combination: 1971, the year they broke ground on the lodge. He tried the handle and was surprised to find it turn. That was strange—Mr. Lowndes never left it unlocked. Had important business papers in there, he said.

Les pushed the door open, reached in without entering, flicked the switch, and gave a terrible shout. "Oh hell, oh hell, no, no, no . . ." He raced in, dropping to a knee and putting a hand to Walter Lowndes's face but it was cold as snow, and he knew at once the man had been dead for more than an hour. "Oh my God, now what? Jesus, what do I do?"

He rose unsteadily, looked around as though seeking help. He was overwhelmed and felt like crying. What was he supposed to do now? Call the police? What if they thought he killed the boss? He was always being blamed for things he didn't do. It had happened all his life. Weird Les, Crazy Les, Lester the Molester . . . Why would things be any different this time?

The dog had followed him into the room and was sniffing around the body. "Get out of here, McDuff, go home, damn you." Les started to shoo the dog away when he noticed that he had blood on his shoes and the knees of his pants where he'd kneeled down. That settled it, then. If he didn't tell the cops and they checked his clothes they'd find Lowndes's blood on them and he'd be cooked for sure. You can't wash blood off so well that the FBI can't find traces. They could probably take fingerprints off the dead man's skin where Les had touched him; he'd seen something like that on TV once. Oh God. . . . *Find a phone, hurry, find a damn phone.*

Les rushed out of the room and directly toward Lowndes's office. He flipped on the light and sat at the desk, something he'd never done before, immediately reaching for the phone. "I hope Mr.

Chavez is there. He's been more decent to me than the others. Even if he did hassle me over that Pooh Bear stuff. Oh God, what am I going to do if Bobby or Todd answers?" But even Chavez had never been exactly friendly to him. No one down there was, he thought as he started to dial. Then his eye was drawn to the open drawer that seemed to be full of photographs, and he took a breath, and slowly set down the phone as a strange lightness grew in his mind.

His heart beating with a sudden new fear he'd never felt before, he picked up a handful of pictures. Kids, little girls, all naked. He began to sweat over all of his body. Hundreds of them, hundreds, girls, all about seven, eight, nine. Posing for the camera, doing things.

His arm wouldn't stop shaking. Using both hands he scooped the pictures onto the desktop, and began to spread his fingers through them in disbelief. This was it, this was what people talked about, a sex molester, a man who did things to little girls. *"Look at this!"* he screamed, and his heart pounded with outrage and hatred; four decades' worth of abuse and ridicule and embarrassment rose at once, choking him.

Hands trembling so much he couldn't hold a picture, he raked his fingers through the pile. Some showed men doing things to the girls, sometimes the girls were doing things to the men, sometimes to other girls, and sometimes to little boys. Cady was sick and disbelieving and trembling with rage and fear and nausea. Then he saw a picture of Walter Lowndes—*Goddamn, it was Mr. Lowndes*—he'd recognize him anywhere, even from the side like that. He was sitting in a chair without any clothes on and a little girl, also nude, was perched precariously on his lap, a look of absolute terror on her frozen face. With loathing Cady brushed it to the floor where it fell with a dozen others. At once he saw another photo of Lowndes with a little girl who was . . .

A moan seeped from his lips. He couldn't look anymore. He stood up so quickly the swivel chair shot out behind him and crashed against the wall. His voice rose in a cry that could have been heard anywhere in the building. *"Noooooo—"*

He spun around, the dog barking at the sudden movement, and his hands went to his face as though to claw his eyes out. "No, no, no. Not Mr. Lowndes, God, please—" The only person who had treated him decently in his entire life. Now Les knew why. Lowndes had needed a scapegoat, someone to draw the attention of the authorities anytime a child was mistreated. For thirty years Les Cady had been taking the blame for the man everyone had congratulated for his humane treatment of the obviously *sick* maintenance worker!

Cady was beside himself; he couldn't hold his body steady, couldn't stop the terrible shaking that racked his arms and legs and torso. Thirty years he had suffered for this man! *His life* ruined so Walter Lowndes could safely run after children who couldn't defend themselves. He pounded his fist on the wall until his knuckles were bloody. His whole life *ruined!*

Crying, screaming unintelligibly, he began to rip pictures from the walls, push over chairs, throw anything that his hands encountered. *Lowndes! Lowndes! Lowndes!* his mind screamed over and over: *My life destroyed because of* him!

In the grip of a rage he didn't even try to control, Cady raced out of the living quarters and into the lodge itself, crossed through the lobby and its huge stone fireplace, past the kitchen, to a utility room where two fifty-gallon drums of gasoline were being stored until Monday when they would be taken up the mountain in the chairlift for use with construction equipment. Hands flying, he opened one, tipped it on its side and, while gasoline gurgled noisily onto the floor, took the other by the top and wheeled it into the lobby where he emptied half of it on the carpeted floor, then pushed the container into Lowndes's living quarters where he dumped out the rest, and watched as it raced down the hallway. His mind quaked with revenge and hatred and the need to destroy, to wipe out the last thirty years with fire.

Hurrying back to the utility room he grabbed a box of matches, lit one and tossed it on the floor. *Whoosh!* Running just ahead of the fire he tossed matches in the lobby and in Lowndes's den, *whoosh . . . whoosh,* and listened as the flames shot upward toward the ceiling and began to consume the lodge. Hurrying down the long corridor to the parking lot, he raced outside to the asphalt, sobbing and shouting with joy as the building trembled and burned.

Then he heard screams from the other end of the building. He stood frozen a moment, cocked his head, and listened. A woman's voice. Mr. Lowndes's nurse. He'd forgotten about her. But there was nothing he could do now.

"McDuff!" His voice was weak with crying but he shouted as loud as he could, and the dog appeared at his side, barking in mad confusion. "Go," Cady yelled. "Go home. Run! Hurry!" He began sobbing again.

"Go!"

101

"Watch your step now," Micah Rollins said as the chair finally approached the top of the mountain. But Mark had already lifted the bar and was on the ground. He turned toward Rollins as the older man gingerly stepped off and moved toward the motor house. "Which way?"

"Hold on, son. I want to turn this here lift off. Ain't doing nothing but wasting electricity. Jesus H. Christ, did you see that lightning? Can't be more than half a mile away. Damn, I hate thunder and lightning. Always makes me think of that scene in *Frankenstein* where the villagers are after poor old Boris Karloff. All they want to do is cut his head off or burn him to cinders."

"Which way, goddamn it?"

But Rollins had gone into the motor room and hit a switch. When he came out he casually turned the knob in the door handle, locking the door shut.

Another jagged crack of lightning exploded across the mountaintop. Mark was looking toward where the restaurant lay in darkness a half mile distant. Micah jumped as he felt the ground move. "Damn, that wasn't a hundred yards from here. Always do get more weather up on top. In January it gets so cold it'll freeze the short-and-curlies in five minutes. That's what we're hoping for—the cold'll send everyone up to the Ice Castle for a rum toddy or big ol' hot steak and Texas fries. Gonna put pictures right here on a lit-up board showing how long you gotta wait at the various runs, then next to it pictures of the restaurant and food. You'll see; folks'll say, 'Hey, hon, forget skiing, I want me some brandy in a snifter, don't care what it costs.' "

Mark was ready to grab Rollins and force him to stop babbling when the man said, "You're on the right track. Keep moving. If they're hanging out at the restaurant we can get there easy enough. Walter had the idea of putting in this horizontal chair-pull—can't exactly call it a lift because it don't lift people, it carries them in a chair a couple of feet above the ground to the restaurant. That way folks don't have to walk. Don't even have to take off their skis to get there. Just hop in and sit for five minutes while you feel around for your American Express card. Anyway, that's what these supports we're putting up are for. Won't be ready till next season, though. Restaurant won't, either, of course. Did I mention it's my construction company doing the work?"

Mark wasn't paying attention. Trying not to think of what might be happening to Lisa if Cady was up here, he pushed ahead in the darkness along the two-foot-deep trench being constructed as a foundation for the chair-pull. Tools, pipe, electrical wire, and bags of concrete lay on the ground everywhere, impeding their way. Mark kept banging his feet in the darkness, and cut his knee on a huge spool of wire but didn't stop to check it out. Every thirty yards or so a concrete abutment rose up three feet, a faint safety light attached to it, waiting for the pylons that would hold the cable for the chairs. "This is idiocy," he yelled over his shoulder. "As soon as the storm came up they should have started down."

Rollins was huffing and puffing behind him. "Hell, would you want to be in one of those chairlift seats when the wind's blowing like the Rapture's here, and thunder's booming in your ears, and lightning's flashing and crackling all around you? Especially with those towers made out of steel! Might as well scratch out your last will and testament and put a lightning rod on your head. Seems to me like they did the right thing. These mountain storms come up, act all crazy, then calm down pretty quick."

"I can see the restaurant," Mark said between breaths as a few drops of rain fell. "Maybe a hundred yards up. Is it enclosed yet?"

"The top's only over the center of the dining room. We're starting in the middle and radiating it out to the edges. But they could stay pretty dry, I reckon."

It started to rain more steadily.

Two minutes later they were there. An electrical cord with low-wattage bulbs at thirty-foot intervals ran along a beam at the level of the roofing supports. A weird-looking horizontal flash of lightning momentarily displayed a collection of construction equipment that seemed out of place on the top of a mountain: a bulldozer, a small crane, two backhoes.

"Lisa!" Mark yelled. *"Lisa. Are you there?"* He was frantic now,

trying to see how best to get into the partially completed structure, looking in the dim light like the skeleton of a huge prehistoric animal.

"Ain't no point in yelling till we get inside," Rollins said. "This wind's going to take your words down to Denver. They'll never hear you in the restaurant." Another crack of thunder rumbled nearby and the lightning flash was almost instantaneous, as was the odd electrical smell of ozone that blew over them. Rollins jumped, and his heart started thumping. "Jesus, got to be right on top of us." He stopped to collect his wits and catch his breath. No way was he going to be able to keep up with the ex–Air Force pilot. Didn't matter anyway. It was too late for Ritter to change the course of events now. And for the second time today the same word occurred to him. *Perfect!* Yes sir, he couldn't ask for things to go any better than this. Wished he had brought a jacket with him, though. It was storming pretty good now. But that was okay, too.

Soaked through with rain, Mark maneuvered around the construction equipment in the dark, stubbing his toes a half dozen times. The workers seemed to have left their tools wherever they were when quitting time came on Friday. Using the light from the bulbs on the roofing beams to find his way, he threaded through to the concrete steps that marked the front of the restaurant. His mind wouldn't stop roiling. Karen had been crazy to bring Lisa up here. A summer hail storm, or a bolt of lightning, could knock out the electricity on the lifts and they'd be stranded for hours.

"Lisa! Karen! Are you there? It's Mark!"

Nothing.

Mounting the steps, he smelled cement that had been recently laid down, and wasn't yet completely dry. Tile, probably for the bathrooms, was stacked on a pallet just inside the building. Steel framing rose up from the floor on all sides and crisscrossed above him where the roof would soon be laid. The wind whipped in from the north and out the nonexistent southern side of the building which hung over the cliff to what was probably a thousand-foot drop, though he couldn't see the bottom from here. Still at the entrance, he tried to get a sense of the place, but couldn't. It was like a strange Neolithic ruins whose purpose was no longer understood, as though Stonehenge had been discovered at the top of the Rockies.

That must be the dining room in front of him. The kitchen was probably off to the side so that the customers could have the prime space overlooking the slopes and the valley below.

"Lisa! Where are you? It's Dad!"

Only the wind responded. Where the hell was Rollins?

He stepped inside.

"Lisa! Karen!" Then, in a voice that quaked, "Cady? You up here?"

It started to rain more heavily, the drops splattering loudly on the bare cement. His shirt and slacks were drenched, and water ran into his shoes, soaking his feet.

Hell, yell all you want, Rollins thought. *They ain't going to be answering unless they learned how to talk through duct tape.* He halted at the front entrance of the restaurant and started wheezing. *Too damn old for this chase stuff, especially at this altitude. Got to figure the young ones are going to run you into the ground, make you look like an oldster.* Then again, the young ones didn't have a gun. He took the automatic out of his pocket and drew a calming breath.

Let's see what's up.

He mounted the steps.

Caroline would be in the basement with her .38, watching Lisa and Karen. Micah had brought Karen, already trussed-up like a calf by Walter, in the chairlift after Caroline took the damn kid, still howling and sobbing her head off, up first. No sense letting the kid see her lady friend all tied up like that. Especially the way Karen kept trying to talk around her gag. Sounded like a hog rooting in a landfill. Then he'd plopped her down on one of those nifty all-terrain vehicles they use in the summer to keep an eye on the bike trails, zapped her the back way to the restaurant, and dumped her next to the girl, who was also tied up by this time, and also trying to cry around her duct tape. Doing a pretty good job of it, too. Jesus, he hated kids; all water and noise.

Caroline was damn well getting on his nerves, though. All this whining about killing a lady and a kid was truly a pain in the butt. He'd told her a thousand times, *Got to do it. Ain't no damn choice. So stop babbling.*

Of course from Micah's point of view, it was all— What do they call it? Academic! *Because Caroline's going up in the explosion, too. Can't have that unstable female running around just dying to tell somebody what Micah did. Fine woman; just too damn queasy, too much of a conscience on her. Never did see much point in having a conscience. All it does is make you feel guilty for what other folks do anyway.*

He stepped into the restaurant. Darker than a banker's heart in here. Couldn't see dumbshit Ritter. Could hear him, though, because the wind had died down. The rain had let up, too. *That's good,* he decided, *let the restaurant burn a little longer. We don't want nothing left but bones and teeth.*

Weird thing was, he could almost smell the fire already. Must be his imagination.

Mark was soaked through with rain and sweat. "Lisa! Karen!"

Nothing, nothing, nothing! Heart pounding.

"Lisa!"

He shouldn't be walking so fast; he kept bumping into things in the darkness. It didn't make any difference, though. *Damn it, where's Rollins? He was right behind me.* "Lisa—"

Hell, they're not here, they're nowhere around here. Can't be. They must have gotten down the mountain earlier. They probably saw the storm coming and hurried to the chairlift. But if they had, why hadn't they been waiting by the lodge? At once his mind reverted to the awful scene in Lowndes's den, the bloodied body of the man . . . dead for at least an hour. Karen hadn't been home; he'd called her. The police were nowhere to be seen even though he'd told Caroline Bellamy to alert them. Had she? He remembered the phone call he'd gotten: Lowndes and Cady had taken Lisa. Did that mean Cady killed Lowndes? He couldn't think, couldn't concentrate. A gust of wind whipped in through the open walls of the restaurant, and the air around him seemed all at once to grow icy. He spun around in the dark, raised his voice again. *"Lisa. Lisa!"*

Suddenly he didn't want to be here anymore. Lisa and Karen were nowhere around. But something was making the hairs on his arms stand straight out and he said in a lower voice, "Micah? You here, Micah?" He couldn't see anything in the darkness and heard nothing but the rain, huge drops of almost warm water splattering around him.

"Cady?" Something kept him from raising his voice. He stood still a moment, listened, then turned back in the direction he had come from and ran into a ladder, sending it crashing to the bare cement floor, now wet from the rain.

"Micah, damn it, where are you?"

He felt his way around the ladder, then jumped when Rollins said, "You see 'em anywhere?"

"*Jesus!* Where have you been? I've been calling you."

"Not as young as I used to be. Couldn't keep up with you. No sight of 'em, huh?"

"No, Christ, let's get down the mountain. They're not here."

"You try the basement?"

"Basement? Where the hell's that?" Suddenly hope sprang back. Of course they wouldn't be out here in the weather if they could take refuge from the rain in a basement.

"Got to go in the kitchen. Basement's going to be a storage area. Actually we had to put it in as part of the damn structural requirements. Cost a fortune digging it out in this ground but the friggin' state's afraid the whole place is going to come tumbling off the mountain. Hell, it's as sound as a Hong Kong dollar."

"Haven't you got a flashlight?" Mark knew he was sounding increasingly panicky but he didn't care. He wanted to hurry.

" 'Course not. Didn't plan on coming up here. Only thought I'd pay old Walter a visit. Didn't expect to find him lying in a pool of blood, and then go off on some kind of quest to the top of the mountain in the middle of a lightning storm. Don't like this at all. Damn spooky up here. Come on, follow me. You can see, can't you?"

In fact the storm had partially blown away, leaving a patch of stars to provide a little light, though the moon was still not visible. Mark said anxiously, "Hurry up, I see you." Just then his leg struck the edge of a metal table and he swore loudly.

"You okay?" Rollins asked.

"Fine. Keep going."

Rollins made his way back toward the entrance, then went through a doorway, still without a door attached, and into another room. "You still back there?"

"Just keep moving." Mark's leg was bleeding, the blood warm and thick on his flesh. He said suddenly, "What's that noise?" It sounded like a low rumble.

"Generator. Haven't got our permanent lines in yet, and power to the rest of the mountain top is shut down in the summer. Got a big old Chrysler 440 engine running a 480 electric system in the meantime. A transformer cuts it to 220. Once the power's in we'll use it for backup when the electricity goes out in a storm. Happens all the time. One more room to go. Stay behind me."

They stepped into a room with no exterior walls. "Stairway leading down's over there. Be careful. Damn light's not on for some reason and there ain't no handrail." *What the hell's going on?* Rollins wondered with a stab of concern. *Caroline ought to have a light on down there.* He'd left a shop light burning from the end of a fifty-foot cord. It didn't really matter, he supposed. Karen and Lisa weren't going anywhere, trussed-up like they were. Neither was Ritter.

"Yoo-hoo, Karen. You down there? How about you, Caroline?" Something made Micah raise his voice, and he felt an icy trail along his spine that made him shiver. But, hell, he knew what he was going to find. Just play-actin' a bit for Mark. Caroline was sitting on the floor with her .38 pointing at the two nosy females. Of course, the gun wasn't loaded now. Micah wasn't about to trust Caroline that much. Didn't tell her, naturally. That made *three* nosy females in his life about to depart for the other side, Micah realized. Couldn't hope for much better than that in a single day.

Mark was on the stairs right behind Rollins. "Slow down," Micah said. "You go pushing and we'll both end up on the floor." Micah felt another shiver. *What in damnation is going on?* He stepped onto the level floor of the room with relief, but was still concerned as hell about the silence.

"Damn it, Caroline, where are you?" Micah moved his foot around, feeling for the power cord on the bare cement floor. *Caroline?* Mark thought again. What would she be doing here? He turned toward Micah's voice just as the older man reached down and picked up the cord, then followed it to the shop light and flicked it on.

Mark gasped as he saw Noel Atchison propped against the wall, a bullet hole in his forehead.

But Micah was more angry than surprised. "God*damn*," he muttered.

The ropes used to bind Karen and Lisa were lying on the floor along with pieces of duct tape.

Mark was stunned. "What the hell is this?"

Micah experienced a moment of pure rage. *That goddamn woman! Was a pain in the butt when we was married and still is.* A few seconds later he regained his normal equanimity. *Don't get upset. Fool woman is still up here. Fell victim to her damn conscience already, didn't she? Going to save the lives of two troublemaking adults and one pain-in-*

the-butt little girl. Don't bet on it, hon. Caroline couldn't get in the motor room, and couldn't figure out how to work the chairlift if her life depended on it. *Which it does, come to think of it.*

Mark bent to pick up a piece of rope. "Goddamn it, Rollins, what's going on?"

Don't have time to have to deal with this, Micah thought. *After all, we got an explosion coming up. Don't want any bullet holes but there ain't going to be much left of the body to autopsy. Hope I don't hit a bone, though. Could be questions later.* "Hey, boy!" When Mark turned around Micah said, "Kinda feel like I owe you an explanation. See, you've been chasing the wrong guy all this time. It wasn't Walter you should have been afraid of—it was the man pulling Walter's strings." He shook his head and smiled. "Guess you feel pretty stupid right now, huh? Well, don't worry none. It don't matter any more."

Micah shot him in the torso, the noise exploding all around them in the small enclosed space. Mark took a step forward and Micah shot again, and watched as his body tumbled face-first to the floor. Mark groaned, and his arm reached out on the concrete, fingers splayed. Then he lost consciousness. Micah bent over and stared at the body. "Might've hit a rib, but I don't think so. Both shots entered on the right side, no more'n two inches apart. Damn good shooting. So much for Survival Training, huh? I'll take squirrel-hunting any day. More practical." Then he calmly made his way up the stairs. Three down, three to go.

"Hey, Caroline! Where 'd you go off to, woman? Your old Pooh Bear's coming at'cha." She used to call him that in bed sometimes, tracing her finger on his hairy round belly. Pooh Bear. She'd say, *Pooh Bear, you hungry, you want some honey?*

"Hey, Caroline, here I come, ready or not." She'd remember what that meant.

102

"Don't make a sound," Caroline Bellamy whispered furiously. "Do you understand me, Lisa? Not a word."

The little girl, frightened out of her mind, moaned and moved her head up and down on the floor of the warming shack, eighty yards down the hill from the restaurant but hidden from it by a growth of trees.

Karen Paige, her back against the wall, shook her head and tried to make sense of the last few hours. "He's crazy. My God, he's as crazy as Walter Lowndes was."

"Walter was sick," Caroline said. "He couldn't think straight. Micah said he hadn't been able to run the resort for two or three years. He thought people were after him all the time, trying to kill him or cheat him. Micah and Janis were making all the decisions." She looked over at Lisa who had already vomited on the floor. "Poor Walter wasn't able to help himself. Ever since Mark and Lisa showed up his mind locked on the past, when Cheryl McAfee was eight years old. But Micah—" She shuddered. "I guess he thought I was too stupid to figure out what he was planning." As soon as Rollins had left for the bottom of the mountain to wait for Mark, Caroline untied Karen and Lisa. If Micah could kill a lifelong friend like Noel Atchison he wouldn't hesitate at killing Caroline. That's when she checked her revolver and discovered he had emptied it.

As they hurried away from the uncompleted restaurant Caroline explained to Karen what had happened after Walter Lowndes had left her tied up in the tackroom. Some of it Walter had told her, some Lisa, and some she managed to put together herself:

After leaving Karen in the tackroom, Walter had taken Lisa to the lodge, to his "Cheryl Room," every inch of the walls of which were covered with huge photographs—black-and-white and color, supersharp or soft-focused or airbrushed—at least a hundred of them, arranged in a dozen settings, real or constructed in the lab, of Lisa Ritter.

Or more accurately, Cheryl McAfee. Permanently age eight. Photos he had saved, and reproduced and played with for forty years.

That was where Caroline had found him, and where Walter had shoved her, slamming the door behind them.

"My God," Caroline whispered, staring around in a panic, and feeling as though she was withering inside her clothes. At the far side of the room Lisa sat cringing against the wall, her hands to her face as she screamed and screamed at the top of her voice.

Lowndes didn't hear her, and continued staring at the pictures, enraptured. Caroline's hand went to her forehead, and her body began to tremble. "God, Walter, no, no."

Some of the photographs showed Cheryl wearing a cowgirl costume and twirling a rope, others had her dressed like an eighteen-year-old beauty contestant in a swimsuit and carrying a rose, others tap-dancing and holding a small cane in her hand, or with a microphone and singing to an invisible crowd—a crowd of one, Caroline knew. Still others showed her nude, legs splayed, smiling a tiny hurt smile at the camera that didn't disguise the horror in her heart and the sheer terror in her eyes.

My God, Caroline thought, *the childhood that poor girl had.* Why hadn't she told anyone? Why hadn't she let her teacher, or a policeman, or anyone know?

But that isn't the way with abused children, she realized. *They trust too much, they know adults would never do something to them that wasn't accepted by other adults.*

She put a hand to her mouth. "I'm going to be sick."

Lowndes didn't hear her. While Lisa screamed without interruption his eyes hadn't moved from the photographs—all four walls, every inch of the room. A shrine. To a forty-year-old fixation that had suddenly come roaring back to seize him in its sick grip.

"Don't, Walter," Caroline managed to say. "Please don't hurt her."

He turned to Caroline with confusion. "Why would I hurt her? She loves me, she came back. I've had these pictures since she left. I like to *look*. To remember. To remember how she loves me. I have more. Would you like to see them? So many—"

Caroline glanced at Lisa, still cringing against the wall and screaming at the top of her voice. "Walter," she said cautiously, "this is not Cheryl. It's not Cheryl. It's Lisa. Lisa Ritter."

The man's eyes shown with pride as he turned in her direction. "She came back, Caroline. I always knew she would. She loves me. And I her. Her mother allowed her to get ugly but now she is again as she was."

Caroline turned to look at the door. A small silver button above the handle evidently disengaged the lock. Reaching out, she took hold of Lowndes's free hand. "Walter, you aren't well. The stroke damaged your ability to think. This is not 1960. Do you hear me? It's not 1960. It's 1998."

The man's deformed face turned on her with contempt. She was speaking nonsense.

Caroline held tighter to his hand, gripping so firmly the old man winced. "Walter, this is not Cheryl McAfee. Cheryl is an old lady now. She is old and fat and ugly and—" Suddenly she shoved Lowndes as hard as she could, screamed, *"Lisa, run, run, run—"* and raced toward the door, pushing the button that unlocked it, pulling on the handle, still shouting. *"Please, Lisa, run, hurry—"*

The child leaped to her feet, still screaming, half grasped what was happening, and raced frantically toward the opening.

"No—" Lowndes shouted with terror. He had only stumbled when Caroline pushed him, but used his cane to catch himself and balance against the wall. As Lisa leaped to her feet he roared toward the door, howling unintelligibly as he saw his forty-year dream slipping away because of the idiocy of a madwoman. "No, no, no. *Stop! Stopppppp—"* He swung his cane at the child but she stumbled past him, hitting the floor, scrambling up, rushing toward the opening. Caroline stepped in front of him, still griping the door, screaming, *"Faster, Lisa, faster!"*

Lowndes momentarily forgot the girl and lunged at Caroline, using his cane like a spear, drawing it back and jabbing the end at the woman as she struggled to keep the door open. "Goddamn you, damn you, damn you!" Saliva spewed like rain onto Caroline's cheeks as he dropped the cane and reached out with one strong hand, seizing her neck and jerking forward. "Filthy whore, bitch, tramp. Let go of the door, let go, let go—"

Lisa's frenzied screams filled the air as she maneuvered around Caroline's legs, hurtled through the doorway—

And was gone.

At once, Caroline pushed the door shut, and a terrible silence engulfed them, the most frightening sound either had ever heard. Lowndes dropped his hand and looked at the woman in a fury of disbelief. "You let her go—" He began to howl horribly.

Caroline slid along the door to the floor, coming to rest with her knees drawn up within the folds of her dress. She began to sob.

"Bitch, whore, filthy—" His mind defeated him; they were the only words that came to his consciousness, and even they died out with a furious rush of air from his lungs.

"Walter!" Caroline raised her hands, rings flashing in the light, and screamed as she stared up at him with wild eyes and a sweat-stained face. *"Walter, stop it, stop it, stop it."* She took a deep breath, balled her fingers into fists, and tried to keep from hyperventilating. "Walter, look at these pictures. *Look!* It's not the same girl. That was Lisa Ritter. Mark Ritter's daughter. It's not Cheryl! Do you understand me? It's not 1960. *It's not Cheryl!"*

He faltered as the words shoved aside some of the rubble that had piled up around his conscious mind, and registered, or partly so, making vague but disturbing connections. "Ritter's . . . daughter?" His thoughts churned like ancient machinery trying to spring back to life, attempted to hold the connections, but the pieces began spinning off into the wind. *Ritter? Who was Ritter to him?* Something was there, but what? He felt suddenly unsure of himself and began to sweat profusely. The stroke had made it difficult to sort out complex relationships or notions, or even bring up the most basic of memories on command. *Ritter's daughter.* Something about that bothered him a great deal, made his heart jump. *Ritter!* But when his eyes dropped to Caroline whimpering at his feet he was filled with rage. Grabbing his cane from the floor he began to slash at her, screaming obscenities.

Caroline pushed unsteadily to her knees, raised an exhausted arm to ward off the blows, and forced her voice into a steely calmness she was far from feeling. "Walter, what's happened to you? Look what you're doing!"

Lowndes paid no attention. "I'm going out there. She can't get away. The doors are locked."

"I came in from the courtyard. That door is open. She's gone by now."

"If she finds it how will she get over the wall?"

"I guess she can't," Caroline admitted. And thought in despair, *Where's Micah? My God, why didn't I call the police? I can't do this all alone!* "Walter," she managed, "Where's Karen? She came out here with Lisa."

"Who?"

"Karen Paige."

He blinked, seemed startled. The pupils in his eyes darted back and forth, then enlarged as they came to rest on her face. "In the tackroom. She can't help you. Now *move!*" He raised his cane, ready to strike her.

"No."

"Move. I'm going after the girl."

Still on her knees, Caroline felt a gigantic sigh rush from her lungs. It was over. She could do no more. Tears rushing to her eyes she slipped aside, reached an arm out to retrieve her purse from where it had fallen, and removed the revolver.

"Walter, not anymore. No more rape." She raised the gun, and her arm shook as if it weighed a hundred pounds.

Lowndes looked at her in genuine confusion. "Rape?" He waved his fist at the walls and the photos. "I'm not going to *rape* her." He faced the woman, his manner so guileless and without threat she almost believed him as she pulled the trigger, the sound exploding as it ricocheted back and forth off the walls of the small room. His expression turned at once to a measureless surprise and then to rage as he stumbled, shouted something, forced himself up with his cane and lunged at her as once again she pulled the trigger. Unable to move quickly enough, Caroline screamed as Walter Lowndes fell on her, hemorrhaging blood all over her face and chest.

103

Shrieking with terror, Caroline twisted from under the still-dying Lowndes as blood poured from his wounds over her body. Yanking open the door, she screamed, "Lisa, Lisa—" lurched into the hallway, ran straight into Micah Rollins, and screamed again at the top of her voice.

"Hey, hold on there, woman. What are you doing?" Micah stepped back and looked at her in distaste. "Cripes, Caroline, you're covered in blood!"

Caroline's screams ground down but she was breathing in heavy sighs, her shoulders heaving as she tried to catch her breath. "Oh God, I killed him. I killed him, Micah!"

"Who you talking about? Old Walter? 'Bout time. Hadn't been you, someone else woulda. Ritter probably. Like I told you, the old fart's been crazier than a loon the last few years. Half the time he didn't know what decade it was. I'd come in here sometimes and he'd be telling me how business was goin' to improve after the war. 'What war you talking about, Walter?' And he'd look at me like I was two bricks short of a load and say, 'The Vietnam War, you twit.' Hell, I told you I've been making most decisions for him for two years now. Me and Janis. Just hand him a piece of paper and say, 'Sign this,' and he did. Usually. Didn't want to tell you because you always was a worrywart."

Caroline braced her back against the wall. "He was going to rape her. Lisa. He was going . . ." She bolted away from the wall. "*Oh my God, where is she?*"

"The kid? Saw her in the bathroom, sitting on the floor, sobbin' like her pet gerbil just died. Looks like she upchucked all over herself but she's okay. Stinks like hell, of course. Kids get over things, though. It's old ducks like us carry it around and get ulcers and such."

"He was absolutely crazy, Micah. He wouldn't leave her alone. Have you seen that room? It's a shrine, a goddamn shrine to Cheryl McAfee."

Micah glanced at the door. "Yeah? Last time I looked in there I found a stack of little girlie pictures under a pillow on the couch, nasty *Shirley Temple Does Dallas* stuff. Didn't look like Cheryl, though."

Caroline took a step back, her head against the wall, breathing erratically, then sank slowly to the floor. Sitting with her knees up and her breath still catching in her throat she asked, "What are we going to do? You called the police, didn't you?"

Micah turned toward the door. "No, didn't do that. Just figured it'd add a complication to everyone's life that we don't need about now."

"But—"

"Now, don't you worry none, Caroline. Let me see what we got here. Or more correctly, what *you* got here since you pulled the trigger on Walter."

Hands in pockets as if he hadn't a worry in the world, which he was positive he didn't, Micah strolled into the room, looked around, and whistled softly. "Gracious' sakes, what a *mess* you made. Old Walter is just *covered* in blood. You do that with the bitty ol' thirty-eight I gave you? She-it, looks more like a forty-five or Tec-Nine. Damn good shootin', though. One in the heart, one in the head. Looks like you got him through the part of the brain that worked. Couldn't have been a very large target." He chuckled to himself.

Leaning back, he scrutinized the walls. "I reckon that's what the shrinks call an 'ob-session.' Man, he had it something bad, didn't he? Thing is, I never could understand how anyone could get turned on by little kids. I mean it's not like they got what it takes for a good tumble in bed. Lacking the *essentials,* you might say. You know what I mean, hon? Hell, of course you do. You and me, we had some fun times, didn't we? Shoot, I've had fun times with all my wives. Till they start bitchin' about takin' out the trash or something dumb like that. You remember that too, don't ya?"

"Micah, for God's sake!" Caroline's voice came softly from the hallway.

"Guess we got some thinking to do. Got us a body, a *bloody* body, and a hysterical kid in the john. Sounds like a real kettle of fish you and your trigger finger got us into."

Caroline didn't seem to answer—at least he couldn't hear anything. He picked up the revolver from the floor, checked to see how many shells it still had in the chamber, and shoved it in the left pocket of the light-weight blue blazer he was wearing. The right pocket held his Beretta 9mm. "Gonna have to clean up in here, Caroline. Can't very well call Housekeeping, can we? Why'nt you go find us a rug shampooer over in the lodge. Get some shampoo, too, and some disinfectant. I'll get these pictures off the walls and make a fire in the fireplace. Don't want to have to explain Walter's hobby to the police. And tell that girl to stop her hissy-fit. It's getting me all cantankerous."

Caroline was suddenly in the room. "For God's sake, Micah, what's wrong with you? He was going to rape her. This vicious old man was going to rape the child. Can't you understand that?"

"What are you talking about, woman? Walter couldn't rape a peach pie. Man's been impotent since his last stroke. Couldn't get his ideas straight, let alone his pecker! He couldn't have gotten it up with a splint and a pint of shellac."

"Then what was this?" She sounded panicky again and waved a hand around at the room.

"You said it, Caroline. It was a shrine. That's all. Old Walter wasn't going to rape her or molest her, or whatever you wanna call it. Shit, I think he forgot what sex was. All he wanted to do was celebrate the child, probably give her some presents—you know, stuffed animals and play jewelry—and talk awhile. You ever read that book he used to yack about—*Death in Venice?* The man in that book wasn't after sex—it was beauty, the beauty of a perfect human child. You should have heard Walter going on and on about her yesterday, thinking it was Cheryl, of course. I reckon his brain hit a speed bump last week and bounced back to 1960. Happened soon as Ritter and his kid showed up. Poor old Walter. Hell, he was harmless as skim milk."

"Harmless? He didn't mean to hurt her? I *shot* him, Micah!"

"That you did."

"But there was no point?" Her face, already wet with tears, had gone red with confusion and rage.

"Didn't say that, darlin'. I figure you did the world a favor. Did *us* a very big favor for sure. With that partnership insurance we got, we take over his part of the business, and his beneficiary—weird Janis-in-the-sky-with-diamonds, I reckon—ends up a millionaire. Or more of a millionaire than she already is. Who's got anything to complain about?"

"But I killed him!"

"Chill out, babe. Frankly, no one gives a flying fuck if you killed the bastard or not. Besides, I figure old Walter murdered that little girl they found raped and dead a few years ago. So you killed a killer. Big deal, the state does that all the time. Except they call it justice."

Caroline was shaking her head back and forth, desperately seeking justification for what she had done. "God, maybe you're right. And he killed Carl Stark—"

Micah had begun carefully removing the pictures from the wall. "Stark? No, fact is, he didn't. Walter thought he did and I kinda let him believe it. Walter just set the fire and skedaddled. Carl was in his cabin at the time, of course. I figured he'd wake up and smell the smoke and call the fire department, then go out and try to put it out. So before Walter got there I went out to talk to Carl, all nice-like, even brought a six-pack of some kick-ass fortified ale. Then when Carl was half-looped and not looking, I bopped him across the back of the head with a big old crescent wrench. Cops thought something fell on him when the cabin went up." He winked at her. "Not *ex-actly!*"

Caroline looked as if she was going to scream. "My God, Micah. What kind of person are you?"

"The kind that's going to get you out of this-here mess and make you a hell of a lot richer than you are, hon. Next year you can be the only person in Harmony with *two* Rolls-Royces. Now you go get that rug shampooer and I'll look around for some way to move Walter over to the chairlift. Going to have to leave him where he is for just a bit, though. Maybe we could use one of those yellow canvas tarps they use to line the fences in the winter."

"The chairlift? What in God's name are you thinking?" She looked at him as if she felt he, too, had lost his senses.

"Well, I think it's what the po-lice call a cover-up. See, you and me, we committed a crime—mine's destroying evidence, yours is murder of the first degree—and now we're going to cover it up so no one knows. And at the same time make us a bundle of money."

Caroline felt herself sink toward the floor. Micah reached out and caught her, knocking them both off balance. "Hey, you all right, hon? You look peaked. But you just killed a guy, right? First one? Well, don't worry none. Your old lover-boy is here to help. Just take a couple of deep breaths, get your control back. You'll be okay in a minute."

"Micah, for God's sake, if you don't tell me what you're planning, I'll kill you too."

He smiled broadly and went back to taking the pictures off the wall. "Killing's like eating snails, ain't it? After the first one the second is easy. Well, like I said, we are going to ensure that we come out okay from the tragic circumstances surrounding the death of the revered founder of the Eagle Point Resort and the father of modern-day Harmony."

"Micah, damn you—"

"The first thing, most important thing actually, is to cover over a little pothole on the road to financial independence. Wish I had a ladder. Some of these pictures are really up there. Say, where's Karen Paige? Speaking of hazards on the highway to happiness."

Caroline wiped perspiration from her forehead, then jumped up. "In the stables, in the tackroom. We have to get her."

"She's alive?" He seemed disappointed.

"I think. Tied up, probably."

Micah frowned, then smiled. "Well, maybe that ain't all bad. Might've caused problems later if she'd been dead. With autopsies and all. Not that there's likely to be bodies to autopsy."

"Jesus Christ, Micah, will you tell me what the hell you're talking about?"

"I'm talking about us not going to prison for the rest of our lives. I'm talking about you and me ending up fifty-fifty owners of this-here resort. Mostly I'm talking about saving your sorry carcass from the executioner, so stop caterwauling and go get that rug shampooer. We got us work to do. Then we got to get the hell out of here before Ritter shows up. From what you told me, that'll be pretty quick."

"What about Ritter?"

Micah had the last poster off the walls. He began to crumple them up. "That, my love, is our most serious problem right now. The fella's pretty sharp. Look what he's done—found his ma when no one else could. He started nosing around old Bill and managed to get someone riled up enough to kill the old coot. You didn't do Bill too, did you? That one's really been bothering me. No, all right, relax. Means someone else out there is killing people, though. Wish to hell I knew who it was. Anyway, Ritter also got Eldon Stallworth killed. The man's a menace and a major-league troublemaker. Can't be leaving him around to trouble us. Know what I mean?"

"So you're going to kill him?"

"Kill him? No way, José. He's going to die in an explosion up there at that crazy restaurant Walter insisted on building on top the mountain. Going to be one of them propane explosions you hear about on construction sites. Along with Karen Paige and that scream-ing brat next door, the Harmony symbol of human perfection, as old Walt would have it. She's about to become perfectly dead. And to make sure you don't suck up a lethal injection at the expense of the state, my darlin', we'll take your dead pal Walter up there, too. All these nice folks having a Saturday-night picnic in the rarefied air of the Ice Castle. Don't need a storm like we got brewing out there but it makes everything easier. More believable, you might say. Soon as they go in to get out of the weather there's going to be a boom you could hear in Utah. Now you hustle along and get that shampooer. I got to burn these pictures. Then we'll take a little ride in the chairlift with several of our closest and dearest friends. Going to have to leave Walter for a while, though. He won't mind. He's been dead for three years."

Caroline stared at him but didn't move.

"Damn it, you heard me. Hurry! Go on!" *Because,* he thought, *we've got to get moving here; a lot of people have to die yet tonight. Including you, my love. Got to start with a clean slate tomorrow, and time's running short.*

104

The wind rattled a board outside the warming shack. "God, what was that?" Karen's intestines clenched as if she was having a seizure, and she bent over on the floor and tried to keep from vomiting. "Is someone out there?" she whispered. Bile filled her throat.

They all listened, and Karen thought, *This is how I die, my face pressed against a filthy wooden floor, smelling urine and vomit, and the stink of my own fear.*

Finally Caroline whispered, "The wind."

Karen shivered and pushed to a sitting position. "Micah's crazy. He's going to kill everyone."

"He's going to kill everyone in the way of his becoming sole owner of Eagle Point. But he's not crazy. He knows exactly what he's doing. Exactly!"

Karen rose unsteadily to her feet. "We have to get out of here. We can climb down the mountain. If we stay here he'll find us for sure."

"You can't do it, honey. It's too steep. In the snow this is a 'double diamond' run. Without the snow it's impossible, especially in the dark. You'd have rocks tumbling within two minutes. We're stuck up here unless someone comes looking."

"Are you sure he's going to bring Mark up?"

"That's his plan. You, Mark, Lisa, Walter—I didn't know about Noel until I saw him—all up here for a picnic when the storm hits, and you take shelter in the restaurant. Then something causes a propane tank to explode and the whole thing burns to nothing. It gets rid of you and Walter, and makes me and Micah sole owners of the resort. But there was no way I was going to get out of that, either. I know how ol' Pooh Bear thinks."

Lisa suddenly bolted up, eyes frightened, mouth hanging open. "Pooh Bear?" She started to sob.

"Jesus," Caroline said softly as Karen kneeled down and tried to comfort the child. "I feel so sorry for her. He had a whole room down there dedicated to Cheryl McAfee. And Lisa. Micah said he was impotent, though; all he wanted to do was be with her, talk to her, experience her beauty. And I killed him."

Still holding Lisa, Karen took Caroline's hand. "You did what you had to do."

"Carl Stark, too. I helped kill him. Did you know that?"

"Please, Caroline. Don't do this to yourself."

"I just couldn't go on anymore. I couldn't be part of more killing. Micah's snapped. I don't know how he ended up like this. Except he got to the point where he hated Walter for taking all the credit for this place. Micah thought he deserved more praise than Walter. He thought magazines should be doing stories on him, Tom Brokaw and Barbara Walters should be interviewing him and not Walter."

The wind moaned against the side of the shack, seeping through the cracks and making them shiver. Lisa had her hands against her face. "I'm scared. I want to go home."

"It'll be all right, hon," Karen whispered, and gave a look at Caroline as she realized how stupid she sounded.

"Maybe you're right," Caroline said after a moment. "Maybe we ought to try to get away from here."

"How?" Karen asked, coming again to her feet. "What can we do?"

"He'll look in all the buildings on top of the mountain. The warming shacks, restrooms, snack bars. Maybe we should try to hide out in the woods."

"And then what? What do we do in the morning? Tomorrow's Sunday. No workers will be up here. He'll find us for sure if we stay on the mountain. He's got all day to look. Can you operate the chairlift?"

"Are you kidding? It scares me just to ride in it."

"We have to do *something!*"

Caroline nodded toward Lisa. "She'll never be quiet enough. Sound travels up here. Especially at night."

"Then we'll hide her. It's easier to hide her than hide ourselves. If we can keep her safe, maybe one of us could make it down the mountain. What about one of those all-terrain vehicles I saw? Can you drive one of those?"

"Maybe. If the key's in it. I doubt it is, though."

"Let's check it out. We're not completely helpless here. Too normal women against one weird man? Shouldn't be a problem."

"The man's got a gun, hon. And his is loaded." She dropped her useless revolver on the floor.

Karen put her hand out. "Come on, Lisa. We're going to find someplace to put you tonight. Okay? Someplace safe!"

The girl whimpered. "I want to go home. I don't want to stay here."

"We've got to keep you from Mr. Rollins, honey. He's not a nice man. He wants to hurt us. All of us."

"Pooh Bear," Lisa said, and began to tremble again.

Karen was startled. "Is that what you meant? *Micah* is Pooh Bear?"

"He talked to me in the store and said he's Pooh Bear."

"Oh my God," Caroline said to Karen. "That's what I called Micah years ago. I hadn't thought of that in ages." She shook her head in dismay and walked over to the door.

"He didn't touch you, did he?" Karen asked Lisa.

The girl started bawling. "He *talked* to me."

Caroline had opened the door and they could feel the wind from outside. Clouds completely covered the stars again, and she couldn't see more than a few feet. The air was heavy with moisture, the smell of pine, and ozone. "If we hide you someplace can you be quiet until we come to get you? Or someone you know comes to get you? You can do that, can't you?"

The girl reluctantly nodded yes. She was terrified of being left alone, but didn't want to admit it since everyone seemed to be counting on her.

Caroline nodded to Karen, "Hurry. He'll be outside soon."

The three of them stepped into the darkness. "Where?" Karen asked.

Just then the white beam of a flashlight raced through the trees sixty yards from them, and they froze. Lisa started to say something but Karen shoved her hand over the child's mouth, and they watched in silence as the beam bounced from buildings to rocks, then swung in their direction, tree after tree lighting up and falling into darkness as the circle of light hurried on. Micah Rollins, invisible in the darkness, stood without moving but the flashlight suddenly made a 360-degree circle as he stared around.

They heard him yelling something.

"What 'd he say?" Karen whispered.

"Sounded like 'Ollie, ollie, oxen free,' " Caroline said, then added, "Jesus, he's heading this way. We have to do something."

105

Les Cady couldn't stand still. He ran back and forth on the parking lot as his dog raced along beside him, barking in excitement and terror. The entire lodge was being consumed by fire, flames leaping sixty feet out of the roof and windows as if they were alive, shooting in the air, sinking, soaring again, and singing with a terrible *whoosh-*ing that surrounded him with beautiful sounds.

Les couldn't remember ever being so happy, at least not since he was a child. For the first time *he* was in control—he had made all this happen. For the first time he was acting, not being acted upon. And the cause of his torment, his thirty-plus years of hell and ridicule and shame, was being destroyed. Les Cady was being reborn, Lester the Molester was dying. The roof suddenly collapsed with an ear-shattering crash and Les shouted, *"Yes, yes, yes!"*

Barking from McDuff alerted Cady to a new danger, and he spun around to see his own house burning from the roof. Cinders from the fire must have blown over there. Again Cady screamed with joy. Not just Lowndes's damn house but the house Lowndes had provided Les so he'd have a convenient sucker nearby to blame things on whenever a girl got molested. For thirty years he'd thought that bastard was helping him, sticking by him when no one else would. *All so he could control my life, blame me for his crimes.* How could someone do that to another human being?

Wait until he told people! It wasn't Les who had been weird, after all; it was Walter Lowndes. Weird Walter. Walter the Molester! Wouldn't people laugh at *that!* He thought he heard a siren. Didn't matter, no sir. It was too late, they couldn't stop it now.

The wind was whipping again and a clap of lightning shot over the mountaintop. *Go ahead and rain! It don't matter, not at all. This here fire's not going out.*

Now he heard another sound, a horrible crashing noise from someplace out of his sight. He ran around to the other side of the lodge and saw the stables going up in flames, the horses tied to their stalls wild with panic and trying to get loose as the flames danced around them. One horse, still saddled and evidently not tied up, had escaped over the corral fence and was galloping toward town, but the others were trapped. "Don't matter," Cady told McDuff again, reaching down and rubbing the dog's head. "They all got to die so we can start over. Got to start clean."

But when he saw the tall grass out near the road catch fire he wasn't sure that was a good thing. The town lay that way. With the wind blowing, the whole town might go up like it almost did thirty years ago.

Maybe that wasn't so bad, either.

106

"Holy Ke-rist, the hell's that?" Micah made a sniffing sound as he tried to figure out if it was what he thought it was. "Smoke, sure as hell."

Stepping carefully, he walked back to the unfinished restaurant, finally maneuvering to the edge of the structure overlooking the slopes and the mountainside below. The smell was obvious here even though the wind was blowing the other way. But he could see a graying in the otherwise black of night that looked for all the world like smoke. "Man, gotta be a big one. The lodge, maybe." But why would the lodge burn? He'd just been down there. He hadn't seen anything or done anything that might lead to a fire. *So what the dickens is going on?*

As he stood near the edge, careful not to get too close, he thought he could see a faint streaking of orange along the horizon. That couldn't be the lodge, though. The resort wasn't visible from here because of the contour of the mountain. That'd be over toward town. The fire couldn't be burning that way, could it? Shoot, maybe it was. It was damn certain if the fire *was* moving, it was going to head straight toward town in this wind.

A bolt of lightning momentarily lit the sky. It was going to start raining up here again; might not hit the bottom of the mountain, though. Never can tell with these Colorado storms. If it did it'd help put the lodge fire out. If not, this wind was going to push the fire toward town faster than anybody would be able to keep up with it. But as far as Micah could tell, and he thought about it now with all his might, there was nothing about that fire that bothered him. Nothing at all. If it burned all night it'd keep people busy, besides destroying any evidence that might exist about what happened in the lodge.

Well, he'd worried too much about it already. Gotta find them females, stick them here with Mr. Mark and Mr. No-el. Everyone having a nice little picnic with the *perfect* girl-child when disaster struck. Who'd be left to write the story for the *Courier? Don't look at me,* Micah thought with a grin. *I'm going to be the hero who finds the bodies when sunup comes and the rescue parties make their way up here.*

The first thing he had to do, though, was find a flashlight. He hadn't expected to be running around the mountaintop looking for these fool women. *There is no place for them to go. None. Not unless they want to head back in the woods,* and he didn't think they'd try that, not with it fixing to storm like it was, and without a light. No, he knew how they'd think, and they'd think *shelter,* probably go in a warming hut or snack bar, maybe split up, hoping at least one would get away. *Okay, girls, we got us about a dozen buildings up here. Take me an hour to check them all. Y'all relax and wait. I'm a-coming.*

Walking carefully in the darkness he'd found the construction shack and rummaged around inside with a match until he discovered a five-cell Maglite like cops used to whack bad guys over the head. *Time to find the gals.*

He stepped outside and began to spray the light around the mountaintop. *They're up here somewhere, probably watching me right now, hushing each other up and peeing their panties. Watch all you want, ladies, 'cause you can run but you can't hide.* Or was it the other way around? Didn't matter. He's the one with the gun. *Bang, bang, you're dead. Fall down!* Just like when he played cowboys-and-Indians as a kid.

He began to sing, the way he did right after he and Caroline got married. Had a pretty good voice if he did say so himself. *"Nothing could be fine*-ah *than to do my Caroline*-ah *in the . . .* moooor-*ning!"* He raised the volume so she could hear. "Recollect that, don't you, Sweet Lips? Remember how I used to sneak up on you while you was making breakfast and grab your titties? Then it'd be off to the races. Had some fine times, didn't we?"

Hearing something that might have been a cry, he swung the light in a circle all around him. Couldn't see diddly. Well, time to start searching. He raised his voice again. "Ollie, Ollie, oxen free. Come out, come out, wherever you are."

So I can send you along to meet old Walter, wherever his immortal soul is residing now. Wherever it was, it had to be warmer than a Colorado mountaintop in a lightning storm. Probably drier, too, he thought as a huge drop of rain splattered on his head.

Well, get moving, won't take but a few minutes to find them. Maybe I'll try that warming hut down the hill first. It's where I'd be if I was them.

He began to sing again, and swung the light in front of him.

107

Mark groaned as he came into consciousness, felt a terrible confusion in his mind as though brain cells were disorganizing and rushing into oblivion. He moved his left arm and felt a pain shoot through his torso, and only then realized he'd been shot. A fragmented picture spun in and out of memory: Rollins turning, saying something Mark didn't hear because there was an explosion of light from the man's hand; then a sharpness piercing his upper body at the same time as he hit the floor with a crash, and darkness that lasted for . . . How long did it last? He rolled on his back, stared at the ceiling. How long did it last? No one to ask.

He brought his hand to his side and felt blood, warm and sticky on the tips of his fingers. As long as he didn't move it didn't hurt, or didn't hurt much. But as soon as he tried to change position the pain cut through his body. *Stay still, then, just lie here.* But if he did, what was next? *Lie here and die because it's easiest.*

There was a light on in the room. He remembered . . . Micah Rollins following a cord with his hand, then turning it on. And shooting him. Why? Had Rollins killed Walter Lowndes, too?

Mark winced as a pain racked through his body, making him tremble off the floor. Suddenly he remembered why he was here. *My God . . . Lisa!* Lowndes had been after her. But Lowndes was dead. It didn't matter any longer. And Lisa was with Karen. Wasn't she? But where had they gone? He had to find them. Because if Micah was after Mark, he must be after them too. But why? What were Mark and Lisa to anyone in Harmony? Except Lowndes.

He wasn't capable of thinking it out. Couldn't even try. His mind spun, unable to focus as though billions of neurons were whipping in the wind, wildly sparking electricity while his brain tried desperately to stay alive. *Don't die,* he heard a voice shout through the confusion. *Don't die. You have to live, you have to find your daughter.*

With an effort he pushed onto his stomach and felt a new pain lacerating his internal organs. Ignoring it as best he could, he pushed onto his knees, then slowly, straining his muscles to the limit, forced himself to a standing position. He turned around and saw Noel Atchison sitting with his back against the wall, staring lifelessly out of dead eyes at him. Mark's knees gave out. He lurched forward, lost consciousness, and tumbled toward the other man's body.

108

"Wait!" Caroline whispered urgently. They had moved up the hill from the warming hut to a clump of fifty-foot pines on the level top of the mountain. Micah appeared suddenly just thirty feet from them, the round beam of his flashlight leaping like a deer over rocks and bushes, before he turned abruptly and headed toward a small storage building next to the warming hut. "Wait until he's inside," she added.

The light from his flashlight vanished as the door to the building opened and Rollins disappeared.

"What's he singing?" Karen asked.

"A song to me. He knows it'll irritate me. He's right. And crazy as a coot."

Lisa began to whine. Karen said, "We've got to do something. We've got to get out of here." *But,* she thought: *what can we do? We're trapped.*

"Now!" Caroline whispered, and grabbed Karen's arm. *"Go!"*

"Where?"

"Just go! Run! As far as we can."

They began to race along the hillside, past a small bulldozer, past a building housing a nature exhibit put up by the Forest Service, past piles of sand and stacks of sheetrock, and, five minutes later, toward the far edge of the ski area, where the woods began. Another chairlift was here, leading down a thousand feet where it ended amid a small snack bar and the original single-seat lift, now almost twenty-five years old, that descended to the resort. Breathing hard, Karen went up the steps of the motor house and tried the door, but it was locked. "Are you sure you can't operate a lift? We could break the window."

"I don't know anything about this stuff," Caroline snapped. "I'm just an investor. Walter was the technical expert."

A bolt of almost horizontal lightning arced through the southern sky, illuminating a whole other line of mountains. "Can we go off that way?"

"We're on the exact top of this mountain, honey. *That* way is the Sawatch range, National Forest land, fourteen-thousand-foot peaks and no way in or out. You'd break a leg, if not your neck, by midnight, trying to get down. And where would you be if you got there?"

"We've got to do something, damn it! We can't just wait for him." Karen moved her head suddenly, and turned back the way they'd come.

"Yeah, I smelled it, too. Fire. Probably a lightning strike."

A terrible peal of thunder exploded nearby, and the ground rose and fell beneath their feet. Lisa began to cry loudly now. Karen dropped down on her knees and hugged the girl. "Please, Lisa. Don't make any noise. Please!"

The girl tried to stop but couldn't.

"We have to hide her," Karen said, rising quickly to her feet.

"Then what?" Caroline wanted to know.

"Then we'll try to get the jump on Micah."

The older woman looked at her and said nothing.

"Caroline, there's two of us. We can do it."

The woman paused. There was no point in reminding Karen of the gun. "Okay. Let's find a place for her."

Karen said, "Micah's going to work his way in this direction. He'll try each building he comes across. We need to backtrack and hide her in one he's already checked."

Caroline darted a glance at the child. "Can she stop crying long enough to get past him?"

Karen again sank to her knees, and looked into Lisa's face. "We need you to be quiet for just a few minutes. You can do that, can't you?"

The girl was beside herself with fear. She wiped her eyes. "When are we going to see Daddy?"

"Soon, honey, soon." Karen turned to Caroline. "We'll go down the backside a little bit. We'll have to be quiet. That means moving slowly and not upsetting any rocks because he's going to be listening for us."

Just then huge warm drops of rain began to fall again. Caroline wiped water from her forehead as she looked at the sky. "Jesus!" She knew, but did not say, that the rain had unsettled the hillside, making it impossible to move quietly now.

The door to the storage shack opened.

109

"Come out, come out, wherever you are."
Nothing.

"Ollie, ollie, oxen free, free, free." Always worked when he was a kid. Say it three times and they had to come out. It was the rule.

Micah's rule, anyway. He swept his flashlight around the mountaintop.

"There aren't a lot of places to hide up here, gal. Just a matter of time until I find you." But he'd sure as hell rather find them now than later. He had things to do yet tonight.

Got to be methodical, though, he thought, looking around. *Do each building in turn. Of course, if I was them I'd double-back, hide in a place I'd already checked. Have to remember that as I move around.*

Keeping the flashlight beam swinging in an arc in front of him, Micah made his way along the path leading to the Forest Service building with its displays of preserved snakes and birds and animals. He always liked that. Especially the snakes. Liked how they looked all slimy and weird, even when dead. Kinda like old Lester the Molester. Or Walter the Intellectual! *Damn strange people I ended up spending my life with! Wonder how that happened, a good ol' boy like me?*

He mounted the steps of the octagon-shaped building and tried the door. Locked. Naturally. The one thing the government knows how to do is keep its buildings locked up when taxpayers want inside. All the windows were intact, and hadn't been tampered with. Okay, another hiding place eliminated. Still, Micah was getting angry. This was taking too much time.

"Goddamn it, Caroline. Where the hell are you?" He yelled as loud as he could, then tried another tack: "Hey, honey, we're supposed to be on the same side here. Why are you causing me trouble? Help me round up Karen and the girl and everything will be hunky-dory with us. Okay?" Ain't no way she would buy that but it was worth a try. It might be better to try the kid. She was probably shitting kid-sized bricks about now. "Hey, Lisa! Pooh Bear's looking for you. Pooh Bear wants to eat you up." He listened but there was no response. *Hell's bells, they got the kid's mouth duct-taped?*

The first few drops of rain turned to a light shower. "Damn it, Caroline, I'm getting wet. Get your ass over here before I get mad."

He listened again. *They're going to try to sneak past me,* he thought. *Can't do it, though.* "Hey, babe, I got ears like a deer. No way you can get by me. I can even hear you *think!* Want me to prove it? Right now you're thinking about being dead. Right?"

He walked over to the edge of the mountain, protected here by a short fence the damn insurance people made him put up, and shot his light along the underbrush and trees below. "Hey, Caroline! You down there somewhere?" *No, she ain't that dumb. Dumb, but not that dumb.* He turned around suddenly and swept the area with his MagLite. Another storage building and a snack bar were up ahead. He'd try them. He was close now, he could feel it. Damn well about time.

110

W*e're like the blind leading the blind,* Karen thought as they moved desperately about in the rain. They could hear Micah yelling but his words were whipped about in the storm, only the occasional threat cutting through the wind. Then his flashlight beam shot suddenly in front of them as it raced toward the storage building to the side. They froze. After a moment both the beam and Micah moved away. Exhausted and soaked-through, they were going to have to hide Lisa before she gave them away with her crying and tripping on the wet ground.

Waiting behind a stand of firs, they watched while Micah shook the handle of the building. The door didn't budge. Something caused him to spin around and aim the flashlight right at them. Karen felt the beam hit her in the eyes but he evidently could see nothing. The light moved quickly away, coming to rest at the large snack bar nearby. Three dozen pink-and-blue picnic tables with attached bench-seats sat in front, rain drumming noisily off their laminated surfaces. Micah set off toward them.

"Now what?" Caroline whispered. "The storage building's locked. We can't hide her in there."

"Wait," Karen said. "See what he does." Lisa's small hand tightened on hers while the girl tried desperately not to cry.

The three of them watched as Micah wandered around outside the snack bar, looking between the tables and on the front deck by the order windows. He kicked a trash can, shouted something they couldn't understand, then disappeared toward the rear of the building where more tables, this time behind a six-foot Plexiglas wall, over-looked the valley below and the town of Harmony. A moment later he was back and tried the door again. When it didn't move Micah kicked with his foot and it banged open, caught by a gust of wind. He went inside, not reappearing for five minutes, then stood on the deck under the overhang for a moment, and looked around. Raising his arm, he aimed the flashlight at his wet face and disheveled hair. "You see me, Caroline? How about you, Karen? I am one very pissed-off person. If I find you now, you're flat dead. You hear? How about you, little Lisa? You understand what I'm telling you? Ol' Pooh Bear's going to make you dead!" The light flashed off.

At once Lisa started to moan. Caroline clamped her hand on the girl's mouth. "Not a sound, damn it! I mean it."

Micah stood for a while without moving, then took off at a quick walk toward the far end of the resort area and the original chairlift.

The moment he was out of sight Caroline said, "Now!" and, grabbing Lisa's hand, hurried across fifty feet of mud toward the snack bar, Karen behind her. The door had been kicked partially off its hinges and whipped noisily back and forth in the wind. The two women and Lisa raced inside, then stared around in the darkness. "Where?" Karen whispered.

"The kitchen."

They moved toward the back of the building, feeling their way in the darkness. Caroline reached out a hand and felt a counter. "Hold on to me," she whispered to Karen. Lisa had grabbed Karen's other hand. They moved cautiously along the counter to an opening, then through it. Caroline bumped against a swinging door. "This is it," she said, and they passed through, the door swishing behind them.

Caroline said, "One thing I know is kitchens. There's going to be closets and storage cabinets here. Lisa can hide in one while we try something else."

What else? Karen wondered silently, but said nothing.

"First get the girl hidden," Caroline said softly, as if reading Karen's thoughts. "Then we'll talk."

Moving in absolute darkness, Karen felt her way to the edge of the room and was running her fingers along the wall looking for cabinets when something darted against her ankle, and she stifled a shriek. "Mice," she whispered, and tried to keep the panic from her voice. "At least I hope it was a mouse." *And not a snake,* she thought, and shivered.

Caroline grunted. "Found it," and a faint light suddenly appeared in the room. "Butane stoves," Caroline said, standing next to a cooktop with a small flame rising from its burners. Karen watched as two more mice scurried along the floor. Caroline pointed to a series of three narrow doors about six feet tall. "In there," she said.

Karen escorted Lisa to one of the doors and opened it. Inside they found a vacuum cleaner, a broom, and two mops. Karen dropped to her knees and wrapped her arms tightly around the girl. "Lisa, we're going to put you in here for a while. But we need you to be very quiet. You can do that, can't you?"

The girl looked at her and nodded through tears. She was soaked to the skin and covered with mud from where she had fallen several times, and obviously terrified. She couldn't stop whimpering. Karen hugged her closer, feeling the girl's heart pound against her own. "You have to stop crying, Lisa. You have to hide from Mr. Rollins. From the man who said he was Pooh Bear. He wants to hurt all of us. If you can stay in here and not make a sound, Caroline and I will get help. You can do that, can't you? You can act like a big girl, and stay quiet."

Lisa nodded uneasily but her eyes were wild with fear, and she continued to whimper. Karen looked helplessly over her shoulder at Caroline, then said, "All right, get inside, honey. Then I'm going to close the door and it'll be dark but you'll be okay. It won't be scary at all."

Lisa glanced at Karen as if she was hoping to not have to do it, then stepped tentatively inside the cabinet. Karen removed the broom, leaning it against the adjacent cabinet, then moved aside the vacuum to give the girl more room. "You can sit on the floor, hon. Maybe you could go to sleep." *Not a chance of that,* she thought, but added cheerfully, "You're probably pretty tired by now, aren't you?"

Terrified, trembling from the cold and wet, Lisa lowered onto the floor, drew her legs up, and rested her head and arms on her knees. Karen, still stooping, reached in and kissed her on the forehead. "Please, Lisa, don't make any noise at all. We'll be back before long. But don't leave until we say it's okay."

She pushed to her feet. "See you soon, raccoon." And closed the door.

The two women stood in the silence a moment and listened. No noise from Lisa. Caroline said, "Wait." She pulled open two drawers before finding what she was looking for. "You can have the butcher knife. I'll take the cleaver. Between the two of us we should be able to slice Pooh Bear into dinner-sized fillets."

Karen took hold of the beat-up fourteen-inch knife with a sense of disbelief. How had she ended up on the top of a deserted mountain in a lightning storm holding a knife, while a maniac with a gun was trying to kill her? Hadn't she recently been complaining how boring her life had become?

Caroline turned off the burner and again the room sank into darkness. There wasn't a sound until she whispered, "Let's get the hell out of here."

111

Soaked through with rain, Micah had walked all the way to the edge of the property, going through the motor room of the old lift, and wandering as far back into the woods as he thought they'd likely try to go. There was no point in heading out to the mountainside in this rain. They were hiding in a building somewhere, one of those he'd already checked, figuring he'd not go back and look again. *Well, guess what, ladies . . .*

He worked his way back to a small storage shed, checked it quickly, moved at once to a larger storage facility, glanced around, came out and stood on the deck with the 9mm Beretta in his hand. *"Goddamn it, Caroline!"* He pointed the gun randomly into the darkness and shot three times, the noise unmistakable even in the wind and rain. "I'm after your ass, woman. You better get up here quick or when I get that little girl you're going to wish Les Cady got her instead. You understand me? Don't you care what happens to her?"

Nothing. *Goddamn her! Goddamn her!*

The main snack bar was up ahead. He'd already checked it once, of course, but it was the logical spot, because of its size and the numerous places to hide inside. That'd suit him just fine since he was damn tired of this rain.

The door was still swinging on its hinges, banging noisily against the wall. Holding the flashlight in his left hand and the gun in his right, he stood just inside, sweeping the circle of light around the dining room, watching it bounce off chairs and counters, hurry over trash cans and under tables. *They ain't going to be here, though; they'll be in the kitchen.*

Pushing noisily through the swinging door, he swept the area with his light. What was that he smelled—the odd, dry odor of a gas flame? Or was it from the fire down below? In the center of the room there was a food-preparation area with two cooktops and three microwave ovens. Several large refrigerators were built into the far wall. Might as well give 'em a look. With no electricity in the summer they'd be the perfect place to hide. Using a broom that had been leaning against a cabinet, he stood back and forced up the latch on each chrome-and-white door. Then he popped the doors all the way open. Nothing.

"Damn you, Caroline!"

There were some closets and storage cabinets on the other wall. And a large pantry to the rear of the kitchen. Maybe he'd check the pantry first, then take a look in the cabinets.

112

Pressed back into the far wall of the closet as though hoping she could disappear into the wood, Lisa squeezed her hands into fists and tried with all her might to stop her body from trembling, but couldn't. Her legs vibrated against the floor, up-down, up-down, over and over, and her chest and stomach hurt so much she thought she was going to be sick again. She had already vomited but almost nothing came out of her mouth because she had been sick so many times at Mr. Lowndes's house.

The thought of Lowndes made her start crying again. He had kept her in that room for so long, and she had been so scared all the time she was there that she kept screaming and screaming, but the old man seemed not to care. He just sat on the couch and talked about stupid things that made no sense, and looked at the walls where all those pictures were. Pictures of Lisa, but not *exactly*, it seemed. Then when that big lady, Karen's friend, came and argued with Walter and pushed him, Lisa had been able to run away.

Later, though, Pooh Bear had tied her up, hurting her hands and wrists, then brought her up here and . . . and what? She didn't understand any of it. Why were all these things happening to her? It seemed everyone wanted to hurt her, and her father wasn't anyplace around, and he was supposed to keep bad things from happening. Why wasn't he here?

She hadn't wanted to go in this dumb closet because it scared her. Karen acted like it might be a long time but she wanted to leave. It was dark in here and smelly, and Lisa was so wet it made her shake with cold. Maybe she'd find someplace else to hide.

Suddenly she felt something on her neck. What was that? She began to shake even more. *Oh please, no!* There was a spider crawling on her flesh. Her heart jumped. She slapped at the spider with her hand and felt it fall inside her shirt. Another spider was on her leg, under her shorts. She ran her hand along her leg to squish it, then heard a noise.

"Damn you, Caroline!"

Was that Pooh Bear? Why did he want to hurt *her?* He was the one who had told her about horseback-riding at the ski place. Now he was mad at her. It didn't make any sense. But she knew for certain he was trying to hurt her real bad.

Another spider was racing along the back of her wrist. She flicked her hand away but the spider ran up her arm toward her neck.

Noise outside the door. Panic gripped her so violently it made her whole body hurt, and she had to go to the bathroom. Pooh Bear was right outside now, not more than a foot from her. She could hear his shoes squeeking on the floor.

"You in there, girl?"

No, no, no. Please! Daddy!

She held her body very stiff and closed her eyes tightly as the spider rose onto her chin and raced across her lips while Pooh Bear huffed and puffed just inches from her. *Daddy, Daddy, Daddy . . .*

Then the door exploded open, the vacuum falling and mops flying noisily through the air, and Pooh Bear seizing her arm in his huge hand. She screamed—"No, no!"—and couldn't stop screaming as he yanked her off her feet, flinging her past the vacuum, out of the closet, and into the darkness.

113

Karen and Caroline didn't know what to do. All they could think of was, *Run, run, run, get away!* After hiding Lisa, they raced as fast as they could through the now driving rain toward the center of the ski area. Panicky, unable to keep their balance on the muddy ground, they stumbled, fell, scrambled up, kept running. Then Caroline hit something with her foot and went flying, the meat cleaver slipping from her hand and tumbling end over end ahead of her. The large woman screamed in pain as she fell on top of it. Karen stifled a cry and hurriedly rolled her friend over. "You have a cut on your shin. That's all. Hurry. We can't stop." She tried to help Caroline to her feet but the woman had difficulty standing.

"My knee's sprained," Caroline said, trying to take a step. She looked down at the gash made by the meat cleaver but merely shook her head.

"You have to hurry. Please!"

Caroline hobbling as best she could, the two women began to run once again, stopping finally under the large metal canopy at the top of the Express lift. Sinking onto the bare ground, chests heaving, they tried to catch their breath. Karen's head hung between her knees and her lungs burned with pain. "What do we do now?"

When Caroline didn't answer, Karen looked over and saw the woman sprawled on her stomach. Her loose-fitting dress, soaked through and caked with mud, had settled around her waist, and Caroline was heaving and coughing into the dirt. Karen gripped her shoulder and shook. "Are you all right?" *Oh God,* she thought, *Caroline's having a heart attack. She's going to die right here.*

But as soon as she asked the question Caroline started sobbing, and her head turned away so Karen could see only the mass of dark, mud-encrusted hair, and the three-inch-long silver earrings dangling toward her shoulders. "Caroline, please—" Karen put her hand on the other's arm and left it there. She didn't know what else to do.

After a minute, Caroline moaned and rolled on her back, then began to cough and choke at the same time. "Sit up," Karen urged. "Hurry. You'll gag on your own vomit if you don't." She crawled behind her friend and began to push on her wide shoulders, encouraging her into a sitting position. Slowly, Caroline managed to raise her upper body. Then she started choking again, her head lurched suddenly forward, and she vomited projectile-fashion toward her feet. "Oh Christ, oh Christ," the older woman muttered, and began to sob again. But instead of falling into despair as Karen feared, Caroline spun sharply on her. "I'm going to kill that bastard!" She picked up the meat cleaver that had fallen next to her and brought it down violently, burying its blade in the hard earth.

"Caroline," Karen pleaded. "We have to hurry. Micah will be here in a few minutes. We have to keep moving."

Caroline turned toward her. Her thick legs were bare, covered with mud, and bleeding in half a dozen places from cuts where she fell; the gash from the meat cleaver was caked with dirt, and water clung like dirty lace to her face and hair. "My knee," she cried, and looked at the blood-swollen mess. She began gasping for air. "It doesn't matter. Where would we go? There's no place left."

Jesus Christ, Karen wanted to scream, *this is your damn resort. You should have some idea of how to get us out of here.* But instead she said, as calmly as she could, "We'll go back to the Ice Castle. It's the last place he'll check. And maybe we can find something to use as a weapon."

Still breathing with effort, Caroline jerked the cleaver out of the dirt. "I can't do it. I can't walk that far. I'm going to stay here."

"Caroline—"

"I'll lie on my stomach with the knife under my body. When Micah comes to see if I'm alive I'll bury it in his goddamn heart."

"Please, Caroline—"

"I'm serious. He'll think I'm dead. He won't be expecting it."

"Caroline, I need your help. You can't stay here. The two of us can work together once we get to the restaurant. There's construction equipment there. There must be something we can use. Either as a weapon or to get help."

The older woman looked at her, continuing to wheeze from lack of breath. Then she put her hand to her heart. "If I get out of this the first thing I'm doing is go in for liposuction. I want to be able to fit in a ready-made casket when the time comes."

Karen put a hand under her arm. As long as Caroline could joke she hadn't given up. "Come on, lady. We got things to do, people to see." One person, anyway. And one thing.

The rain had eased into a fine, crystalline mist that seemed to hang in the air rather than fall, but a rumble of thunder rocked the ground under their feet as they set out. "Feels like it's right on top of us," Caroline said. "Maybe God'll throw a bolt in Micah's direction."

"It's a long way to the restaurant," Karen reminded her. "Watch your step, especially once we get into that trench where the pylons are."

Moving slowly in the dark they made their way west. "I hope the kid's okay," Caroline whispered from behind Karen.

"Can't worry about that now," Karen answered, and thought, *Of course I worry about it. I can't stop worrying about it. But I don't want to* think *about it.*

Bursts of lightning strobed suddenly across the northern sky—*crack, crack, crack,* one after another—followed immediately by peals of thunder that shook the air. "It's going to start in again," Caroline said. Just then huge drops of rain began to fall on their heads. "Mountain storms!" the woman muttered with fury.

In five more minutes they were at the partially constructed restaurant. It was impossible to see anything but the mass of the building pressing defiantly against the dark sky. Karen said, "Maybe we could find something to use as a weapon where they keep the construction equipment."

Caroline's voice sank with despair. "Honey, we aren't going to overcome a man who has a gun with a circular saw or a power nailer. We gotta stay hidden till morning. Then hope someone comes looking. But right now we gotta make ourselves invisible."

Karen stared around in the darkness. She was shivering from cold, and wet, and fear. "How?" she managed.

Caroline thought a moment. "They already built the motor room for the lift Walter's putting in from the Express to the restaurant. Probably no electricity hooked up to it, of course. Just a little building with a window and a door. No reason for it to be locked. But we'll be able to lock it from the inside. No lights so he won't be able to see us as long as he can't get in and poke around. Sound okay to you?"

"Okay," Karen said, but thought, *What alternative do we have? We've run out of places.*

114

Micah was consumed with rage. Holding the seven-year-old girl by the arm he dragged her screaming across the rain-soaked hillside, toward the center of the ski area dominated by the Express and its huge blue metal canopy, where thousands of people arrived every day in the winter. "I've got the girl!" he shouted into the wind. "Goddamn it, Caroline, you hear what I say? I got the damn girl. Gonna put a bullet between her pretty blue eyes real soon if you don't show yourself."

Lisa shrieked and tried to twist away from Rollins but he angrily tightened his grip, his fingers closing on his palm as he grasped her biceps. "Damn you, keep that up and I'll kill you right now. Don't need no troublemaking brat slowing me down." *Ought to just go ahead and kill her anyway,* he decided. She was going to die in the explosion. Still, she might be useful as bait.

The thought of bait gave him an idea. He dragged Lisa back to the trench where he recalled seeing some nylon rope. He uncoiled it. *About thirty feet,* he thought. Not as much as he wanted but it'd work. Still holding Lisa he formed one end of the rope into a hangman's noose, then dropped it over her head and pulled it tight, making her cough.

"Come on, we're going fishing." It was like using a minnow to catch a big ol' lake trout, he thought as they began heading across the mountaintop again. "You wanna run, girl? Go on. Take off." He raised his voice. "Here she is, Caroline. Walter's perfect beauty. Come and get her."

Lisa screamed and sprinted away from him. Micah aimed his flashlight at her but as the rope reached its limit he yanked as hard as he could, and the girl flew off her feet, landing on the ground.

"Come on, ladies. You don't want this poor child hurt, do you?" As he walked toward Lisa the rope slackened, and she burst to her feet and took off again. But again Micah yanked her to the ground.

"She's going to break her neck if you don't come out and help her," Micah yelled, aiming the light at her.

But nothing happened.

"Caroline!" He raised his voice as loud as he could. "Don't you care about this little girl? How about you, Karen? Hey!" He had an idea. "Tell you what, Karen. You come out and help me and we'll go partners in the resort. How's that sound? Make you a millionaire." *And you'll be rich for about one nanosecond before I put a bullet in your back-stabbing, money-grubbing heart. Think I'd trust anyone who'd turn against their friends?*

A bolt of lightning and crack of thunder hit simultaneously, startling even Micah. "Damn! Always did hate lightning. Worst thing about the mountains." Lightning killed more people around here than hunting accidents, he'd heard. And that crap about it never striking twice in the same place was flat untrue; he'd read about a man up in Montana who got hit twice. *A man!* And lived! Kind of guy who ought to buy lottery tickets. Just last year, though, a whole family was wiped out when they tried to take refuge under a tree during a lightning storm out on the prairie. *What a way to go,* he thought, *electricity charging through your body, turning you into a human torch. Man!*

He said to Lisa, "Go on, take off again, girl."

But Lisa wouldn't do it. Instead she tried to pull the noose from her neck.

"Hell," Micah said. "It ain't going to work anyway." He yanked the noose free and dropped it to the ground. Grabbing Lisa's arm he started walking again. *"Caroline, goddamn it, now I'm mad!"*

Five minutes later he was at the Express. He dragged the girl under the canopy to get out of the rain and immediately saw the vomit and wet ground where Caroline and Karen had been sitting. "Goddamn it, stop fighting me or I'll shoot you right here. Do you understand what that means? It means *dead!"*

The water on the ground seemed to drift toward the west. As rain noisily drummed on the metal roof, he dragged Lisa in that direction and saw footprints in the dirt. "Well now. Heading toward the restaurant, are you? What do you think about that, child? Going back where I need 'em. Damn! That was mighty considerate of the ladies. Probably figuring on looking for some sort of weapon once they get there. Well, look all you want."

He pulled the girl toward the trench leading in the same direction. "You are getting to be a royal pain in the ass. Ought to just drop you here. But since you're the star of the show I better have you at the Ice Castle. Go on, get in front here, and follow my light. You try to climb out of this trench and I'll make dog meat out of you. You hear?"

Micah stepped into the trench, pulling Lisa after him. *A half mile,* he thought with irritation. *Well, shoot, gotta do it. Don't have a choice here. Do wish it'd stop raining, though.*

It took almost fifteen minutes because of the puddles and Lisa's struggling, and all the equipment they had to maneuver around. When finally they reached the end of the trench Micah pulled himself out, then stuck a hand down to help Lisa. But the moment he did she turned and began to race back the way she had come, screaming.

"Goddamn little bitch." Micah ran ahead of the girl on the raised ground, then dropped in front of her, grabbing both arms and shaking her, but he tripped over a knee-high concrete form and lost his grip. This time Lisa leaped out of the trench and disappeared into the darkness.

"God*damn* it!" Rollins screamed in pain, dropped onto his seat in a pool of mud, and rolled up his left pant-leg, then aimed the flashlight at his knee, now gushing blood. He needed something to stop the bleeding. Hurriedly slipping from his blazer, he yanked off his shirt and ripped a foot-long strip from its back. Working quickly he tied it around his knee, then jumped from the trench. His whole left leg hurt now, and he put his weight on the right.

"Damn you, girl!" He stood at the end of the trench, the restaurant fifty yards distant, screaming. "Damn you! You'll be sorry!"

Listen!

He froze, concentrated his mind, and moved the light slowly from the restaurant back toward the trench. *Slowly.* Trees . . . piles of lumber . . . a four-foot stack of pipe . . .

Listen! A sound like a motor—almost like the old chairlift, but distant. The generator?

He moved the light again. Cement bags piled under a tarp. . . . A newly graded area where a bandstand was going to be constructed. . . . A flash of movement crossed the light as a body shot from behind the stacks of cut lumber toward the southern edge of the mountain.

Micah swore and tore off after the girl. "Come here, goddamn you!" He caught up to her as she sprinted over the edge of the mountain and tried to race down the precipitous hillside. He reached out and grabbed her shoulder, but she lost her footing and they both tumbled downward, rolling in the mud until they came to a stop against a tree fifty yards from the top. Rollins, shirtless, covered in mud, one pant-leg rolled up past the knee, seized her by the neck and jabbed his gun against her nose, ripping the skin and making it bleed. "Damn you!" His voice echoed through the rain, kept echoing. *"Damn you! . . . Damn you! . . . Damn you!"*

115

The rain had begun to let up, though occasional bursts of lightning crashed overhead, momentarily illuminating trees and buildings. Micah swore furiously as he pulled the girl toward the Ice Castle. Stopping suddenly, he turned toward the edge of the mountain where once again he could smell the unmistakable odor of fire, even through the storm. Seemed like fire had always been a part of his and Harmony's existence—from Contrell's and Stark's fires thirty years ago, to numerous forest fires, to this. Had to be the resort this time. *Looks like we'll be starting over from scratch.* It didn't really matter, actually was a godsend: the place was insured, even for lost revenue. Micah could rebuild in his image now, not Walter's. Maybe he'd do away with that stupid German-Swiss look, and modernize things.

Dragging the girl behind him, he went around to the back of the unfinished restaurant and made sure the generator was still functioning. There weren't any lighting fixtures in the building yet, but shielded construction lamps on long cords offered illumination wherever the workers needed it, while other cords provided electricity for power tools.

Using the flashlight to show the way, he mounted the steps to what was going to be a service entrance in the rear. He flicked on one of the portable lights. Water everywhere. The roof hadn't come out to here yet.

Lisa shrieked as though in pain, pulled suddenly from his grasp and sped away, back toward where they had come from. Micah swore and tore after her, grabbing the girl before she could get out of the building. "Goddamn it, I've had enough of you." Still swearing, he twisted her arm behind her back, jerking it so sharply she screamed in agony. Losing whatever hold he had on his temper, he threw the girl to the floor, and stared around for something to tie her up with. Finding a roll of black plastic electrical tape, he twisted it around her ankles while holding her wrists, then quickly bound her hands behind her back. Grabbing a shop rag off the floor, he shoved half of it in her mouth and used the tape to hold it in place, winding it around and around her head so only her eyes and nose were uncovered.

"Scream all you want, goddamn it," he snapped, and left her writhing on the floor. He raised his voice to the restaurant. "Got the girl here, Karen. Got her bound up like a standing rib-roast. I'm about to put her on the dinner table. Want me to carve, or do you want to do it?" Holding the flashlight in one hand and the gun in the other, he hurriedly checked the dining room and kitchen. They weren't there. The basement, then. They had to be! He'd looked everywhere else. But he felt a sudden bubble of fear rise into his mind. He didn't want to go down there, a dead man and a dying man on the floor. There was no light he could access from here. Did he turn it off when he left? He couldn't remember. Damn it! Had to do it, though. There was no choice.

Holding the flashlight high in his left hand, he slowly descended, stopping on each step, listening, moving the light around. It wasn't Ritter he was worried about—he was in no condition to be a threat. But if Caroline was down there she'd find a way to get at him. He knew how the woman thought. Revenge! Once Micah had threatened her she'd think of nothing but bringing him down.

At the bottom of the landing Noel Atchison's expressionless face appeared in the circle of light where Micah had left him. But Ritter had moved. It looked as if he'd gotten to his feet, taken a step, and collapsed onto his stomach. Ritter's hand was on the construction light; he must have turned it off. Why would he do that? Unless he had been planning to jump Micah when he returned. *Not in your shape, pal.* Micah reached down and turned the light on. As he did so Mark moaned, and one leg twitched against the cement. He opened his eyes and stared into Micah's face. "Lisa—"

The women weren't there. Micah spun around and hurried up the stairs. For maybe the first time in his life he knew what it was to completely lose his temper. *"Goddamn it, goddamn it—"* He was screaming at the top of his voice. "Caroline, you goddamn bitch. I'm going to tear your heart out."

His body began to shake with rage. "You're dead. You hear me? You're fucking dead!" He stormed past Lisa twisting and moaning on the floor, and onto the front landing of the Ice Castle. *"You're dead!"* he screamed into the darkness, standing shirtless, mud thick in his hair and covering his trousers, the left leg still rolled up past the knee. *"You're fucking dead!"* The words roared into the wind and were lost.

Out of control, needing to break something, kill something, he raced back into the restaurant and picked up the first thing he saw, a sledgehammer resting against a counter, and flung it against the wall, screaming his rage at the top of his voice. *They're here!* he told himself. *Goddamn it, they're close enough to hear me. I know it!*

He stormed again through each room on the main floor, switching on the temporary lights, screaming threats at both women, then raced outside and, using the flashlight, strode around the periphery of the building, hurriedly looking under decks, behind construction equipment, and in the storage shed. *They're here!* He'd seen the footprints heading this way. *They're close enough to see me right now. Right now! They're watching me!*

He heard a noise and spun around, heart pounding. Nothing. But Caroline was watching. He *felt* it! Swinging the flashlight beam around, he saw the motor house to the unfinished lift. *Gotcha!* It was the only place he hadn't searched. Hurrying back inside the Ice Castle, he stopped where Lisa was writhing on the floor. Reaching down, he grabbed the girl's arm and pulled her up with one hand. "You're coming with me."

But her feet were bound too tightly to walk. Swearing to himself, Micah shoved the Beretta in his rear pocket and snatched her off her feet. Still holding the flashlight in his left hand, he carried Lisa horizontally, like a small rug, over to the motor house.

Dropping the girl noisily on the just-completed wooden deck, he tried the door. Locked, of course. He went up to the large window, put his hands to his eyes, and peered in, but could see nothing in the darkness. He pounded on the tempered glass with his fist. "I know you're in there, goddamn it. I've got the girl with me. Want to see her? Got her all trussed-up." He pulled the child up to the glass and shined a light on her face. "Get out here now or she dies."

Flattened on the floor behind boxes of tile and cans of paint, Caroline whispered, "He can't see us. He's bluffing."

"What about Lisa?"

"He won't hurt her. He needs her to get to us."

"He can break that glass, Caroline. What do we do then?"

"No choice, honey. We go after him with our knives. You go to the left and I'll go to the right. Maybe one of us can get him."

"Goddamn it, Caroline!" The glass rattled as he hit it with his fist.

"He's going to break it, Caroline. God, he's coming in."

"Get your knife ready. He'll see me first. I'm the one he's looking for now, the one he's furious at. When he grabs me you get behind him and aim for the side of his neck. Get the carotid artery, but don't stop thrusting. Not till all the blood's drained out of his carcass."

Micah was beside himself, storming back and forth in front of the window. "Damn you, woman! Damn you!"

He put his hands to his eyes and stared inside but saw nothing.

Then he had an idea. "Got to break this window, Caroline. What say I throw Lisa through it? Sound like a plan to you?"

"He wouldn't dare," Caroline said softly. But even she knew—

Then they heard movement on the other side of the wall.

Micah reached down and grabbed the girl, holding her like a battering ram. "Got to crack the glass first or she'll just bounce back," he yelled. "This stuff's a bitch to break. Wish I had a hammer. Going to have to use the kid's head instead. Hope she don't bleed too much." He banged Lisa's head against the window. "You sure you don't want to open up?" Without waiting for an answer he again hit the glass with Lisa's head.

"We've got to do it," Karen whispered. "We can't let him hurt her."

"Don't be a fool! Make him come in here." This close to Micah, Caroline's earlier fear had dissipated, and she was thinking coolly now. Micah was the one who had lost control.

"Caroline! goddamn you!"

"Wait," the older woman told Karen. "Patience. He doesn't think well when he's upset. He'll make a mistake—"

The glass rattled again. "Going to toss the girl through."

Karen risked a look from the edge of the boxes they were hiding behind. "Oh God, no . . ."

It was dark outside but she could see Micah's outline on the other side of the window. Shirtless, filthy, hair hanging down in his eyes, he was holding Lisa over his head with both hands, his arms raised like a weight lifter with barbells.

She ducked back. "Caroline, God, he's going to—"

"Wait!"

Nothing happened for a minute.

Then glass exploded all around them and something heavy hit the floor in front of the boxes. The two women jumped up screaming, and a burst of light exploded in their eyes. Micah put a bullet in the wall between their heads. "Step on out, ladies. Be nice about it and drop your weapons or I'll kill the child."

"What—?" Karen's body shook terribly as she looked at the broken window.

"A metal stool," Micah said. "Did the trick."

Caroline opened the door and stepped out. She was covered with mud and her dress was torn in a dozen places. She braced herself against the wall, shook her head, and tried to catch her breath. Then she looked up abruptly. "What's burning?"

"The resort," Micah said. And added between heavy breaths of his own, *"My* resort. It's all over, girls. You lose."

116

Half a dozen times Mark regained consciousness, tried to move, but couldn't make his body obey. Then he heard noises, a man yelling, and tried to get to his feet. He managed to push up so that he was sitting, heard the shouting again, had some vague notion of surprising Rollins when he returned. Then he passed out.

The next time he came to, he was staring at his daughter, dripping with mud, gagged and bound, her face—almost completely covered with black electrical tape—not more than a foot from his on the floor. He was conscious at once as adrenaline pumped through his veins, and reached out to touch her, but a boot shot into his side and he rocketed back into the wall, his head slamming against the cement.

Through the pain he heard rather than saw a commotion, sensed flashes of light, color, movement, and sharp fragments of sound that tumbled through the air. His eyes snapped open as Karen and Caroline fell heavily to the floor next to him. They were soaking and filthy. Caroline's legs were covered with cuts and scratches, and one knee was swollen to twice its normal size. He blinked, saw Micah Rollins, shirtless and drenched, one of his pants legs rolled up to the thigh, holding an automatic at his side.

Madness, Mark thought, still unable to concentrate; it was all madness, his mind playing tricks on him. Rollins was screaming at them, but it seemed to be a senseless repetition of the same words— *bitch, goddamn you*—until he noticed Mark again trying to touch his daughter.

"Hell, go ahead," the man shouted at him. "Say your goodbyes. It's Big Bang time in the Rockies."

"Micah—" Caroline began, a pleading tone in her voice. She rolled on her side and put an arm out on the floor in his direction.

"You shut the fuck up," Rollins yelled at her. "Already wasted too damn much time up here. I ought to be down fighting the fire. Folks might notice I'm not around. Going to have to explain that."

Fire? Mark wondered. *What fire?* And a voice in his mind whispered: *You've gone mad. None of this is happening. You're hallucinating.*

Rollins noticed Mark's eyes wander, his attempt at concentration, and his fury escalated again. "You and your damn kid have been nothing but trouble for the whole of Harmony, Ritter. It's finally going to work out, though." His gaze shot briefly to Lisa. "Old Walter was after her from the moment you two hit town. That's why I tried to scare you away with that phone call and Polaroid photo. Didn't want crazy Walter causing trouble for me or the resort. Not just bad publicity; sooner or later he'd sure as hell start babbling about Carl Stark and the fire in 1968. Couldn't risk that.

"Then I realized what a golden opportunity this all was. Instead of scaring you away, put you and Walter together so he does go after the girl. Soon as he started in on his *Death in Venice* routine I knew it was just a matter of time before he'd have his hands all over her. I figured if you didn't kill the son of a bitch maybe I'd have to, to save the poor child from a fate worse than death. Not only would the old man stop being a thorn in my side, but I'd be a hero.

"As it happened, things didn't quite work out that way, I'm afraid. Caroline here flew off the handle and killed Walter." He saw Mark's reaction, and smiled grimly. "Yeah, she did. A regular Calamity Jane with a six-shooter, ain't she? Anyway, instead of the original plan, we have the backup. Just as good, maybe even better." He waved an arm around the large room. "A group of good friends taking a picnic on the mountaintop. I laid the groundwork for that this afternoon. I let Janis and a few others know about the excursion to the restaurant you folks were going on while I prepared to escort poor old Walter to New York. Unfortunately that trip will never be taken. Of course, while you were up here the rains hit and everyone sought refuge in this unfinished building. Then something—perhaps lightning—causes a propane explosion and the whole place goes up in flames. It should make for quite a sight from below. Unfortunately everyone will be too busy with the fire at the resort to worry about it."

While Rollins was talking Karen leaned toward Mark and began to strip off his shirt. "My God, Micah. What did you do to him?"

She looked over at the man, her voice rising. "What's happened to you? We were friends. We've known each other for years."

Mark's head lolled from side to side. None of this made the slightest sense to him. There was a fierce burning below his breastbone, not where the bullet wounds were, but deep inside, as though he had been operated on without anesthetic. His head spun and his throat was thick with swelling. But when his shirt was stripped off he could see there was little blood on his torso. He stared at it and wondered why. He had been shot, hadn't he?

Karen gasped when she saw the wounds. Her voice rose, and she shouted out as though it was she who had the gun and not Micah. "You're insane! You've lost your mind."

"It's only people on the losing side who say dumb things like that, Karen. I seem to be doing pretty good, I'd say."

Caroline Bellamy heaved a mighty breath, and managed to push up on her seat. She burst out angrily. "Is that why you killed Noel, someone you've known all your life? Because you're doing pretty good? Jesus, Micah!"

Rollins glanced toward the wall where Atchison's body slumped, the head hanging down to the chest. "I'm afraid snoopy old Noel finally figured out who Lisa reminded him of. He called me, wanting to know if I had a picture of Cheryl McAfee as a child. He was so damn excited I thought he'd pop. Then he started thinking about Walter and the fire—well, I'm afraid I just couldn't risk him screwing things up this close to the end. There's too damn much at stake here."

Mark pushed Karen's arm aside and forced himself to his knees. He moved over to his daughter, put a hand on her head. The girl moaned around the gag and black tape, and writhed on the floor, bending at the waist and kicking spasmodically with her feet. Caroline put her arms out, pleading. "Micah, let the child go. Please. She's too young to understand any of this. She's no threat to you."

Rollins used his arm to wipe water from his forehead. "You've gone from dumb to dumber, Caroline. There ain't no way anyone but me is getting off this mountain."

Mark's mind began to clear. If he didn't do something now they all were going to die. He couldn't overcome Rollins but one of the women might. But how to do this without a weapon? His eyes darted around the room, glancing at the tools left by the workers: a small ballpean hammer, a hacksaw, portable welding torches, an electric drill. But even if he could get one to Karen or Caroline, Micah would have time to shoot everyone in the room before she could use it.

Rollins was shifting from foot to foot, trying to shake off the pain in his wounded knee. His tone suddenly angry, he said to Mark, "Everything was just dandy around here until you showed up. We figured we were out of the woods, didn't we, Caroline? It wasn't right having to worry about this shit all over again. But if people started poking round in Carl Stark's death it was just a matter of time until they figured things out. Crazy old Bill knew all along, though. He saw Walter leaving the fire thirty years ago and tried to tell the police, but they wouldn't believe him. Stallworth finally figured it out, just three decades too late. When he saw Lisa he also realized why Walter used to spend so much time out at Annie McAfee's house. Guess he was pretty pissed about how his department had treated Les Cady over the years. But if he had pulled Walter in, in his condition, he'd've had the whole story in five minutes. The guy was in cuckoo land all week. I couldn't afford that. Don't matter none now, though. You all is about to die."

"Guess again," B.J. Blake said.

117

Blake was standing at the bottom of the stairs. He advanced to within three steps behind Micah, an old bolt-action deer rifle pointed at the back of the man's head. When Micah started to turn Blake said, "Uh-uh. First drop the gun." He sounded nervous, as though he didn't like what he was doing, or didn't trust himself with the rifle.

But Micah's fingers wouldn't let the pistol go. Just wouldn't do it. Images rose at once in his mind: All his plans, all his hopes— Micah Rollins, lord of Harmony—dying right here if he gave up the weapon. Better to risk death than throw away the dream.

A .30-caliber slug screamed past his head, slamming with a thud into the unfinished wall beyond. At once the bolt on Blake's rifle operated, metal clanging on metal. Micah's ears rang from the shot and there was a hot spot on his cheek that stung like hell. He had to force himself not to empty his bladder right there. His fingers opened and the Beretta clattered to the bare cement floor.

"Kick it over here with your left foot."

"Got to turn around first." Sounding reasonable now, even smiling, but still forcing himself not to pee. He would not make a fool of himself in front of all these people. And he damn well wasn't going to let everything slip away this close to the end. He'd think of some way to turn things around. Always had before.

Mark used his arms to push himself to his knees. Something was wrong. Micah was not going to give in this easily. He was up to something. The voice in Mark's brain was screaming at him to get the pistol. *He had to have it,* the voice insisted. *Not anyone else. Hurry.* . . . But the exertion made his head spin, and he sank forward on the floor, out of breath.

Blake seemed not to see anyone but Micah Rollins. But he, too, obviously didn't trust the man, even unarmed. "First put both hands over your head, then turn around. Very slowly, Micah. You don't want me to accidentally shoot you."

Moving with elaborately drawn-out movements, the man did as ordered—*step . . . step . . . step*—thinking all the time, until he finally faced B.J.

"Now kick the gun to me."

Again Micah hesitated. His gaze shifted from the gaping black muzzle of the rifle, not more than an arm's-length from his forehead, to Blake's eyes, which seemed to have never blinked. There wasn't a sound in the room now as the two men faced each other across three feet of space. Everyone, even Rollins and Blake, seemed mesmerized by the absolute silence. Unexpectedly a drop of water, followed closely by another, and another, rolled down the stairs from the main floor, falling off one step, then the next, and the next, each time making a loud *plunk*ing sound, and finally trickling to the bare cement, where it began to course over the uneven surface toward the wall nearest Mark. *The rain must have picked up again,* he thought, and wondered, *is that good or bad?* But the voice in his head didn't know. The Beretta was on the floor on the other side of Rollins. *Now!* Mark told himself, and braced his feet for a lunge at the weapon. But Rollins saw the movement out of the corner of his eye and quickly kicked the gun across the floor toward Blake. The mood in the room suddenly changed.

"Check his pants," Blake ordered Karen.

"Haven't got any more guns," Rollins said and smiled, in control of himself again.

"*Do it!*" Blake shouted at Karen, and the rifle wavered in his hands. He was getting tired of holding it at eye level, and his fatigue made him nervous.

Karen eased up behind Micah. "You make a move toward her and you're dead," B.J. warned him.

She felt the rear and side pockets of his trousers and shook her head at Blake. She could scarcely stand, her body was shaking so much, and she moved away quickly, going over to where Mark lay. "My God, B.J., how did you end up here?"

He hadn't shifted his eyes from Rollins. "Saw some funny business down at the resort. Couldn't figure it out, people coming and going in the dark. It sure as hell seemed like something no good was going on. Kinda looked like trouble when Caroline took little Lisa up in the lift. When you and Micah went up it didn't look good at all. I thought maybe your hands were tied but I couldn't tell from where I was. Then Micah came down alone. A few minutes later Ritter showed up and pretty quick left with Micah. None of it seemed right to me. I was about to go in the lodge and check things out in there when I saw Les Cady heading that way. So I figured maybe I'd just come on up here and take a look-see. All those folks going up in the dark and no one coming down. It all was kinda weird. Took my thirty-ought-six with me just in case."

"But how did you get up here?" She helped Mark sit, then ran her fingers over his wounds and shook her head. "God!" Her hands trembled at the discolored flesh. "We have to get you to a doctor as soon as possible."

Mark shook his head. "Lisa!" He winced and nodded at his daughter. "Take care of her."

Karen was about to ask Caroline to take the tape off Lisa but the older woman suddenly lost control, sobbing gently with relief, her back against the wall and her hands to her face. When Karen again turned to Mark's wounds his tone became insistent. "Get Lisa free!" When she hesitated his jaw set angrily. "Damn it, leave me alone. Take care of her!"

"Came up on the old lift," B.J. explained. "The one way over by the government land on the east side, with those dinky single chairs. Wasn't fun in the wind and rain."

Karen began quickly unraveling the tape around Lisa's head. "How did you know how to operate it?"

Blake seemed confused. "Operate? You just push a button. A big red one. Can't miss it."

Karen's eyes went large, then she started laughing, and glanced at Caroline, who was crying and breathing so hard she seemed about to hyperventilate. Then the older woman also began to laugh, but with far less humor. Karen reached over and patted Caroline's foot comfortingly, then began to strip the tape from around Lisa's legs while the girl gasped for breath and shook her head back and forth, choking, crying, and asking for her dad.

"I guess you couldn't hear the chairlift in the storm," Blake went on. "It ain't that loud, anyway. Especially being over at the edge of the property like it is. Then when I saw Micah wandering around with a gun I sorta followed him until I could see what the heck was going on. I guess I still don't rightly know."

Rollins shoved his hands in his trousers pockets. Soaking wet, his hair plastered to his head and his bare belly hanging over his belt, he said, "Why don't you and I have a talk, B.J.? No sense you screwing up a multimillion-dollar deal since you don't understand the importance of what's happening here."

"Don't," Blake warned. He still hadn't moved the muzzle from Rollins's eyes.

"Thing is," Micah began, "I always liked you. Felt sorry for you though, since you never had a pot to piss in."

Mark stirred. *It's starting,* he thought. *Rollins is going to get out of it.* He tried to get up on one knee. His head continued to spin and he braced against the floor with his hand.

Speaking rapidly now, trying to get it out while he could, and push all the right buttons, Micah said, "Always thought you had a rotten deal in life, busting your butt with that Land King crap while Caroline doesn't do a thing but sit in her restaurant all day drinking piña coladas and counting her money. It just never seemed right."

"Goddamn you!" Caroline screamed from the floor. She tried to get up, but abandoned the effort, falling back against the wall, her dress riding up above her knees. "Micah," she managed coldly, "you are the most immoral person I ever met. You even make Walter look good."

With her hands finally freed, Lisa hurried to her father and hugged him, crying loudly. Mark, on his knees, engulfed her with his arms, but his mind was elsewhere.

"Walter's dead," Micah explained to Blake. "Killed by sweet little Caroline over there. But once these folks go up in the fire here in the restaurant, I become sole owner of the resort. That's how the insurance works. I own everything, including all the undeveloped land. I figure it's worth about ninety million. It's a lot of work for one man, though, a lot of responsibility. How'd you like to go partners with me? With your knowledge of real estate, and mine of skiing, I figure we'd work out real well together. And we always did get along, didn't we? A hell of a lot better than me and Caroline and Walter. Hell, boy, we *think* alike—both like hunting and CU football and Johnnie Walker scotch. I figure we hook up and we can be as close as brothers. I'll even draw up a will making you my heir. That way when I die you'll own the whole shebang."

Karen put her hand on Lisa's back, trying to calm the child. "You never give up do you, Micah?" Then she turned to Blake. "We've got to hurry, B.J. Mark has to get to a doctor. He's pretty bad."

Rollins wasn't through. His voice had settled into a calm, continuous monologue. Like a cult leader—Jim Jones or David Koresh—talking his followers into mass suicide, Mark thought: it had that same almost dreamy, singsongy *roll, roll, roll* that lulled its listeners into a semi-hypnotic state. "You go along with these folks and you'll still be flat broke tomorrow, just like you've been all your life. Is that what you want? Look around you, B.J. This is the land of milk and honey, right in the middle of the country of plenty. Come November, you won't be able to drive from one end of town to the other in less than an hour because of the tourists in their damn Mercedes and Jaguars. Shoot, even Ritter comes tooling into town in a sexy little BMW, looking like James Bond. You lived here all your life and you're driving a beat-up old Explorer, must have a hundred and fifty thousand miles on it. Half the time it won't even kick over in the winter. It's not fair, B.J. None of it. Not for a hardworking man like yourself. But you don't have to be one of Harmony's poor folk. I can change that. *Only* me. I'm the fairy godmother with the magic wand. You let me do it and I'll turn you into Cinderella. Just take one minute, and *poof!* you'll have a coach and white horses, and more jewels than you'll know what to do with."

"Micah!" Caroline Bellamy screamed at the top of her voice. "Stop it! Stop it! Stop it!" She pushed away from the wall as though she was going to tackle him.

"Getting married real soon, aren't you? Changes a man's life, it does. You've got a *heritage* now, a destiny—not just a wife but children, and grandchildren, and their children. What do you want them to say about you? That you're the man who began a dynasty for the Blakes? Or someone no one even remembers?

"You give any thought to where you're going to live when you're married? Not that old fall-down house of yours, I hope. How about a ten-thousand-square-foot penthouse for the new missus? Wouldn't she like that better? Doesn't she *deserve* something like that? You've seen Janis's place, haven't you? We've got a better one coming on the market this week. Belonged to Princess Stephanie of Monaco. Got its own enclosed swimming pool on the roof with a disco just below, where you can watch folks swim while you dance. There's an apartment for two maids and a chef so you can have thirty or forty friends over for a little dinner in your thousand-square-foot dining room. Bigger than your whole house, ain't it?"

B.J. was looking uncomfortable.

Mark's head was spinning. "B.J.," he began, but stopped. His throat burned, making it difficult to talk. Why did his throat hurt? He'd been shot in the side. He managed to push away from Lisa and put his hand on one of the footlong propane welding torches lying on the floor. B.J.'s eyes went to him, then shot back to Rollins. Mark saw Blake's arms waver, as though the gun were becoming too heavy to hold.

Rollins must have seen it too, because the muscles in his shoulders and neck relaxed. He said calmly, "This town's too built-up to make any money out of it now unless you're already wired in. You stay here and you're going to die as poor as you are today. A year from now you'll be in the bank begging old Lou Dubbons for a loan to buy baby furniture or a new car. You know how that goes. Man knows you all his life and he says, 'Here, fill out these forms in triplicate, and bring in your last two 1040s.'"

Karen hugged Lisa to her body, trying to staunch the flow of tears. "We've got to get going, B.J. Before another storm comes up." But there was a new note of tension in her voice, too, as though she also sensed something happening that she never could have believed before this minute.

Rollins kept up his chatter with B.J., acting as though no one else were present. "Think of the future. Think of what I can do for you, what I . . ."

Still on his knees, Mark turned so he was facing Karen as Micah's monologue droned on. "Get Lisa outside," he whispered. "Now. Then come back."

Karen's eyes widened in a question.

"Now! As far away as possible," Mark said under his breath. "Don't wait. Go!"

Fed up with Micah's scheming, Caroline Bellamy yelled, "Gag him, damn it, B.J. Then tie him up and get us out of here."

Mark suddenly tumbled over on his face, trying to draw Micah's attention as Karen led Lisa to the stairs, whispered urgently in her ear, and watched as the girl disappeared into the darkness.

But Micah had eyes only for Blake. They were the only two people in the world, and time had come to a complete stop. "Being poor's a crime around here, son. It don't have to be. There's nothing wrong with being rich, let me tell you. I've been poor. Didn't like it. Not one bit. But when I go home tonight I'm going to pour myself some Johnnie Walker Blue Label. It's so dang expensive most folks don't even know it exits. Gonna splash it over some glacier ice from the Arctic that's ten thousand years old. I buy some every year from a company in Norway. It cracks like fine china when the scotch hits it, then kinda floats around the glass, keeping the drink cold but not diluting it. I'll sit back, put my feet up, listen to Clint Black or Jerry Jeff Walker on my stereo. Me and Clint's gotten to be friends, you know. Took me backstage at his Austin show last year. Shoulda seen the groupies back there! Gracious! Eighteen, nineteen years old, wearing those real tight jeans and halter tops. One of Clint's security guys says, 'Go ahead, pick one out. We'll send her up to your room.' Well, I didn't, of course. Thing is, I coulda. And not because I'm some handsome dude, but because I'm Clint's buddy. And I'm fucking rich! And that's all it takes to make folks do what you want. Ain't no one in the world gives a damn if you're a nice papa or honest businessman or loyal husband. All folks care about nowadays is money. And I can give you more money than you even knew *existed*."

Blake said nothing.

"Don't think of yourself, my friend. Think of your wife and kids. How are they going to like being poor when everyone else around here is driving an eighty-thousand-dollar car, and seven-year-olds are wearing Ralph Lauren and riding twelve-hundred-dollar dirt bikes to school. While you're waiting to shop the Wal-Mart over at Copper Mountain on sale days. Is that what you want for them?"

"Jesus Christ, Micah!" Caroline picked up the hammer and threw it at him, hitting the small of his bare back. She forced herself to her feet, drops of water dribbling from her hair and dress. But when she saw what Mark was doing she froze, not certain if she should pay attention or not.

"What kind of partner are you talking about?" B.J. asked hesitantly. He and Micah didn't take their eyes off each other.

"Fifty-fifty." The cult leader's voice again, droning, promising, hypnotic, sucking in the gullible with promises of a golden future, a new and better life. "Everything equal. That's the way it's got to be when two guys trust each other. What's half of ninety million?"

"B.J.—" Karen shouted.

But Blake didn't hear. "That's all fixed assets! What kind of cash flow are we talking?"

"Cash flow? It's more like damn Niagara, son. You couldn't match this if you had a printing press and Treasury Department plates in your basement. Hell, you could swim in it, do high dives—"

B.J.'s arms stiffened. "I want it in writing. Tonight. Before we go down."

Now Karen and Caroline were both yelling at the top of their voices. Caroline moved toward Micah. B.J. squeezed off a round that missed her head by less than a foot. Karen shrieked and B.J. swung the rifle in her direction. Mark turned his back to B.J. Grabbing one of the power cords on the floor, he whipped it over near the two men.

"Deal?" Micah asked above the yelling. Mark could see the man's thick, tree-trunk legs trembling as though he was going to collapse any second.

There was a pause, then, "Deal."

B.J. looked suddenly elated. The rifle lowered. Suddenly nothing in his life was the same. His future was gold-plated. Diamond-studded. Tiffany's, not Wal-Mart. *"A pool on the roof and a disco just below."* No longer poor for life. He was starting a dynasty!

Karen was stunned. "My God, B.J., no—"

Micah's voice instantly turned decisive. "Give me my gun back. Then we'll take care of these folks."

B.J. reached down, grabbed the Beretta from the floor, and tossed it to Micah who checked the safety, then pointed it at Karen. "Get upstairs," he told Blake. "We gotta get moving here, we're already behind schedule. There's a propane tank in the kitchen. Open the valve. The gas is heavier than air and will seep down here. It'll take awhile in this wind, but we need it to make this look right. And hurry, damn it! We're getting out of here and going down the chairlift to fight the fire at the resort."

Blake took off upstairs with Micah's flashlight.

Karen looked at Micah beseechingly. "Don't do this. Please."

"Christ almighty!" Caroline was bellowing at him, and pushing to her feet. "You're insane. My God. You can't get away with this."

"Caroline," Rollins explained patiently, "all this has been thought out. Ain't no way in hell the police are going to figure this is anything but a tragic construction-site accident. These things happen."

B.J. Blake came clamoring down the stairs, an excited look on his face. "Propane's on."

Micah nodded, then shot him in the head. "Dumb fuck," he said as the man fell to the floor.

"Micah!" Caroline screamed, and launched herself at the man.

As Caroline grabbed her ex-husband by the arm Mark sat on his knees and hurriedly switched on the torch. Nothing happened. No fuel. *Jesus!* Panicking, he threw it aside and grabbed another torch. A small flame shot from the end but it wavered, as though ready to go out. At once he aimed it at the cord twisting down the stairs and along the floor. Suddenly it severed with a loud *snap,* insulation melting away from the wires and pooling on the wet cement. Mark dropped the torch and tried to stand, but his legs wouldn't let him. He started to fall but Karen caught him under the arms. She looked at what he had done. "What is this?"

"Make Rollins back up."

"What?"

"Push him if you have to. But don't let him grab you. Make him fall!"

Caroline was fighting with Rollins, flailing her arms ineffectively in his face, reaching for his eyes, screaming. "Goddamn you, Micah. Damn you—"

"Get her away," Mark said urgently, and tried to stand again. "Pull her off of him." Once more he tried to stand but couldn't. *"Make him back up!"* he yelled again, but his throat was so constricted it came out as a loud hiss. *"Hurry!"* Panicking, he twisted away from

Karen and began looking for something made of wood that he could use to push the cord.

Micah, swearing furiously, yanked his arm free from Caroline, and immediately pointed the gun at her. Mark screamed, *"No!"* as loud as he could but Rollins pulled the trigger and shot her in the chest. The woman looked at him in dumb surprise, then sank at his feet. Micah spun toward Mark. "You're next."

Mark was propelling himself on the floor toward Micah, desperately trying to think of a way to move the large man back. But it was impossible. Micah pointed the Beretta.

Caroline cried from the floor, *"Micah, my God—"*

He looked down at her. His face was wet and red with anger, and his hair plastered to his scalp.

"Micah," she screamed. "We were married! Didn't that mean anything?"

He stared down at her stupidly, as if thinking, *What did that have to do with this?* Then she grabbed his bare ankle. "Damn you, what are you doing? Let go of me." When he saw the cord he realized at once what she was thinking. *"Noooo!"* he shouted, the word exploding all around the small room. Panicking, he tried desperately to pull away from her grip, swinging the gun at her head and trying to yank his leg free. Caroline's fingers wouldn't loosen. Crying, *"Micah, Micah,"* her voice half scream and half sob, she reached out with her free hand, stretching as far as she could. But she was inches short. With a final effort of will she forced her body forward, fingers clawing on the bare cement until, still sobbing, she seized the live wire.

Both bodies, joined by electricity, jerked immediately as 220 volts shot through them—the water making them perfect conductors—and continued going through them as it sought an outlet, their flesh turning red and smoking from every pore. Micah's hair and eyebrows caught fire, his lips turned black, and his fingers sparked tiny bursts of electricity into a pool of water. Burning flesh sizzled, the air everywhere stank, and still the electricity flowed, the bodies burned, and smoke and steam rose.

Mark screamed, "Don't touch them. Don't touch anything. Get us out of here! *Hurry!*"

Karen helping him, they stumbled up the steps, while behind them the air turned putrid and black.

"Where's Lisa?" he asked in a panic.

"I told her to hide. If she saw us she was to come out. If not, stay hidden."

"Lisa!" He began screaming. *"Lisa!"*

Breathing heavily, they made it to the front of the restaurant. Karen turned back toward a sound from inside. "What's that?"

"A fire." He hurried outside. *"Lisa!"*

Karen also raised her voice. "Lisa. Come out. Lisa—"

The girl, clothes torn, covered with mud, shot toward them from the darkness, sobbing loudly.

"What's burning in the basement?" Karen asked, panicking. "There's nothing down there except the bodies."

"Hurry!" Mark shouted. "We've got to get out of here. We can't wait!"

Holding hands, the three of them began to run away from the restaurant in the darkness. Three minutes later they saw the outline of the blue canopy in the center of the ski area. "The lift—" Mark said, trying not to pass out. Then a huge explosion, followed almost immediately by another, rocked the mountain. They were thrown to the ground as pine branches clattered on them from above. Stretched out on her stomach Karen looked over at Mark. She couldn't catch her breath. "My God—"

"The propane must have set off the explosives they were using for construction work," Mark managed. He drew a breath. "It wasn't what Micah expected. It probably took half the mountaintop." He tried to stand. "Let's see if the lift still works," then sank into unconsciousness.

VIII

118

Mark woke up in the hospital, near-delirious from painkillers. He moved his arm, and moaned, "Lisa—"

"Right here," Karen told him, and allowed the girl to hug her father. She grabbed so tightly it hurt, but he smiled before losing consciousness again.

At two A.M. the thudding of his heart made the monitors at the nurses' station beep a shrill warning. An RN rushed down, and Karen said, "It's okay. I just told him he's going to get married."

119

Mason Hightower leaned back in his chair and said, "You look pretty good for a man just a week out of the hospital."

"Can't run," Mark said. "Not for another three or four months. Otherwise—"

"How's Lisa taking to the idea of having a new mom pretty soon?"

"She's excited. They're swimming over at the Marriott. I guess it's one of the few buildings in that part of town that didn't burn."

"Worse than 'sixty-eight," Hightower said. "Twenty-three structures lost. Janis is already talking about rebuilding the lodge. Wants to do it exactly as it was. Without the Ice Castle, though. I reckon they'll start on it before winter."

"Bobby Sample missed out. He could have been King of Harmony."

Hightower shook his head. "Janis never would have married him. He was just something to do in a town without a lot of unmarried men. He'll have time to reflect on all this from prison, though. Shouldn't be hard to get him for Stallworth. Janis said he practically admitted to killing someone for Micah. He had a stack of cash in his house. And Chavez found a revolver under the floorboards in his kitchen. He was arrested at the Orange County Airport, you know."

"No. Why?"

"Someone—had to be Janis—called the airport and said a man matching Bobby's description would be coming through from Denver with a gun in his carry-on bag and a wallet full of phony IDs, including a phony police ID. Of course the police ID was real. But so was the weapon. So Bobby was already locked-up when Chavez went looking for him. Poor Bobby went ballistic, claimed he was set up." He leaned back in his chair. "Lies and deceptions everywhere we look, isn't there? Starting with the way Walter kept poor old Les around to absorb the blame for his own sins. Chavez told me Walter even put those pictures he left at Bill's in an old pay envelope he'd handed Cady his paycheck in, so Les's fingerprints would be on it."

"It started long before that."

"When my dad and your folks set up the adoption? Yeah, I guess it did. I reckon that's why they never told you you were adopted, since it was all illegal. Under the law it was actually baby-selling. The Ritters were afraid of losing you."

"I'm glad they didn't," Mark said, his anger at his adopted parents long gone. "What sort of charges did they file on Cady?"

"Arson, murder of Lowndes's nurse, some lesser things. Poor old Les thought people would think him some sort of hero for exposing a child molester. I reckon he'll plead insanity and do his time in a state hospital." Hightower came out from behind his desk and eased down on the other end of the couch from Mark. "Did you hear about the magazine and newspaper articles Chavez found at Micah's house?"

Mark said he hadn't.

"Must've been a hundred stories about Walter. Every time Walter's name appeared in print Micah neatly cut it out and saved it, just like he saved everything from high school. I guess it's what pushed him over the edge. The world just wasn't interested in Micah Rollins, only in Walter Lowndes. The man couldn't stand it. I guess he wasn't the first person driven to kill by ego. Won't be the last, either."

A month later, when he was well enough to drive, Mark went to Dexter. By himself. There were some things to clear up.

Eleanor Dahlquist had her no-nonsense attorney's face on when she reluctantly met with him. "I helped people who couldn't have babies. Is that so bad?"

"I didn't say it was bad. I said it was illegal."

"So go to the Bar Association. Get me disbarred. I'm ready to retire anyway."

"I'm not going to the Bar Association, Eleanor. I'm not even mad at you. There's just a few things I want to know."

She sat back and stared at him across her cluttered desk without saying anything.

"For example," he began, "did you work for Lowndes?"

"I met Walter years ago through Julian Hightower. It was an acquaintanceship; not a friendship. I like to ski so I'd see him every winter. It became an attorney-client relationship in October 1987. He gave me a time-share for winter, and I did a few things for him."

"That was two months after my father died."

"Your mother, your real mother, the woman who raised you for eighteen years, came to see me. She'd been going through some of your dad's stuff and found a copy of a newspaper article someone had sent him years before. It was about a fire at the resort, and mentioned Carl Stark. She knew he was listed on your birth certificate as your father, of course, and she wondered if that meant maybe you were in line for part or whole ownership of the modern resort. I told her, of course not. The land had been sold shortly after Stark died.

"But, as a courtesy, I called Walter and told him. He called me back the next day and said he'd like to set up an annuity for your mom—one thousand dollars a month—as long as I told her it was something your dad arranged long ago. I went along with it. Why not? When I asked him why he was doing it he said because he remembered when you were born and wanted to do something nice for your family."

"Bullshit. He was afraid my mother would start poking around

and get people wondering about that fire. Like I did ten years later."
But that explained the file at his mother's house, as well as the one
in Lowndes's office. The "Payments Received" were from Lowndes.
"That newspaper article was sent to my dad by a local character
named Wild Bill. He sent one to me, too, and the police found more
copies in his house. Bill had seen Lowndes on the mountainside just
as the fire broke out, and assumed Lowndes killed Stark. So did
Lowndes. But Caroline Bellamy told Karen that Micah Rollins was
responsible. He knocked Stark out before his cabin burned."

"I don't know anything about that," the attorney said, in attor-
neyspeak.

"But Lowndes killed Bill. He must have thought the old man was
going to cause him trouble. Then he tried to implicate Bill as a child
molester. He left some pornographic pictures at Bill's cabin. The
police said they were part of the same group of pictures I took from
his desk. He also came up to my mother's house the day after she
died."

Still the attorney was noncommunicative.

"He took whatever evidence he could find of the thousand dollars
a month she was collecting. And went through my folks' stuff. Just
looking for anything incriminating, I guess. He killed Monster, obviously. Thing is, how did he know my mom had died?"

Eleanor Dahlquist scowled at him.

"How much did he pay you?"

"He was my client."

"He's dead. There is no attorney-client privilege."

The woman came forward in her chair and planted her elbows
on the desk. "I told him he no longer needed to send the monthly
checks. That's all."

"Did you know he was my biological father?"

Her eyes widened despite her attempt at nonchalance.

"Our secret, Eleanor. Okay? Not something I want to publicize."

The chair tilted back. "And he knew he was your father?"

"I don't know. Probably not at a conscious level but he must have
always suspected something. I was born nine months after he raped
my mother." All of which, Mark thought, had contributed to the
hostility Lowndes had toward him.

"Interesting," Eleanor said. "Walter told me his daughter was
chasing after you. I guess she didn't know she was your half-sister.
Would've made a curious marriage, wouldn't it?"

Mark ignored her. Removing the picture of Lisa in their Seattle backyard from his shirt pocket, he held it up. "Do you know where this came from?"

"It was on your mother's bedroom dresser. I saw it a number of times. She said you sent it to her."

He put it back in his pocket. "I thought that must have been it. I was always sending her pictures, doing the proud-parent bit. I just didn't remember it." Lowndes had obviously removed it from his mother's house, probably thinking it was Cheryl. Later, when he grabbed a handful of pictures to leave at Bill's, it must have been in the pile.

Still Eleanor said nothing.

Mark got up. He was tired of Eleanor and wanted to get home. "Shakespeare was right. When a society needs cleaning up we should start by eliminating the attorneys. Cuts down on overpopulation, too." He started for the door, then stopped. "By the way, I lied about the Bar Association. I filed a complaint yesterday. Also with the attorney general. They'll be in touch."

120

L isa said, "Can I play on the equipment?"

Mark smiled. "Tell me if anyone in the bushes talks to you."

Lisa giggled and took off, holding her ice-cream cone.

Karen licked a bit of whipped cream from the top of her hot fudge sundae. "I wish she'd call me 'Mom'. But I guess 'Karen' is okay for now. You, on the other hand, can call me 'Mrs. Ritter.' "

Mark smiled at her. "Soon."

The sounds of construction were everywhere around them. The town was rebuilding. Janis Lowndes had been on national TV, interviewed by Barbara Walters. She was a natural at PR, just like her dad.

Mark said, "How much do you think Janis knew about Walter?"

"I asked her," Karen said. "She said she thought he liked looking at pictures of little girls. She thought he may have molested some children a long time ago. He never bothered her, though."

"And the girl that was killed a few years ago?"

"She insists he didn't do it. I don't believe it. I think she doesn't want to know. Of course, she went away to college when she was eighteen, and didn't come back until three years ago. He was pretty far gone by then. It was easy for her to pretend he was always pretty harmless." She hesitated, then said, "She still doesn't know you have the same father, does she?"

Mark shook his head. "Why go into it now?"

"But *you* know. So I'm sure you'll never look at her quite the same way again. Will you? I mean that sort of thing might have been okay for Egyptian Pharaohs but—"

"Not to worry," Mark told her; the idea still made him cringe.

Karen set her ice cream on the ground, and put her arms around him. "I've got an idea," she said with enthusiasm. "Let's make out like high-school kids."

"I'm an invalid. Be gentle."

She tried to kiss him but Mark pulled away. "Speaking of Janis, what was that baloney you gave me about Janis and the graffiti at the cafe? It bothered me for days."

"Graffiti? What graffiti?" An innocent look.

"Janis. 'The artist of sex.' "

"Oh, that." She brushed it aside as irrelevant. "I made it up, of course. To warn you away from her. I've been a bad girl." She put her lips on his. "So do with me as you will."

"Your mouth is cold from ice cream."

"Warm it up."

Lisa yelled from thirty yards away, "I see you!"

Karen smiled. "Does she wonder about suddenly getting a new grandma and grandpa to go along with a new mom?"

"Sure. But it's all pretty long-distance at this point. Cheryl told her family but doesn't want us to visit for a while. I can respect that. It's as surprising to them as it was to me."

Karen glanced at her sundae. "One more little, teensy-weensy kiss. Then I have to turn my full attention to chocolate. Don't forget its aphrodisiac effect. We can test it later. So far it's been an absolute wonder. Such energy, such endurance—"

She put her arms around him. But Lisa came up from somewhere, moving between them, and said, "Stop! Stop! Stop! We have to get married first."

"Next month," Karen reminded her, laughing.

Lisa turned to encompass them both with her arms. "Then I can have a mom." She kissed Karen, then her dad, and ran back toward the swings. Halfway there she turned around and yelled, "And a horse! You promised!"

Mark said, "You didn't—"